FEAR FOR
ME

Also by Cynthia Eden

Die For Me: A Novel of the Valentine Killer

CYNTHIA EDEN

FEAR FOR ME

A NOVEL OF THE BAYOU BUTCHER

Text copyright © 2013 Cindy Roussos

Published by Montlake Romance, Seattle
www.apub.com

ISBN-13: 9781477848340
ISBN-10: 1477848347

Library of Congress Control Number: 2013909621

This book is for my mother—a woman who taught me (very early) to love books.

PROLOGUE

He stared at the same fucking walls day in and day out. The prison cell reeked of piss and vomit, and the heavy stench wouldn't go away. Sunlight never came inside his cell—there was no window to let in anything sweet. Just those three fucking walls, a stained toilet, a bed, and the bars that kept him prisoner.

Day in and day out.

But he wouldn't be prisoner for much longer. He'd planned. Prepared. His time was nearly at hand.

I'll get them. Every damn one of them. They wouldn't get away with what they'd done to him.

Yes, he'd make them pay, and he'd start with *her.*

His fingers curled around the shiv in his hand. He'd spent hours and hours carefully transforming the plastic spoon, turning it into the weapon he needed.

He preferred to hunt with a knife. He loved the feel of a knife in his hand. The hard, cold power of the blade.

He'd have a knife again. Soon enough. He'd feel the blade slice into skin. See the brilliant and beautiful red spray of blood.

Soon.

"Lights out!" the guard barked as he passed. Right on time. Douglas was always on time. "Lights out, Walker!"

1

Jon Walker's shoulders hunched but he made no move to advance toward the crumpled mattress that passed for his bed. Instead, his fingers curled tighter around his weapon. He'd never been one for cutting himself before. He liked to give the pain to others, but sometimes, sacrifices had to be made.

"Medic," he bit out.

The guard's shuffling footsteps halted. "What's that?" Douglas Reed demanded.

Walker sliced the shiv across his stomach and grunted at the lance of pain. Blood dripped over his fingers as he turned to face the guard. The lights were still very much on, so the guard would easily see his wound. "I need…a…medic…" The wound wasn't that deep, but he'd always bled fast and well—well enough to put on a nice show right then.

The guard—short, stocky—swore and reached for his radio. "Prisoner's wounded!" Douglas snapped. "It's Walker, cell block four ten."

So far, everything was going according to plan. It should. He'd had plenty of time to plan. All those days. All those nights. Locked away.

Her fault. She'd been the one to toss him in this prison.

"Drop the weapon!"

More guards were coming. Other prisoners were shouting now as they realized that some action was going down. They all liked blood, as long as it wasn't their own.

Yes, Jon had everyone's attention. It was so hard not to smile, but he couldn't do that. Not yet.

Making a big show, he dropped his weapon. Kept playing his role. They thought he was crazy anyway. That was why no other prisoners were allowed in his cell with him.

They'd tried to put a prisoner in with him, back when he'd first been brought to the Louisiana State Penitentiary. When the bastard had tried to push him around, when the others had tried to attack him, Jon had known just what to do.

Killing his cell mate had been easy. The sweet rush of power was exactly what he'd needed to get through the dark days.

The guards swarmed him. He kept bleeding, but he didn't even feel a sting from the wound anymore. Soon the guards were rushing him to the med ward. At this time, so close to lights-out, the med ward would be nearly empty.

Nearly...

There she is. Not the bitch who haunted him, but one who would give him a chance to escape. A woman who would do...for now.

The doctor spun toward him when he was wheeled inside. Dr. Sheila Long. She didn't smell of piss and vomit. She smelled of hope.

Freedom.

And peppermint. The lady had a taste for sweets. He'd noticed that the first time she'd checked him out. Noticed it. Noticed Sheila with her long, dark hair. Hair she kept pulled back in a ponytail. Her skin was pale, it looked like silk, and he'd wanted it beneath his knife since that first meeting.

Sheila's gaze met his and then dropped quickly to his wound. Sheila never looked straight at him for too long. No one did. He noticed her stare widen when she saw the blood. The blood had soaked the bottom of his shirt, so she couldn't see the wound clearly. Good. She wouldn't know yet that he'd avoided everything vital. After all his knife practice over the years, he knew how to make a cut that bled plenty but left the victim without any mortal injuries. He could keep playing like he was at death's door.

"Get him on the table," Sheila said, biting her lower lip. "I need to see the damage."

One of the guards dragged him up on the table.

Jon gave out a long, pain-filled groan.

Sheila hurriedly went to work on him. "Who attacked this prisoner?"

Two of the guards left, heading back outside to take up what Jon knew were their positions outside of the med room. They'd stay there until the doc was finished with him.

Douglas stayed behind. Protocol dictated that one guard would have to stay in the med room and oversee a prisoner's treatment. One armed guard.

But Douglas had no weapon ready.

I do.

Douglas muttered, "No one attacked him. The dumb fuck did it to himself." A rough sigh slid from him. "Now we'll have to put him on suicide watch."

No, they wouldn't. He'd never been suicidal. He didn't want to see what waited in the next world for him. He liked this world far too much.

His gaze darted quickly around the room. Only Sheila and Douglas were there. The guards had been lazy when they burst into his cell. They'd just taken the shiv that he dropped.

They hadn't even checked him for another weapon.

They should have.

Douglas bent toward him. "Let me cuff him to the—"

Jon lunged up as he yanked out the second shiv. Douglas didn't have a chance to scream before that shiv sank deep into his throat.

Sheila just stood there, eyes wide, frozen.

Fear could do that to a person. Make them freeze when they should flee. Not that he was going to give her time to flee.

He yanked the shiv out of Douglas as the guard's body fell to the floor with a thud. The thud made Sheila flinch. She opened her mouth to scream.

Her scream would alert the guards outside. No one ignored a woman's scream in this hell. The prisoners might enjoy the scream, but no one *ignored* it.

I can't have her bringing company in.

He grabbed Sheila, wrapped his hand around her mouth, and put the bloody shiv at her jugular. "There are two ways this can work." His lips brushed over her ear. The scent of peppermints teased him. So much better than piss. He inhaled deeply, then said, "I can kill you now, or you can be a good girl." He liked good girls. He liked bad ones, too. "If you're good, then you get to live longer." *But you'll still die.* He'd gone too long without a woman's blood staining his hands.

No, she wasn't the bitch who tormented his dreams, the one who'd *pay* for taking so much away from him, but Sheila…oh, sweet Sheila would still bleed damn well for him. She'd give him the rush of power, of pleasure, that he'd missed for so long.

She was his tool. His toy. His ticket out of the cage.

He could feel the mad thunder of her heartbeat against him. Sheila was small, probably only around five foot two. Curved, but she hid her figure under her oversize scrubs. Her features were plain, when he liked his girls prettier, but she'd do.

She'd definitely do.

"Call out to the guards," he ordered her, keeping his mouth at her ear. She was trembling against him. "Tell them you're stitching me up." Because they were just outside that door. He knew that. He let the shiv slice her, drawing forth a long trickle of her blood. *Yes. I missed that.* "If you call for help, you'll be dead before they get in the room." Those words were a promise. Sheila would have read his file. She would know all about the things he'd done.

She would believe him.

She *should* believe him.

Sheila's head moved in a fast nod. This part was the gamble, but really, what did he have to lose?

Nothing. If she ratted him out, then he went back to his cell. He was already serving multiple life sentences—what more could they do to him?

If Sheila didn't scream for help, if she did exactly as he'd ordered, then…

Freedom.

His fingers lifted from her soft mouth.

"I-I'm going to need more time." Sheila's voice grated in his ears because the fear was so sharp in her words. Would the guards hear the fear?

His own heartbeat kicked up. Sweat trickled down his back. The wound in his stomach began to throb.

"Finish your duties!" Sheila called, her voice getting a little stronger. It was lights-out. All the guards needed to patrol right then. "I'm stitching him up now."

"Yes, ma'am."

The guards shuffled away.

Jon smiled. He pressed a kiss to Sheila's head. "Good girl," he whispered as he turned her in his arms.

She stared up at him. Her eyes were wide, stark, terrified. Just the look he loved.

"Wh-what happens now?"

"You stitch me up." First order of business. He couldn't very well escape with a wound that might get infected.

Her breath was panting out as she reached for the needle.

"Now, you're gonna need to be careful." He angled his body so that she could reach his wound—and so he could keep the weapon at her throat. "Because you make one wrong move, and I'll slice your throat open."

The panting of her breath got worse. Her fingers were shaking so badly it took her five tries to get the first stitch in place.

He smiled as he watched her work. He'd always been involved in cutting people open, not stitching them back together. It hurt every time the thread went in, but he found he didn't mind the pain as much.

Not when he got to watch her face and think of all the things he'd do to her. She would be his practice run. A guy could get rusty after so long away from his trade. He had to make sure he was in top form when he delivered the payback that was coming.

Then she was done. Sheila even cleaned him up. Wasn't that nice? What, did she think that if she was good enough to him, he'd let her go?

Not happening, Doc.

But she'd done her part. The rest would now be up to him. He glanced over at the clock.

Jon knew where the scrubs were kept. He'd put them on and slip away at the shift change that took place in ten minutes. *Ten minutes.* That wasn't much playtime.

The other doc—Casey Hall—had left his ID behind. He'd noticed that Hall did that. A mistake, leaving the ID behind on the weekend, but Hall had a bad habit of being a little too forgetful. With Hall's ID, Jon would be able to get out so easily.

So very easily.

He stroked her cheek. "You did a very nice job on me." It would barely scar.

"Will you—will you let me go now?"

Ah, there was hope breaking through her voice.

He shook his head. "No, now..." His smile widened. "Now you die."

Terror leaked across her face as the words sank in. She tried to lunge away, tried to scream but—

There was no time for that. He brought up his weapon, slicing fast. Enjoying the blood and not caring that it soaked his clothes. He'd change soon—for now, he'd *enjoy* this.

Just as he'd enjoy the prey that was soon to come. Only that bitch's death wouldn't be easy. She sure hadn't made things easy on him. Not when she'd stood in that courtroom, day after day, mocking him. Belittling him. Telling his secrets to the world.

She'll pay.

As for Sheila, he would give her a quick death, though he did usually enjoy letting it linger.

Only ten minutes. There was still a lot he could do in that length of time. Every slice of his knife would be heaven then. *Next time, I'll do plenty more.*

He'd made his list of targets. Some should have stood by him. They hadn't. They should have feared him. Not put him on display. Not turned *him* into the freak.

So many deserved to be punished. So many.

Jon held Sheila while she died. He figured he owed her that much. After all, she'd just given him his freedom.

He inhaled deeply, drinking in the scent.

Freedom smelled a hell of a lot like blood—and peppermint.

CHAPTER ONE

"Do you know how many people Jonathan Walker killed?" U.S. Federal Marshal Anthony Ross asked the question quietly, trying to keep his emotions in check.

A real hard job, considering he was currently watching two bodies get bagged and tagged as they were loaded up by the Angola penitentiary coroner.

This should have ended. Walker's path of blood and death should have stopped five years ago.

Anthony had done his job. He'd helped to lock up the killer, sent Walker away for good—or so he'd thought. The bastard had just broken out of the prison that should have been his home until he died.

How the hell had he gotten out of Angola? Once in this pit, no one was supposed to get out. And a killer like Walker—he should have been a maximum-security hold, watched carefully, twenty-four-seven.

The warden—the *new* warden—was sweating bullets and shifting from his left foot to his right. "I believe that Walker was found guilty of killing seven people—"

"Eight, when you add his cell mate," Anthony snapped. Now these poor bodies made Walker's kill total reach all the way up to ten. That they knew of. Anthony had long suspected that Jon's kill list was much longer, but those bodies just hadn't been found. "You knew what he did, yet you let the bastard just walk out of here?" So much for the prison being secure.

The Bayou Butcher. Sonofabitch. That brutal bastard should have gotten a needle in the arm, but no, the man who'd sliced his way through seven women in Baton Rouge had been given consecutive life sentences instead of death.

And now more victims were bleeding for Walker. For the Bayou Butcher.

"He didn't just walk out." The warden, James Miller, swallowed quickly. The guy was in way over his head with this case. When word reached the press, shit was going to hit the fan, and Anthony knew Miller would find himself looking for a new job—because the governor would demand that the man leave Angola. *The Bayou Butcher had escaped on the guy's watch.*

Hell. This was so bad, in so many ways. Anthony would have to make sure all the jurors on Walker's trial knew what had happened ASAP. They'd have to get protection—they'd need to pull in a ton of manpower on this one. He'd have to get his office to contact the victims' families. The DA.

The DA.

His jaw locked.

"He didn't just walk out," Miller said once more, his voice gaining a bit of strength. *Too little, too late.* "Walker took the ID of one of the other doctors. Walker matched him in height and coloring and he—"

"Walked right out the fucking door." Yeah, right, that was what he'd just said. Anthony's gaze drifted over the blood-soaked room. Walker had been quick with his first kill, going right for the jugular with the guard, probably so that his prey wouldn't be able to call out for help.

But then the sick SOB had played for a while with the female victim. Walker always enjoyed playing with his prey.

"Take me to his cell." The dogs were already out, chasing after Walker's scent. But the guy was smart. So damn smart. An IQ that had tested off the charts and a desire to torture and kill had been with him since he was seven.

Age seven—that had been when he'd decided to see what the neighbor's dog looked like on the inside.

Sick, twisted, but *smart*. Anthony knew that Walker must have been planning his escape for a while, and, with that escape in mind, the man would have made sure that he had a getaway vehicle ready.

Did someone help you? It was Anthony's immediate suspicion. Because to get a car, to have that ride waiting, Walker would need assistance. A partner.

Whoever the dumb prick was, Anthony figured that Walker would turn on him, sooner or later.

"I want to see his cell." Maybe Walker had left some clue behind. Some hint as to his partner's identity or an indicator just where the hell the guy was heading.

"Of course." The warden motioned toward two men. "Henry, Alan, escort the marshal to Walker's cell."

Anthony left the warden and the blood-soaked med room. The guards were all on high alert now. Like being on alert *now* was going to do any good. The prison was in lockdown, but as Anthony made his way to Walker's cell, shouts and whistles filled the air.

The prisoners knew someone had escaped. That a guard had died. And they were celebrating.

The guards in front of Anthony shouted for quiet. They didn't get quiet.

Walker's cell opened with a groan and Anthony headed inside. He quickly searched the area. Saw no personal effects. No books. Nothing. He reached for the sagging mattress. Yanked it out and away from the narrow bed railing. There had to be *something* there.

The mattress fell to the floor.

It was a bunk bed, only no one slept on the top bunk. Not since Walker had climbed up one night and choked his cell mate.

Anthony checked the top bunk.

Nothing.

No fucking thing.

"We already searched his cell," the warden told him as he came into the room. Anthony wasn't really surprised that Miller had followed him. "There weren't any more weapons here."

"I'm not looking for a weapon."

He was looking for a destination. A clue. Something that would help him figure out where the hell the guy had gone.

As a marshal, it was his job to track the escaped prisoner. But it wasn't just about doing a job.

The Bayou Butcher had been *his* case from the beginning. He'd been in the courtroom, he'd been there to protect the witnesses.

He'd been there when Jon Walker was found guilty of seven murders.

"Did the guy get mail?" Anthony figured that he *had* to get mail—fucking fan mail, probably. There were always those freaks out there who got off on interacting with killers.

"He did, but he never read any of it," Miller replied as he twisted his hands together. "He gave a standing order for us to destroy it all."

Anthony's eyes narrowed at that. In his experience, many serial killers reveled in the attention of their "fans." Why hadn't Walker wanted that attention?

He rubbed a hand over his face. There had to be *something* there. His hand dropped. Anthony's gaze focused on the bunk bed.

Something.

He bent, craning his head, so that he could see the bottom of the top bunk's mattress. This would have been Walker's view, every single day and night. He would have looked straight up—

There was a picture there. Faded, as if it had been touched so many times. Too many.

Carefully, Anthony pulled down that photo. When he saw just who was in that image, his heart seemed to stop.

Not her.

But he knew that face. Knew it too well. It haunted most of his dreams.

Lauren Chandler. *District Attorney* Lauren Chandler. The woman who'd sent Jon Walker to Angola. The woman who'd pushed for the guy to get a needle in his arm so that Walker would never kill again.

Lauren.

Of course, when he'd known her, she'd still been the ADA. She'd gotten her promotional bump right *after* Walker's conviction. She'd made her career on his case.

And once upon a time, she'd been Anthony's lover.

A lot could change in five years.

He pulled out his phone. Dialed the number he still remembered so easily.

No longer in service.

Fuck.

He glanced up at the sound of footsteps. Finally—the two other marshals under his command had just rushed into the tiny cell. He shoved the phone into his pocket even as he held tight to that photo. It was a Saturday, so the DA's office would be closed.

It had taken the warden twelve hours to notice that Walker was gone. Then it had taken Anthony and his team too many hours to get to the prison.

"We need to find Lauren Chandler." He tried to keep his voice steady as he said, "She's the DA in Baton Rouge. We need to get her on the phone and alert her to the prisoner's escape."

The marshals—Jim O'Keith and Matt Meadows—nodded in near unison.

He glanced back at the photo. Just getting her on the phone wasn't good enough. Not with Lauren's safety at stake. "Meadows, contact the Baton Rouge PD. I want them sending a patrol unit to her house." The photograph was so worn. Walker had stared at it, touched it, for how many nights? He'd been fixating on her for who the hell knew how long.

Rage burned within Anthony. That bastard was *not* getting his hands on Lauren.

But the guy had screamed that last day in court, shouted that Lauren would pay. As the judge had handed down sentencing, four guards had been needed to subdue Walker as he lunged for Lauren.

Are you trying to keep your promise, you SOB?

He would see the Bayou Butcher in hell first.

***

Lauren juggled her groceries as she used her foot to prop open her back door. The milk was sliding, and she was about 90 percent sure the bread was going to hit the floor and end up a smushed mess. She should have waited, carried less inside in one haul, but the dark clouds promised a downpour that wouldn't wait long.

Her phone was ringing in her back pocket, a vibration that was stubbornly persistent, but there was no way she could answer the call then.

She tried to hit the lights with her elbow. They didn't turn on. Just darkness. Great. Fabulous. She hit the lights again, aiming harder with her elbow. Still nothing.

Had the storm already knocked out power? Sometimes the rough wind could do that in this area. She loved her neighborhood, with its sprawling yards, but the pine trees drew the lightning like crazy.

Her phone stopped vibrating.

Stumbling, weaving, she made her way to the counter and dropped her bags just before the milk could slide free.

"Lauren..."

She tensed. Had someone just whispered her name?

The call had been so faint, she wasn't even sure that she'd actually heard it.

The wind was starting to howl outside, and her shutters banged against the side of her house.

It was so dark. She edged back carefully, and her fingers went to the light switch once more. Her fingers jerked the switch quickly. Up and down, up and down.

Darkness.

The lights *weren't* coming on. Her heart was thudding far too rapidly in her chest.

Had she heard her name being whispered?

Fumbling, she reached into the drawer on the right and pulled out a knife. A very sharp butcher knife. "Is someone there?" Lauren asked, her voice a little weak. One hand clutched the knife. The other reached for her cell phone as she yanked it out of her pocket. No one should be in her house. She didn't have a live-in boyfriend. Didn't have a boyfriend at all.

"*Is someone there?*" Her call was louder.

Silence was her answer.

No whispers. No creaks.

Then the shutters started to bang again. She jumped.

Her heartbeat wouldn't slow down.

She'd check the house. Every room. Just to be sure it was safe.

Her job had given her an up-close and far too personal look at the darker side of life. She wasn't about to take any crazy chances. She knew what happened when those chances were taken.

But she also knew that a girl didn't get to call the cops on a storm-filled night just because she *thought* she'd heard a whisper. That was a surefire way to get a not-so-stellar reputation at the prosecutor's office.

Taking a deep breath, she edged forward. She kept her hold on the knife. She took one step. Two—

A scream cut through the night. No, not a scream, a siren. The flash of red-and-blue lights lit up her kitchen. Her heart beat faster. She lunged for the back door, clutching her knife as she shoved her phone into her back pocket once more. As she rushed outside, Lauren saw the cops, already jumping from their vehicle. Her body was on high alert, and something was very *wrong*.

Her feet thundered down the stairs of her back porch. Rain began to pelt her even as the bright light of a flashlight locked on her. No, not just one flashlight.

Two.

"Lauren Chandler?" one of the officers shouted.

Lauren froze. Crap. She still had the knife. Instinct. But she knew better than to approach a cop with a weapon, so she let the blade drop from her fingers. In the glare of the flashlights, she knew the cops would see the weapon fall. "Yes, yes, I'm Lauren Chandler." She kept her hands up. "What's going on?"

The cop on the right took a step toward her. "Why do you have the weapon, Ms. Chandler?"

"I thought I heard something inside." If they'd only witnessed what she had. Hell, if they'd been privy to all the details of her cases, most folks wouldn't even be able to sleep at night.

She'd sure been through her own share of sleepless nights. Sometimes, she'd only made it through after late-night phone calls with her best friend, Karen. Karen knew all about the darkness, too. She never thought Lauren's fears were crazy—not when Karen shared them.

We've seen the monsters out there. Karen's voice, the low drawl that dipped beneath it, whispered through Lauren's mind. *Seen 'em plenty, and we're smart enough to be afraid. The rest of the world—maybe they're better off not knowing. Hell, sometimes, I wish I didn't know.*

But Karen's job was to know. *Just like mine is.*

What would Karen think if she'd seen how scared Lauren had been in that dark house?

She'd probably tell me I need a drink to calm down…and that next time, I should immediately get my ass out of the house.

"Is there anyone else in the house?" the cop asked as he took another step toward her.

"There shouldn't be." She wasn't even sure she'd heard the whisper. Lauren glanced over her shoulder at her dark house.

That was when she realized lights glowed from the homes of her few neighbors. The lots were big and private, but she could clearly see illumination coming from those houses. Hers was the only house with a power outage. The only dark house on the road.

Lauren crept toward the cops. "Why are you here? What's happening?"

"We're under orders to take you back to the station, Ms. Chandler."

"Is this about one of my cases?" This wasn't standard operating procedure. The rain kept falling onto her.

"The order came from the U.S. Marshals' office, ma'am."

Her racing heart stopped. *U.S. Marshal.* "Why?"

"We got word that a prisoner escaped from Angola, and the marshal wanted you to have protection."

"Jon Walker," she whispered through numb lips.

The cop replied, but the rumble of thunder swallowed his answer.

She hurried toward them, her fear making her move faster. Her feet slipped in the slick grass, but she didn't slow down. In the middle of the storm, the uniformed cops looked like the safest port she'd ever seen.

The taller of the two opened the back of his patrol car. "Ma'am, why don't you get out of the rain?"

Grateful, Lauren slid inside. But the cops didn't follow her. They were staring over at her house, and she knew suspicion when she saw it.

"Why aren't your lights on?" the cop nearest her asked. His face was round, his shoulders stooped just slightly.

"The power didn't work," she confessed. Her hands pressed over her jeans as she tried to wipe the moisture from her palms. Part rain and part plain old sweat and fear.

The cops had their guns drawn. She saw the quick nod they exchanged. The taller cop ran toward her house while his partner took up a position near Lauren.

Guarding her.

"We're just gonna do a quick sweep," he told her, flashing a grin that she was able to see in the glow of the patrol car's interior lights. "To make sure that the area is secure."

Right. Goose bumps had risen on her arms. It was an early summer night, warm despite the rain, and she was shivering.

A few moments later, the cop's partner made it into her house. She could see the glow from his flashlight.

"I'm Officer Hank Lane," the man standing near the open car door said. "And you don't have anything to worry about, understand? You're—"

The radio on his hip crackled. They both tensed as Hank picked up the radio.

"Get an ambulance," his partner's voice barked. "Get one *now!*"

Lauren... She shuddered when she remembered the whisper.

Her gaze flew back to the house. She tried to push out of the car, but Hank held her back. No one should have been inside her home.

Get an ambulance...

Someone had been there. In the dark. Waiting for her?

The cop's grip tightened around her.

"Go inside," she said, voice desperate. "Help him!"

Hank hesitated. Lauren pulled away from him. The man scrambled and called for backup and an ambulance.

She could almost smell his fear. He was a uniform, probably new to patrol duty, and he'd just thought he was heading out to pick up the DA for a little babysitting job.

Hank pointed at her. "Stay here, ma'am."

No, no way. If someone was in there—possibly hurt—she had to help. She was the one to run toward those in need, never away. Helping victims was her job.

When he took off running, so did she.

Hank jumped up the back steps. He whirled when he heard her footsteps. "Ma'am, you're supposed to stay—"

"We're wasting time!" Her voice held the whip of command. She was the DA, dammit.

Gulping, Hank spun around and headed into the house.

She hurried behind him, using his flashlight to guide her. The milk had fallen to the floor. Spilled everywhere. Her tennis shoes slid through the white liquid. A few seconds later, she and Hank were in her narrow hallway. Then—

Her bedroom?

Hank's flashlight hit the face of the officer. He was over Lauren's bed. Crouched over the woman sprawled on Lauren's covers.

A woman who wasn't moving. A woman whose eyes stared sightlessly above her. A woman covered in blood.

So much bright, red blood.

The light hit the woman's face. Lauren lost her breath. *I know her.* "Karen?" She tried to rush forward. No, no, that couldn't be Karen.

Hank caught her arms. "No, you need to stay back!"

Because it was a crime scene. Because they were looking at a murder victim. Because they were looking at—

"Karen!" Her best friend. Sometimes…sometimes it seemed Karen was her only friend.

The wail of a siren reached her. It was the ambulance coming to help them.

Coming too late.

Because Karen Royce, Lauren's best friend, was dead.

***

"Why did you have the knife, Lauren?"

Lauren's fingers tightened around the coffee mug. The coffee was ice-cold, pretty normal for the police station's thick brew. It was late, edging toward two a.m., but she didn't need the caffeine to keep her awake.

The image of Karen's mutilated body could do that just fine.

"Lauren?" the detective pressed, his voice deepening as he tried to catch her attention.

Lauren sighed. "Do you really think we need to do the formal game?" She'd worked with Paul Voyt on dozens of cases. And right then, the guy actually had her in the *interrogation* room. Normally, they questioned the suspects together.

Now he was the one questioning her.

Paul exhaled heavily. Face grim, he said, "I'm sorry, but I'm afraid we do. Karen Royce was stabbed at least five times, in your home, and officers on the scene reported that you raced out of your house holding a butcher knife."

She pinched the bridge of her nose. A headache throbbed relentlessly behind her eyes. "There's no blood on the knife. Or on me. Get the techs to check the weapon. They'll see it wasn't used." Her lips wanted to tremble so she pressed them together as she straightened her shoulders. Then, when she hoped that the trembling had passed, Lauren said, "You can't be looking at me for this crime. You *know* me, Paul."

Damn well.

Biblically.

Unfortunately. Their night together had been a one-time mistake that would not be repeated.

She'd been lonely. Weak.

Missing an ex-lover who couldn't stay out of her mind, even though he'd sure moved on easily enough. As soon as the case had been closed, he'd left town without looking back.

If only she'd been able to move on so easily.

"Right now, all I know is that a dead body was found, in your house, in *your* bed, Lauren." But there was sympathy in his voice. Paul was a good guy, and she could tell by his expression that he *hated* doing this part of his job.

"I didn't kill Karen. She was my friend."

"A friend who you were fighting with yesterday."

Her gaze flew to his.

"Yeah. I know about that. Word traveled fast about your little courthouse scene."

"That was…a personal matter." One she didn't want to get into. Karen was dead. There was no need to say or do anything to hurt her memory.

"Don't give me that. I need you to be honest. To cooperate *fully*. Hell, you know the press is going to freakin' flip when they find out that the DA is involved in a murder—"

"Jon Walker escaped." Lauren said the words flatly. "That's why the cops were at my house. They were bringing me here, for protection. But *you* should already know that." She leveled her stare at him. "So why am I being grilled when you should be looking for Jon and not wasting time in here with me?"

"We *are* looking for him. But questions still have to be asked, and hell, Lauren, I thought you'd prefer to talk to me instead of the other detectives out there."

The breath felt cold in her lungs. He was right. If she had to sit through the questioning, she'd rather face him.

"Why was she at your house?"

"I don't know." Truth. "Karen had a key, and sometimes she liked to crash there."

"You're sure you didn't know she was going to be there?"

"No!" The denial sprang from her. She sucked in a deep breath. Held tight to her control. "After our argument, I hadn't talked to Karen. I had no idea she'd be at my place." Not until she'd found her body. A sight Lauren would never forget. "I saw her in my room. I saw what had been done to her." Lauren's gaze held his. "You know Jon's way of killing. You know just what the Butcher liked to do."

Jon Walker had been given the grim moniker of the Bayou Butcher—sometimes shortened simply to the Butcher—for a reason.

Paul leaned toward her, his body on the edge of his wooden chair. His eyes, a steely light gray, raked over her. Paul was handsome, tall, strong. He had one of those golden-boy faces that got witnesses to trust him far too easily, a very handy trick. "You're telling me the Butcher was in your house? Did you see him there? The uniforms told me they didn't see any sign of anyone else."

Like the blood hadn't been a sign of someone else?

She shook her head. "I'm not saying I saw him." Another icy breath. "I'm saying I didn't kill Karen. I wouldn't! Jon Walker has been out for over—" Hell, what was it? She'd asked the cops on her ride there. "Over twenty-four hours. That would have given him plenty of time to get out here and—"

"You think he came for you?"

Her fingers pressed onto the scarred tabletop. "I was the one who put him away." She'd made her career on that case. She'd been twenty-eight when she prosecuted the Butcher. Twenty-eight and secretly terrified of the monster who sat in the courtroom with her. But Lauren hadn't let fear stop her. She'd done her job. Convicted that murdering SOB.

By the time she'd turned twenty-nine, the Butcher had been in Angola and she'd already been the DA. A DA who still had nightmares because of that case.

"Fuck, Lauren." Paul's hand crept toward hers. A crack had appeared in his mask. "I wasn't even on duty when the call came through about Walker and you. The captain just sent me in here when you pulled up with the uniforms. I got the shortest fucking briefing on record." His gaze held hers as his fingers covered her hand. "But if that sick sonofabitch is actually back and targeting you—"

The door opened behind Paul. Lauren glanced up, expecting to see the face of another detective or maybe even someone from her office.

She didn't expect to see U.S. Marshal Anthony Ross standing there.

For a second, she simply stared at him as the memories came rushing back. Once, she would have done just about anything for that man. She'd wanted him more than breath. Needed him with a fierce desire that just wouldn't stop.

Then she remembered...

He'd just walked away.

He'd been so busy walking that he hadn't noticed when he left her in damn pieces behind him.

His gaze—a green that was bright and intense—dropped to her hand. Paul's hand. His square jaw seemed to harden, then he stalked forward, even as Paul leaped to his feet.

"This is an interrogation," Paul began as his body blocked Ross's. "You can't barge in here—"

"It's one cozy interrogation," Anthony muttered. "I bet that technique works wonders with the suspects."

He shouldered around Paul.

Paul grabbed his arm. "Who the hell are you and just *why* are you in my interrogation?"

Anthony yanked out his ID. "U.S. Marshal Anthony Ross."

Paul blinked.

"And I'm here because I'm in charge of tracking the escaped fugitive Jon Walker." Lauren could almost hear the *dumbass* that she knew Anthony wanted to tack on the end of his statement. Anthony had never been gifted with a whole lot of patience—or finesse.

Paul backed away.

Then Anthony bent over her. His hands swept over Lauren's arms. "Were you hurt?" There was a deeper, more intimate note in his voice. One that reminded her far too much of other times.

She shook her head. "I wasn't the one he stabbed."

"No, but you were the target."

That seemed to be the consensus, dammit. Anthony sure seemed certain enough of that. She stared into his eyes, seeing the faint gold around his pupils. Anthony was big, easily six feet three, with wide shoulders that had once done him proud during his college football days.

But he didn't run on the field anymore.

Now he ran down fugitives. Protected witnesses.

Stared at her with a leashed fury in his eyes.

"Are we even sure it's Walker?" Paul's question was quiet, considering. "I mean, there are other killers out there."

He was right. There were plenty of killers loose out there. But Jon Walker was in a category all by himself.

Paul shook his head. "Walker just escaped from prison—shouldn't his first move have been a run for the border?"

Anthony's expression never changed. "Not if he wanted revenge."

Her heart beat faster.

Anthony's stare was unnerving as he told her, "He had a picture of you in his cell. I don't know how or when he got it, but Walker had it pinned right above his pillow, just where he could see it every night."

A shiver slid over her.

"He escapes, then twenty-four hours later, a woman winds up dead, stabbed in your bed, Butcher-style."

Paul stood behind Anthony, silent, but with an avid gaze on them.

"You don't have to be a genius to connect those dots," Anthony growled. "Walker's coming for you. You put him in prison. You're the one he wants dead."

And Karen had—what? Been in the wrong place? Died, for Lauren?

So much blood. She tried—and failed—to shove the image out of her mind.

"*If* he wanted me dead—" She spoke slowly, trying to hold on to her control because of all the people in the world, she would *not* break in front of Anthony Ross.

Stay with me.

Those had been her words to him.

He hadn't stayed.

Hadn't cared enough to do so.

Her shoulders stiffened as she said again, "If he wanted me dead, I wouldn't be sitting here. He could have just stayed in the house, waited for me to get home, then he could have killed *me.*"

Now Paul cleared his throat. "Lauren, you said you heard a whisper when you got home."

Anthony's gaze sharpened.

Lauren gave a slow nod.

"Was that whisper from Karen?" Paul asked.

Lauren hesitated. "The wind was loud. I'd just come inside."

"Was it a woman's voice?" Paul pressed.

She closed her eyes for a moment, blocking him out, trying to block out Anthony, too. If only it was that easy.

But she focused and tried to remember…

The milk was sliding. The shutters banging. Then a whisper. Lauren…

"I thought it was a man's voice." Her eyes opened. "But I can't swear to that." She, of all people, knew how unreliable witness testimony could be.

"If it was a man, he could have still been inside," Paul said, voice tightening. "He could have been there—"

"And he got away when I ran out to meet the cops." The thunder and rain would have masked the sound of the killer's footsteps.

"Uniforms are searching the area," Paul said. "We can—"

Anthony gave a hard shake of his head. "That's not good enough." Then he rose to his full height, a height that put him a few inches above Paul. "Jon Walker grew up in this area. He knows how to vanish in these swamps."

Knew how, and had, for months before during his previous attacks.

Sometimes he'd taken his victims with him into those swamps.

"I can find him," Paul said, voice grim. "I can track him down."

Anthony's gaze burned. "When it comes to fugitive apprehension, I'm in charge of the Walker case. The marshals will be finding him." He stared down at Lauren. "We stop him *before* he gets close to the target he wants so desperately."

CYNTHIA EDEN

Then he backed away. Marched for the door.

Her breath rasped out on a heavy sigh. That was it? He barged in, dropped the Walker photo bombshell on her, then vanished?

She shot to her feet. Almost instantly, she found her path blocked by Paul. Gritting her teeth, she said, "I need to talk to him."

"My captain told me to hold you, to make sure—"

"I'm not leaving the station, but I am talking to him." She was the DA. She'd played nice with him, but she wasn't about to let any of the cops shove her into a corner. "Follow me, but you aren't stopping me." The only way he could stop her would be to arrest her, and she knew that wasn't happening.

Five years ago, Jon Walker had abducted and mutilated coeds. No, he'd *started* with coeds. The first two victims he'd killed quickly, but by victim number three—Gina Richardson—he'd changed his kill method. He'd taken Gina into the swamp. Kept her alive for days. Taken his time as he tortured her.

Hunters had discovered Gina's body a week later. What was left of it, anyway.

The cops had been monitoring every college campus in the area. Extra security procedures had been put into place by the administrations.

Curfews were instituted, and girls had been advised to not walk alone at night on the campuses. With dead coeds, no one had been willing to take chances.

The cops had been sure that they would catch the killer.

But as the security had tightened at the colleges, Walker had just moved on to a new hunting ground. He'd abducted a waitress from an all-night diner. Then a mom of two. A stripper had been his next victim. A teenage babysitter his seventh—and the victim who had finally tripped him up.

Kathy Johnson had been hired to watch the children at 508 Marigold Place—she'd agreed to stay all night for a little extra cash so that the Petersons could enjoy an anniversary night on the town.

Walker had known about Kathy's schedule that night. He'd known about the kids who'd been asleep upstairs—kids who hadn't even realized what was happening in their house.

But Carolyn Peterson had gotten sick at dinner. She and her husband had canceled their anniversary plans and come home early—and they'd found Walker using his knife on sixteen-year-old Kathy.

So many bodies. So much death. And it wasn't over. It *still* wasn't over.

Because she hadn't done her job well enough. Sure, the press had all claimed that she'd done great. Her boss had been impressed. But, deep down, Lauren knew the truth. *If I'd fought harder, the guy would have gotten the death penalty. Not life in prison.*

Now it looked as if he wanted her to be the one to die.

She slipped by Paul and hurried to the door. Her fingers shook as she grabbed the knob. She yanked it hard to the left, then rushed outside of the room, too aware of all the glances that slid her way. Her own stare darted around the room.

She found Anthony's retreating back. Saw him and two other men she didn't recognize. More marshals? Anthony and the men turned for the exit.

"Ross!" Her voice whipped with an order.

Lauren could sound like she had authority when she needed to do it. No one had to know that her knees were shaking.

Anthony looked back at her. The man was still as handsome as ever. High cheekbones. Strong blade of a nose. High forehead.

His dark hair was shorter than it had been before, the faint lines near his mouth were a bit deeper, but the guy was still too good-looking by far for her peace of mind.

Dark. Dangerous.

Her type.

Well, once upon a time, he had been. She was trying—very much trying—to stick with the good guys these days. Guys who were *safe*.

Her tennis shoes squeaked as she hurried across the bull pen. She hadn't exactly been given time to change before being rushed to the station.

Was Paul following her? She didn't hear his footsteps. That was good.

She closed in on Anthony. "We need to talk."

A muscle flexed in his jaw. "Later, ma'am." His native Georgia drawl rolled lightly beneath his words. "Right now, I have a killer to hunt."

She grabbed his arm. Held tight. "A killer who was in *my* house. A killer who murdered *my* friend." *Karen, I am so sorry.* Each time she thought of Karen, it felt as if someone were clawing open her chest. "You aren't shutting me out, understand, Ross? I'm working this with you. I am going to make sure this city doesn't fall back into the Bayou Butcher madness it faced before." When fear had held them all captive.

Fear of the dark.

Fear of the monster who waited in the dark.

Jon Walker had made children—and even adults—fear the boogeyman once more. Because he truly was that monster.

"I tracked him before," Anthony said quietly. No emotion entered his voice or his gaze. "And I can do it again."

Without you.

Unspoken, but the words were still there, hanging between them.

She wouldn't back down. "My office will give you any support you need. We *will* work together on this." She knew the reporters were probably already swarming outside. Paul had been right on that score—a story about her, about the Bayou Butcher—hell, yes, they were talking a front-page spread.

Anthony bent toward her. His scent—rich, masculine— surrounded her. His mouth was close to her ear when he whispered. "Haven't you already come close enough to death?"

She turned her head. Met his stare. "Haven't you?" Because she knew the risks he took, day in and day out.

Even when he'd left her, she'd followed his career. Anthony's cases were the darkest she'd ever encountered. Brutal killers. Sadistic criminals.

Nightmares.

"Not close enough," he told her softly. "Not yet." His green gaze heated as it swept over her. "*I missed you.*"

Then he was gone. Hurrying away with the other two men as they went out on the hunt. When the station's doors opened, she heard the shouts from the reporters.

Yes, they were there.

Her hands had clenched into fists. She glanced around the room, wondering what the detectives and cops saw when they looked at her. Lauren sure hoped she didn't look as out of control as she felt.

Because she felt like she was breaking apart on the inside.

I missed you.

But he'd sure walked away easily enough. Then, and now.

***

Anthony paused as the reporters swarmed around him. When a body was found right inside a DA's house, word sure spread like wildfire.

Especially when the Bayou Butcher was on the loose.

"No comment," Anthony snapped as he made his way through the crowd. When necessary, he knew how to use reporters to his advantage.

However, he wasn't interested in using them at that moment. He wanted to get to Lauren's house. To search the area himself. Every moment that passed allowed Walker to get farther away.

He went straight for Lauren.

Anthony slid into the SUV that waited on the corner. Three seconds later, he was rushing away from the scene.

When he arrived at Lauren's house, he wasn't surprised to see more reporters. They were standing behind the yellow line of police tape—barely behind it. Vultures, closing in.

"Go talk to the trackers," Anthony ordered Jim O'Keith when the other marshal climbed from the second SUV and came to his side. Jim was new to his division, having transferred up just a few months back. This was the guy's first big fugitive case, and Anthony could see the nervous tension in the man's body.

But they didn't have time for fear.

Matt Meadows followed behind Jim. Matt had far more seniority, and a real gift with tech. Matt didn't talk much, but the man was one of the best guys Anthony had ever seen in the field. His ancestry was a mix of Jamaican and Cherokee Indian, and Matt had told him once that his parents had wanted him to be comfortable in *any* world he faced. From what Anthony had seen, Matt could more than handle himself, any place, any time.

Carefully, Anthony made his way past the police tape. He flashed his ID so he could gain access to the house. He'd be taking charge of this case—and this scene until someone with more authority came along and damn well had to kick his ass out.

He would make sure the Butcher went back to jail. And when he did, Walker would *not* be escaping again.

Cops were milling around. More detectives. The homicide captain was there, too. Anthony recognized him at once—he'd worked with Reginald Powers when they'd originally apprehended Jon Walker years before.

Reginald inclined his head as he came toward Anthony. "Been a long time."

They shook hands. More gray lined Reginald's hair than the last time Anthony had seen him, and the guy's dark eyes looked tired.

Anthony wondered if he looked as grim. After the Valentine Killer case, there had been days when he hadn't even wanted to look in the mirror. *That SOB almost took me out.* But he shoved those memories aside. "You knew I'd be the one they sent to track him."

Reginald pulled his hand back. "You are the best, right?"

No, he was just one of the marshals who faced death too damn much.

"Come on. I'll show you where they found the body."

Anthony didn't tell Reginald that he already knew exactly how to get to Lauren's bedroom. Not many people in that town had known about their relationship. Lauren had been too good at keeping secrets.

Reginald led Anthony down a tight hallway. The house smelled of Lauren. Lilacs. He hadn't even known what lilacs were, not until her. After her, he'd never been able to forget the scent.

They rounded a corner, and then they were heading into Lauren's bedroom. The sheets had been stripped from the bed, and Anthony could easily see the bloodstained mattress.

"The ME estimates that our victim died at least an hour before she was found," Reginald told him.

An hour.

"Rigor mortis had already set in, but the uniform on scene…" Another rough sigh. "Hell, it was the kid's first body. He still tried to save her."

Hard to save the dead.

"Lauren heard a voice," Anthony said. "When she first came into the house, she heard someone call her name." His gaze scanned the tidy room—tidy, except for the blood. The scent of the blood smothered the lilacs.

"You think she heard the killer?"

He did.

The killer had been there. Waiting.

Had he wanted Lauren to rush in? To find the body? If so, he would have wanted the perfect place to watch her discovery. "Have your crime scene techs been over the whole room?" He could see one tech bent down on the other side of the bed.

"They're still working. I want them to be as thorough as they can be."

On this case, there wouldn't be room for slipups.

Anthony pulled on a pair of latex gloves. He headed toward the closet. It was located at the foot of the bed. The door had thin, decorative slits running its length. Slits that would allow someone inside to easily see out to the bed.

He opened the door.

"We searched there," Reginald said from behind him as he heaved a sigh. "Didn't find anything."

Nothing looked disturbed inside. Lauren's clothes hung neatly on their hangers. Her shoes were all neatly on the shelves. The scent of lilacs was stronger in the small space.

Reginald came closer to Anthony. "Someone threw the breaker at her house, that's why she didn't have power when she came in. The techs swept for prints there, but it had been wiped clean."

Anthony bent, staring down at the carpet. No shoe impressions. No debris.

He headed into the closet.

Shut the door.

Anthony stared through those slits—and had a perfect view of the blood-soaked bed. His hands rose, hovering above the door.

He reached higher. Higher. The closet would have been the choice spot for anyone who wanted to hide, but if the killer had been in the dark, he would have wanted something close by so he could turn on a light and see his victims—both of them.

His fingers skimmed along the edge of the door's top. His hand slid over the wood, searching.

He wondered if there was a small flashlight somewhere. Instead, his gloved fingers touched the handle of something. A knife. He pulled the weapon down and stepped from the closet.

Reginald let out a low whistle.

Anthony studied the blade. No blood. The knife appeared to have been wiped clean, but the techs would be able to tell for sure.

"Sonofabitch," Reginald muttered.

Yes, Walker was. Anthony raised a brow as he looked at the captain. "I guess your guys missed something." A pretty big fucking something. On a case like this, there wasn't any room for error. No mistakes.

Mistakes meant death.

CHAPTER TWO

"District Attorney Chandler!" a reporter shouted as Lauren paused on the steps of the courthouse. "Is it true the Bayou Butcher is hunting in the city once more?"

Anthony saw Lauren pull in a slow breath, then she pushed back her shoulders. He'd seen her do that move dozens of times in court. Bracing herself. Getting ready for the attack.

She turned slowly to face the crowd, and the sunlight glinted off her blonde hair. She'd changed clothes, put on a sleek skirt and blouse that made her look both professional and far too sexy for his weak self-control.

She'd always been too tempting for him.

"Jon Walker escaped from Angola prison, and the U.S. Marshals Service is currently conducting a manhunt for him." Her eyes, the brightest shade of blue Anthony had ever seen, glanced his way. "I have every confidence that the marshals will have Walker back within custody in a very short time." She gave a nod, and turned away.

"Will they have him back in custody before or *after* he kills again?" the same reporter fired out. A redhead, one with her hair in a twist, and one who was already trying to follow Lauren up those steps. "The Butcher *did* kill the woman who was found in your house last night, correct?"

Lauren glanced back. Even across the space that separated them, Anthony could feel the chill of her stare. "Sharon, you should know better. I cannot comment on an ongoing murder investigation."

Then Lauren hurried up the steps, refusing to give any more comments. Anthony pushed through the crowd and followed her easily. They both needed to see the judge, and if this trip gave him the chance to have a few minutes alone with Lauren, he'd take those minutes.

His ID let him sweep right past security. The reporters were held back, but their questions followed him.

Lauren's heels clicked across the marble as she closed in on the elevator. She slipped inside, turned around, and saw him. He caught the slight flare of surprise as her eyes widened. The doors began to close. He pushed his hand through the doors, triggering the sensor. Then he was inside with her. His gaze held hers.

"Hold the elevator!" a voice shouted.

Anthony glanced over his shoulder. "Get the next one," he ordered, his voice a low rumble as he shoved against the button to send the doors closing.

The guy—older, balding—glared at him but wisely stepped back.

The elevator doors closed. Anthony glanced to the left at the control panel. She'd pushed the button for the fifth floor. Not a lot of time to talk, so...

He pulled the emergency stop knob.

"What the hell?" Lauren immediately demanded as she surged forward. "Why did you do that?"

He turned toward her. *Damn.* Until he'd walked into the station and seen her, he'd almost forgotten just how beautiful she was in person. Photographs had never done her justice.

Up close, he could see all the different shades of gold and blonde in her hair. Natural—he knew that fact intimately. Her face was heart shaped, her cheeks high, and her lips so lush and full. And—

"Stop looking at me that way," she told him, backing up a step. Her forward march had sure stopped quickly enough. "And get this elevator moving."

In due time. He cocked his head and continued to study her. Five years. He'd thought about her far too often during that time. "Back at the station, you were the one saying that we needed to talk."

"Yes, well, I've got a judge waiting on me now. A very nervous judge who I'm going to have to calm down." Her gaze flickered over him. "You didn't find the killer's trail at my house, did you?"

"We knew the rain would wipe away the tracks." Mother Nature could be a real bitch when she wanted to be. "Every cop in this city is on full alert," Anthony said. "I've got my men doing sweeps, and as soon as I talk to Judge Hamilton—" He broke off and gave a grim smile at the surprised expression on her face. "Yeah, I'm here to see him, too."

Judge Pierce Hamilton. The man who had presided over Walker's case.

The judge who was now nervous as all hell because the killer was on the loose once more. Only Anthony didn't think the judge was the prime target for Walker. Walker hadn't been fixated on the judge's image, he hadn't gone straight to the guy's house.

No, Walker's main attention...*is on Lauren.*

Lauren had been the one in that courtroom, telling the world what a monster Walker truly was. It had been her face on the TVs, in the newspapers. Hamilton had banged the gavel, but it had been Lauren who sent Walker to Angola.

Then he remembered the way she'd cut through the courthouse. That sexy rolling stride—the way she'd been *alone.* Back teeth clenching, he gritted out, "I thought the cop was giving you protection." That had been his order to the handsy cop who'd been way too close to Lauren at the station.

Her delicate brows arched. "Don't worry, Marshal. I have a police escort here, and he's waiting outside to take me back to my office once I'm done with the judge. I'm covered."

Not well enough. He sure hadn't caught sight of her escort. "Walker *killed* a woman in your house."

"I'm well aware of that."

She should be plenty aware of the danger. Lauren couldn't pretend like most folks did. Couldn't act like the monsters weren't real.

Her breath whispered out as she continued. "He killed a friend, not just a woman. A *friend.* I'm trying to figure out why Karen was even at my house, and don't think for a minute, not one single minute"—now she was advancing on him once more, closing the space between them as color lit her cheeks—"that I don't feel like someone ripped into my heart. Karen was the best friend I had."

Maybe that's why she's dead. He didn't tell her that. Couldn't. It was too brutal of a truth.

But Walker was a brutal killer. He'd suffered in jail. Locked up for five long years. Maybe he wanted Lauren to suffer now, too.

Anthony's hand lifted and brushed across her cheek. She flinched at his touch and pulled away from him.

"Get this elevator moving," she said, but her voice was husky, reminding him of their past. Tangled sheets. Secrets. "*Now.*"

No, not just yet.

Studying her carefully, he said, "We're gonna need the DA's office to work with my team. Full cooperation."

She stared back at him. "Did you really think I'd give you any-thing less?"

With the way things were between them, he hadn't been sure. He should have known, though. Lauren had always been good at compartmentalizing her life. Hot sex with him in private. Ice in public.

She exhaled slowly. "He killed two people at the prison. That's what Paul told me."

Paul. The handsy detective. Anthony nodded.

"He only killed women before." Her voice was softer now. His hand had clenched into a fist—so he wouldn't reach out to her again. "But this time, one of the victims was a guard?"

Another nod. "It was a fast kill. More necessity than anything else." Cold words. They had to be. He didn't tell her about the doc-tor's body. Walker had been up to his old tricks with her. Staring into Lauren's bright gaze he said, "I'm meeting with the judge, then I'm joining my team. We're going to search every hangout that Walker had in this area. He's in Baton Rouge, and he's going to try to look for security, familiarity."

Her lips pressed together, then she said, "I want to come with you."

"Baby, that's not—"

Her head jerked up. "I'm *not* your baby."

Talk about a slip. He sure hadn't meant for that to roll out.

"What I am…I'm the DA in this town. I want the people here to know we're doing everything possible to keep the city safe, and I want justice for Karen." She swallowed. The faint click almost seemed painful to his ears because he knew she was trying to push away the grief from her friend's death. "I won't get in your way, but I *will* be involved, and if I have to go over your head to do it, then I—"

Static crackled on the elevator's intercom. "Ms. Chandler?"

Her head turned toward the security camera near the speaker in the left corner.

"Do you need assistance?" that crackling voice asked.

She leaned around Anthony, her body brushing lightly against his, and pressed the button to restart the elevator. "No, thank you. We're good."

The elevator rose. Their gazes held.

He hadn't agreed to let her tag along on his hunt.

She hadn't backed down.

Just like old times.

The doors slid open. "I can help you," she said quietly as they headed toward the judge's chambers. "I'm the one who talked to Walker's friends before and after the trial. I'm the one who interviewed the witnesses. I know him and his habits far better than you."

Maybe that was true, but he still wanted her away from the danger.

Not getting up close and personal with it.

She waved to a guard, then paused near the judge's closed chamber doors. The flush had left her cheeks. Now she studied him with a cool gaze. "Unless you don't think you can manage to keep me safe while I'm with you and your entire team of marshals. Is that the issue? Maybe my safety is too much to ask?"

He almost smiled. Would have, if he hadn't been so worried about the twisted killer on the loose. "I can do my job."

"Good. And I can do mine." She turned away from him. Knocked on the door. "Judge Hamilton!" Her voice rose.

The judge's secretary wasn't at her desk. Anthony wasn't in the mood to wait around for the lady to return so that she could announce his arrival. He didn't have time to kill. He pulled Lauren back and shoved open the door.

The judge stood just a few feet away from the door. His black robe billowed around him. His face, pale and haggard, reflected his fear.

"What took you both so damn long?" Pierce Hamilton waved his hands, motioning to hurry inside. "What the hell is going on? How did Walker get out?" He marched around to sit behind his big, antique mahogany desk.

Lauren eased into the lush leather chair across from the judge. Anthony didn't bother sitting. "He stabbed himself with a shiv, got taken to the infirmary at Angola, then he managed to kill a guard and the doctor on duty."

Hamilton flinched but his gaze didn't waver. "Did he have help? Is the bastard working alone?"

Now this was the dicey part. "We haven't found any connection to anyone else...yet." But Anthony's instincts were in overdrive. The guy had gotten away from the prison too quickly. Had transportation been waiting? An old friend—or even a new one—who'd been willing to help the Bayou Butcher? Anthony had someone searching through all the visitor records at the prison. If there was a link to anyone who could possibly have assisted Walker, then he *would* find that link.

Fuck, the last thing they needed was to discover that Walker had an accomplice out there. Someone to help the sick freak with his crimes.

"We're going to talk to all of Walker's acquaintances next," Lauren said, her voice the smooth cream that lulled jurors into believing every word she said. "If he's working with someone, we'll find out."

But her voice didn't seem to be lulling Hamilton.

"I'm going to hunt Walker based on what we already know about him." Anthony could see the judge wanted reassurance that

Walker would be caught. Well, he'd do his fucking best. "Walker was always at home in the swamps. He knows that area like the back of his hand. We're going to search there, because the swamps would be the perfect hiding spot for him. Isolated, secure. He would feel in control there."

"And Walker was always about control," Lauren murmured.

Yes, he had been.

"His cabin," Hamilton said, frowning, "that damn place where he kept all of his trophies—"

Anthony saw Lauren swallow. He didn't like remembering that place, either. "We're going to search it. Trust me, judge, I know how to do my damn job."

Hamilton didn't look reassured. He looked like he was about to break apart. "We're off the record here," Hamilton said as he ran a hand through his graying hair. "So far off."

Lauren glanced over at Anthony, then nodded. "All right."

"I was sleeping with Karen." His fingers flattened on the table as his gaze cut to Lauren. "But you knew that, didn't you?"

It was sure news to Anthony. Karen Royce had been an investigator at the DA's office. He'd met her a few times before, back when they'd all been working the Butcher case.

Hamilton was a married man, tied to old southern money. Had his wife known about the affair?

"That's why you and Lauren fought at the courthouse, isn't it?" Hamilton continued. "You think I didn't hear about that? Hell, gossip travels like wildfire here. You found out about us..."

"I knew," Lauren said softly.

Hamilton's hands slapped against the desk. "And you didn't call to tell me about her murder? A murder that happened right in your own damn home?" Anger ripped through his words. "I had to find out about it on the news. I had to—"

"Right after her body was discovered, I was taken to the precinct, surrounded by cops and reporters. Did you really think that if I stopped to call you *then*, it wouldn't be noted?"

The judge's eyes glittered, but he didn't speak.

"Karen told me you two had broken things off. She told me that I didn't need to worry about her because it was *over* with you."

"We would have worked it out. We would have—"

"You're married." Her voice was flat. "Karen told me she didn't want to be involved with you anymore. She was done—she hated that she'd been with you. Hated that she'd let you *use* her." Anger flashed across Lauren's face. "Dammit, Hamilton, you have a ring on your finger. It's supposed to mean something."

The ring gleamed dully. The judge's eyes narrowed. "My wife knew about Karen. She didn't care—"

"Maybe Karen deserved better than to be your dirty little secret."

He surged to his feet. "Maybe she deserved better than to die in your place!"

Fuck that. Anthony jumped between them. "Judge, you need to calm the hell down."

The judge sucked in a deep breath. "He went after Lauren, didn't he? Her house, her bedroom. Karen was just in the wrong place. I called her—told her I was coming over to her house…" His words tumbled out. "I wanted to talk. I was willing to do *anything* to get her back." His body trembled. "She told me she wouldn't be home. Karen left—went to *her* place, and she died in *her*—"

"If it was Walker, then he knew exactly who Karen Royce was," Anthony cut in before the judge could say anything else. "If he was the one who killed her, then it was deliberate. Maybe he was trying to send a message with her death."

The judge suddenly looked much older as the lines on his face appeared to deepen. "What message?"

Payback.

As he stared at the other man, Anthony saw that the judge understood. The knowledge was in his eyes.

"The DA's getting protection," Anthony said without glancing back at Lauren. "We'll work with the police and make sure you have a guard, too."

"Are you sure that's necessary?" Then Hamilton gave a rough laugh. "Do you know how many killers have told me they were coming after me? How many threats I've received over the years?"

"Walker won't just threaten. He'll slice you apart."

Hamilton shook his head. "Only women. That's his target. That's what all the shrinks and profilers said on the stand. He only targeted women because of need for control and fixation on the female form and—"

"The prison guard was male. He's just as dead as the others."

The judge shut up.

"You're getting protection." The last thing Anthony wanted was another body turning up.

If they didn't find Walker soon, that was exactly what would happen.

***

The judge was nervous when he walked into the courtroom. His steps were too fast, his movements too abrupt.

Good. The bastard should be nervous. He should be shaking. Running.

Dying.

He would be dying, soon enough.

The judge slammed down his gavel. Called everyone to order. The lawyers stood and started preening for the jury.

The judge's eyes were darkened with fear as they swept around the courtroom.

Looking for a killer he wouldn't find. Disguises were always easy enough to manage. Most folks saw only what they *wanted* to see.

The guy had no clue.

He'd been in this courtroom before. So many times. Waiting. Watching.

He'd lost something very important in this same room. He *would* be getting it back.

As for the judge—as for the self-righteous jurors and the slick lawyers—maybe it was time for them to see what it felt like to lose.

To lose everything, including their lives.

He stood and made his way to the back of the courtroom. This wasn't the place, but the time was close. So very close. The next target waited.

He had a list, and he'd be crossing the names off.

One by one.

He paused at the door and glanced back at the judge. The oblivious fool.

I'll be seeing you.

Maybe he'd let the bastard die with the robe still on. Seemed fitting. The robe—the job—would be what killed him.

***

The SUV braked just outside of the small cabin that sat on the edge of the swamp. Lauren climbed out of the vehicle, and her heels immediately sank into the mud.

Gritting her teeth, she trudged forward, or, rather, she went as far forward as Anthony would allow. He threw up his hand, blocking her, while the two other marshals he'd introduced her to earlier, Jim O'Keith and Matt Meadows, made their way toward the cabin.

"It looks abandoned," she whispered. It looked that way because it was. Once upon a time, the cabin had belonged to Jon Walker. After his arrest, the place had been left to rot…and rot it had. The wood was falling down and the windows were smashed in.

The word *BUTCHER* had been spray painted across the front door—a door that swung open. She could see bricks and rocks strewn across the sagging front porch.

Folks in the area hadn't exactly taken kindly to finding out that a serial killer had been using their swamp. Right after Walker's arrest, the place had even been set on fire. The wood in the back and near the roof was charred, and maybe it was her imagination, but she could almost swear she still smelled ash.

Jim and Matt slid inside the open door.

Her gaze darted to the left. To the right. Trees twisted and concealed, hiding the murky green water that she knew wasn't very far away.

"No sign of any other vehicles, at least, not since the rain," she murmured as her gaze slid over the muddy stretch that passed for a dirt road. The only tire tracks she saw were from the marshals' SUVs.

So Walker hadn't returned to his little home away from home. *I'm surprised someone didn't come back and finish burning this place to the ground.*

The victims' families had sure been angry enough to do it.

And the little cabin—the dark husk that remained of it—was eerie. Dark.

Dangerous.

"Clear!" Jim's voice came from inside, and Anthony finally stepped back so that they could head toward the cabin.

Jim met them on the porch. "There's no sign of anyone inside." He was young, probably in his midtwenties, with dark-blond hair and eyes that seemed a bit nervous.

Behind him, Matt Meadows was still doing a sweep of the area. She'd met Matt a time or two over the years. Quiet, intense, the African American marshal seemed the exact opposite of Jim. There wasn't anything nervous about Matt—the guy was too controlled for nerves.

"We'll start a sweep of the perimeter," Matt said as he turned toward the bald cypress trees that dipped toward the murky water. Heavy moss hung from the trees, drooping toward the dank earth.

Anthony nodded. "I'll finish the search in here."

The others slid past them.

There wasn't much to search in the charred remains. Two rooms. No furniture. Dirt. Mold. Decay.

"This is where it started," Lauren whispered as she crept carefully around the cabin. This place. With its wooden walls and small rooms. They'd found Walker's tools in this cabin. The sharpened knives.

The trophies.

Walker had kept trophies from his kills.

Her gaze lit on a heavy chunk of wood that had fallen near the left wall.

"No," Anthony said, "it didn't start here."

The certainty in Anthony's voice had her glancing over at him.

"This is just where it ended. Where it *should* have ended." His eyes narrowed, but his gaze wasn't on her. It was on the wood near her feet. "Where did that come from?"

"It must have fallen—" But she broke off because she'd just looked up and realized that there weren't any missing roof slats from above them, and the wall beside her was charred, but not broken. The wood was broken to the left, way across on the other wall, not in that spot.

His hand closed around her arm and Anthony pulled her back. Then he bent and carefully slid the wood, maneuvering it so he could see underneath it.

She peered over his shoulder.

Something gold glinted in the light.

Gold...

"We're gonna need Detective Voyt and his men out here," Anthony said as his fingers tightened around the wood.

"A necklace." She could see it clearly now. Thin, delicate. A woman's necklace.

"Maybe it's nothing, just something left by some kid, but—"

"It's not." Her voice was sad and certain. She could see the locket on the end. A locket with a rose in the center. Karen's locket. "It's hers."

His head whipped up, his eyes blazing. "Karen's?"

A nod.

"You're sure about that?"

Dead sure. "She was wearing it the last time I saw her alive."

In the next instant, he was pulling her from the cabin. "Don't touch anything else!"

She knew the drill. Evidence was there—evidence they didn't want to contaminate because the cabin wasn't nearly as abandoned as it looked.

Before, Walker had kept his trophies there.

Now that he was back in town, it seemed he was back to his old tricks. He'd killed Karen, then brought his trophy back to the cabin.

It looked like some habits died very hard.

As soon as they exited the cabin, Anthony had his phone out. She listened to him make the call. He was asking for a tech team and telling Paul to get there ASAP.

Then he broke off.

She looked at him, and saw that his gaze had turned back toward the trees that led to the lake.

"We need you now," he snapped into the phone and ended the call. His gaze lit on her. "Stay behind me."

He pulled out his gun.

"The killer could still *be* here."

Her heart slammed into her chest. She crept behind him as they edged toward the line of twisting trees.

"There are old paths all through this place," Anthony muttered. "If you're coming by car, you have to take the dirt road. But you don't have to get here by car."

He slid through the trees. One hand locked around her wrist while his other hand remained tight around his weapon.

The trees bent overhead, blocking out the sky and sending faint streams of sunlight trickling over them. It was summer in Louisiana, which meant that it was already hell hot. Sweat began to bead on Lauren's skin. Every foot or so, her dang shoes got stuck in the mud, so she jerked them off and held them in her free hand.

Insects chirped around them and her breathing seemed far too loud. She was pretty sure she heard the hiss of a snake just a few feet away.

Then Anthony froze. "Tracks."

She could see them, too. Not from a car, but the single indention of a tire. A motorcycle?

The tracks cut through the mud and led deeper into the swamp.

Yes, some habits died very, very hard. It looked like Walker had come home again.

How many bodies would he leave in his wake this time?

***

The dogs were barking as they rushed through the swamp. They'd given the dogs Walker's scent, taken from prison clothes left at Angola. Anthony kept his gun ready, the image of Sheila Long's body too fresh in his mind.

Killers like Walker were predictable. They followed patterns— twisted patterns. After Karen's death, Anthony had suspected that Walker might come back to his cabin. It had been the guy's trophy shop, and sure enough, the killer *had* been back.

Karen Royce's necklace was proof of that.

The dogs began to whine. Hell. Not a good sign. The green water of the bayou waited up ahead.

And the motorcycle tracks ended.

"He didn't just take the bike into the water," Jim burst out as he threw his hands in the air. He glared at the dogs' handler. "Make them get the scent again."

One of the handlers spat on the ground. "Don't work like that." He had on the pressed uniform of the Baton Rouge K-9 unit. "You don't make 'em. They get what's there for them to find." The dogs were sniffing near the water's edge. "This is where he went."

Anthony nodded. "A boat." He could see the indentions on the embankment. The bayou slipped around and branched in at least four different directions. "The SOB had a boat waiting here for him."

A boat that was big enough to hold a motorcycle.

With every discovery they'd made, it was sure looking like Walker must have help. A man who'd been in prison for this long shouldn't have so many resources at his fingertips so quickly.

Sure, he could have stolen the motorcycle, but the boat, too? Maybe. *Doubtful.* Anthony's gaze landed on Detective Voyt's. The guy had hauled ass to meet them. "You got any reports of a stolen boat in these parts?"

Eyes grim, Voyt said, "I'll find out."

They needed to find out yesterday.

He can't be doing this alone. But according to the prison's warden, the guy hadn't read his mail. He hadn't gotten any visitors, other than lawyers. How the hell had they coordinated this?

*An accomplice...*not just an accomplice to escape, but, with Karen's body growing cold in the morgue, an accomplice to murder, too.

If Walker had stumbled on someone to go along with murder...*fuck, are you helping him kill?*

Anthony surveyed the water. A gator was drifting lazily about twenty feet away. "Locals have access to this area." The locals were the ones they needed. "Let's get some boats and see just where the hell he could have gone." He'd need aerial maps, ground maps. The swamp gave Walker far too many places to hide.

It also gave him a huge advantage. Walker had buried bodies in the swamp. He'd kept his victims here—alive, for days—while he'd tortured them. And no one had realized what was happening.

Because Walker had known the area too well.

"We need someone as familiar with this area as Walker." A guide who could help them while they hunted.

While we hunt, Walker's hunting, too.

Which one of them would find their prey first?

When Walker had been on the loose five years ago, they'd used an agent from Fish and Wildlife to help them search. He'd need to see if the guy was still available.

Anthony glanced back over his shoulder. He didn't see Lauren. She'd stayed behind with the uniforms. Watched him walk away with a worried gaze.

Get to her.

The instinct was there, and he found himself turning away from the others. Hurrying back toward the cabin. "Find that guide and get me those boats!" Anthony shouted back to the assembled men.

Each step was faster than the last as he rushed back to the cabin. Back to Lauren. Things were raw between them, rough. Their ending—hell, it had been screwed.

Walking away from her had been one of the hardest decisions of his life, but Lauren didn't know the secrets he carried.

He didn't want her to know them—or his shame.

He'd stayed away, tried to play it safe. Given her time to move on. To settle down. To have a family.

Only she hadn't settled down. She was still single—still just as tempting, and he *needed* her just as desperately as he'd needed her five years ago.

He'd wanted to see her, but he'd never expected to come back and find a killer stalking her.

Lauren was supposed to be safe. Protected. *Always.*

He jumped around the trees. Cop cars had swarmed on the scene. Uniforms were everywhere as they searched the area.

But he didn't see the shine of her blonde hair.

Anthony grabbed the nearest uniform. "Where's the DA?"

The guy blinked, doing a fast impression of an owl. "She got called back to the city. Some judge needed her."

Some judge… "Which judge?" He pulled out his phone. Hamilton hadn't called him.

"She didn't say. Just asked that a patrol car take her back."

The knot in his gut was getting worse. "Get that patrol car on the radio. I want to know exactly where she's going."

Had he really thought he'd be able to turn over her protection to someone else?

He needed her where he could see her. Wanted her close.

That had been the problem for them. He'd wanted her too much.

Until she'd become his obsession.

He knew, better than most, just how dangerous an obsession could be.

He glanced back at the cabin. So much death was there. He could feel the darkness, hanging in the very air around them.

Lauren had asked why Walker hadn't run for the border. Anthony knew it was because the killer hadn't escaped in order to be free.

He'd escaped to get his vengeance.

"Sir?"

He turned back at the uniform's voice.

"She's headed to meet Judge Hamilton. He's the one who called her back." The kid hesitated—and he truly looked like a kid, barely older than twenty-one. The uniform was new for him. "Want me to have her brought back to you?"

He'd wanted her back for years. But he'd stayed away.

He forced himself to unclench his jaw and say, "Tell the uniform to stay with her. Every single minute." He didn't like having her away from him. He wanted Walker back in his cage and as for Lauren…

Lauren with the lips made for sin and the eyes that, even after all she'd seen and done, still glinted with innocence.

He wanted Lauren back in his bed.

Too bad he couldn't always get just what he wanted.

**

"You can stay here," Lauren said as she turned and gave the police officer a weak smile. He'd been shadowing her the entire time she'd been in the courthouse. But she was at Hamilton's office door now. Safe, with plenty of guards close by. And Hamilton's message had said that the judge needed to see her—alone.

She rapped lightly on the door.

The secretary was gone from her desk again. But it was long past five now—past time for everyone to go home.

I can't go home. I don't want to remember Karen. I don't want to see the image of her body.

She'd already talked to Karen's parents twice that day. The grief in their voices had ripped through her.

Grief, rage…it had just made her guilt worse.

Hamilton didn't answer the door.

She frowned. He'd called her less than forty-five minutes ago. Told her it was urgent. That he had to talk to her about Walker.

Her fingers curled around the doorknob. If Hamilton wasn't there, it would be locked. Standard protocol at the courthouse.

"Ma'am?" The uniform came closer to her. Officer Shamus Riley. As far as shadows went, he was a good guy. "Is there a problem?"

She shook her head. "Just give me a minute." She twisted the knob and it turned easily beneath her fingers, but the door ran into something as she pushed. As she leaned against it and opened a space wide enough to enter, Lauren was expecting—hoping—to see Hamilton rush toward her in his billowing black robe.

But Hamilton wasn't there.

And his office had been wrecked.

CHAPTER THREE

Lauren stood inside the doorway of Hamilton's office, her gaze sweeping over the overturned files, smashed computer bits, and cracked glass of photo frames. The place had been trashed. Gutted.

"Where is he?" Lauren asked as she whirled to face the cop. He'd already called for backup and, over Shamus's shoulder, she could see a guard rushing toward them.

Shamus shook his head, worry tightening the lines near his eyes.

"We need to page Judge Hamilton, now," Lauren told the guard. He had a radio on him that connected to the main security system. They could send a call through the courthouse. If Hamilton was there, if it was possible for him to respond, he would.

Then Hamilton rounded the corner. He came to a stop when he saw them.

"Ms. Chandler?" He hurried toward her, sending a quick frown toward the courthouse guard and Shamus. "I was hoping you'd—" He broke off, his eyes widening as he glanced toward the open door of his office and caught sight of the destruction. "What in the hell happened?"

He was okay. Alive. He'd just scared her to death. She grabbed his hands. "Judge, where have you been?"

"I had to sign a warrant for your ADA Crenshaw." He stared over her shoulder at his office. The color drained from his face. "He came looking for me, didn't he?"

It sure looked like he had.

The courthouse guard shifted nervously next to them.

Hamilton rounded on him. "Who came into my office? Who was here?"

The guard's Adam's apple bobbed. "Sorry, sir. I didn't see anyone. There was a scuffle with one of the prisoners on transfer, and I had to go help. I left the area for a few minutes…"

"Security cameras," Lauren said, thinking quickly as she looked at the cameras discreetly perched in the corners. "There's a system on every floor." Had to be, thanks to a bomb threat that had emptied the courthouse a few years back.

The cameras would have captured the intruder.

At least, she sure hoped they had. Because maybe those cameras could tell them where Walker had gone—or even where he was right then. She motioned toward the courthouse guard. "Tell security to pull up the footage, *now*. Find out who was in this area, and where the hell he is now."

The guard nodded quickly and started talking into his radio.

Shamus's voice caught her attention. "Yes, sir…" He was on his phone with someone—Lauren sure hoped that someone was Paul or Anthony. "The office was trashed, sir." The cop's eyes rose and locked on her. "She's right here. Yes, yes, I will."

As he ended the call, Shamus's hand curled around her arm. "Sorry, ma'am, but he told me to keep you by my side until he got here."

"Who's he?"

Hamilton tried to edge around the cop to get into his office.

Shamus moved, blocking his path. "The marshal said I had to keep her close, and he also told me not to let anyone in the room. He wants the techs in there before anyone disturbs the evidence."

So Anthony was leading the investigation. Edging out Paul in a pissing match for jurisdiction.

She pulled her arm away. "You can let me go."

He flushed. "Ma'am, he said I was to keep a hand on you until he got here."

"I'm the DA, Officer Riley." More guards hurried into the area, surrounding a still stunned-looking Judge Hamilton. "I think I'm safe now."

Riley slowly dropped his hand. "That's just the thing. He said you *weren't* safe. That the killer could be in the building." He made no move to back away.

She glanced at the wreckage of Hamilton's office, then she looked at the judge's haggard face. "Why did you call me, Hamilton?" Lauren demanded. "Why did you want me here?"

Hamilton's gaze cut to the cops. The guards. He gave a small, negative shake of his head.

She knew he wasn't going to tell her what she needed to know. Not with so many eyes and ears close by.

Secrets. They didn't have time for them. Not when the killer was this close.

***

Anthony could barely contain his fury. The security cameras turned up jack shit. The guards didn't remember seeing anyone enter or exit the judge's chambers, and Hamilton's secretary, a young woman who'd just graduated from college, had burst into tears when the cops started to question her. She'd left early, heading out to meet her boyfriend, and she hadn't even realized that the judge's chambers had been invaded.

Anthony glanced over at Lauren. Her gaze wasn't on him. It was on the judge, and Lauren looked damn suspicious as she studied Hamilton. Fair enough. He also knew the judge was holding back on him. With a killer hunting, no one needed to hold back.

Time to clear the air.

Anthony closed in on Lauren and Hamilton. "Why did you want to see her?" he demanded.

Hamilton hunched his shoulders. He didn't meet Anthony's stare. "There are a number of cases that her office is working. I just needed to talk about—"

"When you lie," Anthony said quietly, "your gaze cuts to the floor and you rub your chin."

Most folks had tells like that. Only they didn't realize what they were doing. Anthony realized. It was his job to notice.

The judge licked his lips and his gaze slowly rose to meet Anthony's. "It's nothing. Really." His hand fell away from his chin.

"Nothing wouldn't make you call me," Lauren said, voice soft. "On the phone, you said it was urgent. That we had to meet."

Hamilton glanced over at the cops. His stare seemed to linger a moment on Detective Voyt. Then he focused back on Anthony. Hamilton edged closer and, voice even softer than Lauren's, he said, "About two weeks ago, I got a letter from one of the Walker jurors."

Lauren inhaled sharply.

"It was from the juror foreman, Steve Lynch. He said he'd made a mistake. That he wanted to talk." The judge shook his head. "I didn't respond to him, *haven't*—but then I got to thinking about Walker breaking out so soon after the note was sent. I wondered..."

"You wondered if Walker had gotten a letter from Steve Lynch?" Lauren asked. "Something that might have pushed him into breaking out?"

A grim nod. "A letter, or maybe even some help." His voice was barely above a whisper. "The kind of help that can get you a ticket out of prison if someone feels like they owe you." He rocked forward onto the balls of his feet. "It might sound crazy, but I've seen plenty of crazy during my years on the bench. If a juror starts feeling guilty, starts feeling like he sent the wrong man to prison...hell, a guy like that will do just about anything to atone."

Lauren was silent. A little too silent.

Anthony had to ask, "Did this Lynch guy contact you, too?"

"No." Hesitation. Doubt? "At least, I don't think he did. My assistant opens my mail, and she would have told me if a note like that had come through the office."

Maybe.

Maybe not.

He raised his hand. "Voyt."

The detective marched over.

"Judge Hamilton has some intel that he needs to give you." Anthony had his own job to do. He caught Lauren's hand. "Come with me."

Her eyes widened. "Where are we going?"

"You wanted to be in on the hunt, well, here's your chance." After this second attack, no way did he want her out of his sight.

The job is to catch the killer. Fugitive apprehension. He knew exactly what he was supposed to do.

But leaving her behind…hell, no, that didn't seem like an option. When he'd gone back to the clearing near the cabin and she'd been gone, his heart had damn near stopped.

It felt like he'd been coming closer and closer to death on his last few cases. Down in New Orleans, a serial killer had even managed to make him think that he *was* facing death. In what he'd thought were the last few minutes of his life, Anthony had closed his eyes and seen—

Her.

A man's priorities could sure change quickly when he thought death was taking him.

But he'd survived that prick Valentine's attack. And the witness he'd been protecting for so long, the woman who'd had her life nearly destroyed by the Valentine Killer?

I walked her down the aisle.

The monsters didn't always win in this world. Sometimes, good did kick the hell out evil.

Sometimes.

His hold tightened on Lauren's arm. "Come with me." Apprehending Walker was his mission, but leaving her behind? *Not happening.*

"I can handle Lauren's protection for the night," Voyt offered as he stepped closer to them. He gave a little nod toward her. "Come on, Lauren, I'll take you home."

"I can't go back home." Her words broke a bit but she rallied quickly. "It's not clear yet. And with Karen's blood…with her dying in my bedroom…" Her breath rushed out. "I'm *not* going there."

Hell, no, she wasn't. The detective was a dumbass to even suggest she return that night.

A muscle flexed in Voyt's jaw. "You can stay with me."

Anthony's whole body tightened. *Not happening, Voyt. Not. Happening.*

"You know I have the guest room," Voyt added as he took *another* step toward her. The guy needed to learn how to respect personal space. Staring into her eyes, Voyt said, "Stay at my place tonight."

She fucking wasn't.

Anthony's gaze slid between them. He didn't like the look he saw in Voyt's eyes. Not one bit. The detective needed to back off and back *up*.

Since the guy wasn't moving, Anthony stepped between them. "She's coming with me," Anthony said, his words snapping out with a fierce force.

Voyt blinked. Even Hamilton edged back.

"She is?" Voyt sounded confused.

What was so confusing?

Anthony gritted out, "I need her to give me access to Walker's friends and family." Those still in the area. Most had fled, hoping to shed the image of being the killer's kin. For those still there, Lauren *knew* them. She'd been the one to interview them years before. If they were going to talk, it would be to her. "I need her," he said again as he locked stares with the detective. He wanted to make sure Voyt got the message—what he was saying and what he wasn't.

But Voyt was proving to be oblivious. "Lauren needs a place to crash." The guy wasn't backing down. He did step to the side, though, just so he could look around Anthony and tell Lauren, "When you're done helping the marshal, come to me, Lauren."

Anthony's back teeth were about to grind down to dust. *She won't be coming to you.* Whatever was going on between Lauren and this dick detective, it would be ending.

"I'll keep her safe," Anthony growled, and then he was turning away from the cop and pulling Lauren with him. They rushed through the nearly deserted courthouse and burst outside into the thick, hot night air.

Jim had stayed back at the swamp, to work more with the trackers. Matt had gone to the precinct to run down more leads.

And Anthony...he'd run to Lauren.

As soon as he'd learned there was a threat at the courthouse, he'd been desperate to get to her. So desperate that he'd dropped everything else.

She was fucking with his head already, and he'd only been in town for a few hours.

It was edging close to eight p.m. The Butcher had always killed at night. It had been just over forty-eight hours since the guy's escape. *Forty-eight hours.* That timeline was cutting through Anthony.

It had taken the warden far too long to notice Walker's absence and to contact Anthony's office. Then, by the time he'd gotten to the prison—hell, Walker had already been given a huge edge.

Anthony opened the passenger-side door of his rented SUV. Lauren swept by him, her body brushing against his. Memories swept through him at her touch, but he shoved them back.

He had a job to do. A job he *would* do.

Anthony climbed into the driver's seat. His hands tightened around the wheel. "Most of Walker's family left the city."

From the corner of his eye, he caught her nod.

"The guy wasn't exactly social, so there's not a trail of friends in the area."

Not a trail, no, but there'd been one person in particular who had always stood by Walker during the trial. His girlfriend. "Stacy

Crawford is still here," she said, turning in the seat to glance at him.

He nodded. His own intel had already told him that Walker's girlfriend—*ex*-girlfriend—was in town, and he knew exactly where she would be.

"Let's go have a little chat with her." That chat would take them on a visit to another of Walker's favorite spots in the area, a rundown bar called Easy Street.

He pulled away from the curb. The interior of the SUV seemed too small. Maybe it was because Lauren was so close. Close enough to touch.

"Stacy wasn't exactly the most cooperative witness five years ago," Lauren murmured.

Her voice was cool, low. She could have been talking to a stranger.

Not to the man who'd once fucked her every way he could imagine—and even thought of some new ways. She was that damn good.

"She believed Walker was innocent," Lauren continued. "Stacy wanted to help him, not lock him up."

He pushed down on the accelerator. "Let's go see if she's still trying to help him." Help him escape prison.

Maybe help him kill.

Anthony was growing more and more convinced Walker wasn't acting alone. Not this time.

***

Easy Street was far from the hustle and bustle of Baton Rouge. The bar was near the swamp, nestled on a rough patch of land.

Despite its off-the-beaten-path location, the small club boasted a packed parking lot, one full of trucks, motorcycles, and a few tricked-out cars. Music blared from inside the club, seeming to reverberate from the slanting roof that covered the place.

Anthony was beside Lauren, his hand light on her arm. He kept getting too close to her. Touching her far too often. His touch made her nervous, and with Walker out there, she was already nervous enough.

They edged toward the entrance. The bouncer gave them a bored look and waved them inside.

Only Anthony didn't go inside. Instead, he pulled out a prison photo of Walker and held it in front of the bouncer. "You seen him?"

Another bored glance. "No."

"*Look* at the photo." Anthony's voice snapped with command. "Have you seen this guy?"

The bouncer stood. Maybe that move was meant to intimidate, but since Anthony was an inch taller, it didn't exactly work. "You a cop?" the guy demanded.

"Marshal." Anthony kept holding the picture. "And this man enjoys slicing apart women."

The bouncer's gaze snapped back to the photo. This time, he looked. Under the flickering fluorescent light, he seemed to pale. "Nah, I ain't seen that freak here."

Anthony tucked the photo back into his pocket and pulled out a small, white card. "If you see him, you call me."

The card disappeared in the bouncer's fist.

Then they were inside. The music was even louder and the alcohol was flowing freely. The scent of stale beer and sweat filled the air. Bodies were smashed together in the dark spaces—and Lauren noticed that there were plenty of dark spaces.

When she'd come to Easy Street before, it had been during the daytime. She'd interviewed the staff, talked with Stacy Crawford— all when the bright lights were on.

Now, the place seemed so different. With the dark bayou waiting just beyond the small windows, the club held an air of menace.

"How many times did you talk to Stacy Crawford?" Anthony asked.

"Too many to count."

"Then when we see her, you get things started. Maybe she'll respond better to you."

Highly doubtful, but she'd sure give it a try. Since Stacy had actually threatened to kill Lauren at one point, she didn't particularly think they were headed for bosom-buddy territory.

You bitch! You ruined my life!

It hadn't been the first time Lauren had been called a bitch. Not the last either. Not with her job.

Her gaze scanned the crowd and lit on the familiar figure of Stacy Crawford. Stacy's hair color had changed since Lauren had last seen her. Instead of the blue black, Stacy's hair was now an almost white blonde and she seemed thinner, paler.

Lauren pushed her way through the crowd. The waitress was leaning over the bar, slapping her hand on the counter as she tried to get the bartender's attention.

"Stacy?"

Without looking back, Stacy said, "Be with ya in a minute—"

"It's Lauren Chandler." She had to raise her voice to be heard over the blare of music. "I'm the—"

Stacy whirled toward her. "I know who the hell you are."

Stacy's hair color had changed, but the hate in her brown eyes hadn't.

Lauren cleared her throat. "Is there some place we can go to talk?"

"I don't have a damn thing to say to you!" Stacy tried to shove past her.

Lauren caught her arm, her grip light. Anthony was silent, watching. "Walker escaped. He's in the area." *Killing.* She didn't say that. Stacy had never believed Walker was a killer.

A tremble ran over Stacy, but she locked her jaw and gritted, "I know. The damn cops called me and I told them just what I'm telling you—*fuck off.*" Then she yanked her arm away and stormed toward a door marked STAFF.

Lauren stared after her. That had pretty much gone as expected.

"So much for you getting witnesses to cooperate," Anthony murmured.

He had *not* just said that. Lauren knew her eyes had just narrowed to slits. "Who said I was done?" She wasn't some piece of fluff who couldn't get a job done, even though this was *way* past just being a job.

This was about Karen. About a friend who hadn't deserved to die in agony.

So much blood...

Lauren slammed the door on the image and took off after Stacy. The doorknob twisted easily beneath her hand. Anthony was right behind her, shadowing her steps.

Stacy was on her knees, crying, her arms wrapped around her stomach.

As Lauren approached, Stacy's head whipped up. Her stare locked on Lauren. "Get out of here!"

Lauren didn't move. She stood in the doorway, the light coming in behind her and Anthony, and she hurt for the woman.

Stacy might have shouted her support for Walker years ago, but this woman, broken on the floor, looked terrified.

Stacy swiped her hands over her cheeks and lurched to her feet. "This room is for staff only. You can't—"

"You know he killed them all." Lauren's words were soft.

Stacy's shoulders slumped.

"When did you start believing it?" Lauren asked. Stacy had been so solidly behind Walker during the trial. Lauren actually thought that Stacy was one of the main reasons he hadn't gotten the death penalty. She'd kept telling the jury what a good man he was.

He's so good to me. He's never hurt me, never.

A tear leaked from Stacy's eye. "I knew when I found the necklace."

Lauren kept her expression blank. "What necklace?"

"The one with the twined hearts." Stacy's smile was broken. "The one I saw Ginger Thomas wearing in that damn picture that was always on the news."

Ginger Thomas. The mom of two Walker had killed.

"It even had her initials on the back."

They'd never found one of Ginger's trophies at Walker's cabin. The crime scene teams had looked and looked. "Where did you find it?" *Why didn't you turn it in?*

Her lips trembled. "In the bottom of my jewelry box. I didn't see it before. I was looking to pawn some old gold, and—" She broke off, shaking her head. "It was there."

Walker had shouted in court that the cops had the wrong man. He'd said he went into the Peterson house because he'd heard sixteen-year-old Kathy Johnson screaming when he'd been out jogging. He'd tried to help her and become covered in her blood.

When the Petersons came inside, they'd seen him crouched over Kathy, covered in her blood, because he'd been trying to save her.

It wasn't me! Walker's story, over and over again.

"It was him," Stacy whispered.

Anthony pushed closer to Lauren. "Where's the necklace now?"

Stacy swallowed. "At the bottom of the bayou. I didn't want that damn thing anywhere near me."

That was called destroying evidence. "You should have turned it in," Lauren said, her voice hardening. "We could have—"

"Jon was already locked up! What good would it have done?" She swiped away another tear. "I just wanted it *over*."

"It's not over," Anthony said, his voice rumbling. "Walker is out. He's hunting."

Stacy's face seemed to become even paler. "I never did anything to him."

"Neither did his other victims," Lauren said. "He's a sociopath. He kills because he wants to."

"I loved him. You're the one who sent him to jail." Her voice had risen.

Lauren kept her own voice calm. "Have you seen him, Stacy? Has he tried to contact you?"

More of the frantic head shaking.

"Are you sure?" Lauren pressed softly. "You don't have to be afraid." She could all but feel the woman's fear filling the small room.

"The marshals can offer you protection," Anthony added.

"Marshals?" Stacy's voice cracked. "Is that what you are? A marshal?"

He nodded. "I can keep you under guard. I can—"

"Forget it. I don't need protection." Her hands fisted. "I'm leaving town. I got me a new boyfriend, and we're leaving after my shift tonight. There won't be no more people staring down their noses at me. Whispering. I'm *leaving.*"

Lauren didn't blame her. She was surprised Stacy had stayed around so long. "Why haven't you left before?"

"My boyfriend didn't want to leave. He had a job he was doin', but it's over, and we can go now." Stacy pushed back her hair. "After my shift, *I'm free.*"

Stacy tried to slide around Lauren. Lauren moved a few inches to block her path. "He killed two people to escape, and he's already killed a woman since getting out."

Stacy blanched.

"He stabbed her, sliced her, and left her body broken." *I'm so sorry, Karen.* Nausea rolled in Lauren's stomach. "So think about this. *Please* think about this. Has he called you? Sent you any notes? Have you seen him—maybe even seen someone who looked like him?" He would have tried to disguise himself after he got out of prison.

"No." Stacy straightened her thin shoulders. "Now I got to get back to work. I want you both to stay away from me." She hurried away from them.

The door slammed behind her.

Lauren slowly turned to face Anthony. "Do you think she's lying?"

"I think she's scared out of her mind."

So did Lauren. "She figured he'd never get out." She pushed back her hair. "Now she's running scared, and she's about to run fast and hard." *I don't blame you, Stacy. I'd want to run, too.*

A very big part of her *did* want to run, but she couldn't.

"I'll do a sweep around the bar, talk to the bartenders, the waitresses," Anthony said as his gaze left her. "If Walker comes within a hundred feet of this place, I want to know."

Right. Sounded like a good plan.

She stepped forward and found that Anthony's assessing green gaze had come back to her. "You're good at your mask," he said.

She was very much afraid her mask was about to break.

"Good at playing it cool so no one sees what you really feel."

It had taken years to develop that mask, but when there was no choice, she'd learned to adapt. Clearing her throat, she managed, "I'll have to tell the cops about the necklace." Walker had always liked to take jewelry from his victims. Necklaces seemed to be his first choice, but if the vic wasn't wearing a necklace, then he took earrings or rings. Something small. Easy to carry. "We'll see if we can get a team to search for it—"

"Like right now," he cut through her words, "you're still wearing the mask. I can't tell if you're angry or scared or if you don't fucking feel a thing."

She didn't so much as blink. "I guess you don't know me well." But then, hadn't that always been their problem? He saw her surface, nothing more. The way most people did.

The music rose again, and they swept back into the club. Lauren searched the crowd, and saw no sign of Walker. No sign at all. When they questioned the patrons, no one in Easy Street remembered seeing him.

As she walked back out into the night, a small shiver slid over Lauren's skin. Anthony was wrong. She felt—plenty. Right then, she was feeling very afraid. She couldn't shake the feeling that the killer was close, too close, just playing with them as he waited for his vengeance, ready to strike at any moment.

***

The marshal and the DA left the club. They skulked around, did their talking and questioning bit, and then they finally left. He noted the vehicle they were using because he'd be seeing it again.

He had plans. So many plans.

While he'd sat in prison, he'd had nothing but time on his hands. Plenty of time to figure out just what he'd do when he got out.

He hung back, waiting in the shadows. And when midnight finally came, he rode his motorcycle closer to Easy Street. Not too close. He figured the marshal and his cop friends had probably ordered some undercover patrols in the place. He wasn't stupid.

Stacy was.

She burst from the back of the club, rushing fast, nearly falling in her high heels. Then she was there with him, jumping on the motorcycle. His helmet hid his face from her, but Stacy—she'd always trusted him.

Stupid.

Her arms locked around him. "Let's get out of here!"

He revved the bike. Didn't take her toward the main road. He took her back along the twisting trails near the bayou. The trails that only a few knew.

The marshal didn't know about them.

Neither did the DA.

"Where are we going?" Stacy's voice shouted in his ear. He hated her voice. It grated every time she spoke. Had her drawl always been so thick? "I thought we were hittin' the interstate."

He kept driving. They weren't far enough away, not yet.

Her hold tightened. "Ben? Ben, stop the bike!"

He didn't stop.

Because he wasn't fucking Ben.

CHAPTER FOUR

Anthony took Lauren back to his hotel. Her brows climbed as she glanced at the tall, well-lit building, then she looked back at him. "You're not staying with the cop," he said. Just so they were clear. He wanted to be very clear on that point.

"I planned to get a room of my own after I get my clothes and everything else I need." Her voice was so cool. How did she do it? How did she always stay in such perfect control?

He jumped from the vehicle. Hurried around to her side. The valet took the keys and Anthony took her arm. "Your bags are waiting upstairs." He'd made sure everything would be ready for her.

And that her room would connect to his.

Surprisingly, she didn't argue as he led her through the hotel and into the elevator. He did notice that her gaze cut to the stop button on the elevator's control panel.

His lips curved. "Don't worry," he told her, "we'll head straight up."

Her gaze came back to him. The walls of the elevator were mirrored, reflecting her image at every turn. She should have looked exhausted.

She didn't.

"From where I stand, you're the priority," he told her, and it was the truth. The killer had been *in* her house. He'd had a picture of Lauren in his cell.

She was the one he wanted—the one Anthony would make sure Walker didn't get. He'd stay close to Lauren, and when Walker came, the killer would have to face him.

I will take you down.

"The judge has protection," Anthony said as the elevator rose. "And so do you."

The elevator dinged and its doors opened. He'd actually cleared this floor for his men, and for the rest of the task force that would be arriving soon. With word of Walker's escape, the FBI had immediately jumped in the hunt, too. They were sending two agents to join the marshals, agents who'd probably enter a pissing match with the local cops—it was the usual way of things.

He pulled out a key card and opened Lauren's room. "You'll be safe here." They were on the top floor, the best for security.

She glanced around the room. Her suitcase waited at the foot of the bed. "Looks like you've thought of everything." Her head tilted. "Just when did you make these plans? I don't remember you calling anyone from the courthouse."

When the jerk cop had offered her a room at his place.

"I made the arrangements while you were talking to some of the waitresses at Easy Street." Covering his bases was the only smart plan.

She gave a faint nod.

He locked the main door. Made sure to put the extra bolts in place.

"What are you doing?" Lauren demanded. Her voice wasn't so calm right then. It had definitely edged up an octave or two.

There was only one bed in the room. Big, king-size. In his fantasies, he joined her on that bed. Instead, Anthony headed for the connecting door.

The door was unlocked, linking his room to hers—again, per his instructions. "My key opens your room, and my own."

Lauren didn't speak. Huh. That was new. The woman always had plenty to say.

So he did the talking. "If you need me, I'll be just a few feet away."

She still wasn't speaking. The woman who could tear into any defense attorney in the country at a moment's notice wasn't responding. He hesitated on the threshold of his room. He didn't want to leave her.

He wanted to turn back, take her into his arms, and pretend the last five years hadn't happened.

But he'd been the one to walk away back then. To turn away from Lauren. He glanced back at her.

For an instant, he could have sworn he saw pain in her eyes, but then her mask was back, as strong as ever.

Anger pulsed through him and he swung back to fully face her. "Why do you always do that?"

Her shoulders stiffened. "Marshal, you don't know me well enough to say what I always—"

"Cut the *marshal* bullshit." His control was too frayed. She wasn't going to deny what they'd been to each other. "I know you. I know you drink chocolate milk for breakfast, your favorite color's blue, and you never go to see a movie that you *think* might have a sad ending without Googling the damn thing first." His breath hissed out from between his clenched teeth. "When you come, your eyes get even brighter and you make a little moan in the back of your throat."

"Anthony—"

That was an improvement. At least he wasn't *Marshal*. But it still wasn't enough. "I *know* you," he bit out as his eyes swept over her. "As well as anyone can know you. As well as you let anyone know you."

She stepped back. "You're not supposed to do that." Her voice was a whisper. "You're not supposed to make this personal."

It was personal. Always had been. He crossed the room and curled his fingers around her shoulders. He pulled her closer, but it wasn't *enough*. He wanted her flush against him. Wanted her under him. Wanted *in* her. *Hold back. Don't do it.* "What else would it be for us?"

She lifted her chin, exposing the pale column of her throat. He knew her, all right. Knew she'd always liked it when he kissed her throat. The sensitive spot right over her racing pulse.

"There isn't an us anymore. There hasn't been. Not since you walked away."

She'd been an ever-growing obsession for him. He'd needed her, day and fucking night, and she—she'd been so controlled. Holding all of her emotions in check.

Except when they were in bed. That was the only time she let go.

"I asked you to stay, but you didn't."

His eyes narrowed. There was anger in her voice. "You didn't give me a reason to stay."

"I wasn't reason enough?" Then she shook her head and jerked against his hold. "Let me go, Tony."

Tony. She'd called him that, years ago. Her voice whispering with desire.

"You were right about us," she said, "it was just sex. The sex ended. We both moved on."

He'd left town, but he'd never been able to *move on*. Not really. Every place he'd gone, she'd been with him. In his memories. Fucking always. When he'd seen that picture in Walker's cell...

I carry a picture of her, too. Does it make me as fucking twisted and obsessed as Walker?

Judging by his past, yeah, it did.

"Who I'm with shouldn't matter to you," Lauren said.

Maybe if he kept telling himself that another hundred times or so... "I think about you." A confession that was torn from him. "Too damn much." He turned away, and this time, he did cross the threshold that would take him to his cold, empty room. "But that was always one of our problems."

She didn't call out to stop him. He shut the door behind him. Held himself still.

Lauren didn't know about his family. Few people did. Those secrets were buried, just like his parents were.

The father who'd been too obsessed. The mother who'd just wanted to get away.

Death had been his mother's only escape.

I won't ever be like him.

Yet when he was near Lauren, those needs—too strong—rose within him.

From the other side of the door, he heard the floor creaking. Lauren, coming toward him. Coming after him?

His heart began to beat faster. He turned and flattened his palm on the door.

Then he heard the lock click.

His smile was grim. He should have damn well seen that one coming.

***

The motorcycle braked in the woods. The only light was from the moon and stars, glittering faintly in the sky.

Stacy jumped from the bike. Scurried back. "Ben, this isn't funny."

He climbed from the bike. Took off his helmet. Tossed it to the ground as he faced her. "No, it isn't."

Her breath rushed out. Her eyes widened. She stumbled back. Her eyes were wide as she stared up at him. "Jon?" Then she shook her head. "Y-you shouldn't be here. The cops—a marshal—was just looking for you!" Her voice trembled with fear.

She was right to be afraid.

Then her gaze dropped to the motorcycle. "That's Ben's bike."

It was. The streak of yellow-and-gold fire rushing down the side was rather distinctive. The fire was set to reflect in the darkness—a rather interesting touch, he had to admit.

"Where's Ben?"

The insects had quieted down. Her stark whisper carried so easily in the night.

"Ben let me borrow his bike," he said, unable to stop the smile that slid across his face. This was gonna be so much fun. "But don't worry about him right now. This is about us, just us."

Terror was stamped on her face. She'd never looked at him that way before. Stacy had been the one to get dragged from the courtroom as she shouted his innocence. She'd been the one to tell him, again and again, that the truth would come out eventually.

The truth had come out. She'd been too blind to see it.

"What changed?" he asked, actually curious. It wouldn't alter his plans, nothing would change them, but he did want to know when she'd lost her faith in him.

Her hand rose to her neck. Fumbled with the small gold chain there. "I found it."

"Found what?"

"That woman's necklace. Ginger Thomas! You put her necklace in my jewelry box!" She screamed the last at him. There was no one around to hear her screams, but he wouldn't let her scream for long.

He shook his head. "I didn't put the necklace in your box."

She shook her head. "You did! You killed those women and you—"

"I didn't put the necklace in your box," he said once more as he closed in on her. Stacy didn't even try to run. Maybe it was shock. Maybe it was fear. His hands locked around her, and he jerked her up against him. "But just so you know, I *did* kill those women."

Her mouth dropped in surprise.

"And I'm going to kill you."

She tried to scream. No time for that. His knife sliced across her throat.

She stared at him, her eyes desperate and wild, as a faint, keening gurgle came from her throat.

"You shouldn't have fucked around on me, baby. When I told you that you were mine forever, I meant it."

He yanked the knife away and watched her knees buckle. She hit the ground even as her hand rose and tried to stop the blood flow.

Nothing was going to stop that. While she couldn't scream any longer, he bent over her.

He'd known he'd come back for Stacy. To punish her. She'd promised him forever, but she hadn't even come to visit him in prison. Not once.

The knife sliced over her arm.

Not one single visit…

Another slice.

Tears poured from her. So did blood.

***

It was her cry that woke him. Soft, but scared, it penetrated the light layer of sleep that surrounded Anthony and his eyes flew open. In the next instant, he was on his feet and running for Lauren's door.

The sound came again. A gasp, a sob. Hard to tell. He just knew one thing for certain. It was coming from her.

"Lauren?" He raised his voice. Pounded on the door. "Lauren, open the door."

There were no creaks of the floor. No sign that she was coming toward him.

Another gasp. So weak and whispery.

He grabbed his gun. Tension had tightened his body. He lifted his foot, and he kicked in the damn door.

The lock shattered, chunks of wood near the door frame went flying, and the door swung back beneath the blow.

The room was dark inside, but he could make out Lauren's form in the bed. She lurched up, breath heaving, and screamed.

He was on the bed two seconds later. "It's okay!"

She'd yanked the sheet up to her chest. Moonlight spilled through the curtains, revealing and concealing her, but he was close enough to see her eyes, and when he lifted his hand, he felt the wet tear tracks on her cheeks.

"You're safe, baby."

Her head turned. Her gaze fell on the gun in his hands. "Hard to believe..." Her voice was husky, and he shouldn't have found it sexy right then, shouldn't have found her sexy when she was scared, but he did. He always found her sexy. "Hard to believe I'm safe…" she said again, her voice getting a little stronger. "With the gun so close to me."

Right. Carefully, he put the gun down on the nightstand. He turned on the small lamp so he could see her better. He wiped her tears away.

She flinched. "I'm okay."

"You didn't sound okay." He knew fear when he heard it.

Her grip tightened on the sheet. "It was just a nightmare."

He stared at her.

"Karen was my friend. I can't get what he did to her out of my head." Her head tilted down, and the curtain of her hair fell around her, concealing her expression from him. "I know she had to be so afraid. In so much pain, and…no one was there to help her."

He pulled her against his chest. Wrapped his arms around her. Held her. "She's not in pain anymore."

Lauren shuddered. "That *doesn't* make me feel better. I close my eyes, and I hear her. Begging me to help. But I can't. I can't do a damn thing."

He tightened his hold on her. "Yes, you can. We can catch the bastard."

"Before he comes to butcher me, too?"

The question was there, heavy between them, and her words burned right through him. "That's *not* happening."

Her laugh was bitter. Broken. "Tony, we know how these cases go. Criminals want payback against the DA. Against the judge—against the cops who arrested them. We get threats all the time." Her head lifted. She stared up at him. "Walker's different. He likes killing. He likes hurting. And since his victims tend to be women, he's locking on me."

"I won't let him get to you."

"You can't be my shield twenty-four hours a day."

No, but he'd like to be.

He brushed her hair back. The bed carried her sweet scent, tempting him. No, she tempted. Always *her*.

"You ran to the rescue," she murmured. "But that door's gonna cost you."

Screw the door.

His fingers slid down her arm. Her shoulders were bare. What was she wearing beneath the sheet?

"When we were alone"—the words came from him, growling out as tension and need hardened his body even more—"you always burned so hot."

Her skin was like silk beneath his fingers. He bent his head and pressed a kiss to her shoulder.

"Tony..."

That was it. The breathy catch in her voice. The way she said his name with need shaking in the one word. "I missed that."

His fingers rose. Slid through the softness of her hair so that he could turn her head toward him. "I missed you." A guttural truth.

They were alone. No prying eyes.

She always burned so hot when they were alone...

"You said that before," she whispered. "Am I really supposed to believe you? You stayed away—for five years."

No, he hadn't stayed away. He'd come back. Had to see her.

She'd been with someone else.

Anger coiled within him, but he kept a death grip on his control. "Believe this." Then his mouth was on hers. Finally. Fucking finally.

She tasted just like he remembered. Soft, rich, sweet wine with an edge of spice that made him feel drunk almost from the first taste.

Drunk, and wild for her.

Five years.

His mouth hardened on hers. His tongue thrust past her lips, desperate for more of her taste. She was kissing him back. Instead of grabbing the sheet, she was grabbing him. Her nails raked over his shoulders as she pulled him closer.

Closer was exactly where he wanted to be.

His cock was hard, full for her. Just looking at her made him hard. Touching her, kissing her—that made him feel like a volcano. He burned for her, needed her more than anyone or anything else.

The sheet was in his way. He yanked it aside so that he could caress more of her, and he immediately discovered she wasn't wearing anything beneath the sheet.

Christ, not a damn thing.

The longing hit him like a blow. Anthony pushed her back on the bed. The sheets were tangled around them, and he didn't care. He wanted her tangled around him. He wanted to thrust into her so deeply that the rest of the world melted away.

Only her.

Sex had never been the problem between them. It had been part of his addiction.

His hands slid to her breasts. Perfect breasts. Full, round, with pink tips that he loved to have in his mouth. When he kissed them, when he sucked them, she went wild for him.

In so many ways, no one knew her better than he did.

So many.

He tore his mouth from hers. Began to kiss her neck. Right there, over her pulse. Her heart was racing so fast, pounding and pounding in a frantic beat that matched his own desperate heart.

He had her back where he wanted her. Beneath him, in bed. With him.

This was where she belonged.

His fingers slid over her breasts. Stroking the nipples.

This was—

"I—I can't..."

Her voice. The husky timbre rolled right through him, but her words...his back teeth clenched as he glanced up at her face.

Her breath came in fast pants. Her nipples were tight with arousal, but the woman was saying—

"Let me go, Anthony."

No. Never.

That wasn't what the good guy was supposed to do. His eyes closed and he gulped in deep breaths. Then he forced himself to let her go. To bend and pull the sheet up, over her, concealing the flesh he wanted so very badly.

The sound of his heaving breaths seemed far too loud in the small hotel room. Lauren was too close, but she'd never seemed farther away.

"I won't apologize." Not for kissing her. Touching her. He caught her blue gaze. So damn blue. "You wanted me, too. *Want* me." It wasn't past tense, not for either of them.

"Just because you want something..." She shook her head, sending her hair feathering over her shoulders. "It doesn't mean it's good for you."

No, they'd never been good for each other. Too hot. Too intense.

"I'm not ready to get hurt again by you."

Her words sliced right through him. Was that what she thought? That he'd *hurt* her?

"Maybe I should find somewhere else to stay." She tucked the sheet under her arms, making sure to keep her breasts covered. "Until the team is done with my house, I can stay—"

"You're *not* staying with the cop." The words were snarled. His nostrils flared as he drank in her scent.

She stared at him, then whispered, "No."

He shouldn't ask. He *shouldn't*. "You had sex with him." It wasn't asking. It was confirming. The jealousy was back, knifing him in the gut.

She flinched. She was there, naked, everything he'd ever wanted just inches away. But he couldn't touch her.

Lauren had said no.

"What I do…who I do it with, that's my business."

Lauren's mistake had been that she never realized exactly how dangerous he truly was—or how much he wanted her. "How many fucking times?" He surged to his feet. He had to put distance between them.

"I'm not asking who you've been with!" Lauren threw at him. "I don't want to know."

His hands tightened into fists. "That's the difference between us." He looked back at her. In bed. So sexy that his cock ached. "I want to know every damn thing about you."

"You don't have a right to know—"

"Two more minutes, and I would have been *in* you."

Her breath sucked in on a sharp gasp. "Go back to your room."

He was screwing this up. He always screwed things up with her. Never said the right thing. Never did the right thing.

He headed for the door.

Stopped.

Confessed. "The women I've been with…they were you."

"That doesn't make any—"

"At first, it was because I was pissed at losing you. I didn't even realize why I was with the blonde." He glanced over his shoulder. "When I called her by your name, then I knew."

There was shock on her face.

"In the dark, they're always you." He knew it was screwed up. He was screwed up. His jaw locked. He'd pushed enough, and if he didn't get out of there right then, he wasn't sure he'd be able to walk away from her. He grabbed for the door and left.

***

Pierce Hamilton stared out at the darkness just beyond his bedroom window. His wife was behind him, sleeping deeply, the sound of her even breathing filling the room.

There was no sleep for him.

A cop was downstairs. The patrol car was parked right in front of his house. Protection.

Only there were some things you couldn't be protected from in this world.

He'd seen so many murderers step into his courtroom over the years. Seen rapists, child molesters, abusers. He'd done his job. He'd put them behind bars. Some of the cases—they stayed with him. They kept a tight hold on him no matter what he did.

When he'd been with Karen, he'd been able to forget some of the darkness. He'd been able to live, to breathe.

Karen.

Beautiful Karen, with her wide smile and gorgeous, golden skin.

Gone.

He glanced back at the bed. His wife was still sleeping. Did he love her? Had he ever?

Her family's money had made things easier. His law school. His time in the DA's office. Money and connections could make anything easier.

But they couldn't stop the nightmares.

So many killers. So many cases. For fifteen years, he'd been on the bench.

He glanced away from his wife. Stared into the darkness.

He hadn't been able to get near Karen's body, not once it had been transferred to the ME's office. He would see her, though. Once more. He knew just the strings to pull. Just the connections to work.

The attack on Karen had been personal. A dig at Lauren? No, *at me.*

Because Karen was the one thing that had mattered to him in this world. The only thing.

That SOB Walker had known that. He'd told Pierce, that last day in court...*I'll take away everything you love.*

Another threat. He got plenty of those. As he'd banged his gavel and sentenced Walker to an eternity behind bars, he hadn't cared much about threats.

After all, what could the guy do while he was locked up? But he wasn't locked up anymore.

And Karen was gone.

"Hamilton?" His wife's voice. She never called him Pierce. Just Hamilton. "Come back to bed."

He stared into the darkness.

Wondered how much longer it would be before it was his turn to die.

He forced himself to turn and face her. So very different from Karen. Julia was poised and perfect, even when she should have been rumpled from sleep.

Always so perfect.

Ice-cold.

But the killer hadn't come for her.

My Karen.

"The woman who was killed..."

Julia reached out and turned on the bedside lamp. "She was the one you were screwing." Her words were flat. The light fell on the right side of her face. "*This* time."

He locked his shoulders. "I was leaving you, Julia."

She laughed. "No, you weren't." Her eyes met his. "Come back to bed, Hamilton."

He didn't want to go back.

Karen was gone.

Julia shook her head. "At least Walker saved us the trouble of having to deal with her."

The rage burned in him then, so hot and dark that he felt like it would consume him.

Walker should have killed you, Julia. It should have been you.

"Now we can get back to the way things were." She turned the light back off with a flick of her fingers. Cold. That was Julia. She didn't love him. Never had.

He didn't love her.

Never had.

It should have been you.

He headed slowly toward the bed.

***

Stacy Crawford wasn't moaning. Wasn't crying. Wasn't doing anything at all.

Except bleeding.

The life had drained from her eyes. That moment—that one instant—was always so amazing to watch. Like a switch was being turned off, and all that she'd been faded away.

Because of him. Because *he* had that power.

He bent over her and pressed a quick kiss to her lips. He would leave her just where she was. The swamp had a way of taking care of prey for him.

His fingers slid over the earring that he'd taken from her. He tucked it into his pocket, keeping it close to his heart. Stacy had told him so many times she wanted to be special to him.

She was special now.

In death, they were all special. He'd learned that.

He turned away from her. Bent to pick up his knife.

There were more plans in place. Others who would soon find their way beneath his knife.

The Butcher had work to do.

The phone in his pocket began to vibrate. He smiled. Only one person had his number.

He lifted the phone to his ear. "Figured you'd call...just when I was having fun..."

CHAPTER FIVE

The next morning, Lauren, Anthony, and the rest of the team returned to the edge of the swamp, back to the desolate cabin that had starred in Lauren's nightmare last night. Only in her dreams, when she'd opened the worn door, she'd seen Karen inside.

Karen, covered in blood, even as she asked... *Why didn't you save me, Lauren? Why?*

The sunlight was too bright and hot as it burst through the faint trickle of clouds. Insects were buzzing, and at least two cop cars waited near Walker's old cabin.

She stood by the SUV, far too aware of Anthony's body beside hers. They hadn't said much on the drive over. She hadn't known what to say. She'd glanced in his eyes—once—and seen a dark need staring back at her.

Sex had never been a problem for her and Anthony. Everything else? *Yes.*

"Looks like our party just got bigger," Anthony murmured as another SUV pulled up behind them. This vehicle was silver. A man exited it first, a man with light-blond hair and broad shoulders. He wore a business suit, looking incredibly out of place in the swamp.

A woman exited next. She had black hair that slid lightly over her shoulders. She was slender, around five foot five, and dressed in jeans and a T-shirt. When she walked toward them, Lauren saw the holster under her arm.

"Marshal," the man called out as a faint grin lifted his lips. "I was told we'd find you here."

Lauren's gaze swept over the two once more. She didn't need to see their IDs to realize…"You're FBI."

The blond male gave a quick nod. "I'm Agent Kyle McKenzie, and this is Dr. Cadence Hollow."

Cadence's golden gaze assessed Anthony and Lauren. "We've been sent down to assist with the investigation." She offered her hand to Lauren. "You're DA Lauren Chandler."

She took the offered hand. "And you're the profiler who took down the serial rapist in Iowa last spring."

Cadence's brows rose. "You know my work."

Lauren gave a little nod as she dropped the woman's hand. FBI Special Agent Cadence Hollow hadn't just taken down the rapist—she'd taken down plenty of other serials over the years. The woman's name had been splashed in the paper plenty of times. Intent and eerily accurate, Cadence's insights into the minds of killers had earned her favored status in the press.

"It's good to see you again, Tony," Cadence said as she glanced over at Anthony. "It's been awhile."

Lauren didn't let her expression alter. Of course Anthony would know her. They both tracked killers, and she knew Anthony was often pretty tight with the FBI. But…the familiarity in the other woman's tone, the intimate *Tony*—just how close were they?

I told him I didn't want to know who he'd been with. She didn't want to know, because she didn't want the jealousy to knot in her gut.

"Sorry about everything that went down on the Valentine case," Kyle murmured. "Wayne told us just how close you came on that one."

Lauren glanced at Anthony from the corner of her eye. She knew they were talking about the case of the Valentine Killer. The notorious serial killer had finally been apprehended—and killed—months before in New Orleans.

According to the news reports she'd seen, Valentine had tried to kill Anthony, but the stories hadn't provided a whole lot of specific information.

"Less than a minute, huh?" Kyle shook his head and gave a low whistle. "That's cutting things real close, even for you, Marshal."

Less than a minute?

Lauren's eyes narrowed.

Anthony gave a rough shrug. "Not like I had a lot of choice. The bomb was ticking, and I figured I was about to get a close-up look at hell."

Her cheeks numbed. Her entire body seemed to ice. Lauren stumbled back.

Cadence caught her arm, frowning. "Are you all right?"

No, she *wasn't*. Had Anthony just said he'd been a minute away from dying in a bomb's blast?

"The swamp isn't for everyone," a man's low, rumbling voice said before Lauren could reply. She glanced over her shoulder and saw that two others had joined their little party. Paul and the man speaking. Tall, dark, and definitely dressed for trekking through a swamp.

The man wasn't a stranger to Lauren. He couldn't be—she'd known him far too long. Wesley Hawthorne worked for Fish and Wildlife.

He'd just been starting as an agent for Fish and Wildlife five years before, when he'd been pulled in to help search the swamp for more of the Butcher's victims. He'd been the one to lead the searches back then.

It looked like he was about to do the same now.

"You don't need to go in with us, Lauren," Wesley said as his dark eyes met hers. "We've got a day of tracking ahead of us. Your marshal wants to cover all of Walker's old hunting grounds, and we both know this was an extensive territory."

Yes, it had been.

And he wasn't *her* marshal.

"I want to be here," Lauren said. No ridiculous high heels for her today. Hiking boots and jeans.

She'd made arrangements to clear her schedule at the DA's office. Her cases were being handled, her staff fully briefed. *This* was where she needed to be.

For Karen.

"If he's gone back to the swamp, I want to help find him."

If he was still there.

Wesley gave a slow nod. "We'll be heading out in five minutes." A ghost of a smile lifted his lips. "Always a pleasure, Lauren."

She noticed that Anthony's gaze assessed the other man.

Paul crept closer to her. "You doing okay?"

She nodded. "I might look like hell, but I'm hanging in there."

"You could never look like hell." The guy was such a liar. He caught her hand and pulled her a few feet away from the others. "I worried about you last night."

Last night. When she'd been having nightmares and nearly giving in to her wild hunger for Anthony. She forced a calm edge to her words, using the mask that Anthony hated. "Nothing to worry about. I had the marshal for protection." Her eyes slid to the right. To him. He was talking with Wesley and Kyle, but Anthony's gaze flicked to her.

There was a possessive heat in his eyes that made her burn.

"We kept a uniform on the judge all night, and a patrol is staying with him today, too." Paul's breath heaved out. "Your house is gonna be off-limits for a while. I'm sorry, but the tech crew doesn't want anyone in there."

No, they wouldn't. Not until they'd collected every single bit of evidence they could.

"The offer of a place to crash still stands," Paul told her. Her eyes met his solemn gaze. "If you need me, I'm here."

Her lips curved. "Thank you."

He rolled his shoulders. "I want this bastard stopped just as much as you do, Lauren."

Because, like Wesley, he'd worked the case before. Paul had been an officer then, not a homicide detective, but he'd been there the night Walker was arrested. The night the Petersons had come home and found Walker slicing up the babysitter. Paul hadn't been heavily involved in the investigation so he hadn't met Anthony back then, but he was still as tied in with the bloody past as they all were.

"We will get him, and the guy won't escape again," Paul promised.

Why couldn't she believe that? Part of her was so very afraid they wouldn't catch him.

Not until he catches me.

She nodded like she agreed, and then they were loading up. Kyle didn't head into the woods with them. He took his fancy suit and went into the cabin with the tech crew that was still working there. But Cadence had on her hiking clothes, and she joined the group.

Lauren glanced over at her.

Lips curving, Cadence said, "Being here, seeing the things *he's* seen, it helps me to understand him."

"I didn't think understanding killers was a problem for you."

"It's not." Then, softer, she said, "That's the part that's more like a curse."

Frowning, Lauren turned away from the agent. It was going to be a long, hot day, but she was ready to do anything necessary. Staying at the hotel or hanging out in her office wasn't on her agenda. She had to do something, anything, to help in the hunt.

To get justice for Karen.

"I'm sorry about your friend," Cadence said quietly.

Lauren knew her shoulders stiffened. "Thank you."

"Do the cops know why she was at your house?"

"Not yet." But after talking with Hamilton, Lauren had a pretty good idea. *I pressured her to leave him. She was running to me...and now she's dead.*

Because of me.

"She had a key to your house."

"Yes." *Take it, Karen, in case you ever need a place to crash.* She'd smiled at her friend. *My door's always open to you.* She'd been worried about Karen. Getting in too deep with a married man.

Lauren forced herself to breathe nice and slow. Her heart ached when she thought of Karen, and she knew it would always be that way. She'd seen enough horror to know the pain didn't vanish. The scars always stayed behind.

"She was in my home," Lauren said softly without glancing at the profiler. "She died in my place."

"Maybe," Cadence allowed, "or maybe her death was his plan all along."

Lauren looked up.

"Walker has a serious issue with women—he likes to control them, to subjugate them, to hurt them. As far as Walker is concerned, *you* took his life away. You were the one there in court, day after day, telling the world he was a monster." Cadence's gaze held Lauren's. "You were the one he saw, the one he could focus all of his rage on, and *you* are the one he wants to punish."

"Then why is Karen dead?" Lauren snapped out the words, feeling raw. "If he wants me—"

"If you die too quickly, then you don't get to suffer enough, do you?"

Right then, she was suffering plenty. By killing Karen, the bastard had ripped out Lauren's heart.

"For a man who's been isolated the last five years of his life," Cadence said, her voice thoughtful, "he sure was able to gain access to transportation and supplies fast enough."

"Anthony thinks someone has been helping him." So did she. But—*who?*

"Helping him, yes." Cadence gave a slow nod. "But for how long?" Her head tilted as she seemed to consider her own question. "I'll need to see all the evidence from the earlier cases. Every piece of information you had on Walker."

Lauren's heart was beating faster. "The original kills were only on Walker. There was never any sign of someone else—"

"Maybe," Cadence said quietly. "Or maybe you just didn't know what to look for. *Who* to look for." Cadence's lips thinned. "I've been tracking killers for years. I know how they work, and I also know that sometimes, they don't work alone." Her breath whispered out. "We might be looking at an alpha team."

"Excuse me?" Lauren thought her heart was going to burst from her chest.

"An alpha team—two brutal, efficient serials working together. But alpha teams are so rare." Cadence lifted her hand, as if waving the thought away. "I need to see all the evidence," she said again. "Before I can work up any additional profile on Walker, I need those files."

Two serials. Lauren swallowed the thick lump in her throat. "It's just Jon."

It had to be.

It's just Jon.

Cadence's eyes were veiled, guarded, and the fear in Lauren's gut thickened.

***

It was close to noon when Anthony spotted the tire tracks. He and Wesley both stopped at the same time. Sweat had slickened their shirts, and the heat was just getting started.

The tracks—

"They're fresh," Wesley muttered as he bent. His left hand hovered above the tracks.

Yes, they were fresh. Grooves left in the mud, tracks that had been made *after* the last rain.

"Looks like a motorcycle," Paul said as he closed in behind them. "My Harley leaves tracks about an inch wider."

Anthony frowned at him.

Paul shrugged. "If you're going off-road up here, bikes can come in handy."

So the killer was finding out.

The small group picked up more steam as they began to follow the tracks. One of Walker's victims had been found in this vicinity. Well, what had been left of her. She'd been tossed aside and discovered by a local fisherman.

It had taken the ME weeks to make a full ID.

As they drew closer to the old dump site, the tire tracks remained steady.

Anthony glanced over his shoulder. Lauren was just a few feet behind him. Her cheeks were flushed, her hair pulled back into a ponytail. She hadn't talked much during the trek, except for her quiet conversation with Cadence. A conversation that had pissed him off.

He wants to kill me.

Screw what Walker wanted.

He inhaled, turning away from her. The scent of vegetation was thick in the area, but there was something else hanging in the air, too. A harsh odor that grew stronger with every step they took.

A familiar, coppery scent.

He grabbed Wesley's arm. The guy turned toward him, the same knowledge in his eyes.

They pushed through the brush and saw the small clearing.

He's used the same site to dump a body again.

Anthony heard the sharp inhalation that came from Lauren, but he didn't look back at her. He was too busy staring straight ahead, and fighting to keep his fury in check.

A woman lay on the ground, spread-eagle, with her hands thrown out at her sides. Blood soaked her. So much blood. Her head was turned away from him, but he recognized the bright-blonde hair. Recognized the short skirt and the discarded high heels that were just inches from her body.

Stacy Crawford hadn't made it out of the city. She hadn't made it far at all from Easy Street.

"She was supposed to get away," Lauren whispered. "She was leaving..."

But Walker had gotten to her before she could get away.

He heard Paul call for backup. Carefully, Anthony walked around the body. He wasn't about to contaminate the scene, but he needed to see—

Fuck. Her body had been sliced, deeper, harder, than the other victims'. And, unlike with Karen, Walker had sliced Stacy's face. Again and again...

"Betrayal." The word came from Cadence. She'd followed Anthony's footsteps, moving in the exact same way because he knew she wouldn't be risking crime scene contamination, either. "This attack was personal."

Anthony turned his head to study Cadence. He'd had plenty of experience with profilers—some who knew their shit, some who tossed guesses into the wind. He'd worked with Cadence twice before, and the woman fell into the knowing-her-shit category. "Why betrayal?"

"Because there's anger in the cuts. They're deep, wild. He usually slices cleanly, and to go after her face so intently..." An exhale. "He was punishing her. You punish for a betrayal."

She told us about the necklace.

Locking his jaw, he turned to Paul. "We need impressions made of these motorcycle tracks." But he knew the tracks would match the others they'd found before. He *knew* it. "Stacy Crawford was alive less than twelve hours ago, so the bastard is still in this area."

Still hunting. Screwing with them.

I'm hunting you.

With the increased media coverage, the bastard would be staying away from the busier places, sticking to the deserted swamps and back roads on his motorcycle, perfect for easy maneuverability. Anthony had already given orders to put extra patrols on the back roads.

The bastard would have to come out soon enough, and when he did...

We've got you.

While the others had come closer to the body, Lauren had backed away. Anthony focused on her now, noting with alarm the ashen color of her face. Hell, this scene had to remind her far too much of Karen's murder.

He took a step toward her.

And saw her retreat again.

He wanted to put his arms around her. Hold her.

But Lauren had made it clear she didn't want his touch.

Crime scene. Focus on the victim. Not Lauren.

"Looks like he went north," Wesley murmured as he studied the direction of the tracks. "Buckhead Road is two miles north of here. He could have hit it and then made his way back to the city."

Or he could still be in the swamp. Hiding. Waiting.

***

"It doesn't look like anyone is here," Lauren said quietly as she stared at the small home located on the end of Azalea Lane. A neat house, with a trimmed lawn and white shutters on the front windows.

The home of Ben Fort—Stacy Crawford's boyfriend.

My boyfriend didn't want to leave. He had a job he was doin', but it's over, and we can go now...After my shift, I'm free.

There would be no going then. Lauren felt sadness weighing in her heart. Stacy had been so close to getting away.

Just hours from freedom.

"He was supposed to leave with her last night." Anthony drummed his fingers lightly against the steering wheel. "So why the hell didn't he call the cops when she didn't come home?"

The house was dark. No car sat in the narrow driveway. "Maybe he doesn't know," Lauren murmured. She'd had to break the news to families before, and it always tore at her guts to see their grief.

Anthony turned his head to look at her. "You think he didn't notice that his girlfriend wasn't in bed with him when he woke up this morning? It's pretty damn hard to miss something like that."

Ben Fort was a thirty-four-year-old mechanic who'd just gotten a new job in Jackson, Mississippi. Paul had pulled up the guy's record for them. Fort had a few drunk-driving charges, and an assault charge that had landed him in jail for six months.

Ben Fort was also the owner of a 2003 Harley motorcycle.

Anthony checked his weapon. "Stay in the vehicle."

She grabbed his hand. "Why? Because you think he's a victim...or a killer?"

Paul and a team of cops were working the crime scene in the swamp. Anthony had wanted to get to Fort ASAP, especially when the check on the guy had revealed that he owned a motorcycle.

Lauren hadn't wanted to stay in the swamp—*more death, more blood*—so she'd jumped in the SUV with Anthony. But now...

"I think he could be either one, and I'm not about to risk you as I find out what the answer is." He reached into the glove box and pulled out a second, smaller handgun. "Keep this close, and keep the doors locked."

Her fingers curled around the gun. "Be careful."

His smile held a reckless edge. "Always."

Then he was gone. Heading toward the house with a confident, hard march. She didn't take her eyes off him, couldn't. He went to the door and pounded his fist. They didn't have a search warrant. There wasn't enough evidence for that.

Her gaze swept to the property. There were no cars in the drive, but she could see the back of the bike, peeking out from beneath a big, blue tarp near the carport.

Her heart beat faster.

Anthony pounded the door once more.

Ben Fort was home—at least, his ride was there—so why wasn't he answering?

She sat up straighter, her gaze searching the area. If Walker had gone after Stacy, then maybe he'd also gone after Stacy's lover. Maybe Ben wasn't answering the door because he *couldn't* answer.

Was he inside, already dead?

Or...dying?

From the corner of her eye, she saw a flash of movement. Near the carport. Metal glinted, shining in the sunlight. The bike wasn't under the tarp any longer. Because someone was there, tossing the cover away, trying to sneak away.

Victim...

Killer?

Anthony didn't see him. He was on the front porch, peering in the nearby window. The man was rolling the bike away, not cranking it, so Anthony wouldn't hear his movements.

He'd told her to stay in the vehicle, but she wasn't about to let Fort get away.

She shoved open her door and jumped out. "Anthony! The garage!"

At her yell, the motorcycle's engine flared to life with a growl. Anthony immediately jumped over the porch's railing and raced for the motorcycle. So did Lauren. While Anthony was coming from the side, Lauren was in front, trying to block Fort's path.

She had a fast impression of a big, hulking guy, a buzz cut, and hard eyes—and the motorcycle. Bearing right down on her.

She lifted the gun. "Stop!"

The motorcycle swerved and kicked up gravel. The man wheeled the bike around, trying to find another path.

Only he didn't find another path. He lost control. The motorcycle slid onto its side, slipping and twisting away from him. The man flew onto the pavement, hitting with a thudding impact.

Lauren's breath sawed from her lungs.

The guy leaped back to his feet and started to run. Anthony threw out his arm, clotheslining the man right around the neck. Buzz cut fell back, slamming once more into the pavement. This time when he tried to get up, he found himself staring down the barrel of Anthony's gun.

"Benjamin Fort?" Anthony snapped the name.

Lauren tightened her grip on her weapon and slowly advanced.

The guy on the ground spat out a mouthful of blood. "Yeah, and who the fuck are you?"

"U.S. Marshal." Anthony didn't lower his gun. "And that woman you nearly ran down, that's the fucking DA. Asshole, you just stepped into a whole world of hurt." There was a deadly promise in his voice.

A promise that made Lauren tense because it was so dark, so dangerous, and so very certain.

***

Anthony stood with his arms crossed, his control held tight, as he stared down at Ben Fort.

The guy had bloody scratches and scrapes running along his face and arms, but that wasn't even close to the amount of damage Anthony wanted to do.

He'd been aiming that motorcycle at Lauren.

If the SOB had hurt her…

Paul came into the interrogation room, swept his gaze over Fort, then raised a brow as he looked back at Anthony.

"The guy fell off his bike," Anthony said.

At his words, Fort jerked his head toward them. "Because you and that DA were in my way! You come to *my* house, and I didn't even see no warrant and—"

"They didn't need a warrant to come and tell you about your girlfriend's murder."

Fort's mouth hung open. "Murder?" He gave a rough bark of laughter, one that held an uncertain edge. "What're you talkin' about?"

Paul took the seat across from Fort. Anthony was playing by the rules—this time—and letting the detective have a crack at the guy first. But he wasn't about to leave the room. He would stick close to Fort until he got the answers he wanted.

Anthony leaned back against the two-way mirror—he knew Lauren was watching on the other side—and waited for his moment.

If the detective didn't break the guy, Anthony would.

Paul opened up a manila file and pushed a crime scene picture toward Fort. "Do you recognize this woman?"

Fort peered forward. "Yeah, man, that's—" He jumped to his feet even as the color drained from his face. "Fuck! What the fuck happened to Stacy?"

Anthony moved in an instant, grabbing the guy's shoulder and shoving him back down in his seat.

"Stacy is your girlfriend, correct?" Paul asked quietly.

A rough nod. Fort's fingers snaked out, edging toward the photo almost helplessly. "Her face…"

"Stacy Crawford told the marshal here…" Paul slanted a fast glance toward Anthony. "That the two of you were heading out of town last night."

"Got a job in Jackson," he mumbled. His eyes were on the photo. His shoulders slumped. "*Her face.*"

Paul's eyes were on Fort's face. "Why didn't you report that your girlfriend was missing?"

"'Cause she wasn't!" Spittle flew from his mouth.

"If you were supposed to leave with her—"

Fort slapped his hand over the picture, covering Stacy's face. "She sent me a text. Told me that she had to pull an extra shift—wanted the cash since it was her last night. She told me that she would be late gettin' in."

"But she didn't get in at all."

Fort's breath was coming in fast heaves. "When I got her text, I went out for some beers with friends. I got in and passed out. I'd just woken up when—"

"When you heard the marshal banging at the door?"

A nod.

Now Anthony spoke. "Do you always run when you hear a knock at your door?"

He hesitated, then slowly shook his head.

"Then I guess today was special, huh?" Paul asked as he pulled the photo from beneath Fort's hand. "But not so special for her."

***

Did you help the Butcher kill your girlfriend?

Lauren had watched hundreds of interrogations over the years. She knew all the tricks detectives used in order to get a suspect to confess. She'd seen men crumble in an instant, and she'd seen cold-blooded killers refuse to break after hours of questioning.

When she'd had Walker in the interrogation room, he hadn't broken. He'd just sat there, smiling at her the whole time.

Fort was already sweating. Sometimes, the guilty sweated. They sweated plenty. Their eyes darted around the interrogation room—just like Fort's were doing. Their fingers tapped on the table, their shoes kept up a steady pounding rhythm on the floor.

Again, just like Fort.

Nervousness? Fear? A guilty conscience?

We'll find out.

The door squeaked open behind her. She glanced over and saw a uniformed cop hurry into the room.

"Ms. Chandler?"

She waited.

The guy licked his lips. "The cops on scene were searching Fort's home…" It had been easy enough to get the right to enter his home after the motorcycle incident. You didn't get to nearly run down a DA without repercussions. "One of them found a stash of stolen electronics in the back. The serial numbers match a string of recent robberies in his neighborhood."

She glanced back at the interrogation room. Anthony and Paul had wanted to know why the guy ran…

He'd been afraid he was about to get busted. That could explain the nervousness—and the guilty conscience. But was there more?

"Thank you," she said as she headed toward the door.

He raised a hand to stop her. "We also got the report back for the marshal." Another nervous swipe of his tongue over his lips. "The bike's tires—they were a match to the ones at the Crawford scene, to the ones we found at Walker's old cabin."

Lauren glanced through the two-way glass. She hadn't just watched interviews over the years. She understood exactly how to push and bargain with suspects.

"Thank you," she told the cop once more, and headed for interrogation.

My turn.

***

"You knew about Stacy Crawford's ex-boyfriend," Anthony said as he stared at Fort. "And you knew how desperate she was to get out of town."

Fort was sweating. His feet nervously tapped against the cheap linoleum floor. "Stacy hated this town. Hated the way folks always looked at her. Like *she* was the freak."

Fort's eyes were on the manila folder. The folder with Stacy's photo.

"But you wouldn't leave town with her," Anthony pointed out. "*You* made her stay."

The guy's jaw locked. "I had a job here. We were plannin' to leave—"

"Your plan was a little too slow," Paul drawled.

The door creaked open behind them. Anthony's gaze shot to the door, to Lauren.

Still dressed in her hiking clothes, she walked into the small interrogation room with determined steps. Her gaze cut to him, to Paul, then to Fort. "Mr. Fort, do you know who I am?" Lauren asked.

Fort's fingers were tapping against the tabletop now. "The DA. I seen your picture in the paper." Then his lips twisted. "And Stacy fuckin' hated you, so I heard about you plenty."

Her head cocked as she studied him. "Shouldn't you be more upset?" Curiosity had leaked into her voice. A trick, Anthony was sure of it. Lauren never revealed any emotion she didn't want revealed, especially during an interrogation or in the courtroom. "I mean, you just found out your girlfriend is dead—that she was tortured and sliced, and you sit here calmly saying she 'fucking hated' me." She shook her head. "That's not the response I usually get from grieving boyfriends." Then she walked to Paul's side.

Fort's gaze followed her every move.

"Detective Voyt here works homicide, but did you know he also used to handle B and Es? He spent several years working burglaries…"

Fort's eyelids flickered.

She leaned over the table toward him. "The cops found your stash of stolen goods, Fort. That's why you were running from your place, right? You thought you were busted?" She waited a beat. "Guess what? You are."

Fort rocked back, nearly falling from his chair. "I don't know what you're talkin' about!"

"I'm taking about the laptops, the TVs, the phones—all the little items you had stashed in your bedroom." She tapped her lower lip with her index finger, as if considering. "Were you trying to make some getaway cash? For the big move to Jackson? Is that why you—"

"It was Stacy!"

The guy sure gave up his dead girlfriend fast.

"She wanted out of this town in the worst way. Ever since she found that damn necklace in her jewelry box. She said we *had* to leave. Hell, the robberies were all her! She took the stuff!" He raised his hands in the air. "I'm clean, it's her, and—"

"Hard to charge a dead woman with theft," Anthony said. What a piece of work. No grief and all too eager to pin the crimes on Stacy.

Fort's head jerked toward him. "It was her. I'm telling you, she *freaked* when she found the necklace."

Lauren was frowning. "Just when did she find the necklace?"

"Last month. I was with her, we were heading to a party and she pulled out the box, and the freakin' thing was there." Another hard shake of his head. "Wasn't there the week before, I tell you, it *wasn't*."

"How do you know that?"

"Because I would have pawned it! I'd been through her box looking already, but nothin' good was there." He was back to tapping his fingers. Moving almost constantly. "Not then."

Anthony closed in on him. "How long has it been since you got your last fix?"

Fort flinched.

"You're shaking, sweating, your affect is off, and your pupils are dilated." Anthony had seen plenty of guys like him. Anthony's eyes noted the blemishes on the man's arms, on his face—the ones that weren't hidden by the scratches. "You're an addict—meth, judging by the marks on your face and arms—and *you* stole that stuff to feed your habit."

"I would've pawned that necklace!" Fort snapped. "I'm tellin' you, it wasn't there when I looked! It wasn't!" He looked quickly back at Lauren. "Lady DA, I'm helpin' you, I'm tellin' you everything I know." He licked his lips—another sign of his habit. Dehydration. "Let's work a deal. Come on…" he wheedled.

"The motorcycle you were on earlier, that is *your* bike, isn't it?" Lauren asked.

Anthony was surprised the guy hadn't sold it for drugs.

"Yeah, it's mine."

Lauren nodded. Her stare touched briefly on Anthony, then she was looking back at Fort. "The tires from that motorcycle were compared to the tracks left at Stacy's murder scene."

Fort's brow furrowed. "So?"

"So they were a match." Her head tilted. "So that bike—your bike—was out there where Stacy was killed."

"No! That's not—"

"You said you went out with friends." It was Paul's turn to go at the guy. Anthony understood the strategy. Fire questions from multiple sources to distract the perp. It worked sometimes. "Who drove? Did you take the bike?"

"No, my buddy Joe picked me up. Took me to Winders." He raked a shaking hand over his face. "I left the bike at home. Left it, and it was there when I got back."

"You expect us to buy that story?" Paul muttered. "Come on, you can do better than that."

Fort's fists slammed into the table. "It's the truth!"

Anthony tensed, taking a step forward. "Settle down." A snapped order.

But Fort glared over at him. "Or what? You'll shove me into the pavement again?"

I'll do more than that.

"No," Lauren said, her voice calm and quiet. "We'll just shove you into a cell, and you won't get out anytime soon. Murder has quite a long sentence."

"I didn't murder nobody! Stacy texted—told me she was workin' late!"

Same story. More anger.

"So I went out with my friends! We got ass drunk, but I never saw Stacy! I never saw her!"

"That's a pity," Lauren whispered. "Because maybe if you had seen her, maybe if you *had* been there to pick her up, Stacy Crawford would still be alive."

Her gaze slid to Voyt. He gave a small nod. Anthony knew they'd be checking the guy's phone. Would the text be there?

If it was, would it truly have been from Stacy?

She hadn't mentioned anything about working a double shift when they'd talked to her. She'd been too intent on freedom.

She was free now, just not the way she'd wanted to be.

Everyone was free in death.

Lauren headed for the interrogation room door. Anthony followed her, glancing back as Paul continued his questions. He hadn't been looking to pin Stacy's murder on Fort, but now, hell, he wasn't sure what was happening.

The door closed quietly behind them. "You think he's telling the truth?" Anthony asked.

"Yes." She sighed and rubbed the back of her neck. "No cell phone was found near Stacy's body. So either the killer took it, or it was dumped somewhere in the swamp."

Yeah, and good luck finding it if it had been dumped. "We need the motorcycle checked for prints," Anthony said. "If Walker took it, then maybe we can get a print confirmation." Then Fort's story would be a little more believable to him.

Lauren was frowning and he could practically see the wheels turning in her head. "It's so much for one man to do."

His gut clenched. He'd thought the same thing as soon as he realized how easily Walker had vanished from prison.

"Dr. Hollow—Cadence—is going through the old case files. She thinks we might have missed...*someone*."

A partner, back then? Fuck. He'd been so consumed by Lauren during those days, had he missed another killer, one right in the same damn town?

I'm just as consumed by her now. That obsession was leading to mistakes.

To death.

"He's working with someone." Lauren's voice was definite now. "That person—he must have planted the necklace for Stacy to find. Walker was in prison then, it couldn't have been him."

Their gazes held.

"Two killers," Lauren whispered.

Two killers would bring twice as much carnage to the city.

CHAPTER SIX

Lauren eased into the ME's office, her steps quiet. As a rule, she avoided this place whenever possible. The smell, the chill in the air, the bodies stored so carefully...the place made goose bumps rise on her arms.

But some trips couldn't be avoided. Sometimes you had to say good-bye.

She knocked lightly, and Greg Wright opened the door. Greg had been in the ME's office for just over six months, and he'd proven to be incredibly thorough at his job. Greg was thirty-six, not much for talking, but when it came to the dead, he was a master.

"You're here for Karen." His gaze held a touch of sympathy. "I figured you'd be showing up soon."

Lauren took a deep breath and could have sworn she tasted death. "I know she's being transferred out soon. I just...I wanted to say good-bye."

He stepped back, turning to head toward the storage area in the next room. Greg was a good-looking guy, with blond hair that curled slightly. He was called Dr. Death by some of the cops—not an insult, but a compliment because he was so good with the bodies. She didn't know if he minded the nickname or not. It was hard to tell with Greg.

He didn't let much show.

But then, neither do I.

Lauren followed him and waited while he pulled out Karen's body. The sound of the locker opening had her tensing. Then the body was there. Covered in a big, black bag. Greg pulled down the zipper, and the sound of it filled the room.

Then she was staring at Karen. Lauren swallowed. Karen's face was so pale. She could see the stitches on Karen's chest. Karen had been so full of life, so ready to take on the world.

Now only death waited for her.

"I was about to call you and Voyt," Greg said, a hesitant note entering his voice. "I found something else."

Her brows rose.

His gloved fingers pointed to Karen's throat. To the arching line that sliced across her neck. "There was…something in there."

"What?" She couldn't take her eyes off Karen's neck. Off that wound. Almost like a smile, one that had been carved into her.

"It was a small, folded piece of paper."

Lauren took an instinctive step back. "That's not Walker's MO." Walker cut. He sliced. But he didn't leave messages behind.

"Maybe it is now." Greg walked away from the table and picked up a small, sealed bag from his desk. "He left a message for you."

Her heart was beating hard enough to shake her whole chest. "What did the note say?" The paper was so small. So tiny. And stained with blood. Karen's blood. *In her throat.*

He lifted the clear bag and she could see the careful letters…

"It's beginning," Greg read.

Hell. She did *not* want to deal with this. "He's not going on a spree in my city."

Greg looked steadily at her. "Two victims in Baton Rouge killed within forty-eight hours." He took a deep sigh. "It sounds like that's *exactly* what he's doing."

Lauren's eyes fell back on the body bag. On *Karen.*

"I'll give you a minute alone with her," Greg murmured as he backed away.

Lauren didn't speak. Instead, she stared at her friend and hated that a monster had stolen Karen's life away.

Greg's footsteps echoed through the chilled room.

The cold air from the storage area made Lauren's goose bumps even worse. She swallowed, trying to shove back the lump in her throat. Karen was one of the few people who had gotten past Lauren's guard. She'd known Lauren's secrets, and she hadn't been afraid of them.

"I'm sorry," Lauren whispered. It was what she needed to say. *This shouldn't have happened. But I will get him.*

Her gaze slid down Karen's body. So many injuries. So much incredible rage.

Her fingers pushed back the bag as she stared at the marks the Butcher had left behind.

Greg's footsteps returned. "There are defensive wounds there, on both arms."

She could see them. "Karen always was a fighter."

"We found Walker's DNA under her nails. She made sure to leave her mark on him."

It hadn't been enough. "Be very, very thorough with your evidence collection. If there's any more DNA, anything that could belong to someone *other* than Walker, I want to know."

She glanced up and found Greg's dark eyes on her. "When the second body gets in," he told her, "I'll check to see if—"

"If he left a note in her throat, too?"

"Yes."

She was going to have nightmares for the rest of her life. *I'm so sorry, Karen. So very sorry.*

His stare flickered to the body. "I would've headed for Mexico. Run as fast as I could and not looked back. I mean, you can kill folks down there just as easily as up here, right?"

She'd thought that Walker should have gone for the border, too, but not just so he could keep killing. "Dr. Wright, sometimes you scare me," Lauren said. Blunt. True. He seemed to have a hard time connecting with the emotional side of the victims.

He offered her a smile, even as he bent to rezip the bag. "If I wasn't a little scary, do you really think I'd ever be able to do this job?"

No.

"The dead fascinate me. They always have." He paused. "But what's your excuse?"

The door opened behind him. She caught sight of Anthony.

"Someone has to make sure justice is served," she told him.

"That someone has to be you?"

Anthony was close enough to overhear them. "Yes."

"Why?"

The truth was tied to her past. "Someone I loved was taken, a long time ago."

Anthony wasn't speaking. Greg kept watching her.

"I tried to get her back," Lauren whispered as she thought of all her desperate searches, searches that had turned up nothing. "But I never could."

Greg swallowed. "She was—"

"Killed. Or at least, I think she was." Lauren knew her smile was grim. "But it was hard to prove without a body."

His eyes widened.

Anthony's footsteps had come closer.

"Who was the victim?" Greg asked.

The case had happened long before Greg started working as the coroner. The disappearance had happened years ago, when Lauren was just thirteen. "My sister, Jenny."

"What?" The shock was Anthony's. His footsteps headed toward her. His fingers wrapped around her arm. "Why didn't you tell me?"

He hadn't exactly stuck around long enough.

She turned her head toward Greg. "Let me know when you finish the autopsy on Stacy Crawford's body. If you do find another note…" She exhaled, trying to focus back on him. "Call me right away."

"Yes, ma'am," Greg murmured as he started to secure the body once more.

Lauren's gaze dipped back to the black bag. Life could just end like that. In a big, black bag. Zipped up.

Anthony's hands tightened around her. "Lauren…" A tight, hard edge was in his voice.

She couldn't handle talking anymore about Jenny, not then. Not in the room made for death. Lauren pulled away from Anthony. Greg *would* have noted that they'd been too close— hard to miss a grab like that, but at least Greg wasn't the type to gossip.

And why do I care? At this point—why?

Lauren cleared her throat. "Walker left a note with Karen's body. It said, 'It's beginning.'"

Anthony's jaw hardened. "No, it's ending."

She wanted to believe him. But the dead around her wouldn't let her give in to that fantasy. It wasn't ending, and it *wouldn't* end, not until Walker was dead.

"He didn't leave notes before." It bothered her. The FBI profiler was still out in the swamp, but she wanted to talk to Cadence again.

Walker had never taunted the cops or the media. He'd just killed. Brutally. Again and again.

"He's been locked up for five years," Anthony said quietly, but his gaze was guarded. "A lot can change in five years."

Her eyes held his. "And a lot can stay the same." Before she could say anything else, there was a commotion in the hall. She heard the grind of wheels and the rumble of voices as her whole body tensed.

The swinging doors opened, and a body was wheeled in—a body covered in a zipped black bag. Another lost life. Stacy Crawford's start in a new town was just a cold dream now.

A cold, dead dream.

When the transport team saw Anthony and her with Greg, they straightened up quickly and pulled out their paperwork for the ME to sign. Lauren barely glanced at them. Her eyes were on the bag.

She'd talked to Stacy last night. And now...

Greg had wanted to know why she was a DA—it was about justice. She wanted to bring justice to the victims. To their families.

She'd never been able to get justice for her own sister.

She wanted to stop killers and not just watch the bodies of their victims pile up.

The transport team left. Greg watched as she closed in on the body. There was one thing she had to know right away.

"Check her throat," Lauren ordered.

Anthony had closed in on the body, too.

The hiss of the zipper filled the air. Lauren's shoulders locked as Stacy's body was revealed. Stacy wasn't as stark white as Karen had been. Her skin had a more ashen color, and she smelled far more heavily of death.

A fresh kill.

Lauren's spine was stretched so taut that it ached.

Very carefully, Greg's gloved fingers went toward Stacy's throat. There was a slice there, a gaping hole that looked like a twisted grin. Lauren could feel the frantic thudding beat of her heart. It felt like it was trying to leap right out of her chest.

Greg's gloved fingers pressed lightly against the wound on Stacy's throat. He had a pair of tweezers in his left hand.

Lauren leaned forward. Then she lost her breath.

She could see the folded paper that his tweezers had just caught. Rolled up, nestled just inside of Stacy's throat. "He didn't *do* this before," she said again. It just felt so wrong. "Not when he hunted years ago in Baton Rouge."

"Well, he's doing it now," was Greg's response as he finished using his tweezers to extract the folded paper.

They all moved toward the counter where Greg slowly unfolded the bloody paper. It would be checked for fingerprints later. She knew that. The paper would be thoroughly scanned, the handwriting analyzed, but for now…

"'Steve Lynch.'" Greg read the name on the paper, then he glanced at Lauren. "Does that name mean anything to you?"

It did. "He was the jury foreman at the trial." The same man who'd written to Judge Hamilton, saying he'd changed his mind about Walker's guilt.

Anthony grabbed her arm. "We need to find Lynch. *Now.*"

He pulled her out of the room, but the heavy stench of death followed. They rushed into the hall and nearly slammed into Paul. The detective staggered to a stop.

"What's going on?" Paul demanded as his gaze jumped between Anthony and Lauren.

"The killer left a note in Stacy Crawford's throat. The bastard—"

"Whoa, hold up!" He lifted his hand. "Her throat? What the hell is that shit?"

Lauren swallowed and tried to stop her knees from shaking. "He left a note in Karen's throat, too." What the hell did it mean? Why the throat? "The bastard must be playing some kind of game with us. Taunting us."

"Just what did the damn note say?" Paul demanded.

"The one he left on Stacy," Anthony's hard voice answered. "It contained a name. Steve Lynch." His eyes glittered. "The bastard might have just told us his next victim."

Paul swore. "What are we waiting for? Let's go!"

If they could get to him fast enough, Steve Lynch might survive to see another day.

***

Anthony stared at the dark house. No lights. No sign of movement. But Steve Lynch was *supposed* to be in there.

"This is my scene," Paul said beside him, the detective's voice low and heavy with intent. "Understand? You're tracking Walker, but this is *my* city. I'm the homicide cop, and I'll be the one taking lead here."

If he'd been in the mood for a pissing match, Anthony would have said so. Paul had been the one to bring Lauren out there, the one to hold them all back when they wanted to rush inside and immediately find Lynch.

But Paul's captain had given him the all clear to handle this his way, so they were following the detective's orders.

For the moment.

Steve Lynch had no cell phone and no landline. He'd lost his job as a factory manager a little over two months ago. Divorced, childless, he lived in the last house on LeRoy Drive. The very quiet, last house.

Two police cruisers were behind them, but their lights were off. Everyone seemed to be playing the quiet game.

"Stay behind me," Paul said as he checked his weapon. "If Walker hasn't approached Lynch yet, this could be our chance to catch the bastard. We can put a watch on this house, wait for him, and then I'll be the one to take him down."

Anthony stared at the detective. Then he cleared his throat and said, "Or while we stand out here, pissing in the fucking breeze, the guy could be *dying* inside—"

He heard the scream. A high, wild cry. A cry coming from inside the house.

Paul's eyes widened, then he spun and rushed toward the house, clutching his weapon.

"Baton Rouge PD!" Paul yelled as he drew closer to the house. "Baton—"

Another scream.

Paul slammed his shoulder into the door, but it didn't give way. When he hit it again, Anthony was with him, and the door shattered beneath them.

They rushed into the heavy and complete darkness. Anthony yanked out his flashlight and kept it held over his gun. He swept the scene.

Had the scream come from the left?

The right?

A new scream broke the silence. High. Loud. Desperate.

***

Lauren stood behind a uniformed cop. Two other cops had been with her, but as soon as Anthony and Paul burst into the house, the cops had taken off toward the back of the house to block off the escape path of anyone inside.

Anyone being Walker.

She swallowed in an attempt to ease the desperate dryness in her throat, but it didn't help. *Nothing* could help.

The cop beside her was pushing forward onto the balls of his feet. The guy was clearly desperate to get inside to the action.

He had his orders, though. He'd been told by both Anthony and Paul to stick to her like freaking glue.

Another scream shook the night. The cop spun from her and reached into his patrol car. She heard the click from his radio, the crackle of static. "This is Officer McHenry. I'm on LeRoy, and we need—"

A twig snapped. The single sound shouldn't have been so loud, but it was.

It had come from behind her. From the narrow line of woods behind the patrol car.

Her heart raced even faster. The cop hadn't heard the twig snap. He was still talking on the radio. The snap, it could have been nothing. Could have been from an animal. A squirrel. A possum. She sucked in a deep breath. Then one more. She couldn't let the fear push through her.

The threat was inside the house. That was where the screams were coming from. Inside, not out here.

The cop spun back toward her. "We've got more help on the way, ma'am. You should get in the car until—"

His words broke off in a desperate gurgle as the point of a knife came through the front of his shirt. It had gone into his back and *come out of* his chest.

His mouth hung open and under the moonlight, his whole body trembled as he staggered—then fell to the ground.

Lauren whirled away from him. Safety was *in* the house. She opened her mouth and screamed as loudly as she could. "Anthony!"

She was tackled from behind. Lauren hit the ground with an impact that bruised her whole body.

***

Anthony kicked in another door, and in the cavernous darkness, his flashlight fell on the man cowering in the corner.

"Steve Lynch?" he demanded as Paul rushed into the room behind him. It looked like the guy from the grainy photo he'd seen at the station.

The man nodded and lifted his hands before his eyes, as if trying to shield from that bright light.

Anthony kept his flashlight trained on Steve as Paul's light swept around the room. There was no one else in that place. No damn body else, and as far as Anthony could see, there wasn't so much as a scratch on Lynch.

"What the hell is going on?" Anthony asked as he took another step toward Lynch. The more he studied him, Anthony realized how different Lynch appeared from his driver's license photo. Thinner, haggard. Terrified.

"I had to do what he…wanted…" Lynch whispered. "He has…Helen."

Anthony's gut clenched. Then he heard the thunder of footsteps coming down the hallway.

He spun away from Lynch, just in time to see two uniformed cops rush into the room.

Anger pulsed through him. "You're supposed to be outside with the DA!"

The cops froze. "We were securing the back exit, sir!" one shouted.

There was no need to secure the back exit. Walker wasn't here. He wasn't...

Anthony turned back around, frowning. From Lynch's position, he would have been able to look out the side window—a window just inches away from him—and see the cops. "You screamed to get us inside." Shit, *shit*.

"I'm sorry! He made me! He said I had to scream—" Lynch's cry followed Anthony as he raced from the room, but he didn't stop. He was running as fast as he could toward the front door. Paul was behind him, shouting for him to stop. Did the fool not realize what was happening?

Lynch hadn't been Walker's target. The guy had been the fucking bait.

The target was the same one Walker had been focused on all along.

Lauren.

He burst out of the house, shouting her name. One look at the patrol car, with its door swinging open, and he knew something had happened. Something bad.

No!

He jumped off the porch. Leaped for the car. He saw the downed cop. The man had fallen face-first into the earth, a knife shoved deep into his back. "Lauren!" he yelled.

Paul's footsteps thundered after him.

Anthony bent and put his fingers to the downed cop's throat. A pulse still beat there, barely. Damn barely. He whirled to face Paul. "Get an ambulance!"

"Lauren?" Paul said, fear cracking her name.

He didn't know where she was.

Not in the house.

He spun back around and faced the woods. His flashlight cut through the darkness. Near the left, it looked like two branches were bent back. As if someone had rushed through that spot.

He ran into the woods. Twigs slapped at him, but he ignored them. He had to get through the woods. He wasn't losing Lauren.

His foot smashed down onto something. Something that cracked beneath his weight. Fuck, a phone. He froze, then bent, grabbing it quickly. The screen was broken, but the phone still worked, and he recognized the image saved there—he'd seen it on Lauren's phone when she'd used it before.

The SOB had taken her this way. Anthony started running again. Faster, faster. The woods stretched and twisted before he hit a path that split in two directions. Which damn path? Which one? "*Lauren!*"

She wasn't answering his shouts. He wouldn't let himself imagine why she wasn't answering. He couldn't think about that and stay sane.

The squeal of brakes shattered the night. *To the left.* He clenched his gun tight and rushed to the left, moving as fast as he could go. More twigs and branches cut into him, but Anthony didn't care. There was only one thing that mattered to him then. Just one.

He would get her back.

Anthony burst from the woods just as a pair of taillights raced down an old, two-lane highway. The car was fishtailing and shooting up gravel in its rush to get away.

You won't get away. Anthony lifted his weapon, preparing to fire.

"No!" Paul's voice. The detective burst out of the woods behind him. "Are you fucking crazy?" Paul demanded. "Lauren could be in that car!"

Could be? She *was*—and Walker was taking her away. If Walker took her to a second location—

Anthony's eyes narrowed as he took aim at the back tire.

Then Paul jumped in front of him. "You aren't shooting! I don't know how the hell you marshals normally handle things, but you aren't shooting at her!"

The car vanished around the bend.

Fuck, *fuck*. Anthony shoved his gun into its holster, dropped his flashlight, and yanked out his cell phone. Two seconds later, he had Matt on the phone. "Get a roadblock up at the end of— of—" Where the hell were they? He tried to picture the map he'd studied earlier, one that showed Lynch's property. The images flew through his head. "Lincoln Road." That was the road he was on— it was also a road that was surrounded by woods on the north and west. "Walker's out there. He has Lauren—"

"You don't know—" Paul began behind him.

Anthony rounded on him and froze him with a glare. If it hadn't been for Paul, then Walker wouldn't have gotten away. Anthony would have killed the bastard.

Lauren would be safe.

Anthony returned to his call. "He was driving an old-model sedan, one with a busted taillight on the right. The car's color looked dark." His words were tumbling out quickly as the adrenaline coursed through his veins. "Get that car. *Stop* that car." Then he ended the call. His fingers clenched around the phone, nearly smashing it to pieces. "You're not fucking in charge anymore, Voyt," he snarled.

Paul clenched his fists. "I'm the lead detective here, I—"

"Lauren is a district attorney, a person of special interest in the Walker case, and she's *mine*." Guttural. "She's my responsibility from here on out. I'm getting her back." He grabbed the guy because he couldn't control his rage. "And if you *ever* get in my way again, I'll fucking shoot through you."

Under the moonlight, he could see Paul's glare. Was he supposed to give a shit about it? *He's been warned. I* will *shoot his ass.*

Anthony tossed him aside. As much as he wanted to chase after the car on foot, it wouldn't do him any good. He'd never be fast enough. So he raced back through the woods to Lynch's house.

Lynch…

At the station, he'd seen a grainy photo of Lynch, courtesy of the DMV. *DMV.* He'd scanned the photo and also learned that… shit, the guy was registered to drive a '92 Oldsmobile sedan.

Anthony shoved his way through the last of the bushes and was back at Lynch's house. One cop was bent near the fallen officer as another shoved Lynch into the patrol car. Anthony locked his gaze on Lynch. The guy was sobbing. He'd give Lynch something to sob about.

Anthony yanked the cop out of his way. In the distance, he heard the shriek of a siren. Still faint and too far away, but coming.

He grabbed Lynch. His hands fisted in the material of Lynch's shirt. "You gave the bastard your car."

Lynch nodded miserably. His gaze was on the ground.

"You lured us into that house so he could get her." He wanted to rip the guy apart. Lynch had been screaming, yelling so loudly. Had Lauren been outside, crying for help then? And they hadn't heard her over Lynch's screams? "*Why?*"

Paul moved behind Anthony then. Anthony heard the detective speaking into his phone and ordering an APB on Lynch's car.

"He has Helen!" Lynch whispered as his gaze lifted. "You have to understand. I didn't have a choice."

"Helen's his ex-wife," Paul muttered as he stalked closer. Then his voice rose as he snapped into his phone, "Yes, dammit, a ninety-two sedan! Stop the car and approach it with *extreme caution* because we think the DA is his prisoner."

"I still love her," Lynch said, swallowing thickly. "I couldn't let Helen die."

The wounded cop on the ground was gasping for air. Anthony hauled Lynch toward him. "But you could let that guy die?"

The uniform next to the fallen man looked up, the pain clear on his face in the weak moonlight. "McHenry's got a wife, a baby on the way..."

"I'm sorry!" Lynch cried. "So sorry!"

"Fuck sorry," Anthony said. Sorry wouldn't change anything. He was trying not to picture Lauren at that moment. Trying so hard not to imagine her fear, but—

A killer had taken him as a hostage once, too. Anthony had been tied up and left to die. He'd been so sure death would come for him. Hope had bled away, moment by moment.

He didn't want Lauren to feel the same way he had.

But while the Valentine Killer had toyed with him, the guy hadn't tortured Anthony with his knife.

The Bayou Butcher was all about torture.

"Tell us every damn thing you know about Walker," he snarled as the rage threatened to burst free. "Where the hell is he going?"

"I don't know anything!"

Anthony's back teeth ground together. "He told you that if you pulled us in, you'd get your wife back."

A miserable nod. The shrieks from the ambulance were closer now. "I'm sorry about the cop. I didn't think…"

No, he fucking hadn't. If he had, he would have gone to the authorities for help and they could have sprung a trap on Walker.

"How were you getting Helen back? Where were you supposed to go?"

Lynch's tongue swiped over his lips. "The old fishing pier on Rattlesnake Bayou. He said to go there at dawn."

The ambulance was pulling onto the road. The flashing lights lit up the scene. Anthony shoved Lynch away. "Take him to the station," he ordered to the other cop. "Stay with him. Don't let the bastard out of your sight!"

"I'm sorry!" Lynch cried out. "I didn't have a choice!"

Same damn song. The guy didn't even know what sorry was, not yet. If Anthony didn't get Lauren back, he'd make sure the guy knew.

He jumped into his SUV. Revved the engine.

Paul yanked open the passenger side door. "You aren't going without me!"

Anthony wasn't wasting time arguing. He wheeled the vehicle to the left and headed as fast as he could for the old highway.

***

Her head hurt like a bitch. Something wet and sticky was in her left eye. She reached up her hand—*blood*. Her blood.

Darkness surrounded her. The kind of thick, total darkness that made her think of tombs and death.

The Bayou Butcher has me.

A scream built in her throat and burst from her, but the scream didn't do any good. She could tell that the car was moving. There was a grinding sound, like wheels, and she was bumping every few moments.

Lauren lifted her hands and her fingers pressed into a hard surface, one just inches from her face. *The trunk. He put me in a trunk.*

He'd put her in the trunk, and now he was trying to take her someplace. He hadn't killed her at the scene, the way he'd done to poor Officer McHenry. Walker had taken her.

So he could play with her.

She wasn't in the mood to be his plaything.

Lauren twisted her body, shaking and maneuvering so that she could try to search the area for some kind of tool. Her fingers fumbled in the dark. At least he hadn't tied her hands—that would make it easier for her to escape or to fight back. Her nails shoved into the trunk's walls, but she kept searching. The drumming of her heartbeat filled her ears. She was so afraid that, at any moment, the vehicle would stop and Walker would come for her.

Then I'll be dead.

Her fingers swiped over something sharp. She stopped, breath heaving, and her fingers slid over the object. She could tell by its shape that she'd found a screwdriver.

Thank you, God.

Her right hand held it tight, while her left started to run along the trunk's wall. She had to locate the rear of the car, had to find the spot where the trunk locked. Once she found the actual lock, she could try to use the screwdriver to pry it open. If the trunk had a separate release latch, she could try to find that. She would find *something*.

Because she *would* get out of there. Lauren wasn't going to give up. No matter what.

She had a tool now, one that she could use to escape. If Walker came for her before she got her freedom, she'd damn well use the screwdriver as a weapon.

The car bounced, hit a deep hard hole, then jerked forward.

Lauren tensed. It didn't feel like they were on a road anymore. No, the vehicle had turned, and Walker was taking her away from civilization. That was the way he worked, right? *Take the prey into the swamp to torture for hours.*

They were on a bumpy road. A dirt road?

Her fingers were sweating around the screwdriver as she frantically went to work.

***

There was a roadblock up ahead. Anthony saw the flashing lights of two patrol cars at the end of Lincoln Road before the road branched and led back to the city.

He slammed on the brakes and jumped from the vehicle. He'd just gone all the way down the road, and hadn't seen a sign of the sedan. "Where the hell is he?" Anthony demanded.

Matt rushed toward him. "No one's come this way. We were on scene as fast as we could be, but no one's passed our way."

No. No fucking way.

"He got out before you were here," Paul said as he climbed from the car. His voice was flat. "The bastard took her out before the roadblock could be set up."

The road was old, and from what Anthony had learned on his one-hundred-mile-an-hour drive there, not well traveled at all. "He likes the swamp." There was plenty of swamp around. They'd flown by the twisting cypress trees, and he'd seen the black edge of the bayou water gleaming in the moonlight.

Matt took a few more steps toward them. "He *could* have driven through before we got here. We hauled ass, man, but it still took us twenty minutes to get here. The cop"—he pointed behind him to one of the patrol cars—"beat me by a bit, but not much."

It had taken Anthony ten minutes to get there from Steve's house, going hell fast. Matt and Paul were right—Walker *could* have gotten away and gone back to town.

But that just wasn't the way he liked to play.

He's changed the rules. The guy had busted out of prison like some kind of alpha dog, and instead of hiding in the shadows like he'd done in the past, had attacked Karen right away with a brutal in-your-face kill directed to hurt Lauren. *The guy thinks he is in charge, so he's trying to make us dance to his damn tune.* Anthony looked at the dark mass of swamp and woods. "Get Wesley Hawthorne out here." If they had to search the woods, he wanted the tracker.

"Walker keeps his prey out there, he plays with them…he *is* in the area." He just had to find out where. His eyes narrowed as he glanced back at Paul. "We passed a little road, didn't we? A dirt road…" It had been but a blur at the time, but now…

Walker could have taken her down that little road. He never would have made it to the roadblock then.

Paul shook his head. "If we focus our efforts on searching the swamp, and she's not there"—Paul sighed, his face grim—"we could be fucking killing her."

Anthony's back teeth were about to grind to dust. "Then let's divide our efforts. You go to town." He pointed to the darkness behind him. "And I'll search here for her." His gaze flew to Matt. "Get the tracker, and tell him I need him with me, *now*."

Every minute that passed would bring Lauren closer to death.

CHAPTER SEVEN

The killer had abducted the DA.

It was a move that FBI profiler Cadence Hollow had feared, ever since she'd heard about the photo Walker kept in his prison cell.

Walker had fixated on Lauren Chandler. He'd *killed* a woman in her house. Cadence had no doubt the man had gone into Lauren's house intending to kill the DA, but when Lauren hadn't been home, he'd found Karen instead...*you thought you'd make her suffer by killing her friend.*

Every move he'd made had been targeted around the DA, and as soon as he'd seen an opening, as soon as he'd lured Lauren to him, he'd attacked.

Cadence stood at the roadblock, watching the swirl of lights illuminate the scene. One of the marshals, Matt Meadows, was a few feet away, carefully screening a car that was passing. On Detective Voyt's orders, they were checking every car that came their way, in case Walker had switched rides.

So far, they weren't having any luck.

Meadows glanced up at her and slowly crossed to her side. "Not him."

No, she hadn't expected it to be. Her gaze drifted to the woods—she knew the woods stretched for a few miles, then gave way to the swamp. "Ross went in there?"

"Yeah, the Fish and Wildlife guy, Hawthorne, just went after him. Hawthorne said there are a few cabins back that way that Walker might be planning to use."

"He likes to take his victims away from civilization."

Meadows tilted his head as he studied her. "You think Ross is right? You think the Butcher took Lauren back into the swamp?"

"He wasn't planning to kill her quickly."

Meadows stared back at her. She'd never met this marshal before the Walker case, and she was discovering he could be tough and tenacious.

"If he had been planning to kill her right away," she continued, "Ross would have found her body dumped next to the cop's." The cop had been lucky. Very lucky from the sound of things. McHenry was in ICU, but the doctors thought he would pull through. Walker hadn't been interested in killing him; instead, it seemed as if he'd just wanted the cop out of his way.

Walker would have driven a knife into the back of anyone who stood between him and his target.

"He thinks she made him suffer," Cadence said, "so now it's her turn." For the DA's sake, Cadence hoped Ross found her before Walker started to play. Because once he started…

Cadence exhaled slowly. "You said there was a dirt road a few miles away? One that cut right away from Lincoln?"

He gave a nod.

More cops were pulling in behind the roadblock. Backup that she didn't think was necessary, not there anyway.

"Marshal, we need to get out to that dirt road."

That was a whole lot of land out there, and once Walker started cutting on Lauren, he wouldn't stop.

Not even when she begged him to. Especially then.

***

The latch snicked.

It *snicked*. Finally. The screwdriver had slipped in her hand dozens of times, cutting her again and again, but Lauren hadn't given up. When she heard that *snick*, she couldn't remember a more beautiful sound. She shoved against the hood and the trunk popped open. The car was still moving, but Lauren didn't care. She'd take whatever scrapes came her way if it meant freedom. She jerked upright in the trunk. The car jostled, going too fast, bumping along the rough terrain. *Do it.* Lauren swallowed back her fear, then leaped.

Her palms hit the ground first, then her knees, her shoulders, her head. The impact stunned her for a moment, but the sudden screech of brakes got her moving again.

Walker must have seen the trunk fly up, or maybe he'd seen her swan dive. Either way, she wasn't sticking around. She grabbed for her screwdriver a few feet away and surged back to her feet. Then she was running. Running as hard as she could away from the car. Footsteps thundered behind her.

She opened her mouth and screamed, "*Help me!*"

His footsteps thundered faster. Much faster than her own. The bastard must have spent time doing cardio in prison. He'd come out even stronger than he'd gone in.

She risked a fast glance over her shoulder, and saw Walker closing in. He was a big, hulking shadow in the night. One lunge, and he'd have her.

One lunge…

She twisted her body to face him as he came at her.

He lunged, all right, and when he did, she shoved her screwdriver into his side.

He was the one to cry out then. A bellow of fury and pain.

Yes, bastard, that's what pain feels like. He'd made sure his victims hurt over the years. Now it was his turn to feel pain.

She left that screwdriver shoved deep in his side. Then she spun and ran as fast as her legs would carry her.

But soon there were footsteps racing behind her.

He should have been down. The attack should have bought her some time.

A hand grabbed her shoulder. He yanked her back. Caged her between him and the heavy trunk of a tree.

"Your aim is shit, DA," Walker snarled at her as his body shoved against hers. "Fucking shit."

She tried to yank away from him, tried to kick, but he blocked her attacks.

He laughed.

"You're not getting away from me."

His breath was hot as it blew over her face.

"I've planned for this moment, dreamed of it, for too long."

Terror was closing her throat. Choking her. She couldn't get away from him. His grip was about to shatter her wrists. Anthony wasn't there, Paul wasn't there, *no one* was coming to save her.

I have to save myself. Have to get away.

Have to live.

Was that what his other victims had thought, too? When Walker had them under his knife, had they been desperate to live just a little bit longer?

"You stole my life," he whispered as his mouth came close to her ear. "Now I'm going to steal yours."

***

It was so damn dark that they could hardly see any tracks along the dirt road. It sure didn't help that the road had split into three sections as it snaked into the woods and headed for the swamp.

Three sections—three ways for Walker to have vanished.

But Walker *had* been there. Anthony had met up with Wesley Hawthorne, and they'd gotten their lights out and scanned in the darkness. They'd found signs of a vehicle headed this way, a vehicle that had left tire tracks that were consistent with a mid-size sedan.

Walker hadn't returned to the city. He'd taken Lauren and headed for the swamp, the way he seemed to so enjoy when he killed.

Don't kill her.

"There's a cabin about two miles up ahead," Wesley said. The guy wasn't talking much, and that was a good thing. It was all Anthony could do to control the rage and fear twisting through him.

He'd told Lauren he would keep her safe. Instead, he'd just delivered her to Walker. Fucking *delivered* her.

"There's water behind the cabin. The bayou snakes and twists all the way back here."

Anthony's hands tightened around the steering wheel. "If our guy has a boat, then that's how he was able to get from that damn cabin to here."

He pushed the accelerator down even more. He swung the vehicle around some trees, then slammed on the brakes.

The sedan was abandoned, its trunk up, not ten feet away.

Anthony jumped from his SUV. His vehicle's headlights lit up the scene as he advanced toward the Oldsmobile. His gun was gripped tightly in his right hand.

If he'd seen Walker right then, Anthony thought he might have shot the bastard on sight.

But Walker wasn't there. Neither was Lauren.

The car was empty so that meant Walker had left on foot—with Lauren. Both Wesley and Anthony began to search the ground with their flashlights. The dark made it harder to notice any telltale tracks on the ground. Anthony yanked out his phone, calling Matt and ordering that the K-9 unit be brought into the area. They needed the tracking dogs.

To rush off on foot, Walker had to be close.

"Blood!" Wesley called out.

Anthony's body tensed. His flashlight lit on the same spot Wesley had found. Sure enough, he saw the spray of red in the illumination from his light.

Lauren was hurt.

"The blood goes to the left." Wesley was already following the faint trail. He had his gun gripped in his left hand. "The cabin is back that way."

"Then let's get the hell there, *now*." He couldn't stand the thought of her suffering. *I'm coming, baby. I'm coming.*

Their feet thudded over the earth as they followed the blood trail toward the cabin.

She's alive. She's alive. The words played through Anthony's head again and again. Lauren had to be alive. For him, there wasn't any alternative. Because if he burst through that cabin door and she was dead—

He didn't know what he would do.

She's alive. She has to be alive...

***

He'd handcuffed her. The cabin was stocked with duct tape, handcuffs, and knives. Walker had planned out this moment, and now she knew he was going to kill her.

He'd thrust her into a chair, yanked her handcuffed hands behind her, and duct-taped her ankles to the wobbly chair legs. The only light in the old cabin came from a lantern near his feet. His shirt had a dark shadow sweeping over it—his blood, not that he seemed to care he was bleeding.

He barely seemed to notice his wound. He was too fixated on her.

"I want to take my time with you." His words were whispered and made the goose bumps on her arms rise even more. "I thought about you..." He picked up a knife. The guy had a whole set of knives, just waiting. "Thought all about what I'd do to you..."

"The cops are searching for me now!" Lauren yelled. She wasn't going to beg him. Wouldn't give him that pleasure. "You're about to find yourself tossed back into a cage again, only you *won't* ever escape this time! You'll be in for life, you'll—"

He pressed the tip of the knife against her cheek. It sliced into her, and she felt the wet roll of blood on her skin, heavier and warmer than a teardrop could ever be.

"Do I want to start with your face?" Walker asked musingly. "Or your body?"

Don't beg. Don't cry. She wouldn't, no matter what happened. "What the hell happened to you, Walker? How did you wind up this way? You had a normal home, good parents..." She'd done her research. He'd had a great home life, even parents who'd sent him to therapy once they're realized their boy was...different. The therapist had signed off on Jon after awhile, saying the guy was fine. *Perfect mental health.* Bullshit. The guy had just been a good actor, perfect at *pretending* there wasn't a monster inside of him. "Why the hell are you like this?"

He smiled at her, and the sight nearly stopped her heartbeat. Jon Walker was a handsome man, almost boyish in appearance. He didn't look like a monster. He looked like any southern boy—a guy who spent his time chasing women and cheering for his football team.

The guy had even played quarterback in his high school days. Been the freaking prom king.

Now he was…this?

"I had to be shown my true calling," he said. The tip of the knife lifted from her cheek but she didn't take a relieved breath. She was too worried about where that knife would go next. "I was lost, until he found me."

He?

Walker's eyes narrowed on her and even through the shadows, she could see the hate that hardened the faint lines on his face. "You sent me away."

"Because you *killed*! You cut up women—you tossed their bodies away like garbage! You deserved to be in jail!" She actually thought the guy deserved to rot in hell, but she managed to bite that part back. The knife was far too close for that kind of outburst.

"You took me away…" Now the knife was on her arm, and this time, the slice was deep. She bit into her lower lip, sinking her teeth into it even as the blade sliced into her arm. The blood wasn't like a teardrop this time. Instead, it pulsed out, hot and heavy. "You took me away from what I needed most."

"You did that to yourself when you…" Oh, it *hurt*… "Decided to…kill…"

The blade came out of her arm on a slow, bloody, painful glide.

"I stared at your picture. Thought of all the things I was going to do to you..." The bloody knife's tip slid over her shirt, just above her breast. "Before I'm through, you're gonna look like a jigsaw puzzle."

She nearly vomited.

He was bent over her. So close. She let her head sag forward as if she were afraid. He came even closer, laughing at her fear.

She jerked up her head, catching him in the chin. Ramming into him. Swearing, he stumbled back. She twisted her body, and the chair crashed to the floor.

"Fuckin' bitch!"

She'd hoped the chair would break when she fell. It hadn't. And now the knife was at her throat.

Lauren froze.

"You think you're so fuckin' brave, don't you?"

No, she didn't. She was so scared she couldn't even speak. One slice, and he'd cut open her jugular. She'd be dead. She'd bleed out on the dirty floor, and every dream she'd ever had would be over.

"Do you think..." The blade nicked her throat. Just a nick. He was taunting her. "Do you think your sister was so brave?"

Lauren's gaze flew up to him.

"I know," he whispered and he was *smiling*. "All those secrets you carry...*I know*."

She tried to jerk her legs free of the duct tape. Her shoulders were burning because her arms were pinned behind her, but she *had* to get free.

"Jennifer Chandler...they never found her, did they?" She'd broken his nose with her head butt and blood dripped down into his grin. "Not that there was much left to find of dear Jenny..."

"Shut up!" The scream tore from her, making her throat feel raw. She ignored the pain. Rage was pumping through her blood and pushing every other feeling away. "Stop!"

"That's what Jenny said, too. She was crying, begging…"

No, it wasn't possible. He was just trying to make her break. Trying to hurt her more. There was no way Walker had killed her sister.

Was there?

Walker's first victim had been Beth Loxley, a freshman at LSU. She'd been the first reported missing, the first they'd tied to the Bayou Butcher.

The first…

"I watched Jenny. At first, she had hope. Then the knife sliced her…" He touched Lauren's cheek. "This was the first cut for her, too."

No.

She didn't realize she'd screamed the word.

"It took her awhile to die. We didn't know what we were doing then…"

Lauren stopped screaming. *We.* She stared at him with horror, a sick knot in her gut.

He leaned his head toward hers as if confiding a secret. "Bet I could find what's left of her. Just bones now. We buried her… cut her up and buried her…" He gave a nod. "Just like we'll do to you."

Lauren couldn't breathe. Walker was behind her sister's murder? But Walker would have just been a kid then…

Just like Jenny had been a kid. Sixteen years old.

Lauren stared up into his eyes and saw madness.

"It's so funny. She kept mentioning you at the end, saying that she had to pick you up. 'Laurie's gonna be late for piano…Laurie's gonna be late for piano..."' He mimicked. "Like the bitch didn't have more to worry about."

There was no more pain. Even the rage was gone. Lauren was too numb, her whole body encased in ice. This couldn't be happening. Her sister?

She started to hear a faint ringing.

Only the ringing wasn't coming from her and her dulled senses.

Walker swore and jumped back. As she watched, he rummaged in a backpack near him. She tried to twist her head so that she could see him better, but he was too far away. He'd grabbed a phone and scurried back.

She couldn't see him clearly. If she couldn't see him...then *he can't see me.*

She yanked her legs up and down, again and again, trying to break the chair legs.

"What? What the hell are you saying? I've *got her!*" Walker was yelling at someone on the phone.

She felt the wood begin to crack. *Yes.* She kicked again. Again.

"I want to kill her! We were going to kill her!"

Her legs were free. Her heart slammed into her chest.

"*Fuck!*" Walker's roar. It was the sound of a man who'd just lost control.

This was her chance. If she didn't get away now, Lauren knew she was dead. She threw her body to the side, her shoulder popped, but the numbness stopped any pain. So much numbness. Then she was on her feet. Her hands were still cuffed behind her, but she ran for the door.

He was screaming. Yelling. So was she.

Lauren had to get the door open. Had to get her freedom. But her hands were behind her, and it was so hard to twist the knob.

He grabbed her. Shoved her against the wall. "I'm not finished with you."

The one image that flashed through her mind, obliterating the sight of Walker's bloody visage—it wasn't Jenny's face. The face that had haunted her for so long.

It was Anthony's.

Her chance at life, and it had passed her by. Anthony would find her, she knew that. Eventually, he'd find what was left of her body. He wouldn't leave her in the swamp.

As she'd left Jenny?

"We're not even close to finished…" His breath heaved. "But playtime has to wait until he can join us."

Hope nearly broke her heart.

"I've got to get the fuck out of here." He locked his fingers around her chin. "See you again real soon…" Then he slammed her head back into the wood behind her, slammed it so hard that she saw nothing but darkness and never even felt the floor as she fell.

***

Anthony ran even faster when he finally caught sight of the cabin just up ahead. They'd lost the blood trail, and Wesley had taken them down the wrong path as they tried to find the cabin in the dark. Every lost second had been like a knife slicing into Anthony's skin.

He's hurting her. She could be dying.

While Anthony dicked around in the dark.

"Hell, yes!" Wesley shouted out. He'd been briefly separated from Wesley as they both frantically tried to find the old path that would lead them to this place, but now both men ran forward, coming from two different angles.

The cabin was dark. It looked abandoned. *Don't be.* Lauren had to be inside.

Anthony reached the door first. He threw it open and hurried inside with his flashlight positioned above his gun so that he could take the shot he needed.

A shot that would kill the Bayou Butcher.

The light fell on a broken chair. Some pieces of duct tape. A row of knives.

A groan came from behind the door. He yanked the door back, nearly hitting Wesley with it, and there she was. Slumped on the floor, her hair a heavy curtain around her face, blood soaking her clothes.

"Lauren?" His voice was a stark whisper. He fell to his knees next to her. With shaking hands, Anthony pulled her into his arms. Her blood smeared over him, and he just held her tighter. "An ambulance!" he barked over his shoulder to Wesley. "She needs to get to a hospital, now!" He lifted her into his arms, not about to let her go. Her head sagged back, her eyes were still closed. There was a cut on her cheek. A long, thin slice.

And so much more blood on her arm and shirt.

"I've got you, baby," he whispered as he pressed a kiss to her head. "I've got you." She wasn't ever going to get away from him again.

Wesley was calling for the ambulance, demanding that they get some EMTs or a chopper out there freaking yesterday as Anthony carried Lauren out of that cabin.

"Baby?" His hold tightened on her. "Please, open your eyes, look at me."

But she wasn't looking at him. Lauren was out cold, and the fear in his gut was just getting worse with every second that passed.

***

Jon ran through the woods as fast as he could. His side ached where the bitch had stabbed him. He'd wanted to pay her back for that.

He'd wanted to pay her back for so much.

But the marshal had been closing in. The phone call had come just in time.

I won't go back in a cage again.

His feet pounded over the earth. He knew how to hide his trail, but there wasn't time for that now. Blood would be dripping from his wound—dogs would follow the blood. If the marshal didn't already have a dog tracking after him, he would soon.

He knew how men like Ross worked. They didn't stop. Not until they'd run down their prey. Jon knew, because he was just like that, too.

He raced onto the old dock. The wood trembled beneath his feet. The boat was there. A motorboat, but he wouldn't use the motor, not yet. Sound traveled easily in the woods. He jumped into the boat, untied it, and grabbed for the oars.

Going out on the water would buy him time. The dogs would lose him at the water, and if he got to the meeting point, his ride would be waiting. He'd get out of there, and the marshal wouldn't know what the hell was happening.

Then he'd have another chance with Lauren Chandler. Lauren would finish the circle, a perfect ending to a new life that had begun twenty years ago. He'd just have to be more

148

careful. *They* would have to be more careful. Lauren couldn't be protected, not always, and there would come a time when the marshal slipped up, when the uniformed cops weren't watching.

Lauren would be his chance to prove he was the one in charge. The one with all the power.

Lauren would have nothing but death.

***

It was dawn. Cadence stood on the small dock at Rattlesnake Bayou, her gaze on the body that had been dumped like garbage.

Helen Lynch, Steve's ex-wife.

"She's been dead awhile," the ME said as he bent near the body. "Lividity has set in."

"Give us a time frame," Kyle McKenzie said as he waited near Cadence's side. She could feel the tension rolling off her partner's body.

He'd thought they would find Helen alive. Kyle, always the hopeful one.

She'd known better.

If the Bayou Butcher had really taken her, as he'd told Steve, she'd known Helen was dead. The Butcher didn't trade. He just killed. And after being locked away from his preferred prey for so long...

Walker knew he'd kill her from the moment he took her.

Greg tilted his head as he studied the body. "I'd say at least twelve hours."

Long before Lynch had played willing sacrifice and brought Lauren into Walker's web.

"He didn't kill her here," Cadence murmured. That was obvious. There wasn't enough blood at the scene. Not enough to

149

match all of the deep, horrible cuts on Helen's body. The Butcher. He'd earned that name for a reason.

Killers seemed to be getting more twisted every day.

To think, once upon a time, she'd lived without knowing about these monsters.

Now she saw them everywhere.

Cadence looked up and found Kyle's hard stare on her.

"He's getting his payback. Lauren, the judge, Steve." He expelled on a long sigh. "Hell, even Karen was part of the reason the guy ended up in jail. She was an investigator on the case."

The attacks weren't going to stop, either. She knew that. Normally, a serial killer had a dormant period between his hunts. The kill itself almost calmed or controlled him. There was no control for the Butcher. What he was doing—hell, he was beyond anything she'd seen before. "We need to make sure all of the jurors have protection." Those still in the immediate area would need a police watch. Those who'd moved away would need to be on guard.

But the guy might not just be targeting jurors. He could be targeting cops who'd worked on his case years before. Witnesses. The families of his victims. Just how much revenge would he want?

She had to learn more about him. Had to work up her own profile on him, and not just go by the work another agent had done five years ago.

"How the hell is he doing this?" Kyle demanded as he jerked a hand through his hair. "He should have no resources. He should have been fighting to survive!"

The ME was putting small plastic bags over Helen Lynch's hands. Trying to preserve evidence. *I hope you fought him, Helen. I hope you hurt the bastard before you died.*

"Walker grew up running through these swamps," Cadence murmured. "He knows the area back and forth. He can use the land, the water—he can hide from us out here, and he knows it."

"But he had to go into the city to get Helen," Kyle pointed out. "He went into the city for Karen, for the attack at the judge's office…"

That was a whole lot of back-and-forth activity. Too much for one man? The new profile she'd been working up on this case said—*yes, hell, yes.* Cadence didn't think they were just looking for one killer.

She pulled out her phone and called Ross. He'd need to know about Helen's death.

He answered on the second ring, and she could hear a hospital intercom sounding behind him. "Ross." He sounded distracted, worried.

She turned away from the scene. "We found Helen Lynch."

"Hell." He understood. Ross wasn't new to the game. "How long ago did he kill her?"

She took a few steps away, distancing herself from Greg and Kyle. "The ME says at least twelve hours."

"Dammit. I knew this would happen. Steve Lynch should have come to us. We could have helped him."

There would be no help now. Lynch was being held at the PD. Someone would have to give him the news about his ex-wife.

"How's your DA?" The wording was deliberate. She'd seen the way those two looked at each other. Lauren was definitely Ross's, and the rage he had to be feeling after Lauren's attack…

"She's gonna make it." There was rage biting through his voice. "I am tired of this bastard screwing with us."

So was she. "I have to come and see Lauren. I need to talk to her." There were questions only Lauren could answer. She'd see Lauren, then she'd pay a visit to Steve Lynch. But first, she ordered, "We need to up the guards on Judge Hamilton." She'd talk to the police captain about that when she got back to the station. "Are you staying with Lauren?" She knew the answer, but asked anyway.

"She won't leave my sight."

The hospital's intercom sounded in the background as a doctor was paged.

"If I learn anything else, I'll get back to you," she said and ended the call.

Helplessly, she turned back to the victim. Helen Lynch was in her early thirties, with dark-brown hair. Her eyes had been opened in death, a deliberate move, and her lips were pressed tightly closed. The neck bore the same morbid grin—a deep slice right across her throat. The blood had stained the skin there.

She had to ask, "Did he leave us another message?"

Greg glanced up at her.

"Go ahead," she ordered, keeping her voice calm and quiet. There was no room for emotion at a scene like this. If she felt too much, if she empathized with the victim, she'd be lost. "We don't have time to wait for you to get back to your lab. If another victim is out there..."

His gloved fingers rose to Helen's neck. He pressed lightly on the skin, making the wound gape open even more.

I can see the paper.

He pulled it out, slowly, carefully.

Kyle edged closer to her. He wasn't as good at compartmentalizing as she was, but he didn't have to be. Control was all she knew.

Crime scenes pissed him off, and she knew he hated to see a victim's pain. It reminded Kyle of his own past too much.

The paper got stuck in Helen's throat.

Kyle swore.

Greg hesitated, then grabbed for the tweezers in his kit. A few moments later, the paper slid free. Greg unfolded it, and when he read the note, she saw him swallow.

"What does it say?" Kyle demanded.

Greg glanced up at them. His gaze darted to Kyle, then to Cadence. "'Guilty.'"

CHAPTER EIGHT

Anthony stood less than two feet from Lauren. Her arm was being stitched up—a long, slow process because that freak Walker had carved into her so deeply.

Lauren didn't make a sound as the doctor worked on her. Lauren actually hadn't spoken at all since she'd opened her eyes. The blue of her gaze seemed dulled, missing the normal sparkle. Too much pain. Too much fear.

A bandage was on her cheek. The doctor had said the wound wasn't deep enough to need stitches. Her shoulder had been reset—popped back into the joint in a fast, brutal move that had made him swear.

Even as she'd continued to keep silent.

He wanted to take all of her pain away.

Anthony's hands clenched into fists.

"I want you to stay here overnight," the doctor said. She was a woman in her early fifties with dark hair and light-cream skin. "You have a concussion, and we need to monitor you for—"

Lauren shook her head. "I *can't* stay here." There was fear in her voice, a tension that pulled at him. He wouldn't have Lauren afraid. "I hate being in hospitals. They remind me too much— I *have to get out.*"

"Ms. Chandler"—the doctor's voice firmed but Anthony could see the compassion in her eyes—"you need someone to watch you. I don't think you understand the severity of the situation. With a concussion, you—"

Lauren's gaze rose and finally she looked at Anthony. "Will you watch me?"

That soft question almost broke him. *Always.* "Yes." He hadn't been able to let her out of his sight since the cabin. Matt had taken over the hunt in the swamp, and Anthony had gone into the ambulance with Lauren. He'd held her hand the whole way, but she hadn't known. Her eyes had only opened when the ambulance pulled into the emergency area at the hospital, and then the EMTs had pushed him back so that they could get her out.

He hadn't been pushed far. With every step that the EMTs had taken, Anthony had remained close. Fear still twisted his guts, and he wasn't sure if the tight knot would ever go away.

"I'll have a marshal watching me," Lauren said, her voice a strained whisper. "What more do I need?"

The doctor frowned at Anthony. "She's got a grade-two concussion, so when I say watched, I mean I want you in the same room with her at all times. If her pain gets worse, if her speech starts to slur, if she has seizures, you rush her back here right away."

Anthony nodded.

The doctor exhaled as she removed her gloves. "I'll give you a sheet with warning signs, but I don't like this."

"I don't like this either." Lauren's voice was hoarse. It was breaking the heart he'd tried to pretend he didn't have.

Lauren was lying on the hospital bed, a thin gown over her. Her clothing had been taken and bagged as evidence. Voyt and his crime scene guys were going over the cabin, and Anthony was hoping the dogs and their handlers from the K-9 unit ran down Walker.

As much as he wanted to join that hunt, his priorities had shifted.

To her.

"One of the cops is supposed to be bringing you some more clothes," Anthony murmured as the doctor slipped from the room.

Lauren wasn't looking at him anymore. She was staring straight up at the bright lights overhead.

He edged closer to her. Took her hand.

She flinched.

"Lauren, it's all right. He's not going to get you again."

She laughed. He'd never heard such a brittle sound come from Lauren. "He said he would. Told me he'd be back." Her tongue slid over her lips. "He said…" Her words trailed away.

Anthony's fingers tightened around hers. "I don't give a shit what he said. He's *not* going to hurt you."

Her gaze came to him. There were tears in her eyes.

Something broke inside of him.

"He hurt Jenny."

Anthony frowned. He didn't remember a victim named Jenny in Walker's file.

"I wondered for so long. I used to hope she'd come home, but she never did." Her breath rushed out. "He *hurt* Jenny."

Fuck—*Jenny*. The name clicked. Jenny was the sister she'd been talking about in the ME's office. The drumming of his heartbeat echoed in his ears. "Baby, slow down. You've got to start at the beginning and *tell* me what's happening."

"My sister…" She swallowed. The small sound was painful to hear. "Walker killed her. He told me—" A tear tracked down her cheek. "He told me he killed Jenny."

"He was messing with you. His first victim was—"

Her hand twisted in his. Her nails sank into him. "He *told me.* He knew about the piano lessons. He knew..."

He had to take her into his arms. Carefully, Anthony climbed onto the narrow bed. He positioned his body around hers. "The bastard was trying to get into your head. Whatever happened to your sister—"

Her body was tense and hard against his. "She was supposed to pick me up from school and take me to piano lessons. She never came. Never came..."

His jaw clenched.

"He said he watched her get cut up. That he buried her—and that he would do the same to me..."

The door squeaked open behind them. Anthony looked back, expecting to see the doctor, but instead, he saw the FBI profiler. Cadence had sure made good time getting there. He'd talked to her less than twenty minutes ago on the phone.

Cadence hesitated in the doorway. He knew she'd see—and understand—plenty by the way he was holding Lauren. He'd worked with Cadence on two other cases. The woman was private, smart, tough. In so many ways she reminded him of Lauren.

But she wasn't Lauren. That was why they'd never clicked— why he never clicked with anyone but Lauren.

No one could ever be *just* like his Lauren. He could never want anyone else as much.

"I need to ask her some questions," Cadence murmured as she hesitated in the doorway. "But I can give you a few minutes longer."

"She has a concussion." His voice came out clipped. He knew the drill with witnesses, knew they were supposed to tell their stories when they were fresh. But this wasn't just any witness.

It was Lauren, and she was shaking in his arms. "She needs to rest. I'm taking her with me. You can get your answers tomorrow."

"Anthony..." Cadence sighed out his name. "You understand that isn't how it works." She walked into the room, her shoes nearly silent on the tiled floor. "Lauren, surely that isn't how you *want* this to work? You're a DA, you have to want us to catch Walker as fast as we can."

Lauren pulled away from Anthony, putting a few inches between them that he did *not* want. "Someone warned him."

At those words—three simple words—the whole case changed.

"Someone warned Walker that the marshal was on his trail." The trembling of her body increased. "Someone was watching..."

Anthony glanced over and caught the slight flare of Cadence's golden eyes. "How do you know that?" Cadence asked.

Anthony looked back at Lauren. A furrow appeared between her brows. "I heard a phone ring. The guy called Walker. Told him."

"Are you certain?" Cadence pressed as she edged closer.

"I know the sound of a phone." Now Lauren's voice was clipped. Annoyed. "He left me so he could answer it. That was when I managed to break the chair and get to my feet."

Anthony remembered the sight of the broken chair. The duct tape.

The knives.

"I heard him. He told the person on the phone..." She drew in a deep breath. "That he had me."

He'd suspected Walker had been using a partner to get out of jail, but this was different than having a getaway buddy.

Anthony kept silent now, waiting for Lauren to finish.

"He yelled into the phone, 'We were going to kill her.' *We.*" The word vibrated with fear and fury. "Not just him...*we.*"

Fuck. Fuck. *Fuck.*

A fast glance at Cadence showed the profiler was watching Lauren with hawk-like intensity.

"I ran for the door," Lauren said. Her hand lifted. Touched the back of her head. "He stopped me. Said we'd finish soon when… 'he' could join us." Her hand dropped. "Then he slammed my head into the door and I passed out, I guess. I'm not really sure what happened. I woke up and saw the swirl of ambulance lights."

What happened was that Walker had raced out of there. Anthony hadn't given chase, but Wesley had joined the K-9 team and started hunting as quickly as he could. When Anthony had checked in just a few minutes before, Wesley had told him that the dogs had followed Walker's trail to the water's edge.

The bastard sure liked to use boats for escape. The cops were out on their own boats then, too. Cops and deputies—any damn one his marshals had been able to find—they were hunting on the water and on land. Looking for signs of Walker and where he'd taken his boat.

"Walker's been working with a partner all along." Lauren's words were bitter. "Since he killed my sister. He told me that he *watched* her being killed. They killed her! Walker and whoever that sick freak is who helped him!"

Cadence was near the bed. "You're sure Walker said he *watched*?"

Anthony glared at Cadence. Had she missed the whole sister part? This interview was ripping Lauren apart.

"Yes," Lauren hissed. "He watched." Her lips twisted into a chilling smile. "He said Jenny started the circle, and I would finish it."

Cadence inhaled on a sharp breath.

"He could be bullshitting," Anthony said. He wouldn't put it past Walker to screw with Lauren's head. *Another way to punish her.* "Maybe he heard about your sister—"

"*You* didn't even know about her," Lauren said as her shoulders slumped. "I don't talk about Jenny very much. Not anymore. It hurts too much."

It also made him understand her more. Made him understand why she was so determined to get justice for the victims out there.

She'd never gotten justice for her own sister.

The hospital room door opened again. Paul entered and his gaze flew to Lauren, heated. Anthony hated the emotion he saw there.

The cop still had strong feelings for Lauren.

Join the club, buddy.

No, there was no club. The detective just needed to back the hell off.

"I brought some fresh clothes for you," Paul said as he advanced toward Lauren.

Anthony scooped the bag of clothes out of his hands. "I thought you were staying at the scene."

Paul's eyes narrowed on him. "I needed to check on Lauren."

"You *need* to find Walker."

Paul bared his teeth in a tiger's smile. "I thought that was your job, *Marshal*. Fugitive apprehension and all."

Fuck this. Anthony's hand fisted around the bag. "If you had let me take the shot, I would've apprehended the fugitive, and Lauren wouldn't be in this hospital right now." But Paul had jumped between him and his prey. "You pull that shit again, and I won't hesitate."

Paul swallowed. "I didn't think you could stop him without hurting her."

"You think she isn't hurt?" His voice dropped but he knew Lauren could still hear him. "I *had* that bastard in my sights.

Don't ever stop me again." The words came from him in a lethal snarl as Anthony fought hard for his control. He was walking a razor's edge, and he knew it.

"Paul..." Lauren's voice was quiet, a softness in the storm brewing inside of Anthony. "He knew about Jenny. He said he watched her die and that he knew where she was buried."

Paul swore.

As he watched the detective's reaction to the news, Anthony realized Paul knew all about Jenny Chandler. Lauren had shared her past with the cop, but not with him. That fact made his anger twist even more until he realized...

I never shared my past with her. He'd deliberately tried to keep their relationship only in the moment. No past. No future. That had been them.

The whole no-future bit sure had changed when he'd realized Lauren was facing death. Her future had become the most important thing to him.

Paul shook his head. "He was messin' with you—" the detective began.

"Why does everyone say that?" Lauren's voice rose, breaking. "He *knew* things about her...about what she said at the end. And his eyes...I believe what he said. I believe every word. He was there when Jenny died." A sob took the last of her words.

It was time he took Lauren out of there.

"You can talk to her again tomorrow," Anthony said, glancing between the profiler and the detective. "She needs rest, dammit." He wouldn't let her fall apart in front of them.

"Lauren..." Cadence hesitated. "Did he look the same as his prison photos? Has he altered his appearance?"

"I couldn't see his face perfectly, not with the shadows. There was just a lantern in the cabin." Her lips pressed together. After a moment, she said, "His hair was short. And I think he had a beard growing. Stubble on his jaw."

"Did he mention the name of whoever was on the phone?" Cadence asked. "Did he give you any hint about who—"

"He never said his name." Her breath sighed out as she looked up at Anthony.

"Are you sure it's a he?" Cadence pushed her.

Back off. Anthony bit the words back.

"Walker said, 'he.'" Lauren was adamant. "I know exactly what I heard." Then she shook her head. Tears glinted in the gaze that she didn't take from Anthony. "Please, I'm hurting. I want to get out of here. Dammit, I just—I can't breathe in here! I need to get out of this hospital!"

Paul shuffled toward the bed. "You still can't stand hospitals, huh?" His fingers brushed over her uninjured cheek. Anthony realized he hated that intimate touch. A touch that spoke of emotions and a shared past. "They still remind you of your mom?"

She gave a low nod. "After all the time I saw her wasting away..." The sound of her swallow was a painful click. "The place is just a morgue to me."

Paul knew her well, too well, and Anthony felt a jolt of shame rock through him. He should be the one to know the private details of Lauren's life. Her secrets should be his.

Not the detective's.

"I can give you police protection," Paul said as his hand dropped away from Lauren. "That room at my place is still waiting for you."

It can keep waiting.

Anthony didn't say the words because the choice wasn't his. It was Lauren's.

After a tense moment, Lauren shook her head. "Anthony's promised to keep watch over me tonight. Dr. Davis gave him the okay to take me."

I'll watch over you, baby, all night long.

Her gaze stayed on Paul. "I want you to pull Jenny's file. I had a copy at my house but..." She broke off and lifted a trembling hand to shove back her hair. "I can't go there now. I need to see her file again."

"I'll need to look at that file, too," Cadence added.

If Walker had been killing that long ago—and it sure seemed he had—then it would change the man's profile. He would have been just a kid himself back then. A kid with a taste for death.

"If you need me," Paul said to Lauren, as he leaned toward her, "you call me anytime."

"Thank you."

Paul glanced up, and his eyes collided with Anthony's. Anthony wanted that guy *away* from Lauren, and if he didn't move soon...

He backed away. *Finally*, the guy filed out of the room, with Cadence following behind him. Lauren eased to the side of the bed and tried to stand. Her body shook, and he was there instantly, steadying her. "I've got you."

Her lashes lifted and her stare met his. The blue still wasn't the vibrant color he loved, but he'd make sure the sparkle came back. "My parents...they both died without ever knowing what had happened to Jenny." She swallowed. "I think they both thought, hoped, that she was still alive."

He held her tighter.

"Maybe that was better," she whispered, the shimmer of tears sweeping her eyes. "Better to have the hope than to know—"

A tear leaked down her cheek.

With fingers that weren't as steady as he wanted them to be, Anthony wiped away the tear.

Lauren's chin lifted. "I need to leave now."

Any fucking thing she wanted—that was what he'd do. "I'll help you dress," he offered. With her stitches and concussion, she'd need help. He bet Dr. Davis would insist Lauren leave the hospital in a wheelchair. It was usually the way the hospitals worked, especially with liability issues.

She gave a little nod. Very carefully, he untied the hospital gown and let it fall to the floor. Lauren was still in front of him, barely seeming to even breathe. The sight of her body made him ache—he *always* wanted her. But this wasn't about lust. This was about taking care of her. He kept his touch light as he carefully helped her with her panties and bra. She didn't speak at all. Didn't make eye contact with him.

He watched her face when he slid the sleeve of the blouse over her injured arm. She flinched and he froze, but she whispered, "It's all right." He hurried to finish.

It's not all right. Her words were a lie.

It wasn't going to be all right until he had her safe with him.

Until Walker was dead.

When she was dressed, he slipped a pair of comfortable shoes on her and eased her back onto the bed. He went to the door, where a wheelchair was waiting for him. A few minutes later, Lauren was secure in the chair. He started to move behind her, but she caught his arm.

"Thank you."

She shouldn't be thanking him. She'd been taken on his watch.

"I knew you'd find me." Her voice was certain. "I just…I didn't want you to find me dead."

He schooled his expression, but she was already glancing away.

Finding her dead would have been his worst fucking nightmare.

What the hell would I have done then?

***

Cadence watched as Anthony wheeled Lauren out of the hospital. Did the marshal even realize how much his expression gave away? Probably not.

"We never found any indication that Walker had committed other murders. We thought we'd found all of his kills," Paul said as he came up behind Cadence. The detective sounded frustrated, confused, and pissed.

She glanced over at him. "Maybe you did find all of *his* kills."

Paul's brows climbed.

"Did you miss that whole part from Lauren about her sister?"

He gave a low whistle. "Jennifer Chandler. I remember when that story made headlines around here. She was sixteen, captain of the cheerleading squad, class president—you know those kids, the popular ones *everyone* misses the instant they're gone."

"Her murderer was never caught?" Cadence asked.

"Her body was never found. Police weren't even sure it was a murder."

Lauren was at the end of the hallway now. Anthony glanced back at them. Cadence noted that he'd schooled his expression this time. *Too late, Anthony.* She'd seen, and she was pretty sure the cop had, too.

"The detectives back then thought that maybe she'd run away, but her family never bought that story." He rolled his shoulders, as if pushing away a bad memory. "I caught Jenny's file as a cold case a few years ago. That's how Lauren and I got together."

Only they weren't together any longer, and Cadence knew if Anthony had his way, they wouldn't be again.

A rough sigh broke from him. "Lauren has spent her whole life trying to find her big sister, and to discover that Walker was the one—hell, I can't even imagine what she's feeling right now."

Shock had seemed to encase Lauren when Cadence spoke to her. A brittle veneer of ice that had looked like it might crack at any moment. Lauren hadn't just learned about her sister's fate—she'd faced death, too.

When the shock wore off, Lauren would have a hard fall.

Good thing that it appeared Anthony would be there to catch her.

She pushed her hands into her pockets. "Walker told Lauren he watched her sister die."

"Twisted fuck."

"But he didn't actually say he *killed* her." That was the point they all seemed to be missing. She'd have to talk to Lauren again to be sure. Cadence planned to analyze all of the old Bayou Butcher files again. "Are you sure the Butcher was just one killer?"

Paul blinked. "One killer is who we convicted, ma'am."

She waved that away. "The crimes, the abductions…are you certain only one killer could do all of that?" She wasn't. She was convinced it had been two men all along. "If he just *watched* Jennifer Chandler's death, then that means someone else was there to do the actual killing."

Paul shook his head. "No, ma'am. You're wrong on this. The old ME checked over all the Butcher's victims. Based on their injuries, she said they were all killed by a left-handed man, approximately six foot two, one hundred eighty pounds—Walker."

"Yes, but—"

"When that poor babysitter was being carved up, the Petersons only saw Walker in their house. Nobody else."

"Maybe the other killer wasn't killing them." Anger beat through her words. She knew killers, and she understood just how deadly some relationships could be. "Maybe it was his turn to watch."

Two killers. It would sure explain how Walker seemed to be moving so easily between the city and the swamp. Maybe he *wasn't* doing the moving. Maybe he was hiding out in the swamp, where he was most comfortable, while someone else hunted in the city.

"Walker's blood was found on Karen Royce," Paul said. His lips thinned. "I know the FBI likes to run with their theories, but what we've got here is just one sick prick of a killer."

"I actually hope you're right about that." She'd only handled an alpha team once before.

Alpha team.

The term she used for two serial killers—two brutal, incredibly dangerous killers, who just happened to pair up because they recognized the same monster in each other.

In such a team, one man would always be the dominant, the alpha, the one who issued the orders.

The second man—or woman—would be willing to do anything, go to any lengths, to please the alpha.

Separate, they were dangerous. Lethal to society.

Together, they were a walking nightmare.

"I need to talk to Steve Lynch."

"The bastard should have known he couldn't deal with Walker." Anger tightened Paul's face. "We could've helped him. If he'd just come to us…"

The cop wouldn't have been attacked. Lauren wouldn't have been taken. As for Helen Lynch? Would she still be alive?

Maybe.

"Walker doesn't trade," Paul said with a slow, hard shake of his head. "He just kills."

It was time for her to talk with Steve. To let him know that the dawn meeting hadn't gone as he'd hoped. Time to tell him he would never be seeing his Helen again.

She straightened her shoulders.

I hate this part of my job.

***

The hotel room door had been repaired. Lauren stared at the door, her body bone tired, as Anthony secured her room.

"I thought about moving you to a new location, but with the other agents here, this is the safest place for you right now," he said. "I'm working on getting another place for you, but I didn't want you to wait any longer. You need your rest." He glanced toward the door connecting their rooms. He followed her stare. "Sorry, baby, but that's not happening tonight."

He'd called her *baby* before. She turned her head. His voice deepened when he used the word.

His gaze was on her now. "I'm staying in here with you. The doctor said I need to stay as close as possible."

He'd had her naked less than thirty minutes before. There wasn't much that was closer than that.

"You aren't supposed to sleep yet, so I'm just going to stay here. If you want to talk, then talk to me. Or don't say a word. Just sit there, and let me watch you so I know you're safe."

He sounded…afraid.

She'd never heard quite that note in his voice before. He was the big, bad marshal. Anthony wasn't supposed to fear anything. "I need to shower." To wash away the blood that was still on her. To wash away the memories.

Like anything could wash those away.

He gave a small nod, a jerky move of his head. "I can help you. I'll just—"

"No." The word was harsher than she'd meant, but she couldn't stand his hands on her body right then. She was too raw. Too scared. Too needy—too desperate to stop the pain. "I can make it."

His jaw locked. "Fine. I'll wait here." His gaze streaked down her body, then flicked away. "But if you need me, just say the word and I'll come running."

Lauren headed for the bathroom door. On the threshold, she paused. "This isn't your fault."

A rough laugh. "I was supposed to protect you."

"I'm the one who wanted to go to the scene. With my job, I go to plenty of dangerous spots." She looked over her shoulder at him as she braced her hand on the door frame. "This isn't on you. I took the risk. I walked right in, knowing what waited for me." Not what, who.

Walker.

"The cop who was hurt..." Talk about an image she'd never be able to get out of her mind. That blade, bursting from his chest. "McHenry is going to pull through, that's what you said, right?"

Another jerky nod.

Thank you, God. She'd been so afraid the man would die.

"And you're still alive," Anthony said, his voice getting harder, stronger. "The cop is alive. Walker didn't win this time."

"He got away." If he hadn't gotten the call and run, she would be dead. Lauren knew it.

"For the moment," Anthony agreed. "But he can't run forever. No one can."

Lauren shook her head. Her temples throbbed. So did the giant knot on the back of her head. She couldn't stand the feel of the dried blood on her for another second. She walked into the bathroom.

And left Anthony behind.

***

Jon tied his boat to the small dock. The red and gold colors of dawn were streaking across the sky. He'd barely slipped out in time last night. With so many patrols sweeping, he'd needed to alternate between using the boat's motor and paddling with the oars as he made his way to this spot. Whenever he'd gotten a little too close to civilization—even if civilization was a run-down cabin—he'd cut the motor.

He was so much smarter than the cops realized.

The dock groaned behind him.

Walker swore even as he grabbed for the knife he'd strapped to his hip.

"You don't need that with me," a familiar voice drawled.

The tension eased from his shoulders as Walker let go of his knife. He turned to face his partner. "You beat me here."

"Course I did. I didn't have to look over my shoulder every second while I was traveling. The cops aren't after *me*."

Walker swallowed. The guy was still pissed. "I did five fucking years for you. Five years—so don't use that shit tone with me!" He took a hard step forward.

The guy didn't back up a step. He never did. "You did that damn time for yourself. Because you got sloppy. You weren't supposed to go after the girl that night. You were supposed to wait for me."

But the girl had been perfect. She'd smelled so sweet, and looked so good. He could still remember when he'd first seen her at the gas station. She'd run in, her phone glued to her ear, and he'd heard her talking about her babysitting gig. She'd stood in front of him in the line, gabbing on her phone, and she'd said she would be alone.

The girl had even rattled off her address to the friend on the other end of the line.

Too easy. Too perfect of a hunt to pass up.

But the parents came home and screwed everything up.

"You weren't supposed to go for her," that dark voice continued, "and you weren't supposed to go after Lauren so soon. We have a fucking plan, remember?"

He remembered he had his own plan. One that involved him being alone with Lauren. Cutting her. Again and again.

His partner wouldn't watch, not with her.

"She owes me," Jon spat and took another step forward.

"I know." Understanding because he always understood Jon, as no one else ever had. "We're going to make her pay for everything, but first there are others we can take. Others who aren't as protected as the DA."

Others. His mouth went dry. "I get to use my knife?"

"You used it on Stacy."

Was that anger in his tone? His partner had never been angry before.

I gave up five years of my life for him. I could've talked. But I kept quiet.

Five long fucking years. The days, the months, the years had slipped away. He'd waited, but no new trials had come, thanks to

Lauren and that fucking judge. Jon had even tried to use Lynch, tried to force new evidence down the judge's throat.

It hadn't worked.

Escape had been his only option. An escape that had taken too fucking long.

Lauren Chandler is a dead woman.

He wouldn't serve time for anyone. Wouldn't let anyone ever push him around again. He was strong. He was power.

Everyone else was prey.

The man before him had been the one to change Jon's life. Only he hadn't been a man when they'd met.

Just a kid...like me.

So incredibly like me.

They'd grown together, learned together, killed together.

There were some bonds that just couldn't be broken. "I've missed you," Jon confessed.

Silence.

Jon wet his lips. Had saying that been a mistake? Shit, he didn't want to screw this up.

"I think it's time for us to enjoy some good old times again."

Yes.

"We'll make them pay for locking you away. We'll make them all pay." A pause, then, "Tell you what, Jonny..."

Only his partner called him Jonny, a leftover from their days as kids.

"This time, you handle the kill, and I'll watch."

Jon's lips stretched wide. This was it. His turn to show just what he could do.

All he needed was a victim.

CHAPTER NINE

"Anthony!" The cry was weak, thready, and it immediately sent him rushing into the bathroom.

He shoved open the door, and it bounced into the wall. "Lauren!"

She had one hand pressed against the tile of the shower, while the other clutched a towel that looked like it was about to drop at any moment.

"Dizzy..." she whispered.

Shit. He was at her side in two steps. He lifted her into his arms. She was still clutching the towel. *Screw that thing.* He tightened his hold around her and rushed toward the bed.

"I'm calling Dr. Davis." He'd been afraid the shower was a bad idea, but he'd also known she needed the blood off her. He'd wanted to make her happy.

Carefully, he bent and lowered her onto the bed. Her stitches looked dry, but she was so pale. "Did you hit your head?" He stared into her eyes. Her pupils looked normal but—

"Don't call the doctor," she said softly. "I just overdid it a bit." She swallowed. "I should have gotten you to help me sooner."

"Why didn't you?"

Her lashes lowered, even as a ghost of a smile lifted her lips. "Because I was naked, and usually when one of us is naked around the other, help isn't what happens."

His heart slammed into his chest. "You're hurt. I could have *controlled* myself." Was that what she believed? That he'd only think of himself when she was hurt?

Yes, he wanted her twenty-four-fucking-seven, but he'd rein in that need. For her.

He was realizing he'd do just about anything for her.

"I wasn't worried about your control." Her lashes lifted. The blue of her eyes was still too dulled. He wanted the spark—the life—back. "I was worried about my own."

They'd lost the towel during the trip back to the bed. With fingers that weren't nearly as steady as Anthony would have liked, he grabbed for the covers and pulled them over her body.

A body that haunted his dreams. "You..." He cleared his throat. "You made it clear you didn't want anything happening between us."

Crystal clear.

"Maybe I was lying." Her voice was soft. Not slurred, or he'd have gotten the doc on the phone.

Lying? That whispered confession drove right through him. Anthony eased into the bed beside her. He slid his arm under her head and pulled her against him. She still fit him so perfectly. Better than anyone else ever had.

Because no one else seemed made for him. "I lie sometimes, too," he confessed.

"Tell me your lies."

She was awake, talking, in his arms. He'd tell her anything. "Leaving was the hardest thing I've ever done in my life."

He felt her start of surprise.

"Then why go?" Lauren asked.

A hard question. He'd been scared. He'd needed her too much. He'd worried she needed what he couldn't give her.

Instead of saying all that, he figured he should go back. Start at the beginning. His nightmare. "You never asked me about my family."

Her head pressed down onto his shoulder. "Not a lot of time for family talk during all the sex fests."

They'd been some pretty awesome sex fests. As soon as she was better, he'd be on her again.

His cock was swollen and hard right then with need for her, but he was holding back. He'd be what she needed tonight.

"When my parents were happy, when they were getting along, you could almost see the love between them. It was so strong." During those times, things had been good. Close to perfect. "But when they weren't happy..." Those times when his dad's anger had burst free... "I didn't think anything could be closer to hell."

He'd been wrong about that, though. When Lauren had vanished, he'd been given a fast trip to hell.

"My dad would get jealous. If my mom talked to another guy, if she was even five minutes late arriving home, he'd swear she was cheating on him."

Lauren was silent in his arms.

"She was his obsession." That was what it had been. He realized it now. It wasn't love. It was an obsession.

"This story doesn't end well, does it?" she whispered.

Stories like his never did. "I don't know if she'd been cheating on him all along—if his worries were real—or if the jealousy actually drove her to another man." He'd been thirteen at the time, and too grief stricken to focus on the whys. "But when my father found out she was going to leave him, he snapped."

Lauren was silent. Her breath came in fast puffs that hit lightly over his skin.

"He wasn't going to let her go. If he couldn't have her, no one else would."

He'd walked home from school and found a bloodbath. His mother, dead. A shotgun blast to the chest. After he'd killed her, his father had put the shotgun under his own chin and pulled the trigger.

"I'm so sorry, Anthony."

He wasn't telling the story for pity.

"My mom loved me," he said with painful pride. His father might have been a twisted SOB, but his mother had always cared about him. Always. "When the police searched her car, they found bags packed. One for her. One for me." She'd planned to get them both away.

Only the police believed that his father had come home and found her packing.

"He couldn't let her go, and in the end, he wound up being the most dangerous thing in her life." It hadn't started that way, though. He'd seen the wedding pictures. Seen the happy smiles. He *did* remember them being happy. There had been fun birthday parties, family dinners at Christmas.

But obsessions could twist over time. Become so very deadly.

"I'm sorry you found them." Her voice was low. Hesitant. "No child should ever see that."

There were plenty of things children should never see. "You asked me why I left you." He realized his fingers were making light circles on her palm. He couldn't stop. With her, that had always been his problem. *Can't stop. Need too much.* "I wanted you, so damn badly, all the time."

Her palm was soft and still beneath his fingers.

"I wanted you to myself. I wanted you away from any other man out there." To be truthful, he still did. But his control was

176

better now than five years ago. "You were becoming my obsession, and I wouldn't—couldn't—stay here and turn out like him."

She straightened quickly, nearly clipping him in the chin with her head. She turned to stare at him. "That's crazy! You aren't your father!"

"I want you with the same consuming need that he felt for her. The way I feel about you—it's not easy and light. It's dark and dangerous." Consuming.

"Just because you want someone badly," she said, her voice husky, "doesn't mean it's wrong."

"If I'd had my way, I would have been in you every minute of the day."

Her eyes widened.

"My emotions with you are too strong. Call bullshit if you want"—though it wasn't—"but I wouldn't risk you."

"So you left me."

He'd left, but had been helplessly drawn back. "It was supposed to just be sex between us, right? You didn't sign on for an obsession. We were fire behind closed doors, ice in public. I was starting to rage out of control, and you were trying to keep a wall between us."

Lauren flinched. "I was trying the case. I never meant to be...ice."

"Shit, baby, I didn't—"

"I know I have...trouble, okay? I can't connect easily with other people. Even the ones who matter." Her lashes lowered to shield her gaze. "I don't let people in and I don't share my feelings or my past. I don't know how to change that."

One thing bothered him...*I don't share my feelings or my past.* Paul sure seemed to know plenty about her past.

There's the jealousy again. Dark, insidious, creeping.

"I think I stopped letting people get close after Jenny vanished," she whispered. "My parents fell apart. They hurt so much. *I* hurt. The pain was an ache in my chest. Constant ache. A part of me was just…gone."

"Tell me what happened to her." The time for secrets was gone. They were both baring their pasts in the dark, and he knew that after this, things would never be the same between them.

The emotions charging the air were too raw and powerful.

"She was sixteen when she vanished. Just sixteen." She blinked quickly, trying to get rid of the tears blooming in her eyes. "She'd gotten her driver's license the week before, and she was so proud to be driving to school." A ghost of a smile lifted her lips. "She failed the driver's test two times, but the third try was the charm. At least, that's what Mom said. 'Third time's the charm.'"

The memory was a good one. Her eyes started to sparkle.

Then the sparkle faded as the tears came back.

"She was going to pick me up from school and take me to piano practice. At first, I thought she was just running late, that maybe she'd stopped to talk to her friends or something. I was so—so mad." Her voice was hushed. Shamed. "I was standing in the parking lot, the buses were all gone, and all I could think was that I was going to tell Mom. I was furious, shaking. She wasn't *there*."

"You didn't know." Guilt was in her voice. On her face. Any child would have gotten angry in that situation.

"I didn't even know I should be worried until Dad came to get me. His face was white. The piano teacher had called him and told him I never showed up." She shook her head. "He was afraid something had happened to me and Jenny."

Her gaze held his.

So much pain. Walker had brought all of the pain back.

"Only nothing had happened to me. Just Jenny." Her sister's name broke. "They searched everywhere for her, and found her VW at the edge of the swamp, but there was no sign of Jenny. Another car's tracks were there, and some of the cops thought she'd met a boy. Run off with him.

"The cops told us we'd probably hear from her in a few days. They didn't even *search* the swamp. Just said she was off with a boy. Told my parents they should have kept a better watch on her."

Shit. Like her parents had needed to hear that crap.

"Only Jenny never contacted us. The years rolled past. There was no phone call. No letters. Nothing. Jenny just vanished."

She hadn't vanished.

She'd been killed. Buried. Hidden.

Jenny Chandler was out there somewhere, and before this nightmare was over, he'd make the Butcher tell him everything he knew about Lauren's sister.

***

He walked through the swamp. Searchers were all around him. Deputies, folks from Fish and Wildlife, even detectives from the Baton Rouge Police Department.

No one gave him a second glance. He wasn't the prey they were seeking. They were all too busy, all too focused on Walker.

But Walker wasn't there. He'd made sure the guy was safely away. He couldn't risk Walker getting captured and turning on him.

The little bastard had threatened to reveal what he knew. He'd sent a note from prison—sent a fucking note—and the warning had been obvious.

The man had wanted freedom. So he'd given it to him.

But freedom would come with a price.

He stopped by a twisting willow tree. Its long, slender branches brushed the ground.

A smile lifted his lips as he stared at that tree. Coming to this place, it always made him feel better, stronger.

The branches swayed gently. The movement so faint.

His shoulders straightened. His gaze darted to the ground. The lush grass grew easily here.

The grass grew, the willow bloomed—it wept.

His smile slowly faded.

"Hey! We need a search party on the northern banks!"

He gave a quick nod. It was an agent who'd just shouted the order. The guy already had sweat streaking across his forehead, and the man—with his disheveled hair and frustrated eyes— seemed far out of his element in the swamp.

Most people didn't understand the swamp.

He did. Walker did. The swamp had brought them together. The swamp and their love of death.

He turned and strode away from Jenny. He'd come back to see her again soon. He always came back for her. In the meantime, he had a kill to plan.

He tempered his excitement as he joined the search party.

***

Cadence's steps were slow as she headed for the holding cell. Steve Lynch had been kept away from the general population. The guard in front of her unlocked a door and led her down a narrow hallway.

"He's been quiet since he came in," the cop said as he darted a quick glance over his shoulder at her. "Not the way they usually are, ma'am. Most come in screaming and don't stop for hours."

They were almost to the holding cell and she didn't hear any sounds. No shuffle of nervous footsteps. No rustles.

Lynch should be worried about his ex-wife. He should be pacing. He should be demanding answers.

That silence was unnatural.

They rounded the corner. She saw the cell. Saw Lynch.

She froze.

The bedding was twisted around his neck, and his body hung as his feet dangled six inches above the floor. He'd locked the other end of the bedsheet around the bars in the high window. What looked like a bench was overturned on the floor near him.

"Fuck!" The cop fumbled with his keys.

There was no need to hurry. Not now. Steve Lynch was gone.

She stared at the body, pity pushing through her. *You knew we weren't going to find Helen alive.*

He might have hoped, but as the hours slid past, he'd realized the truth. Or maybe he'd realized it when Walker attacked the cop and took the DA.

No, Helen hadn't been found alive, and now they hadn't found Lynch alive, either.

Another life gone, snuffed out in the Bayou Butcher's wake.

Guilty. Lynch had been the one to stand up and read that verdict in court. The verdict that Lauren had pushed for, day in and day out.

She pulled out her phone and called Ross. He'd need to know. So would Lauren.

He answered on the second ring. Cadence tried to keep her voice emotionless as she said, "Lynch won't be able to tell us anything."

More cops were rushing in, hurrying through the narrow hallway.

"Why the hell not?" Ross demanded.

"He hung himself." A silent death. One that had probably taken no more than five minutes.

Dammit. She spun away from the body and tried to suck in a deep breath, but a knot had formed in her throat. She'd joined the FBI to stop crimes, not to keep finding bodies.

It seemed like she kept arriving too late to make a difference. *Too late.*

***

Twenty-four hours had passed, and there'd been no sign of the Butcher.

Lauren glanced up as Anthony paced the length of the hotel room. He'd been doing a whole lot of pacing and it was driving her crazy. "You want to be out there, hunting." She waved to the door. "Go!"

She felt like she was weighing him down.

He gave a hard, negative shake of his head.

"Look, if you're worried about me, send in some cops, send in one of your marshals. Give me protection." She paused. "But you go and do what you need to do."

He stalked toward her. After their early-morning talk yesterday, things should have been easier between them.

Things weren't easy. They were even more tense than before. With every hour that passed, with every moment her strength came back, the tension between them seemed to thicken.

You were my obsession.

It wasn't exactly the tender declaration of love most girls longed to hear. But then, she wasn't most girls.

Had Anthony thought his past would scare her? It hadn't. It made her yearn for him even more.

He's a survivor.

So was she. Dammit, *so was she.*

"You almost died." His green eyes glittered with emotion. "From now on, I'm sticking to you."

If she didn't still have the headache from hell, she might be able to actually enjoy his company.

"They're having a briefing down at the station," she said. She might be sidelined by her injury, but she was keeping tabs on things. "Let's go hear what they've got to say." Even she could handle a trip to the station.

"They've got jack shit." Disgust tightened his face. "All of those hours spent searching, and they turned up nothing."

"Walker has help." Just what she needed—a second serial killer in her town. "His partner could have helped him slip away from the swamp. He could be hiding him right now."

Anthony thought the same thing, she saw it in his eyes. She pressed on. "Staying here isn't doing any good. I'm stronger now." Maybe he wouldn't recognize it for the lie it was. "Let's get to the station. Whoever Walker's working with...if they killed J-Jenny"—she stumbled over her sister's name— "if they've been working together for all of this time, then the partner should be someone who was in Walker's life five years ago."

Maybe the partner was even someone she'd interviewed as she prepared for the trial. She could have come face-to-face with her sister's killer and not known it.

"We've got all the old interviews on file at my office. Names, addresses. We can contact those people. The cops might even walk right into the house where Walker is hiding." Hope—it was all she had to hold on to at that point.

After a moment, Anthony gave a grim nod. "But you stay with me."

"I will." She was already dressed in pants and a top—he hadn't helped her this time. She hadn't needed his help, thankfully, because she sure hadn't been up to handling his hot touch.

Lauren rose and headed toward the door.

"We *will* talk about it," Anthony said.

His words stopped her. Not understanding, she glanced back at him, "We did plenty of talking." Her soul was bare. What more did he want?

All your secrets. That was the answer in his hard stare.

She'd never given all to anyone. Wasn't even sure if she could.

He reached into the nightstand, pulled out his gun, and holstered the weapon. Then, with his eyes holding hers, he closed the distance between them. "You talked plenty about the past, but you didn't tell me a damn thing about what Walker did to you in that cabin."

She hadn't been able to think about it. She'd barely been holding herself together as it was. "I told Cadence." The FBI agent had come to the hotel to interview her again. The other marshals had pulled Anthony away while they talked. She'd actually been glad he left. Baring her soul again in front of him would have been too painful. She tried to keep the emotion out of her voice. "Why bother with that nightmare twice?"

"Talking to me isn't the same thing as giving witness testimony." Anger burned in his words. "Dammit, I can *help* you."

"When you catch Walker, you'll help me plenty."

She turned toward the door.

His fingers curled around her shoulder. "I see what you're doing."

Her heart was beating faster.

"What happened? Did I get too close? You're trying to put the wall back up now?"

Yes. That wall was what helped her get through each and every day. She needed it to survive.

He turned her to face him. "I won't go back to being on the outside." He bent toward her. His lips were just in inch from hers. "I wanted you for too long. Too much. I came too fucking close to losing you." His gaze searched hers. "Everything's changed. Don't you see that?"

He was all she could see.

Then his mouth was on hers. Not hard. Not demanding or taking.

Seducing.

She'd never been able to resist his seduction.

Her lips were parted, but he didn't thrust his tongue past her lips. Not at first. He pressed his lips to hers, stealing her breath, giving her his. Her mouth opened more beneath the light touch.

Helpless. That was the way he made her feel.

His tongue lightly licked her lower lip, then it was pushing into her mouth. Her fingers locked around his shoulders, and Lauren found herself rising onto her toes.

Her body pressed along the length of his. His arousal thrust toward her, but still, he kept the kiss easy. Gentle.

His tongue was against hers, his arms surrounded her. He was all that she could feel, all that she could taste.

She wanted more. Harder. But his mouth was already pulling away even though a moan of protest slipped from her lips.

"I could never forget the way you taste," he said.

Her lashes lifted. His eyes...she pulled in a quick breath...he looked hungry.

Not for food.

"Sin and sweetness, all twisted together. You fucking bring me to my knees."

He wasn't on his knees. She was the one who felt like her knees were wobbling.

"I will have you again." A promise.

One she wanted fulfilled.

"The doctor wants to check you once more. If you get the all clear from Davis...if it's safe for you..."

Her fingers pushed against his shoulders, forcing him back. "It will be." It needed to be. Because she wanted, as desperately as he did.

The look in his eyes—the stark promise of pleasure and passion—it was exactly what she needed to wipe away the memory of fear and death.

It will be.

***

Pierce Hamilton wasn't paying any attention to the case being presented before him. The witness was testifying, going on and on about an alibi that was probably crap, and all he could think was—

Lauren Chandler got away from the Bayou Butcher.

He'd woken to the headline today, screaming from the cover of the newspaper, and then the reporters from the local news had been too eager to blast the same story at him.

The DA was a very hot topic, and apparently extremely good at surviving. It hardly seemed fair she had survived when Karen hadn't.

"Your Honor?" The defense attorney cleared his throat. "I—uh—I objected."

Hell.

He didn't even know what the objection had been about. He slammed down his gavel. "Court is recessed until nine a.m. tomorrow."

The defense attorney's jaw dropped. "But Your Honor—"

Pierce shoved away from his chair and hurried for the door.

The police had said they'd protect Lauren. They hadn't. She'd nearly died.

What will happen to me?

His robe billowed around him. He wasn't going to sit there and wait for the Butcher to come after him. Karen was already gone. He wouldn't roll over and die, too.

If the Butcher thought he would, then the sick prick needed to think again.

He was in a different office today—one that had been empty since Judge Remus retired six years ago. The cops had told him his office was still off-limits.

This office would work, for now.

He pulled open the desk drawer. A gun waited inside. As a judge, he didn't exactly spend a whole lot of time getting patted down. It had been too easy to get the weapon in the courthouse.

He tucked the gun into the waistband of his pants. He'd already hit the bank and withdrawn a nice chunk of cash. He hadn't run after getting the cash. Instead, he'd gone to court.

He'd thought he could try and wait things out. Use the cash only if he got really desperate.

I am desperate. With every moment that passed, the fear grew stronger. He wasn't ready to die.

He wouldn't be the Bayou Butcher's next target.

After tossing his robe, Pierce hurried down the hallway. He took the elevator, an empty ride that coasted quickly down to the parking garage. He was avoiding the cops who were supposed to watch him, slipping right past their guard. If they saw him, they would stop him.

No one was stopping him. He was getting out of town before the Butcher came after him.

When the cops had the killer, then he'd return. Until then, Mexico was looking pretty fucking nice.

Screw any pending cases. Screw the bitch of a wife at home. Screw all of it.

Life was what mattered. He wasn't ready to give his up.

The elevator doors opened, and he hurried into the parking garage.

Footsteps shuffled to the right, and he froze. "Is someone there?"

Silence.

I'm not going to die.

He hurried his pace.

The footsteps shuffled once more.

I'm not going to—

***

"The original profile for the Bayou Butcher missed a few key elements." Cadence stood in the front of the conference room.

The room was filled with cops, marshals, and even the ME. The homicide captain sat in the back corner, his arms crossed over his chest.

Anthony also stood in the back, near Lauren. She'd taken a seat in the last row, and he kept close to her. She seemed too fragile. Every time he glimpsed the cut on her cheek, he wanted to empty his weapon into Walker's heart.

"I don't believe Jon Walker was working alone when he committed his crimes."

The silence in the room was thick and heavy.

"When Walker held DA Chandler, he said he watched the murder of the DA's sister years before."

Several heads turned toward Lauren. Her shoulders tensed.

"Jennifer Chandler died twenty years ago," Cadence continued. Her partner stood by her side, his eyes on her. "If Walker was there at the time of her death, he would have been only sixteen years old."

So young.

"By his own words, Walker watched Jennifer die, so that means someone else—"

"Pardon me, ma'am," Paul said as he rose to his feet. "Maybe the guy just fuckin' slipped up when he was talking. Maybe he killed her and then *stood* back and watched her die." He shook his head. "With respect, I worked those Bayou Butcher cases five years ago. There was never a sign anyone else killed those women."

"Not those women, no," she agreed.

Anthony noticed Kyle had tensed when the detective rose.

"I believe those kills were all his. I also believe *someone* else might have witnessed them. Just as Walker witnessed Jennifer's death."

Lauren must be hating having her sister's death mentioned again and again…Anthony wanted to reach out to her. Pull her into his arms. But she'd never wanted their involvement seen by others.

Screw what she wanted. I can't let her hurt.

He stepped closer to her and put his hand on her shoulder.

She glanced back at him.

"You okay?" he whispered.

Her lips were pressed together, as if she was trying to hide the tremble. She gave a quick nod.

"One watched, one killed. I believe that is the way they've been working for years. Walker *did* kill seven women, the women he was convicted of five years ago. But I also believe there are more victims out there—more bodies—victims who were the prey of his partner."

There wasn't silence in the packed room anymore. There was shock. Paul slowly slid back into his seat.

"A team?" a uniformed cop asked. "I thought those crazy guys killed on their own."

"It's believed that sociopaths have a hard time forming attachments, so sociopathic serial killers do often kill on their own." Cadence paused. "Serial killing pairs aren't common, but they do happen."

"All sociopaths aren't serial killers," Kyle said as he raised a brow and studied the group. "And all serial killers aren't sociopaths. Serial killers strike for dozens of damn reasons."

Yes, they did. Anthony had worked on enough cases to realize that. Sometimes, there was no understanding their savagery.

Kyle stepped forward, fully facing the group. "Some serial killing teams are couples. Husband-and-wife teams. One member of the team will act as bait—usually the wife. She goes out and draws the prey in. Then she might stand back and watch as the husband rapes and murders his victims."

"That was the case with Jonas and Candy Kramer," Cadence said, her face somber. "Their plan was to get a group of sex slaves. Candy would approach the victims, get them to come into the van, and..." She shook her head. "Well, the idea was that their slaves would be disposable, so those poor girls didn't survive long."

Fuck. Anthony remembered that case. It still turned his stomach.

"Are we looking for a couple here?" Matt asked as he tilted his head. The marshal had met Anthony at the precinct door, his frustration with the swamp search clear in the hard lines on his face. Jim was out there, still searching. They weren't giving up. Marshals never did.

Cadence shook her head. "I don't believe we're looking at a man and a woman. From what I can gather, Stacy was the only long-term girlfriend in Walker's life. She was trying to get away from him, not help him."

"So he killed her," Kyle finished.

"It's not a romantic pairing," Cadence continued as her gaze slid around the room. "I think it's an alpha pairing."

From the back of the room, Anthony saw Paul tilt his head in confusion. "What's an alpha pairing?"

"When they began the killings, I believe Walker and his partner were both teens. The partner would have been a few years older. At the time, he was the dominant one, no doubt the one to push for the murder in the first place. He killed, and Walker watched."

Lauren's fingers had clenched in her lap.

"Over time, I believe Walker came into his own. He grew confident at the kill scenes, he *wanted* to kill. So he started his own crimes. Both men continued killing—one would kill, one would watch. Again and again."

"She makes it sound like a competition," the ME muttered a few feet from Anthony.

Cadence's head jerked up. It seemed she had some damn strong hearing. "In a way, Dr. Wright, that's exactly what it became. Walker's killings became more brutal over time. Not just because of an escalation, but because he had someone to impress."

This was a fucking mess.

"He stopped killing just in remote locations. He went right into the house of the Peterson family. He was taking risks because the bigger the risk, the bigger the reward."

Murder was a reward in Walker's sick world.

"Walker started as the submissive part of the team. He watched, he might have even lured in the prey. He didn't kill. All that changed with the death of coed Beth Loxley. He was competing with his partner then, not just standing back and watching. After that, with each of his kills, Walker stepped closer to being an alpha in his own right. Not just one strong killer, but two." Her gaze darted to the board behind her that showed all the faces of Walker's victims. "They're an alpha team, and that is the most dangerous serial killing team I know."

She went to the board and flipped it over.

More photographs stared back. Missing persons reports. Anthony counted at least nineteen of them. "What the hell is that?" he demanded, raising his voice over the cops' murmurs as they absorbed all of the pictures. Too many pictures. Lauren remained silent in front of him.

"These are women who've gone missing in surrounding counties. Some of them are believed to be runaways, but the others…the others are presumed dead." Cadence paused as she waited for the noise to quiet. "I actually think they're all dead."

Shit.

Agent McKenzie's hands had clenched into fists.

Cadence walked toward the first picture. "Walker's partner was smart. He knew if he killed in different counties, it would be harder for the police to make connections between the crimes, especially when people didn't even realize that crimes were happening."

There were so many photographs. Nineteen of them.

Matt maneuvered close to Anthony. "Is this for real? You think Cadence is right on this?"

"Cadence doesn't bullshit."

Lauren flinched beneath his hand.

"How the hell do you know those are his victims?" Paul was back on his feet. The guy seemed to have real trouble staying in his chair. "Look, ma'am, we're not some dumbass cops down here, okay? If we had another serial working here all this time—"

"I told you, the killer was smart. He crossed county lines, so there was no reason for the authorities to connect the dots on these cases." Her fingers were touching the first picture. "Especially since he kept varying the age of his victim."

She was staring at the first photo. "Denise Reed, age seventeen."

Denise stared back at them. A young girl with dark hair and wide eyes.

Cadence touched the second picture. "Sally Samwell, age eighteen." Another girl with a big smile and a dark tumble of hair.

"Rachel Penelope, age nineteen." Her fingers skimmed over the girl's dark hair.

"Georgia Trace, age twenty."

The next photo. "Jamie Snowden, age twenty-one…"

"He's going up a year, every time..." Kyle said, his voice too loud in the quiet room as the cops all made the same connection. "The girls look the same, same hair—"

"And they have the same blue eyes," Cadence said as she glanced around the room. "This killer, I believe—in his mind—was killing the same girl again and again."

Her hand slid over the other photos until she came to a photo that had been circled in red. "I believe he was killing Jennifer Chandler, over and over. The age went up, as Jennifer would have aged if she'd still been alive. That kill—it was necessary to him. He's been doing it every single year since Jenny died."

Fuck.

It was Lauren's turn to rise to her feet. "My sister..."

All eyes turned to her.

"So many women..." Pain whispered through her voice.

"Since I believe Jenny was the first victim, I think she had a personal connection to the killer. They were friends, maybe they dated, maybe she rebuffed him. She *knew* him." Sympathy flashed across Cadence's face, but the determination in her gaze didn't falter. "That means *you* might know him, too. If we can just find him, we can also find Walker."

"We can take them both out," Kyle added.

"That means we need to see every witness from the original Bayou Butcher case, we need to go over every file..." Cadence lifted her chin. Her delicate jaw hardened. "We will be looking for a male, in his midthirties, highly intelligent, attractive—"

"He's good-looking?" one of the uniforms muttered, a little too loudly. "How do you know that?"

"Because all signs are that his prey willingly came to him. If there were indications of a struggle, we would have noticed them at the scenes. Even when Jenny Chandler's car was found"—Cadence's gaze darted to Lauren—"the appearance is that she *willingly* drove out to meet the perpetrator. An attractive man would have a much easier time luring his victims."

Lauren backed away from her seat and moved to stand beside Anthony.

"Jon Walker is also attractive—he used the same luring technique with many of his victims. It's a technique I believe he learned from his partner."

Anthony slanted a fast glance at Lauren. Her body was stiff, and she looked so pale. "Are you okay?" he murmured.

"I don't think I'll be okay for a very long time," she whispered. "*All* of those women. He took them all."

"I'll be adding to the second killer's profile soon. When I do, I'll give an update to all the officers working this case." Cadence reached for files on the table near her. "These men are extremely dangerous. Now that they are back together again, they will keep killing. They won't stop until we stop them."

The meeting ended after that. The cops filed out, Cadence and Kyle huddled over their files, and Lauren—

Her fingers wrapped around Anthony's arm. "I need to get out of here."

He knew desperation when he heard it.

"Please, take me away from here."

Anthony nodded and immediately steered her toward the door. They pushed through the bull pen, heading fast for the exit.

"DA Chandler!"

It was Kyle McKenzie. The guy was rushing after them, his gaze on Lauren.

Beside Anthony, Lauren stiffened.

Anthony's jaw locked. "She's had enough for today, got it? I'm taking her out of here so—"

"I know how you feel, Lauren."

Lauren. Not DA Chandler.

The guy's voice held way too much intensity.

Not just intensity, Anthony realized as he studied the agent with a critical eye. *Pain.*

Slowly, Lauren turned to face the agent. "I don't think you do."

Kyle nodded. "Fifteen years ago, my sister vanished."

Lauren trembled, then she held herself still. Far too still.

Anthony stood close to them. Kyle's voice was low as he said, "There's not a single night that passes for me—not a single one—when I don't wonder where she is. When I don't wonder what happened to her." His gaze hardened. "And when I don't want to make the bastard who took her *pay.*" Fury flashed in his eyes, battling with the echo of pain.

"I'm sorry." Lauren's voice was whisper soft. "I didn't know."

"I've never been able to bring my sister home. I never got any justice for her." He inclined his head toward Lauren. "But I'll do my damnedest to see that you get justice for Jenny."

A tear tracked down Lauren's cheek.

Anthony pulled her closer to him.

Kyle's gaze rose to his face. "You take good care of her."

Always.

"And we *will* stop that SOB out there."

Yes, they would.

As they hurried from the station, Anthony realized if Lauren asked, he'd do any damn thing she wanted. Even kill—in an instant—if that helped to ease the pain that seemed to break her apart.

CHAPTER TEN

The second the hotel room door closed behind Anthony, Lauren turned and wrapped her arms around him. She was desperate. She *needed* him. Needed the way he could make her feel. *Only him.*

"Lauren, why—"

She rose onto her toes. Her mouth pressed against his.

His hands came around her and he tried to gently push her back.

She wasn't in the mood for gentle.

Jenny's killer. All of those women...all of them...

"Baby, you're hurt," he growled the words as he eased away from her. "I can't—"

"I can. The doctor said I'm fine." Mostly true, but right then, she didn't care about some aches and pains. Lauren felt as if she were breaking apart on the inside. On the outside, her skin was chilled. An ice that threatened to consume her.

She needed Anthony. Needed the wild rush of pleasure he'd always been able to give her.

She had to forget everything, in order to be able to live without breaking. "I *need* you."

His gaze darkened. "Baby, you know I'm always desperate for you." Then he was kissing her, but not with the fierce intensity she wanted. He was trying to be careful.

Fuck careful.

Her hand rose between them. She unbuttoned her shirt. Let the soft silk part so he could see the edge of her bra. He might think he was going to take it easy with her, but she remembered everything about him. Including all the ways to make him lose control.

Her tongue met his. Her breasts pressed against his chest. He was aroused, growing more so by the moment, and she wanted him in her. Wanted the drive to oblivion that would let her pretend—if only for a fleeting moment—that everything in her world wasn't a nightmare.

She sucked his tongue. He growled. Good. She wanted better.

Lauren stepped back. Shed the rest of her clothes. He watched her with eyes that burned.

She was his obsession. He'd said that. She wanted to see just how obsessed he could get.

His eyes were on her breasts. In the next second, his hands were, too. Caressing. Stroking. Then he was lifting her into his arms—still being so freaking careful—and carrying her to the bed.

His mouth was on her breast. Licking. Kissing. Laving her nipple and making the hard knot of lust within her grow even tighter. Her legs were parted, and his fingers went straight to her core. No hesitant touch from him. Just a deep thrust of his index finger into her even as his thumb pushed on the center of her need.

"You have to want me…*more*." He whispered the words as he turned his focus to her other breast. "So fucking perfect…"

She wasn't perfect. Far from it. She was barely holding on.

His finger withdrew, then thrust again. Helplessly, her hips arched against him when he pushed a second finger into the heat between her legs.

"Easy." His head lifted. "You have to take care—"

Her eyes flashed open. She hadn't even realized she'd shut them. "No! I don't want easy. I want—" She broke off, lost.

"What do you want, Lauren?"

"Make me forget." It was a broken whisper. "Please."

A muscle flexed along his jaw. "I'll do better than that." His hands found her wrists, and he held them against the pillows. "But you can't move. Not an inch. You stay right there."

He was still being *careful*—

Anthony positioned himself between her thighs. Then his mouth was on her. His lips, his tongue…he was sampling her, exploring her secrets, and she wanted to move so badly. Wanted to arch into his mouth.

But her muscles had locked. Was it by his order? Or her own desperate need? She wasn't sure. She just couldn't move. Couldn't do anything but take the pleasure as his mouth took her.

The pleasure was there. It hit her, striking hard and reverberating through her on a wave of heat that melted the ice surrounding her. Then she was moving, wildly, frantically. Shudders racked her body, her sex contracted and the orgasm seemed to go on and on.

Only pleasure. Only pleasure…

"That's a nice start." His voice was a low, rough rumble.

She heard a faint ripping sound and saw a foil wrapper get tossed to the side.

The head of his cock pushed against her body. Her eyes met his. *Anthony.* His face was savage with need, but his hands were gentle. His control hadn't broken. Hers had.

I'm broken. So lost—

He thrust into her.

Only pleasure.

His fingers twined with hers, keeping her hands pinned to the pillow. His thrusts were slow and deep, driving all the way into her core. She lifted her legs and curled them around him. He made her feel so full. Made her whole body pulse with pleasure—

Another orgasm was already building.

He kissed her when she came. The pleasure rolled through her on hard waves. There was no more fear, no more worries— only the release that held her in its white-hot grip and wouldn't let go.

Anthony thrust deep into her once more, then he stiffened. His mouth tore from hers as he growled her name. She looked up at him as he came and saw the flash of stark pleasure that swept over his face. His cheeks were flushed, his eyes blazing— he was so sexy that he made her lose the breath she'd finally just caught.

Slowly, so slowly, the pleasure ebbed. Her heartbeat became less like a wild drumbeat and more of a slow, steady thud.

He slid out of her, and she hated that. She wanted to stay a part of him, but he was already sliding to the side of her body, cradling her. Anthony kept his fingers entwined with her right hand. "I missed you." His stark confession came as the sunlight poured through the blinds and fell on their bodies.

"You didn't have to stay away." Her words were a whisper. Her throat felt parched, as if she'd been screaming.

Had she? For the sake of any folks rooming close by, she hoped not.

"How do you know I did?"

His question had her brows pulling together. "Of course you stayed away. You left and—"

"Sometimes, I just needed to see you." He brought her hand to his lips. Kissed her palm. "Sometimes it was too hard to let you go."

The shock must have showed in her eyes.

"I told you," he said, giving a slow, almost sad shake of his head. "Obsession. It's dangerous."

He rolled away and went to the bathroom.

The chill came back on her skin. What had she thought would happen once they had sex again?

I hadn't been thinking.

She'd just wanted to stop feeling. She'd known sex with him would give her that delicious oblivion she needed.

Her hand fumbled and yanked the covers over her naked body just as the bathroom door opened again.

Silently, he came toward her and lifted the covers she'd just so desperately tried to arrange. He slid in bed next to her and pulled her close. "I didn't want to hurt you."

"You didn't." Were they talking about the sex or the past?

"Sometimes it's too easy to hurt the ones who get close to you. No one has ever gotten as close to me as you." He studied her carefully. "Did I hurt you?"

"No." Not if they were talking about the sex.

His gaze seemed to look past her. "A few months ago, when I was working the Valentine case down in New Orleans, that bastard managed to get the drop on me."

Her fingers clenched the covers.

"I was searching for him in the woods. There'd been an explosion at the scene a few minutes before. I was hurt, but not badly enough to stop the hunt."

She knew he never stopped a hunt if he could help it.

"The bastard hit me from behind. When I woke up, I was tied to a chair, and there was a bomb strapped to my chest."

The heat that had just filled her cheeks cooled instantly. She'd heard he was involved in an explosion while apprehending Valentine, but the bomb *had been strapped to his chest*? Dear God.

"I knew how much time I had. Valentine made sure of it. The guy fucking hated me. I'd kept his fiancée hidden from him, for years, and he wanted me to suffer." He ran a hand through his hair. "So I suffered."

She should say something comforting, but she couldn't speak past the heavy fear in her throat.

Strapped to his chest.

"After awhile, it wasn't about hours of survival. It was about minutes. I was in the middle of nowhere, and I didn't expect a rescue." His gaze turned back to her. He paused a beat. "Did you?"

Yes. She'd expected him to find her, too late.

"When you lose hope, you think about the things that mattered. In those last few moments, all I could do was remember."

In those last moments when she'd been so sure that Walker was going to kill her, she'd remembered, too.

Anthony.

"You were the woman in my mind. The woman I would die thinking about—wishing I'd been able to see you one more time."

She swallowed down the hard ball of fear.

"I thought about the things I could have done differently, what I *should* have done."

Lauren pushed back her hair. Her fingers wanted to shake.

"Once I got back here to you, everything just went to hell once more." His hands had fisted. "I want to be with you, but the last thing I *ever* want is for you to hurt."

"You're not the threat to me." He had to see that.

His gaze raked over her body. "You were attacked. You've got bruises on you, stitches, a concussion, and I still want to fuck you until you can't move."

Her breath caught.

"Trust me"—his words were little more than an angry growl—"I'm a threat, and I'm doing my damn best to keep my control."

The control she'd wanted to see shatter.

The phone rang, breaking the stark silence that had fallen between them. Anthony turned away to answer the call.

Lauren tried to *breathe*.

"What?" Anthony barked. The shock in his voice had her head jerking up. "You're sure? *Shit*. Right. Yeah, I'll be right there."

His hand clenched around the phone as he whirled to face her.

Not again. She understood what those deep lines on his face had to mean. "Walker."

A grim nod. "Judge Hamilton's missing. The guy ditched the guards on him—he's *gone*."

***

Paul met Anthony and Lauren at Hamilton's home. The detective was waiting outside on the wide, wraparound porch. When he saw them arrive, he waved them over.

Anthony slanted a worried glance Lauren's way. He should have kept his hands *off* her. Denying her anything, though, was beyond him. She'd looked at him, with tears gleaming in her big, blue eyes, and he'd been a goner.

The minute he'd actually *tasted* her, he'd known there was no hope of stopping.

"Are you sure—" he began, his voice low.

"Do *not* ask me if I'm okay again. I'm the DA, a judge is missing—I am staying with you. This is my job, Anthony."

He wasn't going to argue, mostly because he wanted her with him. He only felt secure about her when she was within sight.

They quickly closed the distance between them and the detective.

Paul yanked a hand through his already tousled hair. "This is so screwed," he muttered.

"You think Walker has the judge?" Lauren asked, tucking a strand of hair behind her ear when it blew with the gusting wind. A summer storm was coming, the kind that would flare with lightning across the sky, erupting hard and fast.

"At first, I did." Paul glanced over his shoulder toward the house. "But then the wife checked her bank account and realized Walker had cleared out twenty thousand dollars, *cash*."

Anthony whistled. "And there was no sign of an abduction at the courthouse?"

"The cops said Hamilton dodged them. Deliberately slipped out a back exit. His car's missing, and I've got cops looking for it but…" He gave a shake of his head. "My money says the guy decided to cut and run."

Anthony wasn't so sure, not yet anyway. "His office was trashed. He was the one who sent Walker to prison."

"He was also the one who gave the guy a life sentence instead of death. From the way I figure it," Paul said, "Walker owes the fellow a big-ass thank-you. Not any payback."

Lauren cleared her throat. "But Paul, Judge Walker has a career here, a family—"

"He also has a dead mistress and a serial killer stalking the streets. He would have seen coverage of your attack on the news."

"Was there video of him leaving the courthouse?" Anthony asked. A video would let them know whether or not the judge had left on his own.

"There was some security footage, yeah. It showed Hamilton looking over his shoulder a few times, running fast for his ride, but the cameras didn't catch anyone else with him."

It was sure looking like Walker had fled, not been abducted.

Anthony still wanted to talk to the wife. He wanted to follow every piece of evidence, any trail that might lead him to Walker. And the judge—well, Walker had already showed a marked interest in the guy.

Anthony and Lauren followed Paul into the house. When Mrs. Pierce Hamilton came into view, Lauren crossed to her side.

"Julia," Lauren said, her voice soft, "I'm very sorry for—"

"He left me." The words seemed lost. So shocked. "He took the money and he *left* me."

"We don't know for—"

Julia, a thin woman with carefully streaked blonde hair, gave a bitter laugh. "Don't lie to me, Lauren. I know what's been going on. I know about the girl he was screwing, I always know about the girls..." Her sentence trailed away as her fingers clenched around a white handkerchief. "I don't usually care. We have an arrangement, you see."

Anthony didn't see and he didn't exactly want to.

"He was never supposed to leave. What will people say?" The handkerchief was about to rip apart in her hands. "What will I do?"

What could they do? The judge was an adult. If he wanted to cut town and run, he could. He'd broken no laws, so they had no legal reason to hold him or to hunt him.

Julia's red-rimmed eyes locked on Paul. "Can you find him, Detective? Can you ask him *why*?"

Sympathy slid over Paul's face. "Ms. Hamilton, you know Judge Hamilton convicted Jon Walker—"

"This isn't about Walker!" She jumped to her feet. "My husband isn't in danger! He's *leaving* me! I can't let him do that! I can't let—"

"We're going to search for signs of foul play because of the Walker case," Paul continued, his voice staying calm and low. "But ma'am, if the judge willingly left the city, there isn't anything that can be done."

Julia's narrow shoulders hunched. "I gave him so many years. I let him screw around with those whores, and this is what he does? He *leaves* me?" She ripped the handkerchief in two. "Let Walker get him. I don't care! If the bastard dies, it will be better for me." Her breath was ragged. "Better to be a widow than the fool he left behind."

***

Pierce Hamilton slowly opened his eyes. His head hurt. It throbbed. He squinted as he tried to see around him. *Where the hell am I?*

"Waking up, are you?" The voice was taunting. "Sure as fuck took you long enough."

With effort, Pierce turned his head to the side.

Jon Walker smiled. "Did you think you were running somewhere?"

Pierce's memory flooded back. He'd left the courthouse in a rush, but his car had been nearly out of gas. He'd filled the thing up a day ago, so it should have been able to go for miles.

He'd found himself drifting into a small, run-down station on the edge of town. He'd started to fill up his tank…

Then someone had slammed his head into the side of his BMW, hard enough to break the fucking window.

"I went to so much trouble to get back to you and Ms. Chandler." Walker shook his head. "Did you think I would just let you walk away?" He took a step toward Pierce. The knife in his hand glinted. "You and I…we have some unfinished business."

Fear rose in Pierce's throat, nearly choking him. "I'm not the one to blame! I was just doing my job!"

"If you had *done* your job, you would have paid attention to the letters you got. Those damn letters said I should go free."

His heart was about to jump out of his chest. "How do you know about those?"

"I know plenty." Walker glanced around. "Like the fact your fishing cabin was empty, sitting all alone up here, waiting for someone to stop by for a nice little visit."

Pierce's eyes widened. This *was* his place. He hadn't been here in at least two years. Julia hated the cabin, so he'd found other entertainment to keep him busy. But the antlers on the wall, the bear rug, the gleaming wood furniture—

Mine.

"Never would've guessed you loved to hunt and kill so much, Judge," Walker drawled. "Looks like we have more in common than I thought."

"We're not alike! We're *nothing* alike!" Pierce strained at his bonds. He was in one of the kitchen chairs. Behind him, his hands were wrapped with what felt like duct tape. He looked down and saw the gray line of duct tape around his ankles. He was trapped. Helpless.

The knife was so close to his skin.

The Bayou Butcher. He'd seen the crime scene photos, seen *everything* during the trial. He knew just how Walker liked to torture his prey. He also knew—

"You don't kill men," Pierce blurted, because what the hell else did he have to say? But it was the truth. Walker liked to hurt women, not men. It was part of the profile that had been revealed in court.

Walker laughed. "Tell that to the prison guard I gutted on my way out of Angola."

Pierce shook his head. He wasn't stupid. He'd had plenty of shrinks in his court over the years, so he understood more than most about the minds of killers. "It was fast, though, right? You don't enjoy it when you kill men. Just women." He licked his lips. "You would have enjoyed it if you'd gotten to kill Lauren."

Walker's face hardened. "I *will* kill the bitch."

"Yes, yes, you will." Pierce spoke quickly. "Call her, tell her I'm here, that you have me, and she'll come running." She'd also better come with that marshal who seemed glued to her side.

Or with the detective she'd screwed once upon a time.

Walker glanced down at the knife in his hand. "Women have softer skin. The knife just slices right through it."

Sick *freak.*

"I sliced your girlfriend." Walker glanced up with a sly smirk on his face. "Didn't realize who she was to you, not at first. Just thought she was some dumb bitch friend of Lauren's. And any friend of Lauren's can damn well find herself under my knife."

Pierce jerked at the duct tape. *Don't think about Karen.*

"Karen, right? I found out her name later. I just called her *bitch* when I was slicing her."

Pierce's hands fisted.

"She started screaming that she had a powerful boyfriend, a judge who would give me anything if I let her live." He laughed. "So stupid. She was your side piece. You wouldn't give up anything for her."

Pierce thought of Karen's laughter. Such a sweet sound. He thought of the way she'd made him feel, like he should do more than let his life fade away. Like he should have dreams again.

"Call Lauren," he managed to say, swallowing heavily. "Tell her—"

"I'm not calling anyone."

Hell.

Walker stood directly in front of him now. "I was in that prison for eighteen hundred and sixty-five days. While I was behind those bars, in that fucking tiny room, you were out. You were screwing your whore, riding in your fancy car, eating your fine dinners."

"You *killed*. A jury found you guilty—"

"One of the bastards changed his mind! He wrote to you!"

Pierce understood. "You made him write, didn't you?"

The smirk was back.

"How? What did you do?"

"Let's just say I found the right motivation to *convince* him I needed to get out of jail." He laughed, bitter, mocking. "When you apply the right pressure, you can get a man to do just about anything."

Pierce couldn't get out of the bonds.

"But his notes didn't work." Walker's jaw tightened, the smirk slipping. "So things had to get bloody for him. The bastard *owed* me, and I made sure he paid. Just like I'll make sure you pay."

He was staring at death. Walker's slow, wide smile confirmed the hell that was coming. "You shouldn't worry about other folks right now, Judge. Instead, you should probably be more worried about what's going to happen to you."

***

Paul whistled softly as the judge's wife stormed away. "That is a woman with a whole lot of rage." He shook his head. "Guess that's what happens when you screw around on someone too long. They want their revenge."

Lauren had seen the fury in Julia's eyes, but she'd also seen the pain. At that moment, she wasn't sure if Julia knew what she really wanted. Her husband being carved up by a serial killer? That might not be what she was praying for.

Paul's phone rang. He held it up to his ear. "Voyt." His body snapped to attention. "What? Hell." A brief pause, then, "I was hoping the guy had just run."

Anthony's gaze met Lauren's. They both knew who Paul was talking about.

"I'm on my way. Get the techs to check the vehicle for prints and see if the station attendant saw anything." He ended the call with a long, rough sigh. His gaze drifted to the door on the right, the door Julia had exited seconds before. "I guess she's getting her wish."

"Is he dead?" Anthony asked. It was the same question on Lauren's lips.

"We don't have a body yet. The judge's BMW was found abandoned at a gas station near Pontraine Lake. The attendant realized the car had been out there for a while. He went to take a look and found blood dripping down the side of the busted passenger window. The judge was nowhere around."

Lauren's heartbeat raced. "Walker took him. Just like he took me."

A muscle jerked along Paul's jaw. "I'm driving to the gas station. If I find out anything else, you'll know. Count on it." He focused on Anthony. "You'll be staying with her." It wasn't a question.

Anthony nodded anyway.

"Maybe you two can get the wife to tell you something else— something we can use. Sometimes, spouses know a hell of a lot more than we think." He headed for the front door, moving with quick, long strides.

Lauren's fingers twisted in front of her. "Walker was ready to start cutting me the minute he had me alone."

Anthony stepped closer to her. "That's because the bastard gets off on hurting women. He enjoys their pain."

She flinched. He'd sure enjoyed her pain.

"The guard at the prison—the man he murdered—Walker killed him quickly," Anthony said. "The judge won't have as much time as you did. Hell, Hamilton could already be dead."

"*What?*"

Oh, hell. Julia had come back into the room. Lauren hadn't even heard her footsteps. She glanced over her shoulder.

Julia was frowning at them. "Did you just say Hamilton is dead?" Her face had turned a stark white.

Lauren took a steadying breath as she faced her.

"Where's Detective Voyt? What's happening?" Julia seemed a whole lot less enraged now, and much more afraid.

"Detective Voyt received a call," Lauren told her, fighting to keep her voice level. "Pierce's car was found at a gas station near Pontraine Lake."

"What?" Then Julia smiled. "Oh, Pierce must have just been going to the old fishing cabin." The tension seemed to leave her shoulders. "I knew he wouldn't leave me, of course. I'm the one constant he always has. He *needs* me, you see. We're a team, we're—"

"The car was abandoned," Lauren said softly. "The judge wasn't there."

Julia trembled. Her smile faded.

Lauren had to tell her the rest. Julia deserved the truth. "There was blood found on the passenger-side window."

"Pierce's blood?"

"It's too early to tell that." Anthony's voice was a low rumble. "The crime techs will have to test the blood before we can determine that for sure."

The hope had vanished from the woman's face. Julia's knees seemed to give way as she collapsed onto the lush leather couch. "I didn't mean what I said." Her voice was a whisper.

Lauren sat next to her and reached for her hand.

Julia's lower lip quivered. "I loved him once, but somewhere along the way, we both got lost." Her lashes lowered. "I was the first to cheat," she confessed in a voice heavy with emotion. Pain. "He worked so much, all the time, and I just wanted someone to notice me. Maybe I wanted *him* to notice."

"We don't know anything for certain about Pierce right now," Lauren said, trying to keep her voice reassuring. "I got away. Even if Walker has him—"

"We were broken after I cheated. Going through the motions. Hurting each other, but never letting go." Julia's lips pressed together into a thin line. It took her a few moments to say, "Maybe we should have let go."

"Julia." Lauren injected command in her voice.

Julia looked up at her.

"He isn't dead yet. You've got to keep hope going, okay?"

"I haven't had hope in a very long time."

Lauren glanced over at Anthony. His gaze was so watchful as it weighed Julia.

"The reporters..." Julia whispered. "They're going to find out, aren't they?"

"Don't worry about them." Lauren had already scheduled a press conference to talk about Walker. She could handle any questions the reporters had about Pierce, too. "I'll talk to them. I can—" She broke off as an idea formed in her mind. "Maybe we can even use them."

A big maybe. A tricky gamble, but what did they have to lose? "The abduction is still new." She faced Anthony. "We know the spot Walker took him from. We've got the general area. If we get the word out now, maybe someone will see Walker or even Hamilton. Maybe we can get a witness to help save the judge."

Julia's nails bit into Lauren's arm. Lauren glanced at her. Tears streaked down Julia's cheeks. "We truly loved each other once."

"He isn't dead yet," Lauren told her again. Please God, maybe he wouldn't be. She yanked out her phone and called the lead reporter for Channel Six. She had Caroline Kramer on her speed dial. The woman answered on the second ring.

"We're moving up the press conference," Lauren told her. "I've got a story I want you to cover *now*."

Taking a judge in daylight when so many people were out and about was a ballsy move—one that just might prove to be a fatal mistake for Walker.

CHAPTER ELEVEN

"I've got money!" the judge said, his face ashen, "I can pay you anything you want!"

"I already took the big bag of cash you had in the back of your car." Walker grinned at the jerk. That much cash would sure come in handy, once he'd finished his business in Baton Rouge. He'd disappear with the money, start fresh. "I figure I don't need a whole lot more."

The judge strained against his bonds.

Walker's smile faded. The judge was a big guy, a couple of inches taller than Walker, and the man had about fifty pounds on him. Hamilton might even be able to get out of the bonds if he struggled hard enough.

Walker glanced toward the door. His partner should have been here by now. He'd waited, only using the knife on the guy a little bit.

His skin isn't like a woman's. It doesn't tear like silk. It's too rough. Ugly.

It was time to kill the judge. Time to shut him up and watch him die.

"Let me go, and I can give you *anything.*"

He liked it when the guy begged, though. Power rushed through him with every plea. Once upon a time, this rich fool had been the one with the power. Sitting up on that fancy bench, wearing a big, black robe. Slamming down his gavel.

Sending me to rot.

His fingers tightened around the knife. He wanted to shove the blade deep into Hamilton's chest. But he could use the guy first. Get some information from him. "Tell me what you know about Lauren."

"The DA?"

Who the fuck else would it be?

"She's not staying at her house." Which made hunting her so much harder. "Where is she?"

"I don't know—"

Wrong answer. He shoved the knife into Hamilton's shoulder. Blood spurted as he twisted the blade. *Not the same.* The blade didn't cut right on the man. In a woman, it would have sliced deep, and the pulse of pleasure from the slice would have traveled all the way through him.

The normal pleasure didn't come. He twisted the knife again, jerking it hard to the left. "You're a fucking judge! You should know where the DA is!"

"Probably with the marshal. He's sticking to her every minute." Hamilton's breath panted out as sweat beaded his upper lip. "That's—ahh, stop, please!"

"Tell me something useful, and I will."

"I—I think they're sleeping together..."

How was that useful?

"Saw the w-way he looked at her—stop, *please!*"

"I don't give a shit who she screws." It was just about the kill. About payback. Punishment. She'd taken so many years from him. She should have been dead long ago.

He'd gotten out of Angola. Started his own path. This time, he wasn't going to stand in anyone's fucking shadow. It was his game. His rules.

That was why he'd left her a note.

It's beginning.

He wanted her to understand. It was all about him. About his power. His control.

The Bayou Butcher's run in Baton Rouge wouldn't end, not until Lauren Chandler's blood soaked his skin, and she drew her last breath.

A breath he'd be the one to take from her.

"Th-thought she was still sleeping with the detective..." Hamilton gasped. "Karen told me about them."

The detective.

The knife pulled out of Hamilton's shoulder with a slow, wet glide.

"What detective?" There were plenty who'd worked on his case before. Plenty who deserved—

"Voyt. Paul Voyt."

Well, well.

"They were..." Hamilton sucked in deep, gulping breaths. "Screwing for a while. If she's not with the marshal, you can probably find her hiding out at Voyt's place."

"That is helpful," he whispered.

The front door opened. He'd left it unlocked. Why bother locking it when he only expected one person? The footsteps were heavy as they thudded over the hardwood floor.

He turned, deliberately keeping his smile in place.

His partner stood there, cheeks flushed, eyes glittering. "What the *hell* were you thinking?" he demanded. "The judge wasn't on our list."

"No, not our list." He wiped the knife on his jeans, smearing the blood across the rough material. "*My* list." *It's beginning. My beginning.*

The judge gasped behind him. "Help me!"

The fool should have realized by now. Help wasn't an option.

***

"We are asking for the public's help in locating Judge Pierce Hamilton." Lauren's voice was smooth and calm as she stared into the circle of camera lenses around her. "Judge Hamilton's BMW was found abandoned at Quick and Fill Gas Station, near Pontraine Lake, a few hours ago. Investigators checked the scene and determined there were signs of foul play."

Anthony had realized very quickly that when the DA said *jump*, the reporters flew into the sky. Right after her call, she'd had the top reporters in Baton Rouge assembled, all ready to go live with a noon broadcast of her story. The broadcast would hit people on their lunch breaks, and maybe the hotline would get a lucky tip—some driver who saw Walker or Hamilton. Something they could use.

Voyt had called back from the scene, and the attendant hadn't remembered seeing anyone. There were no security cameras. Just jack and shit.

"Are you saying the Bayou Butcher has the judge?" a blonde reporter demanded.

"I'm saying that, at this time, we are searching for Judge Pierce Hamilton, and we would greatly appreciate the public's assistance in finding him."

"But *you* were abducted by Walker just yesterday, were you not?" the same reporter fired. "Is Walker targeting the people who sent him to prison?"

Just yesterday. Walker sure wasn't wasting any time. A week ago, Anthony had been finishing up a case in Texas. Walker had been locked away in his cell. Now the bodies were piling up—fast. A rising tide of blood and death.

Lauren cleared her throat. "Only Walker can tell us that," she replied. He knew she was trying to walk the line and not reveal too much information.

Not enough to compromise the investigation, but just enough to get help.

"If the public spots either Walker or Hamilton, we need to be contacted. Manhunts for Walker have been ongoing since his escape." Her gaze darted to Anthony, then back to the cameras. "Authorities now believe Walker has been working with someone in the Baton Rouge area, someone who has helped him avoid detection."

The reporters pounced. "A partner?" a male with an artful spray of gray at his temples asked. "The Bayou Butcher has a partner in crime?"

Lauren's focus shifted to the reporter. "It appears someone is hiding Walker from the police. Walker is an extremely dangerous, unpredictable killer. Even the person working with him cannot be assured Walker won't turn on him. Walker kills—that's just what he does, and we need the public to help us stop him." Her shoulders straightened as her attention spread to the full group of reporters once more. "As I said before, Walker should *not* be confronted by any citizen. If you see him or have information to share, call our tip line. Do not approach him on your own."

Anthony backed away as she concluded the press conference. The FBI profilers were there, too, and he knew Cadence would be talking soon. While they were busy milling in the front of the police precinct, he saw an opening. There was someone he wanted to talk with.

Inside the precinct, he found Julia Hamilton huddled in a small office. She had a Styrofoam cup of coffee cradled in her hands. She wasn't drinking it, though. Just holding it and staring into space.

"Mrs. Hamilton?"

She flinched and carefully set the coffee on the desk. "They said I didn't have to talk to the reporters." Her hands smoothed over her pants. "Lauren was going to handle all of that."

"Yes, ma'am, she is." He crouched in front of her. "But I was hoping you'd talk to me a bit."

Her gaze focused on him. "You aren't a detective. I haven't seen you around here before."

"No, I'm a marshal. I'm in town to catch Walker."

Lines of grief had settled on her face. "Will you catch him before or after he kills my husband?"

He wasn't going to give her false hope, so he didn't answer. "You said the gas station was near an old fishing cabin your husband had?"

She nodded. "On Pontraine Lake. It was actually his father's place. Pierce never seemed to enjoy going there." Her lips twisted. "His father was big into hunting and fishing. Pierce didn't like killing." Her breath expelled in a rush. "That's why he sentenced so few to death, even when they deserved it. Like Walker did. He should have sent the man to die, but he didn't."

The cabin was so close to the site where Pierce had vanished. Could it be a coincidence? Anthony wasn't sure he bought into those. "Would you mind if I searched the place?"

She blinked. "You think Walker has him there?"

"I don't know. Walker is familiar with the area." A little too familiar for someone who'd been sitting in prison for five years. "Maybe he realizes where the cabin is." Maybe he'd been looking for a quick spot to vanish and found one a few miles down the road. "I'm going to need an exact address."

While she scribbled down the address, Anthony pulled out his phone. A few seconds later, Voyt was on the line. "Have you checked the judge's cabin on Pontraine Lake?" Anthony asked.

"What cabin?" Paul barked. "What are you talking about, Marshal?"

He took a few steps away from Julia and lowered his voice. "Judge Hamilton's father owned an old fishing cabin near the abduction site. It's possible Walker knew about it. We should search the place. Make sure it's clear."

"Send me the address," Paul said. "I was waiting for Hawthorne to meet me, so I'm still in the area. I can check the place."

"A marshal and I will be on the way, too," Anthony said. He needed to be out in the field stopping the bastard. "We'll be there as fast as we can." He ended the call and took the address from Julia. With a quick text, he sent the info to Paul.

"Please…" Julia's voice stopped him as he headed for the door. He glanced back at her.

"I don't want to bury my husband."

***

The interview was over, and Lauren felt exhausted. Her stitches ached, her head ached, and her heart hurt.

I don't think we're going to find Hamilton alive. She wanted to have hope, but she didn't.

"Come with me." She turned at the sound of Anthony's voice. He led her back into the station and pulled her into the conference room that the task force had been using.

As soon as they were inside, he shut the door. A glance to the right showed Lauren that the profile board had been moved. She knew Cadence had ordered it be removed for the time being, because she hadn't wanted to risk any reporters sneaking inside for a look.

Even though the board was gone, Lauren still shivered, remembering all of the faces.

Jenny's face.

"Matt and I are going to meet up with Paul and Wesley at Hamilton's fishing cabin."

Her heart started to beat faster. "Did Paul find—"

"No, it's a hunch. My gut is telling me the place would sure as hell make a perfect kill site."

She flinched.

"Jim has orders to stick with you."

He was leaving her behind. Her brows climbed. "I thought we were a team on this."

He brushed back a lock of her hair. The back of his palm lingered on her cheek. "I can't hunt him if I'm worried about you. You need to stay here. Where you're safe. Where there are a dozen cops right beside you." He bent and brushed his lips over hers. "You're hurting, don't you think I know?"

She didn't answer.

"I'm not taking you back to the swamp. I won't put you in his path again."

"You didn't put me there before." She didn't want him blaming himself. "I did that all on my own." Apparently, she'd been in

Walker's path for years—long before the trial. Back when she'd just been a kid.

"Stay with Jim. Let him and the cops keep watch—"

"I have to go back to my office." She needed to check in with her staff. Make certain the cases they had to prosecute were set. Walker wasn't the only killer out there.

His lips tightened. Well, tough. She had a job. People who needed her. She wouldn't let Walker destroy everything she had. "I have to go."

"Fine, but then Jim goes, too. So does a patrol." He was adamant. "I won't have you unprotected. I *can't* do my job if I think you're unsafe."

She nodded. "I'll take Jim and the patrol." She wasn't stupid and she sure didn't have a death wish.

His forehead rested against hers. "I can't get you out of my head."

She had more of a problem keeping him out of her heart.

"No one else has ever been like you." His confession could have been hers.

She swallowed and whispered, "Go."

He pulled back and studied her with a guarded gaze. "Even when I catch Walker, this isn't over."

The words sounded like a warning.

He left as Jim eased into the office and gave her a weak smile. "I promise, ma'am," he said, with a little nod, "you can count on me."

She was in a police precinct—the safest place on earth. She wasn't afraid for herself right now.

It was Anthony she was worried about.

Her gaze slid after him.

Come back to me.

***

Walker shoved the knife hilt deep into Hamilton's chest.

Blood soaked Pierce Hamilton's shirt. The life drained from his eyes, and his head hung forward, sagging toward the gaping wound in his chest.

"One more down."

It was becoming something he now *had* to do. He walked toward the old desk, found a slip of paper, tore it in half, and made the perfect size he needed.

"What are you doin'?" Jon's partner asked.

"Leaving Lauren a message." With blood still staining his fingers, he scrawled, *The blood is on you.*

If Lauren had just died like she should have yesterday, he would have left this rat hole town already. Hamilton would have gotten to keep living. Sure, he'd thought about killing the judge, and he'd sure enjoyed trashing the guy's office, but *Lauren* was the one he really wanted.

Only she'd gotten away. So he'd had to take other prey. Had to slake the thirst for vengeance that grew and grew inside of him.

He folded the paper and stalked back toward Hamilton. The judge didn't look so high and mighty anymore. If it took the cops a few days to find him, he'd be rotten. Stinking. Decay and garbage. Exactly the end he deserved.

He yanked the knife from the judge's chest. "Open wide," he muttered and then he sliced the bastard's throat. His fingers jammed the piece of paper into the bloody opening.

The floor creaked behind him. His partner came closer. A hard hand landed on Jon's shoulder and yanked him around. "That's *not* how it's done." Rage darkened his partner's eyes.

"That's how I do it." Jon had learned from this man before. Done everything *his way*. For so many years. *Too many*.

He'd even gone to jail, keeping *his* secret.

He wasn't going to be anyone's little bitch anymore. Prison had taught him one thing—true power went to the strongest. He was the strongest.

After he'd killed his cell mate, the others in Angola had stayed away from him. Rapists, robbers, murderers—they'd all feared him.

Strength is power. I have the power now.

Jon shook his head and offered his partner a small smile. "I do things differently now. I do what *I* want." It felt good leaving the damn notes—letting them know *he* was the one in charge. He'd wanted to leave messages years before taking credit for what they were doing, but his partner—oh, hell, no, *he'd* been against that. Said messages would be traced.

Nothing had been traced yet.

Nothing would.

They can't stop me.

"We fucking tried doing what you wanted before." Rage snapped in the words. "I let you pick your own prey, and you got caught slicing up the teenager. If you'd listened to me, you never would have—"

Jon lifted the bloody knife. Put it against the other man's chest. "I'm rising."

"What the fuck does that mean?"

"I don't need you to tell me what to do anymore." Power flushed him. Killing the judge had given him a rush. A rush nearly as good as the one he got when he sliced into his usual prey. "I know how to kill. I'm even better at it than you."

His partner's rage-filled stare dropped to the knife Jon held so tightly. "You think you're going to kill me?"

Jon hesitated. That wasn't part of his plan. His partner was the only one who truly knew him. His only connection.

His family.

He lowered the knife. "Of course not." Jon tried a rough laugh.

The other man didn't laugh back. "You shouldn't have brought the judge to this place. It's too close to the abduction site. The cops are going to come out here."

Let 'em come.

"They're going to keep searching until they have you." A hard shake of his partner's head. "The marshal won't just walk away from this case. He's not giving up."

"Because he's screwing her!"

"*You* screwed up in front of her. You mentioned Jenny."

Jenny. She'd been so beautiful, covered in blood. A work of fucking art. He'd tried to make Karen look just like her in death. He tried to make all the women look like Jenny. Broken, bleeding dolls, frozen forever in time.

"You mentioned Jenny, and now they're gonna want to open her case again."

Jenny had been too good of a secret to keep any longer. "Do you still remember where she's buried?" his partner whispered. "I do. I can find her, anytime I want."

Jon had learned so much since Jenny. They both had. Jenny's death had been messy and beautiful and so fucking good. But Jenny had fought. She'd scratched his partner. "You left a part of yourself with Jenny." That was part of his new power, too. "I could tell the marshal, I could tell the DA. If they find Jenny, they find you."

His partner stared back at him. "We were brothers, you and I." Brothers born from blood. "I've been helping you all along," he continued. "I'm the one who took Helen Lynch—I made the phone calls to Steve. I *convinced* him to contact the judge. I'm the one who told him just what the fuck would happen if he didn't make sure you got out of prison."

Convinced him by putting Helen's life on the line.

"Don't act like you didn't enjoy cutting on her…" Jon said. The guy had kept Helen, played with her.

"I let *you* finish her," his partner shot back.

He had let him. She'd been a gift. A beautiful, bloody doll for his collection.

"When Hamilton ignored the letter, I came up with a different plan, didn't I?" His partner snarled.

"*My* plan." The guy was trying to take credit? "I'm the one who got to the infirmary—"

"And I'm the one who had the car waiting, just like I said I would. I had the car waiting for you. New clothes. Cash. I'm the one who made sure no one would know about the communication we had—do you even know how hard that was? I did it, *for you*."

His voice vibrated with fury, and Jon hesitated. He didn't like to make him angry. But something was fucking bothering him. "You put that necklace where Stacy would find it. If you wanted me out, why the hell would you—"

"The bitch wasn't respecting you." It was said with barely contained fury. "She needed to know who she was pissing off—and she needed to know what was going to happen to her."

It did happen. I cut her so deep.

She respected him now.

"Hell," his partner blasted, "I've been doing everything for you. I even took you to Lauren Chandler's place, and I let *you* kill the whore there."

He'd done all of that for him. Kept him hidden. Brought him food. But… "*Five* years—"

The other man exploded. "You shouldn't have fuckin' taken the babysitter! That was stupid! They caught you red-handed. What the hell was I supposed to do? I *got* you out!"

Not soon enough. Too many days and nights had passed. Now he couldn't stand to be confined. He'd taken to sleeping out in the open because he couldn't bear to be in the cabins near the swamp. Not anymore. The walls closed in. He couldn't breathe.

"I even let you target the ones you wanted for payback, when they weren't the prey I would have chosen."

He only liked to hurt women—the ones like sweet Jenny.

I even let you...

His partner's words rang in his head. The anger erupted. "You don't *let* me do anything." Not anymore. I'm the leader now," Jon said, straightening to his full height. A height that put him a good two inches shorter than his partner. "We do what I say because if the marshal gets close again, I will tell him all about Jenny. And you."

His partner's face flushed dark red. "They already know about me. Lauren *told* the cops you were talking to me. They *know*."

Walker backed up a step, the move instinctive.

No, don't back down. You're in charge.

His partner glanced toward the door. "They're gonna find this place. I told you, it was too fucking obvious a choice. You need to get the hell out of here before the marshal comes or before the dogs hunt you down. You need to run."

"I'm sick of running. I want Lauren," The scent of blood was clogging his nostrils. Driving him wild.

He wanted it to be her blood. When Lauren was dead, when he finished the circle that had started with Jenny, his partner would *see* he was the one in charge. He wasn't the student. He didn't need to be taught.

This was his game.

His power.

In the distance, he heard the growl of an engine. Not just one engine. Two.

"Told you," the other man said with a sigh. "How many escapes do you think you've got in you?"

"Plenty. Because *you* have to help me. If you don't, I'll send sweet Jenny home at last."

A muscle jerked in the man's jaw. "Go out the back. Run through the woods on the north side. I came in that way. My boat's still there."

Yes.

He spun, gave one last glance at Hamilton. Already rotting.

Not so high and mighty.

Soon, Lauren would be rotting, too.

***

Anthony braked his SUV, sending dust and dirt flying around his vehicle. He and Matt weren't the first on the scene. To the right, he saw the Jeep with the Fish and Wildlife logo on the back, and he knew Wesley had already arrived—Wesley *and* Paul. The detective stood on the steps of the cabin, his gun held tightly in his hand.

There was another car at the scene, too. A beat-up sedan was parked near the side of the cabin. He noticed Wesley had parked his vehicle behind the sedan, blocking it in.

Maybe Wesley and Paul thought it was Walker's stolen ride. They weren't about to give the man the chance to escape in it.

Good move.

Anthony and Matt exited their SUV quickly. They drew their own weapons as they swept the scene.

"Wesley?" Anthony asked. He couldn't see the guy.

"He went around back to block the exit." Paul inclined his head toward the front door. "We just got here, freaking seconds before you."

No need to wait any longer.

Anthony gave a nod. At the signal, Paul lifted his foot and kicked in the door.

The cabin wasn't small. It wasn't some shack. Instead it snaked and stretched back. But it didn't take the men long to find the judge.

He was in the den, blood soaking him, duct tape still holding him trapped to the chair.

"Hell," Paul muttered. "Too damn late." He rushed toward the judge anyway, checking for a pulse.

With that much blood, Anthony didn't expect Paul to find one.

"No pulse," Paul said quietly, his voice thick, "but he's still warm."

A door crashed in from the back of the house. Anthony ran toward the sound and saw Wesley coming. He had a gun in his hands.

"He's not out back," Wesley said with a shake of his head

The body was warm, though, so he was fucking close.

"The house is clear," Matt said, hurrying up behind them. "He must have fled before we arrived."

Not by car. There was only one road that led to and from the cabin, and they hadn't passed any other vehicles.

Paul called for backup, giving the person on the other end the news that the judge had been found.

"We need to split up and search," Anthony said. There was a hell of a lot of ground to cover, and not enough time.

Paul shoved the phone back into his pocket. "They're ten minutes out."

They weren't waiting ten minutes. They kept their weapons close and headed out the back.

Twisting trees met them.

"It's a fishing cabin, so where's the water?" Anthony demanded. Water—it was the way Walker liked to escape.

Wesley pointed. "To the north."

Maybe he was trying a different exit strategy this time.

Good thing there were four of them. Time to split up and cover as much ground as possible.

***

The boat wasn't there.

Walker staggered to a stop on the rickety dock, the bloody knife still gripped in his fist.

The boat wasn't there.

The dock bobbed lightly as the hot summer wind tossed the waves. Lightning flashed across the sky. The storm was finally rolling in.

The storm should have helped him. It would have covered his tracks. He would have slipped away again.

But the fucking boat wasn't there.

Snarling, Walker spun around. Shock and fury and fear battled inside of him. Fear—it had been so long since he'd felt fear. He wasn't supposed to be afraid, not any longer. His partner had told him that, after the first kill.

We don't have to be afraid of anything or anyone. They fear us. We're the power. They're the prey.

His feet thudded over the dock as he rushed back for the trees.

He partner had lied to him. Had sent him running for a boat that wasn't there. *Why? Why would he do that to me?*

They were family.

Brothers of blood.

He froze, breath heaving, surrounded by gnarled trees. He'd heard footsteps. Rushing toward him.

They're hunting me.

He was all alone. No partner. No help.

Just him. In the woods.

His fingers tightened around the knife.

He wasn't going back to jail. He *wasn't* finished. The circle wasn't complete. Lauren wasn't a beautiful, bloody doll.

It wasn't over.

I have the power. He also had the big-ass knife.

***

The swamp seemed too quiet. Far too quiet. Even the insects had stilled. Anthony paused and glanced at Paul. The detective nodded and pointed to the left. The dock. They could both see the edge of the wood.

Anthony eased forward while Paul branched to the left a bit, still searching the line of trees. Anthony's gaze surveyed the scene. No sign of a boat. No sign of Walker. But...

Wait. There was a *sign* of him. A shoe impression, just a few feet from the dock in the loose dirt. Anthony turned, body pumping with adrenaline, as he followed the impression. One step. Another. Another—

"Help!"

His head jerked up. It was Paul's voice—Paul, who should have been close behind him. Anthony whirled and ran toward the voice.

He burst through the bushes and saw them. Paul was on the ground. Bleeding.

Walker—tricky SOB—he'd circled back and come up on Paul from behind. Paul was on the ground, blood dripping down his back as he tried to crawl for his weapon. Walker was lifting his knife once more—

"Freeze!" Anthony yelled.

Paul kept crawling.

Walker froze for an instant, his head lifted, and he locked his gaze on Anthony.

"Drop the weapon!" Anthony yelled. "Drop it *now!*"

Walker shook his head. "I won't go back."

"You don't have a choice." Anthony advanced on him. "Now *drop it!*" Or he would put a bullet in him.

Walker glanced down at Paul. "I have the power."

He lunged for the detective.

Anthony fired his gun, sending a bullet straight at Walker's heart. At the same moment, Paul rolled over and came up holding his weapon. He fired. His bullet hit Walker just seconds after Anthony's.

Walker's eyes widened as he stumbled back. The guy's mouth dropped open and shock swept over his face.

The knife fell from his fingers. He fell back and hit the ground.

Anthony raced to him. He kicked the knife farther away. Two bullets were in the bastard's chest, and Walker was coughing up blood as he struggled to bring in his last breaths.

Crouching and keeping his gun trained on him, Anthony said, "You aren't going to be hurting anyone else."

Walker tried to turn his head toward Anthony. "W-Weep…"

"What?" Anthony demanded.

"W-weepin'…wil…low…tree. T-tell…Lau…"

A gurgle ended the words. A rough rasp that was the last breath the Bayou Butcher would ever take.

"Is he dead?" Paul gasped.

Anthony's heart slammed into his chest.

"Yeah." *About fucking time.* "The bastard is on his way to hell." *Try escaping that prison. You want hurt Lauren, you piece of shit. You won't hurt anyone, not anymore.* Anthony hurried back to Paul's side. "Now let's make sure you stay alive."

Matt leaped out of the brush, breath heaving. A few moments later, Wesley appeared. They took in the bloody scene and saw Anthony working to stem the blood from Paul's wound.

More backup arrived. Cops. EMTs. Paul was loaded into the back of an ambulance. He was lucky—the knife wound wasn't lethal.

A survivor.

Judge Hamilton hadn't been so lucky.

The ambulance's siren screamed as Paul was driven away. Anthony watched the vehicle vanish, the knot in his gut still tight.

"You did it," Matt said as the other marshal came to his side and slapped him on the back. "You caught the Bayou Butcher."

"Killing him isn't the same thing as catching him." The Butcher's last words replayed in Anthony's head.

"It is to me." Matt's gaze was dark and steady. "Now he doesn't get to torture anyone else. Our job's done."

The job of tracking down and apprehending Walker, yes. But what about the bastard's partner?

The only person who knew the man's identity was being zipped up into a body bag.

"It's not over," Anthony said.

Not yet. Not even close.

CHAPTER TWELVE

Anthony didn't go back to the police station. He called Jim and was told Lauren was at her office. When he was clear, Anthony went to her. He wanted to talk to her—alone—without all of the prying eyes at the police department.

Word of the Bayou Butcher's death had spread like wildfire. Even as he drove to Lauren's office, he heard the DJ talking about the death on the radio.

"Folks can rest easy in Baton Rouge tonight, the Bayou Butcher is off the streets. I for one am glad the bastard is burning in hell…"

Anthony leaned forward and pushed the dial, ending the broadcast.

He should have felt relief. He'd already gotten a call from his boss congratulating him.

Yeah, he'd stopped Walker, but Hamilton had still died. Stacy Crawford had died. The doctor at Angola—dead. The guard—dead. Walker had left a bloody trail in his wake.

A trail that had finally ended.

But one that still raised questions.

He showed his ID at Lauren's office and got a fast track to her. There were two uniforms in the lobby, both wearing big grins.

Everyone seemed to be celebrating Walker's death, but didn't they get it?

Another killer is still out there. A killer who'd taken far more lives than Walker had. A killer who could be hunting, even as they whooped and hollered.

Jim met him outside of Lauren's office and offered his hand. "Good job, sir."

So he kept being told. "I should have brought him in alive."

Jim lowered his voice. "Why? To me, it's better this way."

Jaw locking, Anthony passed him and entered Lauren's office. She was sitting behind a wide desk with a slew of papers in front of her. When she saw him, Lauren jumped to her feet and hurried toward him. "I heard—"

He caught her in his arms and pulled her tightly against his chest. Her sweet scent filled his lungs, banishing the coppery stench of blood that had clung to him since he'd found the judge's body.

Her body felt warm and soft against his. Delicate. Fragile. He thought of Walker, charging with his knife.

He'd used that knife on Lauren.

When he'd pulled the trigger, Anthony had seen Lauren in his mind's eye. The truth—brutal, dark—was that he could have shot the knife out of the bastard's hands. He could have done it. He was a good enough marksman to have made it work.

But he hadn't. He hadn't wanted to just stop Walker.

He'd wanted to kill him.

I should have kept him alive. I wasn't thinking, just feeling. Now we don't have a link to the other bastard.

She pulled back and stared up at him with the gaze that had always seemed to see too deeply into him. "Is Paul going to be all right? I wanted to go to the hospital, but Jim said I should stay here."

It had been Anthony's order to Jim. Anthony hadn't wanted her to leave until he got to her.

"Walker killed the judge before we got there. He stabbed Hamilton in the heart."

Her eyes widened. "Does Julia—"

"She knows." Cadence had made sure of it.

Lauren nodded. Her hands slid away from him. "I'm glad Walker's gone." A stark confession.

Tell her. His jaw locked, and he couldn't speak. She said she was glad, but it was the heat of the moment. She didn't fully realize the stakes.

If Walker had lived, he could have taken them to Jenny's remains. Lauren could have finally brought her sister home.

"What is it?" She stared up at him, a faint furrow between her brows.

His hands tightened around her. "The last thing he said, it was about you."

The stark understanding sank into her eyes. "Jenny."

Anthony nodded. "Walker said, 'Weeping willow tree. Tell Lauren.'" His jaw locked. "He didn't have the chance to tell me anything more."

Her lips parted as shock slacked her face.

"He wanted you to know, so I'm thinking..." *Fuck.* "She's buried near a willow." He'd gone over those words, again and again, in his mind. That was the only thing that made since to him.

The shock slowly faded. "A willow tree? My sister?" Her face was pale.

"I think if we find that tree, we'll find her." One tree in a fucking huge search area.

A knock sounded at the door. Lauren stepped away from him, putting at least two feet between their bodies. He frowned at her as she said, "Come in."

The door opened. Jim was there with a petite woman with short, red hair.

"Lauren, the reporters are already calling," the redhead said as she shifted nervously from her left foot to her right. "You're going to need to release a statement soon."

"Of course, Bridgette. I'll be out in just a moment."

Bridgette nodded, and after a curious glance at Anthony, she slipped from the room.

Jim pulled the door closed behind them.

"Your job's done," Lauren said softy as her eyes found his. "Walker's gone. No more fugitive apprehension needed." Her gaze was carefully shielded, showing no signs of emotion.

Anthony could already feel the walls coming up between them. He could damn near see them. *Not happening this time.* "I told you before, this isn't over." He couldn't keep his hands off her and didn't want to try. He closed the space between them once more, his fingers curled over her shoulders, and he pulled her against him. They had a few precious moments alone, without any threat from a crazed killer. "The case may be over for me, but you and I aren't done."

He pressed his mouth to hers.

As soon as his lips touched hers, a wildfire of lust seemed to explode between them.

The heat was always there for him, simmering just beneath the surface. No woman had ever made him want the way she did.

Her body slid closer to his. Her lips parted, and her tongue thrust against his.

He'd seen too much death in his days and nights as a marshal. When he was with Lauren, she made him think of life. Passion. Hope. Every damn thing he'd ever wanted.

Right then, what he wanted most was her. His cock stretched, thrusting toward her. In his mind, she was already naked. They were on the big desk. He was *in* her.

His heart was a drumbeat pounding in his ears. Her scent seduced him, her body tempted him, and her tongue, her lips—they made him so hard.

The kiss stopped being gentle. It became rougher. Wilder. Her taste was all he knew. All he craved.

But someone was fucking knocking at the door again.

Growling, he pulled away from her and spun to face the door. "Don't," she whispered.

He glanced back at her. Lauren's cheeks were flushed, her eyes shining, her lips red and full from the press of his own.

"It's my assistant again, trying to get me out so I can talk to the press."

He sucked in a deep breath. Tried to calm the fury within him.

"The briefing won't take long, then I'll be done here for the day." She slid her tongue over her lower lip, as if still tasting him, and his back teeth ground together as his cock ached for her. "Will you still be here then?"

Still be here? "We've covered this." He said it slowly. Deliberately. "We aren't done."

He didn't know that they ever would be.

Lauren gave a small nod. "I was told I could go back to my house today." Her fingers brushed over the edge of her desk.

"But I can't do it. I can't stay there. I don't know that I'll ever be able to go back, knowing what happened to Karen there."

"You can stay with me." As if he'd want her anywhere else.

"In the hotel?"

Tonight, he'd do something different. He'd gotten a call the new location was finally ready. With Walker dead, it would be the perfect time for the move. "Trust me."

She smoothed back her hair. Straightened her clothes. "I always have, Tony."

He was surprised by the truth he heard in her voice.

Lauren headed for the door. Sure enough, Bridgette's nervous face was waiting when the door opened. Jim was there, too, with a few uniforms scattered behind him.

Time for the big press briefing. Time to say the Bayou Butcher would never kill again.

He was too busy already roasting in hell.

***

"Jon Walker, the man once dubbed the Bayou Butcher by the press in Baton Rouge, was killed today." Lauren's words were flat and cold as she stared from the television set.

He watched her, rage twisting through him. This wasn't the way things should have ended for Jon.

This *wasn't* the way things would end for him.

"Walker was tracked by a task force consisting of local Baton Rouge PD, U.S. marshals, and FBI agents. Working together, this team hunted Walker, and a few hours ago, U.S. Marshal Anthony Ross fatally shot Walker."

The TV flashed a rotating headline beneath Lauren's somber picture: Bayou Butcher Killed by U.S. Marshal.

"My sympathies go out to all of the families who lost loved ones as a result of Walker's actions..."

Fuck them. Fuck *her*. She was standing up there, all but gloating, and the marshal was right behind her. He was always right behind her. From the instant that bastard had come into town, he'd been sniffing at her.

She'd fallen right back into the guy's bed. He knew because he'd been watching them very closely.

She was still talking about the families. About the pain they'd felt. About how it was time for healing.

Blah. Fucking blah.

He glared at her. It felt as if someone had shoved a knife into his chest and cut out *his* heart. Something was gone, missing, and he didn't know what the hell to do.

Jon had been with him for so long. Someone who understood the darkness. Someone who knew what it was like to want the blood and the screams.

Jon had been there for the first kill. They'd stalked their prey together. Planned every moment. Every single detail. Getting caught hadn't been an option.

His Jenny had been so perfect. His first.

You never forgot your first.

He could still smell the blood. The death.

Jon had vomited after she was dead. The guy had been so shaken. Shaken, but he'd still understood the power they had. The power of life and death. Total control.

Jenny. Perfect Jennifer Chandler. The girl all the boys wanted. And all of the girls, they'd wanted to be her. She was the best one. Why would he have ever settled for anything less than the best?

If Jenny hadn't tried to break up with him back then, he might not have realized just how powerful he truly was. But she'd wanted to leave him.

You'll never leave me now.

He'd made sure that Jenny, his sweet Jenny, stayed with him forever.

Just as Jon should have stayed with him—*forever*. But Lauren had screwed that up for him. The bitch.

Even when Jon had been in prison, the link had still been there. He'd known Jon would be free sooner or later. Jon would be free, and he'd come back to him. They could continue, finish what they'd started.

The kills weren't as fun for him if Jon wasn't there. He needed Jon to watch. Needed someone to appreciate what he was doing. Needed someone to realize…*I'm the best. I have all the power.*

But prison had changed Jon.

Anger beat at the fucking hole in his chest. Jon had threatened to turn him in. That would have ruined *everything*.

The minute Jon said those words, he'd known the end was near. *I couldn't let him turn on me.*

Only now that Jon was gone, the darkness within was growing stronger.

"Thank you," Lauren said. "Now Marshal Ross will make a brief statement."

She backed away. Her arm brushed against Ross's. She tensed for an instant, and her gaze jerked up to meet the marshal's.

Ross's fingers slid down her arm. Lingered a second too long before Ross stepped into the center of the circus ring. He started talking about how Walker had died and that the Baton Rouge PD would still be—

"...investigating the mysterious partner who is believed to have helped Walker escape from prison and kept him hidden in the area."

Fuck, fuck, fuck.

They were still looking for him. Even with Jon dead, they were *still* hunting him.

They weren't going to stop. They were going to wreck his life, the life he'd built with so much blood, sweat, and savagery over the years. His perfect life. Jenny had taught him to be perfect.

No, Lauren and the marshal weren't going to stop.

So he would have to stop them.

***

"Why aren't we staying at the hotel?" Lauren asked as she settled into the passenger seat of Anthony's car and watched the buildings slide by her.

There was a beat of silence, then Anthony said, "Jim and Matt will both be in their rooms tonight, and I didn't want us to have to worry about any kind of...noise control."

That made her laugh. She couldn't remember the last time she'd laughed.

No, she could. It was with Karen, just last week. They'd gone out for drinks and—

"I lost you."

She blinked at his words.

"Stay with me tonight. Focus on me. Not on the Butcher, not on all the shit he did. He's gone, and I want to be with you."

Her hands pressed against her thighs. "What about his partner?" *Alpha team.* One killer was down, but another killer—Jenny's killer—was still out there. "That's not your job, is it? You were here to catch Walker, and you did that."

She'd gotten the feeling most of the cops were taking a case-closed attitude after the press conference. The homicide captain had sure been pushing that vibe. When Reginald Powers had spoken to her, he'd been clear that there were no bodies to be found, just missing victims and the hunch of FBI agents.

"I called my boss after the press conference," Anthony said as he turned the wheel to the right. "I told him I was taking some long overdue time off."

Surprise hit her.

His gaze slanted to her, holding hers for just a moment. "I'm not leaving town. I want to help you find out what happened to Jenny."

Her heart beat faster. "Thank you." For so long, it had just been her, hunting and hoping all by herself.

"Walker was the key to her murder. With that discovery, we *will* solve her murder."

Murder. Not disappearance. Not runaway. Not all of the terms cops had thrown out for so long.

"But for tonight—just tonight—I want it to be you and me, Lauren. Just us." His fingers tightened around the wheel. "I think we deserve that time."

She wanted that time.

They drove in silence for a while, then he was taking the long, winding path that led to a two-story, gleaming antebellum home nestled on a private road, away from the bustle and lights of the city.

He parked the SUV, then came around to her side and opened the door. "I had a bag brought over for you," he said as he took her arm.

He'd thought of everything.

Lights gleamed from inside the house. "How did you get this place?"

"I had a friend who owed me a favor."

They walked up the gleaming steps and entered the house. Her gaze drifted over the marble floor, to the glittering chandelier and the spiral staircase. "Some friend."

"When you've spent years finding safe houses for witnesses and informants, you make a lot of connections."

He locked the door behind them. Set the alarm. Then his arms wrapped around her.

His touch was warm and strong, and there, in that perfect house with him, she wasn't going to let the shadows of fear pull her down.

"I remember the first time I saw you." His lips feathered over her temple.

Her breath whispered out in a little sigh.

"You were in court, wearing a black skirt that stopped two inches above your knees—"

"Two inches? You remember that exactly?" she teased.

"Uh-huh, I measured. A sexy skirt and black fuck-me heels."

Her jaw dropped. "I would *never* wear those to court—"

"Trust me, I looked at those shoes and wanted one thing."

He still wanted that one thing. She could hear the arousal in his voice.

"You were a fantasy I could never give up." His lips pressed to hers. "No matter how many miles were between us."

"There aren't any miles between us now," she told him, her voice husky. He was the fantasy that had slipped into her mind too many times. A fantasy that wasn't out of reach any longer.

A flesh-and-blood man, a man who wanted her, not a dream.

"There are just too many clothes between us," he muttered, "but I think I can solve that problem."

She was sure he could.

The marshal had great problem-solving skills.

* * *

Cadence Hollow shoved open the door to the morgue. "Dr. Wright!" She knew Walker's body had been transferred to the morgue, and she wanted to see the Bayou Butcher herself.

Dr. Wright didn't respond.

Her footsteps tapped over the old floor. Goose bumps rose on her arms as the chilled air swept over her. Most people didn't like morgues. FBI agents and cops she'd met would often tell her that dealing with the dead was their least favorite part of the job.

That wasn't the case for her. In order to hunt killers, it was best to study the victims. The victims held the secrets. They could show *why* and *how* the killers had acted.

The ME's office smelled of antiseptic and bleach. Everything was in a briskly organized fashion. She crept closer to Greg's desk. She'd done her research on him, as she did on *everyone* working her cases. Obsessive, that was her. A negative side effect of the job.

Greg had taken the ME's position about six months ago, transferring from New Orleans. He was originally from Baton Rouge, and had left years ago to attend med school at Tulane.

"What are you doing?" His voice—sharp, definitely annoyed—called from behind her.

She turned from his desk. *No pictures. No adornments of any sort.* Her gaze swept over him.

He wore a pair of scrubs, white gloves, and a clear shield over the lower part of his face. She could just see Dr. Wright's eyes, so incredibly dark, studying her.

"I'm here to see Walker. He was brought in earlier, wasn't he?" She'd gone back to the scene of his death, searched the area, studied it, and come back here as the darkness swept across the city.

"He's here." He tossed aside the face mask.

Greg Wright was classically handsome. His blond hair slanted away from the strong planes of his face, curling just slightly.

She'd heard some of the cops call him Dr. Death.

She didn't exactly go for the pretty boys. She had a rule about that. Men who were too good-looking often came with far too many flaws on the inside.

Cadence cleared her throat. "Show me the body."

Instead of showing her the body, Wright stepped forward and placed himself in front of her, effectively blocking the door leading to the mortuary area. "I was in the middle of an autopsy. Things are graphic in there right now."

She stared up at him. "I track serial killers for a living. Trust me, there's nothing you can show me that I haven't seen." Had he forgotten she was the one who'd been behind him at Helen Lynch's crime scene? Had she gotten shaky and sick then?

No. Some poor uniform had been the one to lose his breakfast.

A ghost of a smile lifted the ME's lips. "Aren't you a surprise."

"No, I'm not." She was a licensed doctor—she could handle blood just fine. She waited. He didn't move. "The body?"

"Right this way, *Agent*."

***

She was so fucking beautiful that she stole his breath.

Lauren lay naked on the big, four-poster bed, her hair fanning behind her. Her body was pale and perfect, a temptation that would never get out of his head.

He stared at her and wanted to feast.

"I like the way you look at me," she told him, her voice like sin. "When you look at me that way, I know just what you're thinking."

That he'd kill to have her? That he'd do *anything* to get close to her? He hoped she didn't know what dark thoughts raced through his head. She might be afraid then. He never wanted her to be afraid of him.

"I'll be easy," he promised her as he tossed his shirt to the floor. He knew her injuries still hurt her.

Lauren shook her head. She rose and sat up. Her breasts thrust toward him. Round, with pink tips that he wanted to lick all night long.

"That's not how it's working tonight."

He slowly removed his holster and put it on the nearby table.

"You don't get to call all the shots." She reached for him, her hands a silken heat on his flesh. "I get my turn tonight."

"But you're—"

"I don't even have a headache." Her fingers slid down to the snap of his pants. A few seconds later, the zipper eased down with a hiss. "I've got other things in mind."

Then her mouth pressed against his and he couldn't *think*. He could only feel. Her lips. Her tongue. She was licking him. Sucking him. Stroking with both her fingers and her mouth. He thrust helplessly forward, because Lauren—hell, the woman drove him *crazy*.

His hands rose, but he didn't want to touch her head. Didn't want to hurt her. So he fisted his fingers even as his hips surged. Her mouth feathered over the head of his cock, her tongue licked him, and his breath hissed out as the pleasure pulsed through him.

"Stop." It came out a growl. If she didn't stop, he wouldn't be able to hold back.

She licked him again.

"*Lauren...*" He pushed lightly at her shoulders.

Her head lifted. Her eyes, so bright, stared up at him. She smiled. "I love the way you taste."

Hell. He could feel his control ripping away. The control he always held—no problem—with other women.

Not her.

Her fingers slid down his erect length. "I think I'd like to taste more."

He would go insane. Anthony shook his head. "My turn."

"But—"

It had to be his turn.

He pushed her back against the covers. Then just drank her in, memorizing every detail of her body with his eyes, his fingers, his mouth. When he kissed her breasts and licked those sweet nipples—better than candy, so much fucking better—she moaned his name.

His cock was so full and heavy that he hurt. He wanted to drive deep into her, as hard as he could.

But she wasn't ready yet.

And he wasn't done with her.

His head lifted. His breath was sawing out, but he had to say, "If I hurt you—"

"You *won't!*" Demand sharpened her voice.

"Tell me to stop," he finished. He'd stop, no matter what, for her.

She shook her head. "I want more! I want you." The demand was even stronger now.

His fingers slid between her thighs. She was wet. Hot. *Fuck.* He thrust two fingers into her. Lauren's hips arched as her breath rushed out, then she bit her lip.

Yes. She was still thrusting her hips against him.

"You don't have to be quiet." There was a reason he'd ditched that hotel room. He loved it when Lauren screamed for him.

He would make her scream.

He pushed her legs farther apart and put his mouth on her sex. He sampled every inch of her, letting his tongue trail over her silken skin.

"Anthony!"

It wasn't a scream. Not yet. Which was good, because he wasn't done.

He thrust his tongue into her even as his thumb pushed over her clit. Her whole body seemed to tighten around him. He kept tasting her, kept drinking her in, knowing he'd never be able to get enough—

"*Anthony!*" Her nails sank into his shoulders, and he reveled in the sting of pain. "I need you in me."

His head lifted. He licked his lips, savoring the taste. Her cheeks were flushed, her gaze demanding.

He was about to explode.

He pushed the head of his cock against her body. Creamy heat. So good, so—

There was nothing between them.

Shit, he had to take care, had to protect her.

Lauren's legs wrapped tightly around him. "I'm on the pill. Clean…"

He was, too. He'd never gone without a rubber with any woman. Yet right then—

I want all of her.

His eyes held hers. His control was threadbare. She arched against him, and he drove into her.

The last of his control tore away.

There was no restraint. No holding back. She closed around him, her sex so hot and tight and wet that he thought he'd go out of his head. He thrust deep into her, plunging wildly again and again. There was nothing but her. Only pleasure. Only the heat of her body.

His hands curled around her hips. He lifted her up, holding her tight. The bed groaned beneath the force of his thrusts. His heartbeat slammed into his ribs.

This was what he wanted. *She* was what he needed.

Her sex clenched around him. Her climax was coming. Good, because his was fucking about to implode on him.

He angled his body, sending his cock sliding right over her clit as he drove into her.

Then she was climaxing and—*yes*—she screamed for him.

"Tony!"

He loved her scream.

Anthony erupted inside of her, still thrusting, still desperate for every single moment with her. Her climax sent her sex contracting around him, ripples of release that made his pleasure intensify.

He was hollowed out, so empty from the release that he'd pumped and pumped into her, but he wasn't done.

Not yet.

Not ever.

He stared down at her, his body slick with sweat. Her breath heaved, matching his. Her smile—oh, damn, that smile was sin.

He felt himself hardening within her again. "Did I hurt you?"

Lauren shook head.

Good. He began thrusting.

***

She'd gone to the morgue to see Walker's body. But as she followed Greg, Cadence's gaze was drawn to the autopsy table. To the body on the table. Judge Hamilton. "I've already bagged and tagged Walker's clothes and belongings." Greg motioned to the right. Cadence saw the evidence bags in a neat pile.

She advanced toward the judge. His eyes were closed, his body the ashen, yellowish color that came soon after death. His chest was a mess—not just stabbed, but carved open.

"The Butcher must have been pretty angry when he killed Hamilton," Greg noted as he came toward her. "He twisted the blade and cut his way straight through the guy's heart."

She swallowed. The sight was grisly, all right, but she'd seen worse. *I have plenty of images that still haunt my nightmares.* Despite her tough words to Greg from moments before, she knew this scene would haunt her, too. "Were there any defensive wounds?"

"I bagged his hands at the scene."

She knew the drill. The hands were bagged to preserve any evidence, and when the body had been transferred to the morgue, Greg would have checked under the nails for skin samples or trace evidence that had been left behind.

"The judge must not have been given the chance to fight back. His nails were clean." His gloved hand lifted and gestured near the judge's head. She saw the dark bruising and cuts on his forehead. "I found chunks of glass that I believe will match up to the broken window from his BMW embedded in the wounds. It looks like Walker knocked him out, and when the judge woke up…" He pushed past the sheet, revealing the dark bruises around Hamilton's wrists. "Hamilton was bound."

"No chance to fight," she whispered. Walker had wanted the power. She understood that. In court, the judge had been the one presiding. The one who got to decide Walker's fate.

In the cabin, Walker had been the judge and the executioner.

Her gaze dropped to Hamilton's throat. "Did he leave us a note?" After the first two notes had been found, she'd realized it had become a part of Walker's process. Killing, leaving the note. A taunt, but not for the cops.

The taunts had been personal.

For Lauren Chandler.

"There was a note," Greg said as he reached for an evidence bag.

She glanced over her shoulder. The other body bag would contain Walker's remains.

She still wanted to see him.

Cadence took a step toward the black bag.

"Here," Greg said.

She froze and glanced back, quickly reaching for the evidence bag.

She read the scrawled letters. *The blood is on you.*

"We'll get the techs to confirm that the handwriting is the same, of course," Greg murmured, "but it looks like a match to me."

It looked like one to her, too. "He was blaming Lauren."

Greg frowned at her. "How do you figure that?"

"All of the notes were for her."

"Listen, Agent—"

"When he killed her friend, Walker wanted Lauren to know her punishment was just beginning." She rolled her shoulders, trying to push away the never-ending tension. "Then he sent her to Steve Lynch's house because that was where he planned to abduct her. He was laying his trap for Lauren. Only she got away."

One brow rose. "Why would that mean the judge's blood is on her?"

"Lauren was the one meant to die, not Hamilton." Cadence shook her head. "Lauren was the focus of Walker's rage. She was the reason he came back here."

It's beginning.

"Tell me something else," he muttered. "Why the hell is the guy slicing their throats and putting the notes in there? I've seen some twisted shit in my time, but—"

Knowing what she did about Walker, this part was actually easy for her to understand. "He slices their throats because he's taking away their voices. They can't speak, they can only carry his messages. It's control." Her temples were throbbing, her shoulders aching. Sometimes, she just hated these cases. "Even in death, he's controlling them completely."

"Sounds like he's trying to control Lauren, too."

Of course, he was. She turned toward Walker's body bag. "I want to see him."

"I haven't started evidence collection yet. There's not much I can tell you." He walked around the table and approached the zipped body bag.

The slide of the zipper seemed overly loud in the small room.

Then she saw Walker's face. In death, he almost looked peaceful. Death had a way of doing that to people, even the monsters of the world.

Her gaze slid to his chest. Two gunshots. One had come from Ross. One from Voyt. They'd made sure the killer didn't get away again.

Based on the statements from the men, Ross had fired first. Then Voyt.

Her gaze swept over Walker. The clothes that covered him looked old—faded jeans, a dark T-shirt. He wore hiking boots. Soil on the bottom of those boots might give them insight into all the places he'd been.

"You really think there are two of them?" Greg asked as he waited beside her.

She glanced up at him. "Yes, I do." She was actually certain of it.

"I heard talk from the cops. They don't think that's the case. There aren't any bodies, and the only one who is sure another killer exists is the DA. And she's remembering overhearing a conversation after she'd gotten her head slammed into a wall."

Their gazes held.

"Speaking as a doctor," he murmured, "those with concussions don't make for the best witnesses."

Her head cocked. "Why do I feel like you're trying to warn me?"

"Because I am. The police captain was down here earlier, wanting to make sure I thought Walker was behind all the recent kills. Walker and *only* Walker." A beat of silence. "One serial killer is bad for business. Two in the same town? That's just a shit storm."

One she was betting the captain and the mayor didn't want coming. "They're going to try and push this away, aren't they?"

A nod. "No bodies, no deaths."

"I won't let this investigation end." She glanced back at the body. "Where's his cell phone?"

"No phone was recovered with the body."

"But Lauren said—"

"Concussion, remember?" he murmured. "The guy might never have even had a cell phone."

Bull.

"Or maybe it's lost in the swamp," Greg continued. "He spent so much time out there. Maybe the guy ditched it."

Maybe. Kyle was out in the swamp searching the area around Judge Hamilton's cabin. The techs had investigated, but Kyle liked to get up close and personal with the kill sites.

It was how he worked.

Talking to the dead—that was how she worked. She glanced back at Walker.

"Just what is it you hope to find by studying his body?" Greg leaned closer to her. Curiosity deepened his voice. "We know who killed him. Ross and Voyt admitted to shooting him. It's no mystery how this guy died."

"The mystery isn't his death, but what was left behind." She reached for a pair of gloves.

"What are you doing?"

"I went to med school, too." She gave him a grim smile. "What I'm doing is assisting you. I'm not leaving this room until I learn every secret Walker carried on his body." Secrets she would not let him carry to his grave.

CHAPTER THIRTEEN

"This city has been under the grip of terror for long enough," Mayor Louis Daniels said as he crossed his arms over his barrel-like chest and lasered his gaze around the room. "Walker is dead, and it's time to move on."

The meeting had been called at seven a.m., in the mayor's office. Lauren and Anthony had been given a thirty-minute warning, and they'd had to rush over to meet the mayor and the chief of police, Jeremiah Dodge. The homicide captain, Reginald Powers, was there, too, along with a very tired-looking Paul Voyt, the ME, and Anthony's two marshals, Jim and Keith. In the back of the crowded room, the two FBI agents stood at attention, and Lauren could clearly see the tension in Cadence's body.

"Now, I've read the files the FBI prepared about the so-called alpha team, but I don't see one single piece of evidence that actually supports the claim that someone else has been working with Walker all of these years."

Lauren's heart was drumming in her chest. She'd dressed carefully, grateful for the suit that had been in her travel bag. She knew a power meeting when it was announced, and she wasn't about to leave this meeting without getting what she wanted.

"Most of those missing-persons cases aren't even in our jurisdiction," the mayor continued, voice hard. "And without bodies…"

"We still have crimes," Paul said, his own voice low.

Should he even be out of the hospital? He was so pale. Lauren cast a worried glance his way.

"Crimes that our DA would have a damn hard time prosecuting." Louis's dark gaze cut to Lauren. "Without the body, the jurors always have doubt in their heads. They always wonder, did she just run away? Did she just get tired of the life she had and decide to vanish? Hell, people up and abandon their lives and families every day. It happens."

"This *isn't* abandonment, mayor," Cadence said, stepping forward. "These are very specific victim profiles that match our killers. The ages increase, every year, and the victims share the same hair color, the same general build, the same—"

"Why wouldn't Walker have rolled on this guy?" the police chief demanded. "He was facing death. The guy should have bargained with everything he had."

Cadence shook her head. "That wasn't how it worked in Walker's partnership. He and his partner had an agreement. When Walker went to prison, turning on the other perp might not have even occurred to him. They don't *think* like regular people do. They think of blood and death and—"

"The city of Baton Rouge *appreciates* all of your help and cooperation on the Walker case," Louis interjected smoothly, with a dismissive wave of his hand, "but the Walker case is over now, and so is your job."

No. Lauren sucked in a sharp breath. She'd worked with Louis for a long time. Fury wouldn't work with him. Emotion never did. "I heard Walker talking on the phone to his partner. He *exists.*"

Louis's lips thinned. "You were terrified, Lauren. You thought you were going to die. You were bleeding, you had a concussion—"

"He didn't slam my head into the wall until *after* I'd heard the phone call."

The mayor sighed. "I read your medical report. You also had an injury to the front of your head. One you probably sustained during your abduction."

She remembered hitting the ground. Everything going dark.

"You *were* concussed then. I can't be sure that your memory isn't faulty." He paused as he studied her. "Be honest. If you had a witness who described the same situation you did, would you put her up on the stand?"

Damn him.

"Without any other evidence to back her up, would you let that woman testify to a jury? Even if she *did* testify, would that jury believe her?"

"There are over a dozen missing women who match the profile," Lauren gritted. "Are we just going to ignore them? Act like they don't matter?"

Louis shook his head. "No, we aren't."

"That's something," Anthony muttered, not sounding impressed.

Lauren wasn't exactly impressed, either. She was pissed.

"Detective Voyt will pull the files for the women missing from Baton Rouge. Clyde will contact the police chiefs in the surrounding areas and alert them to the possibility that—"

"Possibility?" Cadence's face had flushed. "There is no possibility. There's reality. Listen to me, I am *telling* you, there is a killer still out there. A brutal, brilliant killer who has been hunting since he was a teen. He's only gotten better over the years. He isn't stopping."

"How do you know that?" Louis demanded. "Sounds like you're just going on a hunch."

"I'm a profiler." Her eyes glittered with anger, but Cadence's voice was flat. "My job is to figure out killers. And I am damn good at my job. I've analyzed Walker, I've analyzed the abductions and deaths related to this case. There is a second man. One who has been going under the radar for far too long."

Louis and Clyde exchanged a long, hard look. "If those police chiefs should want the FBI's assistance on those cases…"

"What if it were your daughter? What if she was on the list of who we *think* the guy killed?" Cadence pushed.

Beside her, Kyle's face was a dangerous mask. A muscle jerked along his jaw. "They need to know what happened to these women," Kyle gritted. "They deserve to know."

Cadence slanted him a fast, worried glance, then she shifted her attention back to Louis and Clyde. "If it were your daughter, would you still be turning us away like this?"

"We *don't* have the evidence." His hand pointed to Greg. "The ME says all the victims within the last few days were killed by one man—Jon Walker. His DNA was found at the crime scenes, on the victims. Just his. No one else's." His shoulders straightened. "As far as I'm concerned, until we have conclusive evidence, your services are no longer needed."

Silence.

Lauren's cheeks had been flushed with fury, but now they felt ice-cold. After a moment, when her heart stopped shaking in her chest, she pushed back her chair and rose to her feet.

She could feel everyone's stare on her. "You didn't answer Cadence's question." The words were still without emotion. "You didn't say what you'd do if your daughter was one of his victims."

Louis glanced away.

Fine. She exhaled slowly. "You know me, Louis. You've worked with me, time and time again. You've trusted me on dozens of cases, why won't you trust me now?"

He still didn't look at her when he answered, "The city can't have any more fear. We need to heal, not start searching for new monsters in the shadows."

He was spinning political BS at her. "What happens when those new monsters come out of the shadows? What then?"

"It's not going to happen." The words held plenty of bluster, but not enough confidence for her. "The people here are safe again."

She considered that. Him. "Maybe it's easier to pretend that, when it doesn't hit close to home." She kept her eyes on him. "It's close for me. My sister *is* the first victim. Walker *told* me he watched someone kill her. I didn't imagine it. I didn't dream it up in my concussed mind. For you to suggest I did…" Now she was walking toward him with slow, sure steps. "It's an insult to me and to every one of those victims."

He flushed and started to stammer. He'd do a lot more than that before she was done with him.

"You're so worried about politics, about the press, that you're willing to let a killer roam free." Lauren shook her head. "I'm not doing that."

A chair scraped behind her. Footsteps, strong and certain, as they crossed the room following her.

"I'm not going to give up on these people. I won't give up on Jenny. I'm going to keep looking, and I *will* find the man who has taken all of these lives. Then I'm going to make certain the justice system takes what is left of his life."

"And I'm going to help her," Anthony said, only his voice was much rougher and angrier than hers.

She glanced over her shoulder and saw the hard fury on his face.

"With respect, *Mayor*"—the word was a snarl from Anthony—"I don't answer to you. Neither do my men. If I want to stay in this area, if I want to hunt that bastard, that's exactly what I'm going to do." Disgust tightened his lips. "I'm sure the press will love to discover how disinterested you are in all of these missing women."

Louis blanched. "I'm not—"

"We'll find your evidence," Anthony told him. "I guarantee it. Then you can try to dig your way out of the grave the press will make for the mayor who didn't give a shit about all of the lost lives."

Louis's gaze fell to the floor once more.

"By the way…" Cadence's voice rang out.

Louis stiffened.

"Here's a tip to remember…" She and Kyle strode toward Louis. "You don't get to tell the FBI that we're done. We don't need you to tell us when to investigate a crime, especially one we believe crossed *state* lines."

His rose to his feet. "What—"

"You should have read the case files better," she said, cutting over him. "One of the victims was last seen just over the Texas border. If we've got a multistate killer on our hands, which I believe we do, the case follows under our purview. We *will* keep investigating, with or without the Baton Rouge PD's assistance."

His cheeks couldn't flush much darker. "I think this meeting is over."

"Yes," Lauren agreed, "so do I." She'd already taken steps to have her office covered for the remainder of the week. Cases had been taken, schedules rearranged. She'd made sure the DA's office was set so nothing would fall through the cracks.

She wasn't giving up. Not now. Now when she was so close.

They left the office. Lauren's steps were far too fast as she hurried down the stone steps outside of city hall.

"Lauren!"

She stopped at Cadence's call. The other woman rushed after her. "I'm not giving up," Cadence said.

"Neither am I," Lauren vowed. She couldn't believe Louis. He was more worried about PR, about Baton Rouge being killer central, than he was about the victims. About *saving* lives.

"I examined Walker's body last night," Cadence told her. Kyle wasn't with her. Had he stayed to tell Louis just what he thought of him?

"What did you find?" Anthony demanded. His shoulder brushed against Lauren's.

"Inside the grooves on the bottom of his hiking boots, I found dried seeds from a weeping willow."

Lauren's heart stopped.

"I know that doesn't seem like much, but willows aren't exactly thick on the ground in the swamp. And it *did* come from the swamp. I got a botanist from LSU to look at the seeds and based on the soil embedded in the seeds, he figured out an area where he *thinks* the willow could be located." She gave a little nod. "The area is in a ten-mile radius around Walker's cabin."

She almost couldn't breathe.

"Before he died," Anthony said, his deep voice rumbling, "Walker mentioned a weeping willow tree. He wanted me to tell Lauren about it."

Cadence's eyes widened. "The tree holds significance for him. Sometimes"—Cadence's voice was soft as she continued—"killers will mark a space that is special to them by planting certain flowers or using a marker to—"

"You think Walker and his partner planted the willow near Jenny." It was what Lauren thought, too. It had to be Jenny. Why else would Walker try to send the message to her?

Cadence nodded. "Maybe one of the killers even felt remorse for the act."

Remorse shown by a willow that would weep year after year. If they'd planted a tree for Jenny...*could they have planted trees for other victims, too? Others we didn't even know about yet?*

"I'm heading for his cabin," Anthony said.

Paul was coming down the steps.

"No." Lauren shook her head. "*We're* going."

Anthony gave her a grim smile.

"Lauren..." Paul called out.

She hurried toward him. Hugged him. "Why aren't you in the hospital?"

"Like someone else I could name, I'm not exactly a fan of those places." His gaze darted over her. "I'm sorry. Louis is being a dick. I'll keep working the case. You know I won't let your sister just—"

"Thank you." She stepped back from him.

Cadence had hurried away, moving to talk with the ME, and Anthony stood behind Lauren, steady, silent.

"Thank you for all you've done on this case, for Jenny. For me." Over the years, he'd always been a good friend. They hadn't made it as lovers, but that was because she *couldn't* love anyone else, not when she longed for Anthony so much.

Paul was looking over her shoulder at Anthony then. "You saved my life in the swamp."

"I did my job."

"Yeah, that job involved saving my ass. If you hadn't burst through those bushes, if you hadn't distracted Walker, I'd have a knife in my heart, too."

Paul offered his hand.

Anthony took it. The shake was brief, solid.

"We think we may know where he buried Jenny's body," Lauren said quietly.

Paul's head turned toward her. "How?"

"Cadence. She found evidence in the autopsy that's given us a search area in the swamp."

"An area around Walker's cabin," Anthony added.

"Fuck, you mean…" Paul stepped back. "All along, she might have been right *there*?"

Lauren nodded.

"We're going to search," Anthony told him. "While we've still got daylight to use."

"I'm coming with you," Paul replied, before staggering back.

Anthony caught his arm. "I think you need to leave the swamp to us…for now."

"Dammit, I want to help—"

"Then you dig up the case files. See if you can make any new connections between the victims."

Sweat had appeared on Paul's upper lip.

That hospital stay was looking better and better to Lauren. "Get rest," she told Paul softly. "Then you can help us."

Jaw locking, he nodded. "I'll call Hawthorne. Tell him what's happening. He can come out there, even send some of his men. The more bodies you have on the ground, the easier the hunt will be."

The hunt.

That was exactly what they were doing. The killer wasn't getting away scot-free. They were the ones hunting now, and they wouldn't stop.

Not until he was found.

***

They hadn't listened to the mayor. He'd had to talk in that bastard's ear forever just to get Louis to call the meeting, and they were still going to keep looking for the killer.

They were heading for the swamp. Back to the old cabin. This was so fucking bad. If they found the body...

They can't tie her to me. It's been years. So much decomposition. There's no way the evidence could still be used. It's far too compromised.

He didn't want them bringing Jenny out of the ground. Jenny was at peace. Jenny shouldn't be disturbed.

Not Jenny.

If they found Jenny, they'd look for others. They'd keep going.

Jenny's blood had soaked his hands. He'd *felt* her life flow away. The power, the rush, had been the most amazing thing he'd ever felt before.

Animals—animals didn't compare to humans. Nothing compared with staring into someone's eyes and *seeing* the life drain away. It was the ultimate power.

Jenny had tried to take his power away from him. He'd wanted to love her. He'd tried. But she'd told him that he scared her.

So I fucking really scared her in the end.

Jenny had consumed him. Obsessed him. He'd taken to following her, watching from the shadows because he'd wanted to see her—all the time.

Other boys had tried to come around her. Had tried to take what was *his.*

He'd known then, there would be no letting her go.

She was his. Always *his.*

Getting her to meet him that day had been so easy. Jenny had always been far too trusting. He'd told her he wanted them to be friends, that they just needed to talk once more.

She'd been smiling when she got out of her car.

By the time he and Jon had her in the swamp, she'd been begging.

Too late. Jenny had made her choice. There was no going back for her then.

Only...

I missed her. After she was dead, after that wonderful rush was gone...he'd wanted it again. Wanted her. The need had built within him, and he and Jon had planned again.

Another girl. Another who reminded him of his perfect Jenny.

Again and again, he'd killed. Again and again...

But the others had never been as good as the original. Never as good or perfect as Jenny.

Would Lauren be as good? He'd come back to this town to be close to Lauren. She was Jenny's sister. Staring at her always reminded him of his first kill. That wonderful power.

Maybe when he looked in Lauren's eyes at the end, maybe it would be just like it had been with Jenny.

The rush. The pleasure.

Soon, he'd find out. Because Lauren Chandler wasn't going to live much longer in this world.

She'd die begging, too.

***

The swamp was full of bald cypress trees, with thick trunks and knotted knees growing in the muddy water. Spanish moss hung from the branches, coiling down as Anthony passed.

He looked to the left. To the right. Lash pine, swamp tupelo, even swamp chestnut oaks were scattered in the area.

No willows. Not one damn weeping willow.

"Maybe your expert was wrong," Wesley Hawthorne said as he stopped, putting his hands on his hips to survey the area. "The willow doesn't have to be out here in the swamp. Hell, Walker killed in the city, maybe someone out there was growing one in a backyard."

"The soil found with the seed matched this area," Lauren said. "The swamp's soil isn't like a backyard. You *know* that, Wesley." She'd pulled her hair back into a ponytail. Like the others, she was dressed for the hike.

She'd been so determined as they searched. The hours had slid away. They kept looking, kept widening their parameters, but so far...

Jack. Shit.

Where the hell is the tree?

"Like finding a needle in a haystack," Wesley murmured. "The swamp goes farther than most people realize."

They wouldn't give up.

Lauren turned away and went south with one of Wesley's men at her side. Anthony kept his gaze on her.

"I know she wants to find her sister." Wesley closed the distance between him and Anthony. "But do you think it's fair to give her false hope?"

The man was pissing him off. "It's not false when it's real."

Wesley shook his head. "I remember when Jennifer went missing."

Anthony glanced over at the Fish and Wildlife agent. "I didn't realize you knew her."

"A swamp rat doesn't exactly run in the same circles as the society belle, at least, not back then." A sad smile twisted his lips.

"I went to a different high school, but at football games, well, everyone noticed Jennifer. It was hard to miss her. She was always flying through the air, captain of the cheerleading team…"

The American Dream.

"There were rumors back then, stories that floated in the schools, about Jennifer hooking up with an older guy. That they'd run away, headed out to LA for a fresh start." Wesley's gaze had turned to Lauren's back. "She never believed that."

"Because it didn't happen."

Wesley faced Anthony. "I searched for Jennifer out here."

Anthony gazed steadily at the other man.

"If you want to dump a body, the swamp's the best place to go. I looked, over the years…"

Strange, for a man who hadn't known Jenny.

The suspicion must have showed because Wesley's jaw hardened. "When I get word of any disappearance, I always search. It's as necessary as breathing for me." He waved his hand toward the swamp. "My grandfather was half Choctaw. He taught me early to love the land and treat it with respect." His head shook sadly. "The swamp isn't a dumping ground. It's not where those girls should have ended up."

"You never saw any signs of them?"

"No. Never found any clothes, any shoes, any tracks at all that told me they'd been here."

"Maybe because the killer was just as good at tracking as you were." Walker had known the area like the back of his hand. Anthony bet Walker's partner had, too. "Who do you know who's like that? Who can slip into this area, know every trail and every path, and leave no trace behind?"

A man who'd be the perfect killer.

"Did I ever tell you…" Wesley rocked back on his heels. "That Jon Walker and I went to high school together?"

Sonofabitch.

"Hated the bastard back then. He was a mean jerk who got off on bullying weaker kids." Wesley's gaze had returned to the trees. To Lauren. "If you're looking for someone who knew Walker back then, for someone who could never get lost out here, but someone who *could* make a body vanish into the swamp…then you're looking right at me."

Yes, he was. Anthony's question had been deliberate, to see what Wesley's response would be.

His response had been chillingly cold.

Wesley's eyes narrowed. "Do you suspect me?"

Anthony waited. When he didn't speak, Wesley's stare came back to him. "I knew you went to school with Walker." Like he hadn't gotten his hands on Walker's old yearbooks first fucking thing. "I asked if you knew someone who'd fit the profile." His smile sharpened even more. "And you just listed yourself."

Wesley grimly shook his head. "Go look somewhere else, Marshal. I'm not the killer. If I were, I wouldn't be trying to help you find the body, would I?"

"*Anthony!*"

Lauren's cry. High. Excited. In the next instant, Anthony was racing toward the echoing sound. His feet thudded over the earth still wet from an afternoon shower.

He turned to the left. The right.

He saw her with Matt at her side, beneath the sloping branches of a weeping willow tree.

The willow had been hidden, crouched beneath tall pines and cypress trees, blocked by moss.

But it was there. Not too big and with branches bleached light by the sun.

He touched Lauren's shoulder. She flinched and spun toward him. "Is she here?" Lauren asked, her voice filled with hope so desperate that it hurt him.

There was only one way to find out.

Anthony glanced at the men who'd circled them. "We need the shovels."

***

Lauren stood back while the uniformed men worked. Louis might have tried to shut her down, but she was the freaking DA. She still had pull and plenty of cops and techs who owed her. If her sister was in that ground, then Lauren was doing this scene right. There'd be no blunders with evidence as shovels were driven into the dirt. No contamination.

Every care would be used. Every. Care.

The pile of dirt grew. The silence in the area was thick as the men worked.

Lauren's stomach was twisted into knots. Her hands were shaking. Every whisper of movement from the deepening hole had her adrenaline spiking.

Anthony was at her side. Watching. Waiting. Every few moments, his assessing gaze would drift to her. She knew he was worried about her. About what she'd do if they found the body.

And if they didn't.

If she's not here, I won't give up. I won't ever give up.

Her parents had kept looking for Jenny. They'd offered rewards, sent out so many missing posters, even bought a few billboards.

Her father had flown to LA twelve times, following rumors that Jenny had run away with an LSU grad student.

She didn't run away.

Her parents had been so determined to never give up on Jenny.

Then cancer had ravaged her mother. Taken her so quickly, in the blink of an eye.

Her father had been the only one left for Lauren then. He'd still been searching for Jenny, always searching, when a heart attack took him far too soon.

Lauren had been nineteen.

Alone.

She wanted to reach out for Anthony. With him at her side, she didn't feel so alone. But so many eyes were there, watching them, noting her every movement and gesture.

I'll pick you up after school, okay, Laurie? Jenny's voice, the memory of her smiling face, darted through Lauren's mind. They'd been at the kitchen table, fighting over pancakes, rushing for school. *Since I'm all street legal*—Jenny had flashed her new driver's license—*Mom said I can take you to piano today.*

She'd rolled her eyes. *You just want a reason to drive.*

So?

Don't be late, Jenny. I've got to practice for my recital—

I'll be there. Jenny had given half her pancake to Lauren. *Count on me.*

More dirt rose from the ground.

Count on me.

The men working in the hole stilled. "We've got something!"

Her heart stopped.

I'll pick you up after school...

Paul shouldn't have been there, but when they'd called the station to get the crew, he'd come. Shaking and pale, he'd been determined to join them.

Now he made his way to the hole.

Lauren found that she couldn't move at all.

Anthony took her hand in his. His fingers were warm. She felt ice-cold. "Lauren?"

She forced herself to speak. "What did you find?" Her voice was too high.

Paul stared down into the hole. His face looked even paler. The lines near his eyes and mouth appeared even more defined. After a tense moment, he looked back up at Lauren. "Bones."

Count on me…

A tear slid down Lauren's cheek.

The men continued working in the hole.

"There's clothing down here, too…"

Clothes and bones would be all that remained. Lauren's lips pressed tighter so she wouldn't cry out.

"Looks like a red shirt…" The words seemed to drive right into Lauren's heart.

Part of her had stubbornly clung to hope. Hope that Jenny was alive somewhere. Alive, happy.

But…

Jenny had been wearing a red shirt when she vanished. A red shirt. Blue jeans. Her brand-new boots—Lauren's birthday present to her.

"I want to see," Lauren said. She took a step forward, locking her knees.

Anthony blocked her path. "Do you really want to see her that way?"

The image of Jenny as she'd been, dark hair gleaming, her wide, slow smile lighting up her face, was in Lauren's mind.

I'll pick you up—

"We don't know that it's her," Paul was saying, voice thick. "It could be any of the missing girls."

No. It was the weeping willow tree. The tree Walker had wanted them to find. They'd do a DNA test, but in her heart, Lauren already knew.

She stared up into Anthony's eyes. His face had locked into a stark mask, but his green eyes shone with emotion. He bent his head toward her. "Don't do this to yourself," he whispered. "Remember the way she was, remember—"

"I have to see her." Didn't he understand? It wasn't over. Couldn't be over, until she saw her sister again.

Anthony shook his head. Pain flashed in his eyes.

The men were clearing the area to bring the body from the earth, the earth that didn't want to let her go.

Lauren stepped closer and heard one of the men swear.

"Sonofabitch. Her hands are severed."

Lauren's body trembled. Anthony was there—always there—to steady her.

"Don't, Lauren," he said again.

It was her sister. She had to see.

She took another step.

Dirt. Roots, twisting through the dirt. And...bones. Bones darkened by the soil. An old red shirt, the edge of blue jeans...

A skull that stared up at her.

Something broke inside of Lauren.

She broke.

Anthony's arms closed around her, and he held her tight.

***

He wanted to fucking *kill.* Anthony barely held his rage in check as he watched Lauren make her way to the ME's office. She'd gone to meet with the mayor in a closed-door meeting—just her, the mayor, and the chief of police—a few moments before, and he sure as hell hoped she'd ripped the dick a new one. They had their evidence now, and there was no way the mayor could shove the body under the rug.

The press would know what was happening. Anthony had already made sure of it with a fast phone tip to some of Lauren's contacts. No one would forget Jenny Chandler or the other victims.

Lauren's steps were slow, her shoulders sagging, as she headed toward him.

He caught her hand before she could open the door to the morgue.

"No, not yet."

Dark circles lined her eyes, from pain, horror, and grief that were ravaging her. He wanted to take it all away. He wanted to find the bastard who'd made her hurt and *destroy* him. Death would be too easy.

The man needed to suffer, as he'd made Lauren suffer. And Jenny suffer. And all the others.

He glanced over his shoulder. He saw an empty room and pulled Lauren toward it.

"Anthony, what—"

His mouth took hers. He had to kiss her. He wanted her to feel something, anything, but sadness and grief. He wanted her to know she was alive, dammit, and there was still hope.

Hope for her. For them.

But he could taste the salt of her tears. He hated the taste of her grief. Lauren should know joy.

I will kill the bastard.

Her arms curled around him. Her lips parted, and she kissed him back with an almost desperate need.

Her body trembled, but she pressed tightly to him. Her nails sank into his arms as she rose onto her toes.

Her lips broke from his, just long enough for her to whisper, "Make it stop."

He stared into her eyes. Saw the gleam of tears.

"I can't breathe. It hurts so much. Just *make it stop.*"

He kissed her again. His fingers sank into her hair. He angled her head up so he could take her mouth. Her lips. Her tongue. There was desperation in the kiss, a maelstrom of lust and need. And fury. For what had been lost. For the dangers that waited ahead.

The nightmare hadn't ended with the discovery of the body. Would it ever end?

"I want to take you out of here," he told her, growling the words when their mouths parted again. "I want you with me. I want to *help* you."

"You have." Her words were ragged.

His hold tightened on her. "Lauren…"

She pulled in another deep breath, and eased away from him. He could see her trying to school her expression, but she looked so damn fragile—*breakable*—that it tore into him. He wanted to stand between her and any pain.

Every pain.

But he couldn't stop the agony she was feeling, and it drove him crazy. She wanted it to stop, she'd asked him to *make* it stop.

I will.

"I have to see the ME," Lauren murmured. "I have to talk to him about Jenny."

"I'm going with you." He'd waited for her, because he'd be damned if he let her walk into that room of death alone.

She gave a small nod. "Thank you."

Screw thanks. He caught her hand. "When we're done, I'm taking you out of here with me. You're not staying on your own."

"I've still got U.S. marshal protection?"

"You've got me." *Always.*

"Thank you."

There it was *again*. He didn't want her gratitude. Just her. As long as the killer was on the loose, Anthony didn't plan on letting Lauren spend any nights alone. Walker had targeted her, so what was to say the second killer wouldn't, too? With Walker's death, the man might be jonesing for vengeance. *Just like Walker.*

He followed her out of the room. When he opened the door, he saw Paul heading down the hallway, making a determined march for the ME's office. When Paul saw them coming from the darkened room, he paused. One brow lifted.

Anthony leveled a hard stare back at him.

Paul cleared his throat, then held open the door that would take them all in to see Dr. Death.

CHAPTER FOURTEEN

"We're in the process of obtaining your sister's dental records," Greg said as he stood beside the carefully covered remains. "Once we have those, we'll be able to see—"

"They'll show it's Jenny." Lauren was certain Jenny was wrapped up in that bag. Lauren had never needed the icy wall she used to separate herself from others more than in that moment. On the inside, she was falling apart. No, splintering. On the outside, her hands were flat at her sides. Her body still.

Greg glanced at Anthony, then back at her. "No jewelry was found at the scene."

"She had on a necklace when she disappeared." Her words were quiet and calm, a direct contrast to the scream inside of her. "A cross my mom had given her." Given them both, the last Christmas they'd had together. Lauren still had her cross, nestled in the bottom of her jewelry box at home.

The home she couldn't enter any longer.

"We've still got crews searching the area," Paul said as he slid into a nearby chair. Pain and exhaustion were etched onto his face. "They might find it."

"Not if the killer took it," Lauren said. Her lips twisted. "Walker took jewelry from his victims. If Cadence is right and

Walker learned from his partner, then maybe he *saw* this man taking jewelry, too, and figured he'd keep little mementos as well."

"Trophies," Paul growled.

Yes, that was the perfect word.

"Are the cadaver dogs hunting?" Anthony asked.

Paul gave a grim nod.

The killer might have buried other victims close by.

"Her shirt was covered in blood," Greg said as he backed away from the table. "Maybe we'll get lucky. He could have left his own DNA behind."

"He cut off her hands." Paul's words were as quiet as Lauren's had been. They hit her with a brutal punch. "The guy knew how to make sure he didn't leave DNA evidence behind. She probably scratched him, and he took the hands to make sure we wouldn't track him."

The kill had been so long ago. Before DNA testing had really advanced.

Lauren's lashes swept down as the sound of her heartbeat filled her ears. "Was she still alive when he—"

"No." Greg said quickly.

Good. Her lashes lifted. She met his stare. Anthony had stepped closer to her, and the heat from his body seemed to reach out and surround her.

"That's actually the odd thing," Greg added. "From what I can tell, the perp didn't originally cut off her hands. He went back and did that…later."

She swallowed the bile that rose in her throat.

"He got smarter," Anthony said from beside her.

Sicker.

Anthony's eyes were on the body. "He realized he'd left his DNA behind."

"You think she scratched him," Paul said, sitting at attention now.

"My sister was a fighter." Lauren knew that when most people had looked at Jenny, they'd seen a piece of fluff. An always-smiling cheerleader. But Jenny had spent ten years in gymnastics. Five in Tae Kwon Do. She wouldn't have gone out easily. Not easily at all.

"He figured out what he'd left behind." Anthony's voice was a dark rumble. "He went back to fix his mistake."

Paul yanked a hand over his face, his frustration plain to see. "Then we aren't finding his DNA on her clothes. The bastard wouldn't take the hands and leave his blood behind."

"You'd be surprised at what we can uncover today." Greg's jaw hardened. "All I need is one tiny hair, one microscopic drop of blood from our perp. Hell, maybe the guy was even sweating when he dug her grave—either time—I just need a little sample. If he's in our database, we'll have the man's identity."

The nightmare could be over.

Greg nodded as he focused on her. "As soon as I learn more, I'll tell you."

"Thank you." She glanced down at the evidence sheet. There wasn't much left of her sister now. There should be more to show for a life. Lauren licked her lips. She *had* to ask, "Have you been able to tell...what happened to her? What did he do?"

Again, Greg glanced at Anthony.

Anger pulsed through her. "Tell *me*."

"There are nicks on her bones that are consistent with stab wounds. I have to study her more—"

"How many wounds?" She cut through the BS. Greg was very good at his job. He would already have a strong idea, she was certain, of exactly what the killer had done to her sister.

"Seventeen."

The ice cracked. "So many?"

She realized Anthony had taken her hand. When had he done that? Both Greg and Paul noticed the move, but so what? She wanted Anthony holding her. She wanted him. Her fingers curled around his. Tightened.

Anthony squeezed her hand. "If she was his first kill, he wouldn't have been as controlled with her. That many slices of the blade—hell, Cadence will tell you that indicates rage. Loss of control."

The killer was angry at Jenny. Enraged.

"There's a reason she was first," Lauren said. She tried to breathe slowly but the stench in the room was making her light-headed. "Jenny was personal to him." It was the way of crimes like this.

"The crazy SOB probably thought they were all personal," Paul muttered. "Freaks like that always do."

"First kills usually *are* personal." Anthony's voice was thick. "The first victim is often a trigger for many serials. Once they get the rush that comes from the kill, they get addicted. They want the power. The control. They want the release that they can only get from taking lives."

All eyes were on him.

There was a grim certainty in his voice. Anthony had dealt with far too many monsters over the years.

"All signs are that Jenny was his first victim." Anthony's hold was strong and what she desperately needed then. "According to Cadence's search, her disappearance dated back the longest. When we discover why Jenny was the trigger, then we understand our killer."

"Sometimes you can't understand crazy." Paul was adamant as he stood near the autopsy table. "All you can do is put a bullet in the killer's head and stop him before he can hurt anyone else."

Lauren felt very cold. "He knew her, didn't he?" That much rage...the loss of control...

"I think he did," Anthony said. "I think he knew her very, very well."

"People thought she ran away with a boyfriend. That was the story that circulated." She rubbed her chilled arms. "Maybe she didn't run away with him—"

"Maybe he killed her?" Anthony finished.

Lauren nodded. She was splintering apart on the inside. "The cops...they talked to all her friends. They said she wasn't seeing anyone. She was always home. I didn't think there was a guy."

"He could have been her secret," Paul murmured.

A secret that had killed her.

***

"I need to go back to my house," Lauren said, her voice soft in the confines of the SUV.

Frowning, Anthony glanced over at her. She'd been too quiet after they'd talked to the ME. Too quiet. Too pale. Keeping too much in.

There were no more tears from her. Just a brittle mask.

"I didn't think you wanted to go back there." She'd told him that before, several times.

"There's something I have to get. Please, take me there."

If that was what she wanted, he'd do it. He'd take her anywhere.

He turned the SUV around, pushed the accelerator down, and cut across the dark road. Rain was falling lightly, beating against the windshield, and the wipers swiped across the glass.

They didn't speak again, not until they were pulling into the drive that led to her house. The headlights cut across the area, and Anthony saw the yellow line of police tape still blocking her door.

He shut off the engine and turned toward her. "Tell me what you need. I'll go inside and get it." There was no need for Lauren to walk into that house. Her mattress had been taken away. An evidence trail would still mark her bedroom. After finding her sister's remains, he didn't want her dealing with that, too.

"I should go in," she whispered, her gaze on the house lit by the headlights. "I *should*—"

"Fuck what you *should* do," Anthony snarled. "Just let me do this for you, okay? You don't have to face down any more ghosts. You don't have to do a damn thing but stay here and let me take care of this for you."

She turned her head toward him. He couldn't see her clearly in the dark so he reached out and trailed his fingers across her cheek, trying to feel her emotions.

Her cheek was wet with a teardrop. The brittle mask wasn't holding.

"In my closet. In the bottom of my closet, there's an old jewelry box. My cross is in there. The cross just like Jenny's. It's stupid, I know, but I want it. I have to have it."

He brought his mouth to hers. Kissed her lightly. "It's not stupid." She was breaking his heart.

"It's all I have left of my family. Everyone's gone." Her breath blew lightly over him as she gave a ragged sigh. "I knew she was dead, I told myself, for years..." Her head shook. "But when we found her body, it was real. It was finally real. Jenny won't ever come home again. I'm alone. They're all gone, and I'm—"

He curled his hand around her chin and forced her to stare into his eyes. "I will never let you be alone."

"Your life isn't here. Your job takes you all across the country, and we're—I don't even know what we are."

He kissed her once more. Harder. Deeper. "I'll tell you what we are. We're just fucking starting, got me? You're not alone, I won't let you be alone. You have me." *You always had me.* Even when he'd been gone. Miles away. She'd been in his head.

In the shell that passed for his heart.

There would be no more miles between them. No more pain for her. Everything was changing for him.

He reached for his weapon. Handed it to her and curled her fingers around it.

"What are you doing? Why are you giving me this?"

"The last time I left you outside alone, a fucking killer took you from me."

Not happening again.

"You keep the doors locked. You keep that gun loaded. I'll go into the house, I'll get your cross, and I'll be right back." He just needed to get the house keys from her. He'd be in and out in a flash and—

"I'm going in with you."

"Dammit, *why?*"

"Because I won't hide from my own life, no matter how horrible it is." She handed the gun back to him. "I can't hide from it. I can't. I can't let what's happened break me."

"You don't have to see what's inside—" He stopped because those were the same words he'd given to her when they'd been back in the swamp.

But she had seen.

Lauren didn't shy away from the darkness in life. She faced it, let it hurt her, but kept going.

He wanted to protect her, but Lauren wasn't the type to let others fight her battles.

"Let's go," he told her instead of arguing any more.

She turned away from him. Reached for her door.

He climbed out slowly, holstering his weapon. Lauren's nearest neighbors were at least an acre away, judging by the distance between their yards. The night air was hot and heavy as it pressed down on him.

His body tensed as his gaze swept the area. The houses down the street were dark. It was nearing eleven o'clock, and Lauren's neighbors had obviously turned in.

The shadows around her home seemed to stretch and twist. He hurried to her side, his body on alert.

Lauren used her key to cut the yellow police tape. It fell away, fluttering toward the window on the right. Lauren's fingers were shaking as she shoved the key into the lock. When the door opened, the dark cavern of the house awaited them.

Lauren didn't cross the threshold.

I can get the necklace for you. He locked his teeth to hold the words back. Lauren felt like this was something she had to do.

"It's just a house," she whispered and stepped into the darkness.

He followed right behind her.

Just a house.

One heavy with the memory of death and pain.

***

She'd gone back. He'd figured she would, sooner or later. After her sister's remains had been found, he'd known Lauren wouldn't be able to stay away from the house much longer.

She'd kept her own case files on Jenny over the years. Kept a memory box of her sister's belongings. With today's discovery, Lauren would want those items more than ever before. She'd had to go back.

So very predictable.

And the marshal was by her side. Where else would the man be?

They were the reason the investigation had continued. The reason the dead were being pulled from their sleep. If it hadn't been for Lauren, Jenny would still be exactly where she belonged.

Pulling her from the ground had been a crime, and now he'd be sure to put Lauren *in* the ground.

Lauren. He'd always wanted to be close to her. Being close to Lauren, it was like being close to Jenny. They had the same eyes.

He hadn't planned to kill Lauren. Not originally. It had been nice having her there. Seeing her—it always brought his best memories back. It had taken awhile to get close to Lauren, but he'd been patient.

Jon had been the one to want Lauren's pain. Jon had been so angry, so determined to make her suffer.

After prison, he'd figured that Jon deserved to enjoy some vengeance. And the two of them killing Lauren—maybe it would have been as good as that first time.

Only Jon hadn't gotten his payback. Lauren and her lover had killed him.

She'd taken Jon away. She'd dug up the past. *Ruined* Jenny.

Lauren had to die.

She should have paid more attention before she'd gone into the house. But Lauren had been so focused on what waited inside that she hadn't noticed the threat all around her.

Pity.

He smiled.

***

She hated the darkness. Lauren's fingers flew out and slapped against the light switch. The darkness vanished instantly, and she was staring at the familiar sight of her living room.

Her couch.

Her photos. Her TV and the stack of DVDs she kept handy for the nights she couldn't sleep.

Her grandmother's afghan was still tossed over the back of her couch. The home looked just as it had days before.

But the chill in the air was new. So very new. With the Baton Rouge summer blaring down on them, the cold should have been the last thing she felt.

Squaring her shoulders, she strode down her hallway, turning on every light she passed. She wanted the darkness gone.

By the time she reached her bedroom, her palms were sweating. The door was shut, and she hesitated.

Anthony didn't speak. She knew he didn't want her in there, but she had to do this.

She wouldn't let fear control her.

Her fingers curled around the knob. She turned it and pushed open the door.

***

The lights had flooded on inside the house. He could see the shadows moving—the bodies of Lauren and the marshal—as they went down the hallway. He had to hurry.

286

It was a good thing he'd learned to be so quiet and careful over the years. One had to be careful when stalking precious prey.

He grabbed his weapon—not the weapon he would have preferred, but one that was going to have to work in this case—and slipped close to the house.

The front door was locked, but that didn't matter.

He had his own key.

***

The bedroom door squeaked open. More darkness. And the scent of death. Lauren's breath was coming out harder now as she fumbled with the light. When it was on, she saw her room.

The mattress was gone, just as Anthony had said. The sheets, the covers—everything was gone from the bed. There were bloodstains on the floor. Spatter on the walls.

Karen's blood.

Anthony swore behind her.

She wanted to do more than swear. "He's burning in hell." Walker had gotten exactly what he deserved.

Karen hadn't, though. She'd never deserved this.

Lauren tore her gaze off the bed and hurried to her closet.

The hardwood floor creaked beneath her feet.

Lauren...

The whisper seemed to be in the air, but it was just a memory. Her memory. It had never been Karen's voice. It had been Walker, trying to lure her to the spot he wanted her. The perfect kill.

But she'd gotten away.

She was nearly at the closet. When she'd bought the house, she'd fallen in love with the closet. Walk-in heaven. A paradise for her shoes.

Now she just wanted her necklace.

Lauren opened the closet door.

She lost her breath. The closet had been trashed. Boxes were everywhere. Her clothes slashed. "Anthony..."

He was already there. Pulling her against him. Holding her tight.

"It wasn't like this before." The house hadn't been ransacked by Walker. Paul had told her he'd checked the house.

Where's my jewelry box?

She heard the creak of wood.

Only the sound hadn't come from their steps.

It had come from outside the bedroom.

She knew the nightmare was happening again.

Lauren...

Before they could leap for the bedroom door, the light went out, thrusting them into darkness.

This time, Lauren didn't imagine what she heard...

Laughter.

***

Come out, come out...I'm waiting for you.

He'd prepared so well. They were going to be such easy prey.

It had been easy enough to throw the breaker switch and plunge the house into darkness. He liked to hunt in the dark. He'd spent so many nights in the darkness of the swamp. First as a child, wandering deep and far to get away from the prying eyes of his family. Then, later, with Jon on their hunts.

Unlike others, his night vision was strong. So very strong.

Sometimes, he even let his prey run from him in the swamp. He hunted on the darkest nights, when the moon was gone, when the stars were clouded. He could see his prey easily in the swamp. See the shadows as they fled.

He would see Lauren and her marshal just as easily in the darkened house. Shadows that would be targeted.

He lifted his weapon. It wasn't his weapon of choice—he always preferred the intimate touch of a knife. Tonight, a gun would have to get the job done.

Brutal. Cold.

I like the knife better.

The knife let him feel his victim's pain. It cut right through the skin. So gentle. So much better than the brutality of the gun.

He'd lured his prey just where he wanted them. Made the wreckage of the closet to pull them in even deeper, so he'd have the chance to get to the breaker box.

And now...

Come out, come out...

The marshal would be first. He knew it. He'd wait for the marshal's shadow, wait to hear the telltale creak of wood, then he'd shoot. When he went down, Lauren would be desperate. She'd try to save the marshal, because she cared for him. She'd pull him back into the bedroom.

His leg brushed against the gas container at his feet. He was counting on Lauren saving her marshal.

Lauren was always trying to save the world.

It was time for her to watch the world burn away.

Then he heard it. The faint creak of the wooden floor. Then the dark bulk of a body, trying to move from the room.

Fabric whispered. Another soft creak.

He stood there in the darkness. Waiting. Needing the marshal to come just a bit closer.

Light. Fucking light.

The marshal had a flashlight in his hand, and he was shining it right at him.

Fuck.

He fired. The bullet missed the marshal, hitting right above him on the wall, but it made the marshal duck back.

He fired again. Again.

He heard the thud of his bullets and—was that Ross's groan?

Hurry, have to hurry.

He grabbed the gas can. Poured it down the hallway. Tossed the can toward Lauren's room.

He jumped back, trying to put distance between himself and the fire that was about to come.

His smile stretched as he grabbed for the matches and lit the whole damn place up.

Only…gasoline was on him, too, on his fingers, and he screamed when his hand caught fire.

The *whoosh* of sound that came from the sudden eruption of flames—the giant whoosh that rocked the house and sent him flying back—drowned out his cry.

***

Blood dripped down Anthony's arm as he grabbed Lauren and pulled her into the bedroom. The flames were white-hot, scorching and destructive as they moved toward him.

He and Lauren hit the floor. The fire was in the doorway, blocking them, burning red and gold as it lit up the room.

The bastard had followed them to the house, and he was trying to make sure they never got out again.

Think again, asshole.

Smoke was filling the room fast. The flames spreading too rapidly. *Gasoline.* He'd caught the scent of gasoline just in time to jerk Lauren to safety.

Gasoline would burn fast, especially when the freak had used a whole damn can to drench the place.

"The window!" he barked. There was no way they were getting through those flames. They wouldn't get to the killer that way, but at least they could escape.

Lauren pulled away from him. She ran not to the window, but to the closet.

"Lauren!"

The smoke was getting too thick. They needed fresh air.

He raced to the window. Shoved the curtains out of his way and realized—

I'm a perfect target. Standing there, silhouetted by the flames, he would be easy to take out. The killer had made it so they only had one way to freedom. If he was waiting out there now, he could make sure both Anthony and Lauren died.

No choice.

Anthony yanked on the window. Only it didn't open. He yanked again, harder.

Then his fingers found the nails.

The killer had nailed the window shut.

Screw that. There was still an easy way to get that window open.

He used his gun to break the glass. It rained down on him, the ground, and sweet, clean air drifted inside.

Anthony glanced back, but didn't see Lauren. "*Lauren!*"

The closet door was still open. He hurried to the door and found Lauren on her hands and knees, searching through the wreckage.

"No, baby, we don't have time for this." The fire was spreading too quickly. "We have to get out! Come on!"

She wasn't listening to him. She was shoving clothes and boxes out of her way. "It's here!" Lauren said. "I know it is!"

The fire was there. It was the thing they needed to worry about. If she wasn't coming willingly, then he'd have to carry her out. He locked his hands around her hips.

"I've got it!"

She scrambled around to face him. Her hands were clutching a small, black box. She jerked open the box.

It was empty.

"Where's the necklace?" she said. It was hard to hear her over the crackle of the flames. "*Where is it?*"

The killer had taken it, just like he was trying to take their lives.

Anthony lifted Lauren into his arms and rushed toward the window.

Smoke billowed around them as he shoved away the rest of the broken glass.

The killer could be out there.

If they stayed inside, they were definitely dead.

"Stay low, and run as fast as you can toward the SUV." He pushed her through the window and followed right behind her, trying to use his body as a shield for her.

But no gunfire erupted. No bullets tore into him.

He heard a siren in the distance. The wail was long and mournful.

"Over here!" a woman's voice called. Anthony's head jerked up, and he saw an older woman and man, both wearing robes and slippers, hurrying toward them. The man had a blanket in his hands.

"My neighbors," Lauren managed to gasp. "Jim and Suzy Baker…"

When Jim and Suzy Baker got a good look at Anthony and the gun clutched in his hands, they stopped rushing to the rescue.

They both froze, and Suzy looked like she might pass out.

"I'm a marshal," he called out. He was not putting that gun away. "There's a killer here. He was in the house."

"We saw a man run…" Jim pointed to the right. "That way. He was in a Jeep, and we yelled for him to stop."

A Jeep?

"But he didn't." Suzy was creeping closer again, holding out the blanket to wrap around Lauren. "He just revved the engine and drove even faster."

The fire truck was coming closer, the siren wailing louder.

Behind them, Lauren's house burned. The heat of the flames was hot against his skin.

He brushed Lauren's arm, trying to get her to step farther away from the fire.

The flames were crackling. The wood collapsing. The house that had known death was burning to the ground.

They could have burned with it.

Was that the killer's plan? To shoot them, then burn their bodies? When the fire spread too fast and the neighbors had come running, he'd been forced to flee.

The fire truck raced around the corner. The lights swept over the scene.

"Did you see a tag number?" Anthony demanded of the Bakers.

Jim shook his head. "Too dark. He didn't turn on any lights when he rushed away."

"Anthony!" Lauren had just lifted her hand. He could see the dark liquid staining her fingers. "You're hurt!"

He didn't know if the blood came from the bullet that had scraped across his arm or from the glass that had still lined the window. He'd made sure the glass cut into him, not her, as they fled. "It's nothing." He could handle a little blood.

He caught her hands in his and held them tight. He was so sick of killers screwing with them.

His gaze darted from Jim to Suzy. "Did you see anything that could identify the driver? Any specific details about the Jeep?"

Jim straightened his shoulders. The house was still burning. Lauren was staring at the flames.

Jim was staring at him. "It...looked like a Jeep Wrangler, the top was off, the color was...dark..." He shook his head. "I was so worried about Lauren, about who might be inside, I didn't look long enough..."

Jeep Wrangler.

Wesley had a Jeep Wrangler.

Coincidence?

I don't believe in them.

Wesley knew the swamp. Wesley had been in the area at the time of Jenny's disappearance. Wesley was the one who'd said he'd help them locate Walker in the woods...only they'd never located Walker when Wesley had taken them out. And when they'd been searching so desperately for Lauren, it had been Wesley who'd mistakenly led him down the wrong path, though Wesley swore he knew the area better than anyone else.

The wrong way...

Because he purposely led us the wrong way?

The firefighters leaped into action. Patrol cars rushed to the scene. An ambulance raced up the road.

"Help!" Lauren called out when she saw the EMTs. "He's hurt!"

Anthony tightened his hold on her. "Forget that." He'd deal with the scratch later. He grabbed the first cop he saw. "We need to put out an alert for a Jeep Wrangler that left the scene."

The fire reflected in the uniform's wide eyes.

"The driver of that Jeep just tried to kill us."

Could the driver be Wesley?

One way to find out.

"Get Detective Voyt on the radio. Tell him to head out to Wesley Hawthorne's house."

"Why?"

"Because I want to make sure the man's not a fucking killer."

***

He raced from the scene as quickly as he could. The fucking fire shouldn't have burned him. He'd tried to keep the gas off him, but the shit had splashed back.

Now his fingers were blistered, red, and that was a condition he couldn't easily explain away.

Shit, shit, shit!

He slammed his hands into the steering wheel. They throbbed even more at the impact. *Stupid.* He'd planned this so perfectly. Even let the neighbors catch sight of his vehicle...all so he could have his end game.

The DA wanted Walker's killer stopped. The marshal wasn't giving up the hunt until he had a body. Well, he'd intended to give them that body.

I still will.

He just had to find a way around his injury. He could make this work.

There was still time.

He could do this.

His fingers fucking hurt.

The pain fueled his rage, and he couldn't wait to get back to the victim waiting for him. He was so ready to kill.

CHAPTER FIFTEEN

After finding Karen's body in her house, Lauren had known she'd never be able to live there again.

Now she didn't have to worry about that. The house was gutted, the flames only now sputtering out thanks to the firefighters.

The fire had burned so hard. So fast.

He was there. He took my necklace. He's tried to take everything.

She had the blanket around her shoulders, but she wasn't cold. With that much heat in the air, how could anyone be cold?

Anthony had gotten patched up, only because she'd dragged an EMT over to him.

More cops swarmed the scene. Paul rushed up on his motorcycle. The guy always liked to ride it when he was off duty. He shoved down his kickstand and raced toward her.

"Lauren!" He grabbed her. Held her tight. The scent of smoke was so strong in the air. "What the hell happened?" He pushed her back. "Why are you even *here*?"

"She wanted her necklace." Anthony was the one who answered. "Only the bastard was waiting for us."

Anthony glanced back at the charred remains of the house. "Jesus," Paul said.

"Did you find Hawthorne?" Anthony demanded.

Paul shook his head. "You can't actually think he—"

"A Jeep Wrangler left the scene. Our killer *knows* the swamp. Hell, when it comes to the swamp, you told me yourself, no one knows the area like Hawthorne."

Paul's shoulders dropped. "He's a friend. We've been friends since high school. We were on the football team together."

"I don't care if you were fucking frat brothers together, I want to know *where he is*." Anthony's control was gone. Burned away.

So was the ice that had protected Lauren. She was raw and desperate.

Anthony was enraged and dangerous.

"I sent a patrol by his home." Paul swallowed. "He wasn't there. His Jeep was gone."

"*Where is he?*"

"His boss said they got a report of some nuisance gators in the area. He thinks Wesley went into the swamp to check things out." Paul's words tumbled out fast. "He's just out doing his job."

"Is he?" Doubt was heavy in the two words.

Paul straightened. "I'll find him. His boss is gonna page him. Gonna send some men to help me go out and meet up with him, but I'm telling you...*it isn't Wesley*."

"When we find him, we'll know for sure."

Lauren dropped the blanket.

"Look, the task force is meeting at the station," Paul said. "The FBI agents want you both to come in, then we can figure out what the hell our next move is."

Anthony wasn't moving.

"You have to come in," Paul said, his voice almost beseeching. "The police chief ordered us all back. After this..." He threw another glance at the fire. "He wants a full rundown of every detail Greg has discovered with his tests. *Come in.*"

"I want Hawthorne."

"We'll find him!" Paul backed up a step. His hands clenched. He was wearing his riding gloves. She saw the dark outline of the gloves when his knuckles curled. "But the chief wants us there within the hour."

Anthony stared steadily back at him. "Fine. We'll be there." He took Lauren's arms. "Let's go."

Shock held her silent. This was it. They were just…walking away. In his car, a bubble of hysterical laughter nearly broke from her. "It's never going to end."

The killer would keep coming for her until she joined her sister in death.

"Yes. It fucking is." He jerked the gearshift into reverse and spun them out of the drive. She glanced at him and saw the muscle flexing in the hard line of his jaw.

"Tony?"

He had his phone out and at his ear. "Matt? Where are you?"

She couldn't hear the other marshal's response, but Anthony said, "Good. We're on the way. Call the techs. I want them to run a trace on this number." He rattled off a telephone number. "It belongs to a Wesley Hawthorne. Yeah, the agent with Fish and Wildlife. I want to know the location of his phone. Hell, yes, the techs can figure that. If the phone is on, they can trace the signal and tell us exactly where he is."

Her fingers hurt, and she realized it was because she had them so tightly twisted in her lap.

"I'll be there in five minutes," Anthony said and ended the call. The SUV started to move faster.

She swallowed to ease the dryness of her throat. She could taste the fire. "You really think it's Wesley?"

"I think I want the cops pulling over every Jeep Wrangler that's out on the streets tonight. I want the tags and registrations for every guy who drives a Jeep, every guy who matches Cadence's profile." He slanted her a fast look. "But right now, we already know Hawthorne matches that profile, so I want to know just where the hell he is."

She wanted to know where he was, too.

"If Voyt won't question Hawthorne, then the marshals can find him." He flashed her a tiger's smile. "And we'll do the questioning on our own."

***

Anthony rushed through the hotel lobby, heading fast for his old room, a room still booked in his name because he controlled the hotel block for the task force. Lauren was at his side, looking shaken and scared.

The elevator doors slid closed behind them, sealing them inside.

"There's ash on your cheek." He stepped toward her. Cupped her cheek. Wiped away the smear on her delicate flesh.

It could have been so much more than ash. The killer could have shot her. Burned her body. Burned us both. The house would have become our grave.

He wasn't ready to die yet.

"I have a backup weapon in my room. I want you to take it and keep it with you."

She nodded. "What are you planning to do?"

"If Hawthorne has used his phone in the last hour, the techs will trace it." Big Brother was most definitely watching, in ways most people didn't even realize. "We've got satellite links tracing his phone's signal. We can pinpoint his location, and we *will* find the guy tonight."

There would be no more vanishing into the swamps. No more taking prey.

Not gonna happen.

The elevator doors slid open.

He took her hand. The doors to Matt and Jim's rooms were shut. He brushed past them and headed to his room. In less than a minute, he'd opened the safe in his closet and pulled out the backup weapon. He checked it, loaded it, and made sure that it would blow a hole in anyone dumb enough to go at Lauren.

He turned back to her.

Her head was tilted down, her blonde hair shielding her face. She looked so damn small and breakable.

The fire could have taken her from me.

No. He never would have left her alone in the fire. He *couldn't* leave her.

When he'd walked away before, he'd left part of himself in Baton Rouge. The obsession hadn't ended. It had just grown deeper, wilder.

Because it wasn't just an obsession?

He glanced down at the gun. What the hell was he doing? Planning on dragging her out to confront a killer with him? She'd been through enough. He tucked the gun into the waistband of his jeans. "I'll take you to the station." She was the DA. She got her justice in a courtroom. Not in some gator-infested swamp.

At his words, Lauren's head whipped up and her eyes locked on him. In her bright, blue stare, he didn't see anything fragile. He saw fury. Determination. Strength.

Lauren stalked toward him closing the distance between them. "You honestly think I'll sit back and let you go out there, after all he's done?"

"It's not your job to hunt—"

She shook her head and held out her hand. "Give me the damn gun."

"Lauren…"

"My life. My sister's life. You think I'm going to sit on the sidelines *now*?" Her laugh was bitter, piercing. "Hell, how do you even know that isn't exactly what he wants? To separate us? To divide and conquer. Divide and kill? He couldn't take us out when we were together at my house, so what if the plan now is to go at us separately?"

I want him to come at me. I just don't want him going after you.

"Where you go, I go." Her voice was flat, but her eyes gleamed with a combination of strength and fury that was truly the sexiest thing he'd ever seen. She was so beautiful he *hurt*. "I'm not backing away. I'm not *running* away. I am going to finish this. I owe it to Jenny to finish this."

Lauren looked down at the gun in her hands.

He had to ask, "Could you shoot to kill if it comes to that?"

Her head tilted back so she could meet his eyes. "He stabbed my sister *seventeen* times." There was no mask on her now. Raw emotion shone on her face. "Yes, I could do it. I could do it in an instant."

Lauren was talking about revenge. He knew she deserved the justice she'd wanted for so long.

Taking a life wasn't easy. *What would killing do to her?*

His fingers closed around hers. Around the weapon he'd given to her. "I will kill him for you." A promise. He wasn't talking about bringing the guy in. Wasn't talking about forcing Lauren to go through a long trial and, then, Christ forbid, another situation like Walker's.

Her lips parted in surprise. "You're the good guy, Anthony. You catch the criminals."

Not kill them.

But for her...to keep her safe...

He took the gun from her. Put it on the bed. Backed her up against the nearest wall and caged her with his body. He wanted her to see him exactly as he was. Far from good. Far from perfect. With a darkness inside that would always burn.

"I would do any fucking thing if it meant you were safe." His hands flattened on either side of her head. "Don't you know that?"

Her eyes widened.

"*You* matter." He growled out the words. "You're the thing in this world, the only fucking thing, I can't live without. I know, I tried living without you for years, and I was so damn miserable. A hole was in my chest, and every day, I was just going through the motions. Hoping no one saw just how lost I was."

Because when he'd left her, that was exactly what he'd been...*lost*.

"I went through my days, and my nights...at night, I dreamed of you. Fantasized about you. Wanted you in my bed and in my arms so fucking badly."

His mouth took hers. He couldn't hold back. She was there, and he needed her more than breath. The kiss was frantic and hard with the desperation that drove him. Her lips parted beneath his. His tongue thrust into her mouth.

Lauren tasted of hope, of every dream he'd ever had.

No one would take those dreams away. *No one* would take her away.

Her breasts pressed to his chest. He could feel the tight nipples, and he wanted them in his mouth. Wanted her naked. Wanted his cock driving into her so deeply she didn't know what it was to be apart from him. He wanted to give her pleasure, so much pleasure that it washed away her pain.

He wanted to give her *everything*.

And he would.

Using all of his control, he pulled his mouth from hers. "I love you."

Maybe he shouldn't have snarled the words. He could have tried romance and class, dining and—

Screw that. They were surrounded by death, and he wanted her to know just how he felt.

Only now she was staring at him in shock, her mouth swollen from his kiss, her cheeks flushed, and her brilliant eyes glittering.

"I always thought love made you a better person," he whispered to her. "That it made you good. That it was gentle and kind." Wasn't that what all the books said? All the sappy movies?

Lauren was still staring up at him, and he couldn't tell what she was thinking.

So he kept talking.

"The way I feel about you isn't…gentle." How could he make her understand? He was screwing this up, but he had to tell her. Before anything else happened. Before another monster was at the door. "The way I feel about you—it's wild and it's dark. I want you with me all the time. I want your body, your heart. I want you to need me as much as I need you."

It fucking sounded like obsession, and that wasn't what he wanted. He was trying to explain that it was more than just a dark need. He'd discovered it was more.

Anthony sucked in a deep breath. "I want you happy." That was love, right? Only…*I'd kill to make her happy*. "You're the dream I've had every night for the last five years. You're the first thing in my head each morning. When I think about my future, I want it with you." Anything, as long as it was with her.

"Why are you telling me this *now*?"

The door banged a few feet away. "Ross!" It was Matt's voice. "I got the tech on the phone! We've got a hit!"

Why now?

Because if something happened, and he didn't manage to survive the killer's attack, he wanted her to understand how he felt about her. That it wasn't just sex, wasn't just the lust that would never be slaked.

Matt's fist hit the door again. "Ross!"

"Because you're the person who matters to me. The only woman I've loved, and no matter what else happens, you need to *know* that." He wasn't asking her to love him back, but he wanted her to.

So badly.

He stepped away. Summoned his control once more.

And headed for the door.

"You won't leave me behind."

Never again.

He glanced over his shoulder and saw she'd grabbed the gun.

"I'm not afraid of what waits in that swamp."

He knew she was, but she was still ready to face it anyway.

How could he not love her?

He yanked open the door. Matt was there, glaring at him. His fist was still up, probably because he'd been ready to pound through the wood.

"If you're finished making out—"

Matt's words ended in a gasp. Anthony had grabbed the guy and shoved him back. "I just crawled out of a fucking fire, dodged bullets, and was left to *die.*" His breath was ragged. "Don't push, not now, and sure as hell not about *her.*"

Matt's eyes widened as he hurriedly straightened his shirt. "Ah, like that, is it?"

Anthony's hands fisted. "Yeah, it's like that."

Lauren crept up behind him.

Matt gave what was as close to a smile as possible. "That would explain some things…"

Anthony growled.

The whisper of a smile faded. "We got two satellite hits on Hawthorne's phone. His first call was made about two hours ago." He cocked his head as he delivered his news. "From a location right outside of Lauren's house."

It was him.

"He turned the phone off after that, but it came back on again about five minutes ago, when he made a call to our friendly neighborhood detective."

"Paul," Lauren whispered.

"Where was Wesley when he made the call?"

A rough sigh slipped from Matt. "It's hard as shit for the techs to get a location out in that swamp, right? It's not exactly easy to—"

"Where?" Matt wouldn't be talking to him unless he knew a pretty damn close approximation.

"From what the techs could tell it looked like the guy was calling from a spot near Judge Hamilton's place. Figures that Hamilton's family would have built the cabin in the one location where the cell service was pristine."

Hamilton's place.

"I tried to contact Voyt after we made the connections on the calls." Matt's stare dipped to Lauren. "But he isn't answering his phone."

What the hell?

Jim came out of his room, heading toward them with determined steps. The guy was armed. Ready to go.

They all were.

Three marshals. One DA.

One killer.

He'd take those odds.

But he'd also stack the deck. *Lauren always has to be safe.*

He yanked out his phone and had Cadence on the line within seconds. "I think you're gonna want to take a little drive to the swamp."

***

The noise from the police station almost drowned out Anthony's words. Cadence turned away from the bull pen, putting her hand over her left ear so she could hear him better.

"We got a hit on Hawthorne…" Anthony was telling her. "He just used his cell phone out at Judge Hamilton's cabin."

Her heart was beating too fast. She caught Kyle's stare and inclined her head. The police chief had gone into the captain's office. They'd just spent ten minutes trying to tear apart her profile. When they hadn't succeeded, they'd retreated for a little pow-wow. They could retreat and come back to attack all they wanted.

I know my job.

"He fits your profile," Anthony said. "His vehicle was just spotted at Lauren's house."

She knew that. She'd been briefed on the fire that had nearly killed Ross and the DA. "Are you all right?"

"I will be when the killer's stopped."

That wasn't exactly an answer. "You don't know it's Hawthorne."

"He made a call near Lauren's house, right before the fire. He was there."

And he did have a strong knowledge of the swamps. He'd been in the area when Jenny Chandler disappeared and his job would have taken him all around Louisiana. Into the cities and counties where the other women had vanished.

"He and Walker went to school together," Ross told her. His voice was distorted, as if he was running or moving quickly. *He's going after Hawthorne.*

She already knew Hawthorne had gone to school with Walker. "Detective Voyt went to school with both men, too. He's not—"

"Where is Voyt? He's there, right? Ask him why Hawthorne called him a few minutes ago, ask him—"

"Voyt isn't here." She spoke slowly as her gaze swept the bull pen. She couldn't remember the last time she'd seen the detective.

"Fuck. He could have gone after Hawthorne on his own."

She checked her weapon. Kyle was at her side. "You're on your way out there, aren't you?"

A pause. "Aren't you?" he tossed back.

She glanced toward the captain's closed door. "You have your men with you?"

"Damn straight."

"I'll meet you at the cabin." She shoved the phone into her pocket and marched for the captain's office. She didn't bother knocking. She just shoved the door open.

Kyle whistled behind her.

He'd told her before he loved it when she got rough. She was about to get plenty rough.

Both men spun to face her.

"You will not be impeding our investigation any longer," she stated as she stood firm in that doorway. "What you *will* be doing is shutting up, listening, and getting the hell out of my way."

***

Wesley Hawthorne opened his eyes. The back of his head throbbed, hurting like a bitch, and he groaned as the pain and nausea rolled through him.

"Don't worry, it won't hurt much longer."

He glanced up at the voice. At the *familiar* voice. Wesley shook his head in automatic denial.

A wave of nausea rose in his throat.

"I know what you've done, Hawthorne."

He hadn't done anything.

"You've killed women. So many women, and you've dumped their bodies in your swamp."

"No," he rasped, "I—"

"You did. And tonight, you tried to kill the DA and her lover. You went to her house. You shot at them. You set her house on fire."

"*No...*"

"Neighbors saw you. They identified your vehicle. The same vehicle will later be tested by crime scene techs. They'll find ash and debris from the fire on it, *in* it, tying you to the arson."

He hadn't been there. He'd been at a bar, Rattlesnake. He'd been drinking. He'd gone to the back parking lot...

I don't remember what happened after that.

"You also made a phone call right before you set the fire. A phone call that will be an extra nail to prove your guilt."

I'm not guilty. "I...never...killed..."

"When you're found, with your head blown open and Jenny Chandler's cross cradled in your hand, the cops won't look for a second serial killer anymore. The cases will end, with you."

Not me.

Something cold and hard pressed under his chin. He glanced down and could see the barrel of the gun.

"The only question I have…" the smug voice continued, "is this: Should I shoot you from this angle…" The gun rose. Pressed into his right temple. "Or should I shoot you here?"

"No!" He jerked but saw that his hands were tied to the chair. Tied but…what the fuck? Padded? Cloth was beneath the ropes on his wrists and ankles.

His heart nearly burst out of his chest. The padding was there so he wouldn't bruise. So that when he was dead, his body could be staged. Positioned.

No one would ever know he hadn't put the gun up to his own head.

"I actually hadn't planned for you to wake up. It's harder to use your own hand to fire the shot when you're awake."

He wants gunshot residue on my hand.

"I guess I have to make sure you're out again. That's kind, isn't it? So you never see the shot coming? I can be kind."

What the guy could be was a "Sick…fuck…" Wesley managed to say. One who'd been hiding in plain sight.

He should have been able to see the evil in their midst all along. Why hadn't he? Why hadn't any of them?

The face above his hardened. "I'm not the sick fuck. That's you. You're the one who killed and tortured all of those girls. You're the one who did it all. The one who had to come back to the scene of his partner's last crime because you couldn't keep going without him."

Wesley tried to yank free of his bonds. The judge had been bound in a chair like this. He'd fought to get free, too.

But Hamilton hadn't escaped.

Hamilton's blood stained the floor.

Mine will, too.

"The city will be glad to see you die." The man lifted the gun. "I think it's time you did just that. Go join the Butcher."

He twisted the weapon so the butt was like a club.

Wesley tried to jerk back. Only there was no place to go.

"Don't worry," the man's voice soothed. The devil's voice. That was what it was. "The gunshot blast to the head will guarantee no one sees the bruises..."

He slammed that gun into Wesley's head.

Dark spots swam before Wesley's eyes. The nausea built again. Pain rolled through him, but he didn't black out. He was fighting to hang onto consciousness with every bit of strength he had. Wesley yanked against his binds. The chair fell back.

The killer swore.

An engine growled in the distance.

***

The cabin was a dark, hulking shadow. Storm clouds hid the stars and the only light to shine on the area came from Anthony's headlights as his vehicle pulled onto the graveled drive.

His headlights hit the cabin, and the Jeep Wrangler was parked right next to it.

"It sure doesn't look like he's hunting nuisance gators to me," Anthony muttered.

Lauren didn't speak. Right then, she couldn't. *We asked this man to help us. To hunt Walker.*

All along, he'd been leading them in the opposite direction.

Another set of headlights lit up the scene. More marshals, arriving mere moments after them.

"I thought Paul was supposed to be here," she finally managed, shoving down the fear in her throat. "I don't see—"

Wait. She'd just caught a glint of light near the trees. "Is that his motorcycle?"

Anthony parked the SUV. They both hurried out of the vehicle, then joined Matt and Jim. Anthony stared at the line of trees. "That sure as hell looks like it to me."

Where was he? The cabin was pitch-black. Everything seemed so quiet.

Too quiet.

A gunshot rang out. The sound thundered through the night and shattered the silence.

The sound had come from inside the cabin.

"Take the back door, and don't let *anyone* out," Anthony barked at his men.

Matt and Jim raced toward the back.

Even in the dark, she could feel the burn of Anthony's gaze on her. "You stay behind me, Lauren. Every step, got it?"

"Got it."

They ran for the cabin. When Anthony reached the front door, he kicked it open, and the wood shattered as it flew back. He hurried in with his gun up and his flashlight positioned above the weapon so he could sweep the scene.

In the circle of illumination from his flashlight, she saw Wesley Hawthorne. He was on the floor. The fingers of his right hand cradled a gun, and blood poured from the wound in his head.

Beside Wesley's prone form, Paul had frozen, his own hands up, as he crouched over the body.

CHAPTER SIXTEEN

"What the hell happened here, Voyt?" Anthony demanded as he kept his gun up and aimed at the detective.

Behind him, Lauren let out a gasp and tried to go toward the men. *No way, baby.* He immediately moved his body, blocking her.

Hadn't they had this talk? She was supposed to stay *behind* him.

There was blood on Voyt's hands. The detective started talking, his words tumbling out quickly. "I just walked in. I found him like this!" His fingers were shaking in the light. "I haven't even called for help yet! We've got to get help!"

"We will." Anthony didn't drop his gun. "Lauren, get your phone out. Call for an ambulance. Then I want you to go outside and make sure Jim and Matt get their asses in here."

"But I can—"

"*Go!*"

He wanted her out of the room.

He heard her dialing nine-one-one, then her footsteps rushed for the back door.

"Why do you have that gun on me?" Paul demanded. His eyes squinted against the light. "We need to help him." He ripped part of his shirt away and tried to use the torn material to stanch the flow of Wesley's blood.

"Is he still alive?" Anthony asked, not moving.

"Yes," Paul hissed, "but he won't be for long. He fucking shot himself in the head!"

"No," Anthony said softly. "He didn't." Anthony stepped forward. The back door had just slammed shut. Lauren was out of the cabin. She was safe. "I want you to stand up, keep your hands where I can see them, and back the hell away from him."

Paul stared at him. "Are you crazy? He needs my help!"

"What he needs is for you to get back. Now, I'm telling you for the last time…" His fingers tightened around the weapon. "Move the hell away from him."

Paul shook his head. "He shot—"

"A left-handed man wouldn't use his right hand to kill himself."

Paul frowned, then looked down at Wesley.

"You should know which hand your *friend* uses," Anthony pushed, as he aimed dead center at Paul's forehead. "That was just sloppy. Maybe we got here too soon for you, and you had to act fast. You were so rushed that you made a mistake."

Paul was still staring at Wesley. "He *is* left-handed," he whispered. "He always threw the football with…"

"You didn't back away." The guy really needed to. "And I can't see your other hand."

Paul's head snapped up. "You think *I* did this?"

Hell, yes, he did.

"I didn't! I got a garbled phone message from him, saying to meet him out here. I just got to the cabin, and I *found* him like this."

Bullshit. "You were *in* the cabin when the shot was fired."

"No, I was outside, I saw you pull up. I ran in—" He lunged to his feet.

Anthony prepared to fire.

***

Lauren shoved open the back door. "Jim! Matt!"

They weren't there.

She stumbled to a halt, catching herself before she fell down the back steps.

"Matt?" Lauren called again, her right hand gripping her cell phone. She'd shoved the gun into her waistband while she called for help. Now she fumbled fast, grabbing for the weapon once more.

The marshals should have been there, but they weren't.

"*Lauren...help...*"

It wasn't a voice from her nightmares. It was a real voice— weak and thready and coming from the darkness of the woods that edged toward the swamp.

"*Hel*—" The word ended in a garbled gasp.

Lauren jumped off the steps. "*Matt!*"

She ran through the dark when her legs slammed into something warm and soft. She tumbled to her knees, letting out a cry as she fell. She twisted around and yanked out her phone, using it as a flashlight. The light hit—

Jim. Bloody, unconscious—*please, please, please not dead.*

A twig snapped behind her. Lauren whipped her head toward the sound and saw the knife coming right at her.

She screamed.

And then felt something sharp slice across her throat.

A knife.

***

Anthony froze. Had that been a scream? The sound faded away as quickly as it had come, but every muscle in his body tensed.

Lauren should have been back inside by now. She should have returned with Jim and Matt.

"Why isn't Lauren here?" Paul asked. He'd jumped to his feet, but hadn't advanced on Anthony. The guy had finally lifted his hands—showing he had no weapon, and he stood, still as a statue, a few feet away from Anthony.

Anthony glanced toward the back door. *Lauren.*

"Cuff yourself," Anthony snarled as his eyes snapped back to Paul.

Paul blinked at him. "What?"

"You've got your cuffs on you. I see 'em at your hip. *Cuff yourself!*"

Paul pulled out the cuffs. Snapped them in place as he glared at Anthony.

"Now don't fucking move," Anthony ordered. "Because if you run out after me, I will put a bullet in your head." He wasn't staying in that room any longer.

Lauren should have returned.

Where was she?

He ran for the back door. Shoved it open. No Lauren. No Matt. No—

Jim was on the ground. The glow from Anthony's flashlight made it look like black liquid soaked Jim's clothes, but he knew what that blackness was.

Anthony hurtled off the porch and flew to the marshal's side. He put his fingers to his throat.

Dead.

Jim was dead. Where was Matt? Lauren?

"*Help...*" A low, weak plea from the line of trees to the right that led farther into the swamp. Tightening his hold on his weapon, Anthony followed the sound. His flashlight cut through the trees, both helping him to see and making him a target.

There wasn't any choice. He needed the light.

"*Help...*"

Christ. The light landed on Matt. Like Jim, blood soaked Matt's clothes, but he was still alive. Barely.

So much blood.

"He got...Lauren..." Blood dripped down Matt's face. "Heard...him...take..."

"Who is it?" Anthony demanded. "Who the fuck has her?"

It couldn't be Paul, he'd left him cuffed inside. Wesley Hawthorne was struggling to survive, so who the hell—

"Me," a hard voice said from the darkness.

A hard...*familiar* voice.

Anthony surged to his feet and turned toward the taunting voice.

***

Kyle rushed into the cabin, shoving aside the already broken door, with Cadence right on his heels. Her partner had his gun ready as he swept the room.

It was too damn dark. She grabbed for the light switch, but nothing happened.

Kyle had already gotten out his flashlight. She fumbled for hers and saw—

The detective—Paul—trying to unlock a pair of handcuffs. Wesley Hawthorne was at his feet, a bloody mess.

"*Freeze!*" Kyle roared.

Paul's shoulders stiffened. "Not again." He looked up. "It's not fucking me!" He raised his cuffed hands and pointed toward the back door. "Ross went out that way. Lauren's missing...*go find her!*"

Emotion shook beneath his words. She wanted to believe the guy, but she couldn't ignore the wounded man at his feet. Cautiously, Cadence advanced so she could check on Wesley.

When she got a good look at him, her breath hissed out. With that kind of trauma, the guy was lucky to still be breathing. Actually, she wasn't quite sure *how* he was still breathing.

"Cadence?" Kyle stood protectively over her, his weapon drawn.

"*It wasn't me!*" Paul screamed. "Look, Ross is out there. The other marshals should have been helping him, but something happened. If you won't help them, I will." He lunged forward and slammed into the barrel of Kyle's gun.

"You aren't going anywhere," Kyle growled, his voice lethal. "Now you settle the hell down."

"*Know...*"

The grated whisper came from Wesley.

She leaned forward, heart racing. "Stay still." She wasn't sure how long the guy had. He needed to be airlifted out of there, freaking ASAP. A trauma unit would have to be on standby for him. Looking up at her partner, she said, "Kyle, we need a medevac—"

"*Know...shot...me...*"

Wesley had a giant hole in his head, and the man was still managing to speak. Talk about a fighter.

"Was it Paul?" she asked, leaning close to see his response.

"*No...*"

"What did he say?" Paul shouted. "Did he say it wasn't me?"

"*Was...right...*"

"Right? Who's—" She sucked in a sharp breath, understanding. Not right. *Wright.* Her head snapped up. "Kyle, get out there! See if you can find Ross!"

He hesitated. His gaze slid from her to Paul. He didn't trust the detective. Neither did she, not with this scene, no matter what a bleeding man was telling her.

She'd learned long ago not to take risks.

Cadence lifted her gun. Centered it on Paul. "I've got this." She'd stay until help arrived for Wesley. She'd keep Paul covered.

Kyle gave a grim nod, then headed for the back door.

"Fuck," Paul yelled, his body vibrating with tension. "I can *help.*"

"Yeah, you can. Come over here and help me to save Wesley's life."

***

Dr. Greg Wright held Lauren in front of him, his knife at her throat. Her *bleeding* throat.

Anthony lifted his weapon, aiming for the man's head. He could take the shot, easily missing Lauren, but…

Would the man have time to slash her throat before Greg went down?

"You don't want to risk it," Greg said as he backed deeper into the swamp. "You know if you so much as tighten that finger around the trigger, I'll kill her long before your bullet can hit me."

Anthony walked with him, matching the killer's steps. Lauren was dead silent, her body shaking. He kept his flashlight on them. The gun was a solid weight in his hand.

It's okay, baby. It's okay.

He couldn't say those words because they weren't true. Instead, Anthony said, "It's over, Greg. Cops are going to swarm this place any minute. There's no place for you to go."

Greg's laughter cut through his words. "I know this swamp. I can disappear in five minutes, and your damn dogs and your cops won't be able to catch me. I can *vanish*."

"You'll be a wanted man. Hunted."

Lauren sucked in a sharp breath when the knife pressed deeper into her skin. Blood slid from the wound.

"*They shouldn't have known about me!*" Rage bit through Greg's words. "Walker screwed up the deal. No one was supposed to know."

Anthony's shoulders and arms had locked as he took his aim. He would *not* drop the gun. "You were the silent partner, right? The one always pulling the strings."

Greg backed up a few more steps. The trees were twisting around them, blocking out even more of the faint light. The murky water of the swamp waited just yards away.

"I taught him," Greg said, the words little more than a whisper. "He knew *nothing* until I showed him. He couldn't even kill without vomiting everywhere!"

Lauren's hands lifted. She curled her fingers around Greg's arm and yanked. "Let me go!"

He held her tighter. "I knew he was like me." Greg's eyes were on Anthony. "I could tell the first time we met…I could tell."

"Tell what?" Anthony demanded, fighting to keep his own rage and fear under control. "That he was another sick freak?"

"That he had the *need*! We were meant to be more than fucking cattle, like everyone else in those schools. We weren't meant to shuffle down the hallways. We were meant to be more."

Lauren stopped struggling. Just froze. "Did you become more when you killed my sister?"

Another low, chilling laugh came from Greg. "She liked me, did you know that? Liked the boy who couldn't play football and who wasn't the fucking class president. She'd meet me after school. Let me kiss her. Touch her." He gave a hard shake of his head. "Then she tried to *leave* me!"

"And you killed her?" Pain broke Lauren's words."

"Jenny was mine. She should have known. I was never going to let her go." More steps backward. A gator's eyes gleamed from the dark water. "When you love someone, you want that person to stay with you forever." He laughed once more, and it was a taunting sound. "Don't you feel that way about her, Ross? I've seen the way you look at Lauren. Don't you want to be with her *forever*?"

"Yes," Anthony gritted.

"I showed Jenny just how strong I was. In the end," Greg's voice whispered, sliding through the night. "She knew."

She knew you were a fucking killer.

"But the DA didn't know," Greg said, his mouth brushing over Lauren's cheek. "I was beside you, Lauren, for so many days—and you never knew." Rough laughter. "It felt so good to be that close, and now…now you'll finally *see* what I can do."

"No!" Anthony shouted back at him. He huffed out a hard breath. "I'll drop my gun, if you *let her go.*"

Even in the darkness, he could see Greg shake his head. "It was supposed to be so easy. I had it all planned. Hawthorne was the killer, it was *him*."

"Hawthorne's still alive, and he's going to tell the world what you did." Maybe. The guy hadn't exactly been showing a whole lot of life thanks to the fucking bullet in the head.

Another frantic shake of Greg's head. "He shot himself! He shot—"

"He's left-handed." Anthony took a slow, gliding step toward Greg and Lauren. He hated the smell of her blood. Hated her pain and fear. "That was a stupid mistake for someone like you to make."

"Left-handed?"

"Yeah, if he'd wanted to blow out his own brains, I think he would have used his dominant hand, don't you?"

Rage twisted Greg's face. "Voyt was coming! I heard his motorcycle! I had to hurry—"

Another gliding step forward. "You panicked and screwed up. There's no escaping now. No pinning the crimes on someone else."

The night was thick with fury, but eerily silent. So silent.

Greg was clinging tightly to Lauren, backing her up even more, moving them toward the rickety dock. Toward the boat that waited there.

Just like Walker. Greg thought he'd get away on the boat. But then, Greg had admitted he'd taught Walker everything.

Including how to escape.

"You let me get on the boat," Greg spoke feverishly. "When I'm clear, I'll let her go."

"No, he won't! He'll…kill…me!" Lauren gasped the words out against his hold.

Anthony didn't buy for a minute that Greg would just let Lauren walk away from this night.

"You aren't getting her on that boat." He couldn't let it happen. If Greg got Lauren on that boat, she was dead.

Greg was just a few feet from it.

"There's no escape for you," Anthony told him. "Not this time."

"What are you gonna do?" Greg taunted. "Shoot me? Shoot her? You're the hero. The hero doesn't get to shoot the victim!"

The hero didn't let the woman he loved die.

"I won't be shooting the victim." Anthony's voice was calm and certain.

Then it happened. The moment he'd been waiting for, praying for. Greg stumbled on the dock, on a loose piece of wood, and his grip on Lauren slackened. Lauren lunged away.

Anthony fired. The bullet slammed into Greg's chest. The ME stumbled back. He hit the edge of the rickety dock, and tumbled into the water.

Anthony jumped forward and grabbed Lauren. "Baby, are you okay?" His fingers rose, checking the wound on her throat.

She gave a weak nod. "Anthony…"

She'd just scared twenty years of his life way.

The wound on her neck was still bleeding, but it wasn't too deep, thank Christ. He pulled her against his chest. Held her tight.

Then he heard the rustle of water. Anthony immediately hauled Lauren behind him, shielding her with his body. But the rustle hadn't come from Greg. It had come from a gator sliding from the bank and sinking beneath the water.

"Where is he?" Lauren asked, her fingers tight on Anthony's arm. "*Where is he?*"

Anthony flashed his light across the area. The surface of the water was black. The gator had vanished, and there was barely even a ripple of movement in that water.

"I hit him." He knew he had. He'd heard the thud of impact. "But I don't think I killed him."

His hold tightened on his weapon.

You have to come up for air sometime, bastard. The guy would come up for air, and he'd try to go for his boat. His escape.

There would be no more escapes.

Anthony gave Lauren his flashlight. He kept one hand on her, and the other stayed securely around his weapon. He slid back one step, and another, wanting to get her off the dock.

The dock.

Greg would have needed to come up for a gasp of breath by then. *If you want air, without anyone seeing you take it, you go under the damn dock to get it.*

Anthony stilled. He aimed his gun at the small gaps between the slats of wood of the dock. He waited…waited…

"Anthony?" Lauren asked quietly, fear roughening her voice.

He saw a glint of light below. A glint that would come from the knife Greg had held. *Kept your weapon, huh? That's not gonna help you.*

He fired even as he pushed Lauren back. Once, twice, he fired his weapon, wanting to make Greg move, wanting to draw the bastard out so he could finish him.

But nothing happened. No jostling of water. No cries of pain. Silence.

His gaze slid to the boat. That was Greg's escape. He'd need to disable it, and then they could—

"Ross!" It was the FBI agent, Kyle, breaking through the brush and running toward them. "What the hell is happening? Where's—"

A motor roared to life. The boat. Shit. Anthony spun around just as the boat began to lurch away from the dock.

No escape.

He rushed forward and jumped off the dock, flying through the air as he chased after his prey. His prey wouldn't kill again.

Behind him, Lauren screamed.

***

"Is he gonna make it?" Paul's voice was a low whisper, as if he was afraid Wesley would hear his words.

Wesley wasn't going to hear anything else.

"No." His blood covered her hands. She'd tried, but there had been nothing she could do. She hadn't even been able to ease his pain.

Wesley wasn't struggling to speak anymore. No more gasping breaths.

No more pain now.

"Shit, he's dead?"

Cadence glanced up at Paul. She nodded even as she tried to shove down the ball of impotent fury in her throat.

Kyle hadn't come back. Fear was snaking in her heart. Everywhere she looked, she seemed to see the dead.

Not Kyle. The man knew how to handle himself better than any other agent she'd met. Hell, he'd saved her ass more than a few times.

I need to be out there. With him.

"The key to the cuffs—I dropped it on the floor over there."

She stared back at Paul.

"Dammit, *trust me*, I'm your backup, I—"

Cadence bent and grabbed the key. "We find Kyle, we find Ross, and we *stop* Greg Wright."

Then she heard it—the blast of a gunshot. She scrambled with the key, hurrying to unlock the cuffs. The second the cuffs dropped to the floor, she and Paul ran through the back door.

Another gunshot thundered.

She saw the marshal. Jim. Down. Her fingers pressed to his pulse.

Dead, dammit. Another dead.

They ran through the woods. They found Matt—*still alive.*

Who else was alive?

Who else was dead?

Kyle...not him. Please not him. Kyle had to live. She needed him.

An engine kicked to life. Cadence had to leave the wounded marshal as she ran desperately toward the sound.

CHAPTER SEVENTEEN

With horror filling her, Lauren watched as Anthony flew over the dock and into the small boat. His body slammed into Greg's. Greg swiped out at Anthony with the knife he still held.

Anthony drove his head into Greg's. The knife glinted once more as Greg shoved it at Anthony.

No one was steering the boat. It bounced on the waves, rattling hard, and then—

Greg slipped on the edge of the boat. He tumbled toward the black water. He grabbed Anthony's arm, sending them both crashing into the water.

The boat rushed away, heading into the dark.

Lauren ran toward the dock, with Kyle rushing to her side. "Where are they?" Lauren demanded. Her throat hurt, a raw, burning pain from the slices. Blood soaked her skin, but she didn't care.

She only cared about Anthony.

A dark head broke the water. The flashlight fell on him. *Anthony.* Her breath rushed out.

Greg's upper body shot out of the darkness. Water flew around him, and he drove the knife in his hand straight at Anthony's unprotected back.

"No!" Lauren screamed, and she jumped in the water.

A gunshot fired behind her.

Kyle's bullet had missed its target. The knife had thrust into Anthony's shoulder. As she tried to get to him, Anthony spun around—never crying out in pain, never making a sound—and knocked the weapon out of Greg's hand. Fighting, both men sank under the water, only to jump back to the surface moments later.

Greg won't stop. Like one of those twisted horror show killers, he just wouldn't freaking stop.

Not until they stopped him.

Something hard and rough brushed by Lauren's feet as she fought to swim. *A gator?* She recoiled. Then she swam faster. Faster.

The knife was thrust at Anthony again.

Something splashed behind her. *Please be Kyle coming to help. Not a gator.* With all the blood in the water, the gators would be drawn in fast.

Anthony and Greg vanished once more.

The boat's motor was a low growl in the distance.

The splashing behind her was louder.

She whirled.

Kyle. Kyle was there. With his face grim and gun still clutched in his hand.

"Lauren..."

The voice came from behind her.

It wasn't Anthony's.

She grabbed for Kyle's gun, but he held tight. They both aimed it as they spun toward Greg.

He wasn't advancing on them. He was staring at Lauren—shock, longing, pain—all twisting in his face.

Anthony was behind him.

He had Greg's knife. It was now pressed to the killer's throat.

"It's *over*," Anthony snarled.

Lauren pulled her gaze from Greg and saw Cadence and Paul swimming toward them.

"Don't kill him!" Cadence yelled. "Dammit, Ross, *don't!*"

Lauren knew Anthony wanted to kill him. She wanted him dead, too. The temptation was so strong, and Lauren knew all she had to do was tell Anthony…

Do it.

And he would.

"Think of the victims!" Cadence cried out.

She *was* thinking of the victims. *Jenny.* Lauren's lips parted.

"Their families! They need closure. He can take us to the bodies. He's the only one who knows where they are."

Dammit.

Anthony kept the knife at Greg's throat. Lauren knew he was waiting for her response.

She shook her head.

The families.

They all needed peace.

Anthony held tight to the killer. Kyle was at his side. They *had* the bastard.

The water was cold against Lauren's skin. Tears burned her eyes. Tears she wouldn't shed, not yet. She was frozen in the water as the others closed in on the killer.

Paul cuffed Greg. The men towed him to shore while Cadence helped Lauren back to land. Cadence checked Lauren's throat and asked her over and over if she was all right.

All right didn't come close.

She couldn't take her gaze off Greg. His head was down, his shoulders slumped, and he wasn't saying a thing.

Sirens wailed in the distance. The rest of the cavalry, riding to the rescue. But the battle was over.

Wasn't it?

He took Jenny away. She pushed away from Cadence and walked toward Greg.

Anthony stepped into her path. Anthony—her strong, tough marshal. The man who'd just stopped her nightmare.

He wrapped his arms around her. Held her tight. His clothes were soaking wet. So were hers. She shivered as she reveled in the hard power of his body.

Yet over his shoulder, her gaze fell on Greg. Kyle was on Greg's left. Paul on his right. Greg was cuffed…

His head lifted. He smiled at her.

Then he drove his arm into Paul's gut. In the next second, he rammed his face into Kyle's nose. Greg lunged away from the men and raced toward her and Anthony. There was a gun gripped in his hand, a gun he'd taken from Paul.

Lauren shoved Anthony out of the way.

The gunshot hit her, slamming into her chest.

Anthony roared her name. He rushed at Greg even as Lauren fell back.

She saw Anthony's hands fly out. He ripped the weapon away from Greg. Twisted the weapon, turning it back on the ME—

Then fired.

The blast seemed to shake the earth. Then she realized she'd shaken the earth as her body slammed into it.

"Lauren!" Anthony's voice was roaring again. His head was over her. "Lauren!"

He was there. Safe. She wanted to smile.

"No, baby, *no.*" His hands were on her chest. It should have hurt. He looked like he was pressing so hard.

But she didn't feel his touch.

She wanted to feel him.

Cadence's face was above her, too. The profiler ripped away Lauren's shirt. Applied her own pressure to the wound.

Lauren couldn't feel any of it.

Before she'd fallen, her heartbeat had been so loud. Almost as loud as the shots. Now, she could barely hear it at all.

"Don't you do this," Anthony ordered her, but the words sounded ragged. "Don't! Lauren, look at me."

She wouldn't look anywhere else. She knew what was happening. She wanted him to be the last thing she'd see.

The best thing.

He'd said he loved her.

She should have told him how she felt.

He was the only man she'd ever loved.

"Baby, *please...*" Then he raised his voice. "Stop the blood, Cadence, *stop it!*"

"Tony..."

Just saying his name made her feel so hollowed out and weak. It was getting darker, so dark that it was hard for her to see him at all.

"Hold on, Lauren, you're going to be okay. Cadence says the medevac is coming. You'll be—"

"*Love...*" The word was a rasp, but she was determined to tell him. "*You.*"

"I fucking love you, too. If you *think* for a second I'm letting you go, think again. I've got you for the next thirty years. Hell, I've got you forever. We're getting married. We're having kids, and we're telling them to stay the fuck away from swamps and—*Lauren!*"

Her lashes were closing. "*Yes...*"

"Lauren?"

Yes…I'll marry you. She didn't get to tell him. She didn't get to tell him anything else.

***

A low, constant beeping pierced the darkness around her. Lauren slowly opened her eyes, squinting against the onslaught of light.

Everything was so bright and white.

She tried to move and found tubes running over her body. She tried to speak.

Panic hit her.

Something's in my throat.

Lauren twisted, clawing, and a long, hot burn rushed across her hand.

"Lauren!" Anthony said. His voice was rougher, raspier than she'd heard before.

Her gaze flew to him.

"About fucking time," he whispered. He leaned across her and hit the call button. "It's okay," he told her, his eyes staying with hers. "You're safe."

In a hospital. *I hate these places.*

"He almost got your heart, it was so close."

She frowned at him, noting the hard lines on his face. Deeper lines. She tried to talk again.

His jaw tightened. A nurse burst into the room. He still didn't look away from Lauren. "You've got a breathing tube in your throat. You can't talk, baby, not yet."

Her eyes stung.

He looked so worn.

How long had she been there?

"Seven days," he whispered, as if he'd heard her question. "Seven of the longest days of my life."

Another nurse came into the room. The doctor followed.

They tried to push Anthony back, but he was putting something in her hand. The hand that had burned before. The object felt cold.

Her head turned so she could see it. She'd yanked out an IV. The machines beeped wildly. In her hand, clutched between her fingers, he'd put two necklaces.

Two crosses. Two perfect crosses.

Merry Christmas, girls! She could hear her mom's voice rising with laughter and love.

Her hand clenched around the crosses.

"Greg had the crosses on him. I think he meant to plant them on Hawthorne, but he didn't have enough time. After..." He cleared his throat. "Cadence found them after."

After Greg had shot her.

After Anthony had shot him.

Tears tumbled from her eyes. The nurses went to work on her. The doctor tried to soothe her.

Anthony stayed by her side, and brushed away her tears.

***

"Where am I supposed to go?" Lauren asked, her voice still not as strong as Anthony would like. He'd just put her in his SUV, and they'd left Our Lady of Mercy Hospital behind them. Finally.

Two long weeks.

The first week, when she'd struggled so desperately to live, he'd nearly lost his mind.

Anthony glanced at her from the corner of his eye. He *had* lost his mind. Cadence had been forced to pull him off one of the doctors—a prick who'd said Lauren only had a 10 percent chance of survival.

Screw that.

He'd stayed by her side. Day and night.

"I don't exactly have a house anymore," Lauren murmured. "And hotels are nice and all but..."

"I have a place for you."

He'd always have a place for her.

Her lips, still not the healthy pink he loved, curved. "Is it a no-tell motel?"

Damn, but he loved her. Only Lauren would try to joke with him after the hell she'd been through.

Only Lauren.

"Better," he whispered. Promised.

Her smile widened.

His heart cracked.

When she'd been airlifted to the hospital, he'd been so helpless. His Lauren, still and bloody.

I should have killed him when I had the chance. Instead, she'd suffered.

"Don't." Her smile was gone.

His hands tightened around the wheel.

"Do you think I don't know what you're thinking? It's on your face, Anthony. It *wasn't* your fault."

He'd bear the guilt for the rest of his life, no matter what she said.

"Anthony..."

She'd risked her life to save him. He cleared his throat. "Promise not to ever do that again."

"Promise not to get into a battle with a crazed serial killer?" Lauren said. "Done." It was that low, husky voice he loved.

But then, he loved everything about her.

They drove in silence, the SUV eating up the miles, taking them back to a place where they'd been safe. A place where they'd been happy, even in the middle of hell.

"Wait, isn't this...?"

He turned onto the drive that would lead them to the ante-bellum home. He hadn't been there since Lauren had been in the hospital, but then he hadn't been *anywhere* since she'd been in the hospital.

"I lied," he told her when he brought the SUV to a stop.

She was frowning.

"It's not a friend's." He climbed from the vehicle and hurried to her side. She tried to walk. He wanted her taking it easy, so he scooped her up into his arms and carried her into the house. "At least, it doesn't belong to him anymore."

She glanced around the house. "What's going on?"

"I bought this place, right before Walker broke out of Angola, before everything went to hell."

Her wide eyes found his. "Why?"

"I was coming back to you. I was going to fight for a second chance with you." He eased her into one of the lush leather chairs. Everything there had been picked with her in mind. "Whatever you don't like, we can change. I'd had a decorator working on the place. I was just trying to get things in place..."

"In place?"

"For when I came back begging you for another chance." After the Valentine case in New Orleans, when he'd had only moments to live, he'd known exactly what he wanted to live for—

Her.

He bent down onto one knee. "I don't have a ring."

Her delicate brows climbed. "A house, but no ring?"

Was she laughing? God, he hoped so. He wanted her to spend the rest of her days smiling and laughing and banishing the ghosts and demons from the past.

"I'll give you any ring you want," he promised. "I'll give you *anything* you want, just please, stay with me."

Her gaze searched his. "I remember what you said to me."

Hell, during those desperate hours in the hospital when he'd been a deranged fuck?

"Marriage," she whispered. "Kids."

He had to swallow the thick lump that rose in his throat. He wanted those things with her, so badly.

"I tried to tell you then..."

She had the two crosses around her slender neck. A neck that still showed the wounds Greg had given to her.

"I tried to tell you yes."

All of the breath left his lungs. He surged up. Wrapped his arms around her and held her carefully, so carefully.

Her hold on him was tight and hard—and so perfect.

"How is this going to work?" Lauren whispered. "With your job, how?"

He pulled away, just a few inches, so he could stare down at her. "I'm not a marshal anymore."

"What?"

"I'm officially retired." He gave her a smile. "I'm going to open a security business in town." Giving up the job had been easy for him.

Wherever she was, that was where he needed to be.

"What happens now?" Lauren asked.

Her eyes were shining. Her lips waiting. Love...it was right there for him to see and touch and taste.

"Now we live." He put his mouth to hers and knew their life together was truly beginning.

***

"It was a beautiful service."

Lauren turned to see FBI Special Agent Cadence Hollow heading toward her. Kyle had flown back to Virginia, but Cadence had stayed a little longer.

Cadence had been checking in on Lauren, and helping Paul find the last of the victims.

When the police had searched Greg's home, they'd discovered journals, diaries—dozens of them. All talking about his kills.

He'd planted a tree over each body. A special tree for his special girls. Love could be twisted for some.

Anthony's hand brushed lightly over Lauren's arm.

And love could be dark and dangerous and *perfect* for others.

"Your sister's at peace now," Cadence continued quietly. "You got justice for her."

Lauren glanced at the flowers on the ground, the spot that would mark her sister's resting place. A perfect spot right next to their parents. The service had been a long time coming, and now...*I still miss her just as much.*

"What happened to him?" Lauren asked the profiler. "What made Greg turn out..."

Like this?

"We talked to some of his old neighbors. As a kid, he was caught killing a lady's cat. Skinning a dog."

Lauren shuddered.

"The behavior stopped after his parents sent him to a group therapy home, so they thought everything was back to normal for him."

Anthony wrapped his arm around her and pulled her close against him.

Cadence's stare moved between them. "Sometimes, it's hard to stay what turns one man into a killer but makes another the hero. The protector. Both have the same capacity within them for good and evil."

Some were just evil, hiding behind good.

"From his journal entries, we learned that Greg and Jon actually met at the therapy group. Their parents were trying to get them help, but it just didn't work." The wind lifted her hair, and Cadence brushed it back. "He helped Jon get out of prison. A week before the escape, Greg was at Angola, supposedly for a consult. We think he found a way to talk with Jon then."

"Do you believe some people are born evil?" Lauren asked.

"Yes." Her voice was flat. "After all I've seen..." There were ghosts in Cadence's eyes, shadows of terrible memories. "I do." Cadence straightened her shoulders and offered Lauren her hand. "I'll be leaving tonight. Got a call about another case."

"There's always another one," Anthony murmured.

Always another monster waiting in the wings.

Cadence nodded. "But at least we took two down." She shook Anthony's hand. "Enjoy your happiness. Few people ever get to be truly happy." Her eyes were sincere. "I envy you that happiness."

She turned away and walked slowly from the cemetery.

Goose bumps rose on Lauren's arms as she watched Cadence leave. The woman spent her days in the minds of killers—why?

I prosecute to give victims their justice. I do it because of Jenny.

What had made Cadence so determined to go after real-life monsters?

"Are you ready to go?" Anthony asked as she turned to face him.

A line of stubble darkened his hard jaw, making him look even sexier than normal.

Her sexy *ex*-marshal. "I'm ready."

Ready to walk away from the past and start looking toward the future.

The future that waited, with him.

ACKNOWLEDGMENTS

Thank you so much to the wonderful Amazon Montlake team! Working with you is a pleasure!

And to my amazing readers—thank you (from the bottom of my heart!) for all of your support. Thank you for the e-mails and messages that you have sent to me. Your support is truly incredible.

Don't miss the next chilling romantic suspense from
Cynthia Eden!

SCREAM FOR ME
A NOVEL OF THE NIGHT HUNTER

Available spring 2014 on Amazon.com

His prey stumbled through the dark parking lot, teetering in her high heels, swaying as she tried to brace her body against the old sedan. Her blonde hair was pulled back into a ponytail, and her slender shoulders were slumped.

Voices and laughter drifted in the night. The last few bar patrons slowly staggered away.

They didn't acknowledge the woman. They were too busy *trying* to stay upright.

He was the only one who watched her.

She wasn't drunk. That wasn't why she swayed. The woman was bone tired. Lily Adams had worked a double shift, staying far later at Striker's than she normally did. She had to be so very weary.

She shouldn't work so hard. If she wasn't careful, little Lily was going to work herself straight into an early grave.

She finally got the car door unlocked. Lily slid into her sedan. Cranked the engine. It sputtered, then died. Lily tried again, obviously used to this routine.

It was a routine he'd watched before.

A few minutes later, after a few more false starts, her car backed out of the lot.

He waited a beat, then followed her.

When she turned on the old, long stretch of highway that would take her back to the little ranch house she had off of County Road 12, he was close. So close. His headlights were turned off, and sweet Lily Adams had no clue she was being hunted.

The hunt was always so much fun. Not the best part, of course, but still…

He enjoyed it. The hunt built the anticipation. Let him know of the pleasures to come.

He kept track of the miles as they passed. It was important to keep track because he'd planned this so perfectly.

Up ahead, her car began to slow. To sputter. *Right on time.*

When the sedan stopped completely, he smiled and flashed on his lights.

The road was instantly bright, the headlights falling straight on Lily and her car. She hadn't gotten out of the vehicle. Sometimes, they did. When their cars stopped, they would jump out. They tried to lift the hood, tried to see what was wrong.

Tried to fix what couldn't be fixed.

But Lily wasn't moving.

He parked behind her. Took a breath. Let the anticipation build even more. Then he slid from his vehicle and headed toward her.

Lily's windows were rolled up. Were her doors locked? He didn't pull on the handle to find out. Not yet. He knew better than to be too eager.

"Ma'am?" He shone his flashlight into her window. "Are you having some trouble?"

She turned toward him, her eyes wide and worried. Fear was on her face.

She had a cell phone to her ear.

His back teeth locked. She needed to ditch that phone.

"Do you need some help?" he asked her, making sure his voice had just the right amount of concern. He knew she couldn't see him clearly, not with his cap pulled low and the light aimed at her, not him. It was too dark for her to see his face.

Lily Adams didn't like the dark. It was why she tried to avoid the late shifts at Striker's. She would hate being out on the road all alone.

Hate it. Fear it.

"I'm fine!" Lily called out, and she didn't roll down her window. Good, cautious girl.

He liked girls like Lily. They were the ones who followed orders so well.

"Help is coming," she told him with a little nod.

Poor Lily. Help wouldn't get there in time.

He deliberately angled the light so it fell on his own body. Not his face. Just his body. "Help's right here, ma'am."

The flashlight glinted off his badge.

His knuckles rapped lightly on the window. "Now, roll this down so we can talk."

Lily hesitated. He saw her eyes dart to the rearview mirror. Probably trying to make out his patrol car.

He'd left his bright lights on, so she wouldn't be able to clearly see his car.

This wasn't his first time. He knew better than to make any mistakes.

The window slid down with a faint grinding sound.

He didn't smile, but he sure wanted to.

"What seems to be the trouble?" he asked as he leaned toward her. With the window down, her scent wrapped around him. Strawberries. Beer.

"I don't know, Officer. My car just stopped." She still had her phone clutched tightly in her right hand. Was someone on the other end?

He let a worried frown pull his brows low. "Why don't you step out of the vehicle and we'll take a look, okay? If I can't get it working for you, then I can always give you a ride home."

She nodded, her full lips quivering a little. Lily was scared.

"It's not safe for you to be alone out here," he chastised her. "You never know what's waiting in the dark."

Lily put down her phone.

No one had been on the phone. Her line about help coming had been a bluff.

She reached for the door handle, then her hand froze. Lily tilted back her head. "I don't recognize you."

Why would she? She hadn't *seen* him, just heard his voice—heard what he wanted her to hear.

"I thought I knew most of the cops in this area."

Lily was going to make things difficult. He'd thought she would be easy prey. For the most part, she had been.

He adjusted the flashlight, making sure it fell right on her face. "Have you been drinking?" his voice snapped. "Ma'am, I smell alcohol on you. Step from the vehicle, *now*."

"No! I—" She shoved open the car door and rushed out. "I work at a sports bar, Striker's. Some beer spilled on me earlier, and I—"

He grabbed her. Shoved one hand over her mouth even as the other yanked her tightly against him. His flashlight fell to the ground with a clatter. "I know just what you've been doing, Lily."

Her screams were muffled against his hand.

She tried to fight him, but Lily was small, petite. Weak. He lifted her up, carried her easily, and in seconds, he'd dumped her in his trunk.

Her cries rose from the trunk. Loud. Desperate.

It was two a.m. They were in the middle of fucking nowhere. Who did she really think would hear her screams?

He whistled as he walked back to pick up his flashlight.

Then he shut her door. Left her purse and phone behind.

When he climbed back into his car, Lily was still screaming. He wasn't ready to enjoy her screams, not yet. He turned on the radio.

And drove away.

ABOUT THE AUTHOR

A Southern girl with a penchant for both horror movies and happy endings, *USA Today* best-selling author Cynthia Eden has written more than two dozen tales of paranormal romance and romantic suspense. Her books have received starred reviews from *Publishers Weekly*, and her novel *Deadly Fear* was named a RITA finalist for best romantic suspense. She currently lives in Alabama.